RECON STRIKE

1

SAN Salvador. Music filled the night, the jukeboxes and the bands of the cafés competing with the stereos of the passing cars to create a cacophony of rhythms and melodies and voices. Groups of teenagers crowded the sidewalks. The boys wore fashions seen in American rock videos, the girls styles from *Cosmopolitan*. Waiters in white jackets wove through the strollers to deliver trays of Suprema beer to the young men at the curbside tables. Steps away, the cars of the wealthy idled on the Paseo General Escalón.

Lidia Rivas watched for the Marines. She sat at one of the wrought-iron tables of the Club Mediterranée, her slim legs in tight jeans, her breasts sharp through the red silk of her blouse. A gold chain with a crucifix circled her throat. Her hands flashed with gold bracelets and rings.

A very lovely young woman, the features of her fine-boned, oval face showed her Castilian ancestry. Her gold, her silk, her French jeans, her Italian sandals, the chic styling of her lustrous dark hair marked her as one of the elite of Salvador. The oversized shopping bag on the table— the yellow plastic marked with the red letters SASSON— contributed to the image.

A box inside the Sasson bag concealed a 9mm Beretta 92S autopistol with fifteen rounds in the magazine and one under the hammer. She had hacksawed an X in the tips of all sixteen bullets. If she had the opportunity to use the pistol, she did not want the slugs punching neat and easily sutured channels through the Marines. She wanted the bullets to

1

explode, for the fragments to tear vast gaping wounds through the Americans who served the fascist regime.

"Señorita . . ." A waiter set an iced orange drink in front of her. Rivas swirled the ice as she sipped from the plastic straws, her eyes watching the faces of the passing crowds. Some of the young men smiled at her, but she looked away, searching for the faces of the Marines.

She heard English. She saw the waiter showing two *norteamericanos* to a table—an English-speaking Chicano in his forties and an Anglo in his fifties. The men waited as a Salvadorian couple left a table. Taking a chair, the Anglo thanked the waiter in bad Spanish and passed him a folded bill.

Businessmen, Rivas guessed. In Salvador to exploit the poverty and suffering of her people. Legitimate targets for revolutionary justice. If they stayed at the restaurant and the Marines came, the businessmen died also.

"¿Chicles? ¿Dulces?" A ragged, barefoot girl offered the diners at the tables gum and candies from a wooden tray. The child's clothes had been stone-washed until the fabric disintegrated. Stitches and patches kept the rags together. Rivas shook her head, no. The girl went on to another table. Diners waved her away. The Anglo *norteamericano* bought a pack of gum and paid the girl a U. S. dollar. The girl looked at the dollar, worth four Salvadorian colones on the black market. She counted through a handful of coins, trying to make change. The Anglo told her to keep the change.

The girl laughed and dodged away, calling out, "Benito, Benito."

Another street child appeared. The boy wore pants so patched they appeared to be assembled from scraps of cloth. The children marveled at the foreign green and gray money as wealthy Salvadorians walked around them.

Two men in cheap suits eyed the crowds. Her body went tight as she recognized the men as officers in the National Police. She had seen the two men and other plainclothes officers several times in the past month as she waited for the Marines. The plainclothesmen operated independently of the uniformed police patrolling the street on foot and in squad cars. Other comrades in her unit had reported that the plainsclothesmen watched for suspected guerrillas and foreigners, using walkie-talkies to order document checks or arrests, but never confronting suspects themselves.

If they ordered her questioned, if the police not only checked her documents, but actually detained her while they confirmed her identity in the national records, she faced interrogation and death. Her *cédula* and her passport carried the name of Marianela Quiñónez—a woman who did not exist.

Not looking at them, she watched the plainclothesmen with her peripheral vision. Fear stirred in her. She had come to the cafés many nights, sitting at a table and waiting—alone. Perhaps they had questions for the uniformed police to ask. Her hand went to the Sasson bag on the table but stopped—putting her hand on the pistol could only betray her.

A whistle startled Rivas. Blasting rock-and-roll came from a Mercedes idling only a few steps away. The four smiling young men inside looked out at her.

"Want to go to a disco?" The young man had his hair permed in pin curls. "And dance, dance, dance?"

Horns blared. A motorcyclist pulled back his throttle, the two-cycle engine screaming, blue-white smoke clouding against the headlights and neon.

"Dance? Dance? Fuck?"

She heard laughter as the Mercedes accelerated away. Rich boys, Rivas silently cursed. She had no interest in rich boys. She wanted to meet American Marines. Groups of Marines from the embassy often came here to meet Salvadorian girls. Four times in the past two weeks she had waited. They had not come. Tonight, if they came, they died.

Faces passed her. The plainclothesmen disappeared into the people. She saw the short-cut black hair of Salvadorian soldiers on a night out from the barracks. A middle-aged man looking for a woman other than his wife paused when he saw Rivas alone at the table. Giving her a wide-jowled grin, he started toward her. One of his friends pulled him back into the stream of walkers. The men argued and Rivas looked away.

A young boy wove his bicycle through traffic. The headlights and taillights gleamed from the chrome of the bicycle's high V handlebars and the white vinyl of the long seat. Red reflective tape had been woven through the spokes of the twenty-inch wheels. In the lights, his wheels looked like circles of flame radiating silver rays. He glanced at Rivas. She ignored the boy and he passed without slowing.

Then she saw the five tall men. Despite their sports shirts and slacks, they looked like soldiers. They walked in a group, all towering above the Salvadorians walking around them, their voices and laughter loud even in the noise of the music and boulevard. The young men had the very short hair of Marines. She mentally checked their faces against the collection of photos she had memorized. Rivas called out in English:

"Don't I know you from the embassy?"

"What?" One man asked.

"Oh, yeah!" Another answered. "You know us, I know you know us. Is this your table?"

"Would you like to sit down? I'm waiting for a friend."

"Who's your friend?" one Marine asked. He turned one of the iron chairs backward and sat cowboy-style, leaning over the back of the chair. "Think I know her?"

"Oh, I don't think so," Rivas laughed. "She's shopping and she said she'd be here, but you know, I've been waiting and waiting."

The other Marines dragged chairs to the table. One tried to get the attention of a waiter. "Your English is very good, miss. Would you like to have a beer with us?"

"Oh, no, thank you. I'll be leaving soon—"

"No! Why? We just got here and now you're going. Stick around, you're beautiful, I'm in love—"

"Hey, Larry, quit it," one Marine interrupted. "Show some respect. This isn't Oceanside, you know."

Rivas smiled at rude Larry, the Marine who sat cowboy-style in the wrought-iron chair. How strange that this Marine would soon be dead. She deliberately looked him over, her eyes going from his face to the lines of muscle in his neck to his shirt-straining biceps. He straightened. His eyes met hers and he smiled.

"I was in Oceanside once," she told Larry. "I lived in Los Angeles for years and years and one time we went to San Diego. We stopped in Oceanside. Salvador's different, isn't it?"

The Marines laughed. "Different, yeah . . ." one said.

"One of the Marines at the embassy told me," Rivas prompted, "that you can't leave the city."

A Marine with jutting ears answered. "Yeah, can't leave the city. Don't want us to leave the embassy, but there's a limit. Got to get out sometime."

Larry kept his eyes on Rivas. "Where did you live in L.A.?"

"Near UCLA in Westwood." Rivas took her Sasson bag off the table and set it beside her chair, the rectangle of yellow and red plastic facing the street. "Isn't this like Westwood? The cafés and discos—it's so nice here. Like Westwood."

"Westwood?" Larry asked. "I wouldn't know about Westwood. That's for rich people. I mean, not everyone in the United States is like those people you saw in Westwood and Beverly Hills. Some of us work."

Across the Paseo, Anna García saw the signal with the red on yellow bag. She hurried around the corner to a parked Toyota taxi. The driver waited behind the wheel. Anna got into the back seat. "The Marines are there."

The driver pulled the microphone of a CB radio from under his seat and spoke. An answer came immediately. The boy on the bicycle appeared seconds later. Skidding to a stop beside the driver's window, he said:

"She put the yellow bag out. Now I go?"

"Go." The driver nodded. "Ask them."

Whipping the small-wheeled bicycle around, the boy ped-aled through the traffic, weaving and swerving around cars and trucks. He slowed near the table where Rivas talked with the young men and hopped the curb.

"Change money?" he asked in English.

"Go away, kid," a Marine told him. *"¡Sáquese!"*

"You Marines? Want change dollars? *Mejorĕ que el banco."*

The Marines laughed. "Locked in on us."

5

"Thought we were in camouflage," one Marine joked, pointing to the gaudy Hawaiian shirt he wore.

"Do you think," Rivas asked, "that Salvadorians cannot recognize that you are soldiers? Very few *norteamericanos* come here now, in our time of trouble. Only *distorsionados*—you know—"

"We aren't journalists!" a Marine countered.

"—reporters who come to write lies and make money. And Marines. Who come to fight for our country."

"Did you hear that?" the Marine in the Hawaiian shirt asked the others. "Miss, I'm Greg. Thank you very much. Six months at the embassy and finally I hear somebody say something good about us. Thank you, miss—"

"Marianela." Rivas smiled as she gave him the name of one of the martyrs of the revolution. She turned to the boy and gave him the confirmation. *"Por favor, niño. No moleste a esos Marines."* Then she pointed to the other Americans two tables away. *"Esos norteamericanos allí tienen dólares. Pregúnteles. Váyase."*

Chafa followed her instructions, asking the businessmen, "Change dollars? I pay high price."

"No, thanks."

"¿Cambia dólares? ¿Dólares?" The other patrons ignored the boy. Bouncing off the curb, the boy pedaled into traffic. He continued to the next corner, then looped back to the taxi.

"They are Marines. And there are two other gringos there. Two tables away."

The driver spoke into the CB radio again, then started the engine. He screeched into the flow of traffic, braking and swerving to cross the traffic lanes. After a series of turns to reverse his direction, he joined the flow of traffic.

At the table, Larry glanced around at the other Marines, then corrected Rivas. "Miss, we're not here to fight. Our duty is to the embassy. And to American citizens in your country. That's it. We got nothing to do with your war. Can't even carry a weapon off grounds."

Rivas studied the face of the sincere young Marine. How strange. He served a government allied with the fascist regime ruling her nation, yet he did not talk of killing communists or fighting for the government of El Salvador. He only talked of his duty to the United States Embassy. She had expected stories of war. But soon, his death would be a story—a story to tell her comrades.

Brakes squealed as the taxi stopped parallel with Lidia's table. Anna García opened the door and called out: "Marianela. *Estoy lista.*"

"Oh, I must go now." Taking a few colones from her Gucci purse, Rivas waved to the waiter.

Horns sounded behind the taxi. The Marines stood up as she started away. Larry followed her toward the taxi. "But we just started talking. Did I say the wrong thing?"

"Oh, no. But I must go. Good-bye. Maybe I'll see you again sometime."

Anna stepped out of the taxi. She smiled to the Marine and asked Rivas, "*¿Quién es tu amigo?*"

"*Nosotros somos norteamericanos, señorita.*"

"Oh, and you speak our language, how charming." Anna shook hands with Larry. "Will we see you at the disco tonight?"

"Which one? We'll see you there."

"Why don't you wait for us here?" Rivas suggested.

"You're coming back?"

"Wait for us a few minutes, okay? I live only a few blocks away. We will come back very soon."

"Sure!" Larry shouted over the blaring horns. "We'll wait. Promise to come back?"

"I promise."

"And bring some friends!" one of the Marines at the table added.

"Of course. Many friends." Rivas laughed as she closed the taxi's door. The driver accelerated away.

Leaning over the front seat, Rivas asked: "When does the unit come?"

"They are coming now."

"Turn around."

"What?"

Rivas waved as they left the Marines. "I told the gringos that I would return. And I will. To watch them die."

Larry watched the taxi fade into the lines of taillights, then went back to the table. He put out his hand to the others, palm up. "The man scores again! Her friend said they're coming back."

One Marine slapped his hand. "Why do they go for crude dudes?"

Greg laughed. "She ain't back yet. And I'll make odds she don't come back."

"Done!" Larry told him. "Beers until she comes back, you pay. She doesn't come back, I pay. All right?"

"Longer you wait, the more you pay."

The Marine with the jutting ears laughed at the wager. "The make-out kings. Don't think you're Don Juan. All they want's citizenship. Get out of this rat-hole country."

"Hey," Larry protested. "She's rich. She went to UCLA. She's got a green card."

"She said," the jutting-eared Marine countered. "Order a beer for me. I'm going to take a piss. This could be a long wait."

"We got a table, didn't we? And when you're in there, tell that waiter to come back."

A heavy pickup truck rattled through traffic. Salvadorian soldiers in fatigues sat on the sidewalls, M-16 rifles in their hands. Larry glanced at them.

"Look at those pukes. Cruising the Zona Rosa with rifles. What do they think they're doing? The guerrillas don't have the money to make this scene."

As they watched, the truck stopped. None of the cars behind the truck honked. The soldiers jumped from the truck and spread into a skirmish line. Their rifles pointed at the silent people watching from the sidewalk—the Marines at the table, the businessmen eating dinner, the arm-in-arm teenagers passing, the waiter with a tray.

"What the . . ." Larry began, then autofire from several rifles hit the Marines, high-velocity 5.56mm bullets tearing through their bodies.

One Marine staggered from his chair and stumbled away, his polyester shirt already patterned with blood. Riflefire tracked him, an arm flailing, gore exploding from his gut. Blood misted from his skull and he dropped.

The line of Salvadorian soldiers swept their rifles over the entire area. Patrons died at their meals. Teenage strollers screamed and fell as bullets hit. Ricocheting slugs whined from the iron tables to shatter windows and neon.

Across the Paseo, Rivas watched as the line of soldiers changed magazines, then resumed firing as they walked through the tables, shooting the Marines point-blank where they sprawled on the concrete.

Rivas craved the hard plastic grips of an M-16 rifle in her hands. She fantasized pointing the rifle at the head of Larry and feeling the jerk of the rifle as the bullets shattered his skull. In the planning of the next action, she would take the privilege of making the executions.

The shooting continued as the soldiers executed the wounded. Screams came as the crowds ran from the scene. Tires screeched as drivers tried to escape backward from the truck and smashed into other cars.

"They're killing our people!" Anna gasped.

Rivas pushed her comrade into the taxi. "They're liquidating the witnesses. The Annihilation Unit has orders to kill everyone."

"But we were only to kill the American Marines!"

"So a few more die. Let the bourgeoisie share the terror of our people."

The soldiers of the Annihilation Unit rushed back to their truck, their rifles spraying bullets wildly. Car windshields shattered, glass exploded. A bullet zipped past Rivas and broke a sheet-glass window. The soldiers cheered and waved their rifles as the truck sped away. A last burst of autofire destroyed a flashing neon sign, the light suddenly black, glass tubing showering down on sidewalks. Rivas finally stepped into the taxi.

Flooring the accelerator, cranking the steering wheel hard to the left, the taxi driver careened through the intersection, the Toyota skidding sideways with the tires smoking. The driver straightened the car and eased off the accelerator as he passed the café.

They saw shattered windows, sprawled bodies, spreading pools of blood.

"Dead gringos!" The driver laughed. "Revolutionary justice for the televisions of the Yankee empire."

Lidia Rivas stared, the image searing into her vision. As the taxi raced through the side streets of San Salvador, her eyes saw only dead Marines tangled with dead Salvadorians, a vast stream of their mixed blood flowing into the gutter. Then, in her fascination and exultation, the image fused with the horrors in her memory—the Marines and Salvadorians, fly-swarming corpses in ditches, the photos of students hacked to death by the army, the closed coffin of her mutilated father; the Marines who had laughed and competed for her attention now joined the thousands of corpses in the war against the fascist regime ruling her country.

"We killed the first Marines in the war!" Rivas shouted. "We will be famous! Famous!"

2

IN the lantern light from the shack, the men crowded around Niles as he put on the deep blue fatigues of the FDN—the Nicaraguan Democratic Force. Bands of light and shadow moved on the impassive faces of the men as they studied his body, looking at him like a piece of used equipment. They saw the strength of his legs and the lean, sinewy muscles of his torso and arms. Veterans of years of war, they recognized the scars on his body as old combat wounds—a leg shot through-and-through, the fading slashes from shrapnel on his legs and back, the fishbone lines of field hospital stitches.

"An old one," a teenager with a Fabrique Nationale FAL rifle commented. The hard-eyed teenager wore camouflage fatigues. "But he is still strong."

One of the older men pointed at a red welt that scarred Niles's ribes. "A bullet. He was unlucky this year."

"And there, on his arm."

"From bullets."

The perfect line of the wound marked the inside of his left forearm and continued across the curve of his ribs. Only months before, in the Bekaa Valley, Niles had made the mistake of trying to take a wounded Iranian Revolutionary Guard alive and received a point-blank pistol shot as thanks.

"And on his back. Scars."

"Made by the hands of a woman," he lied, speaking the same peasant Spanish as the fighters. Some of the men laughed at his joke.

One asked, "Was her name Kalashnikov?"

Niles laughed but did not answer. He had not come to the

11

mountains of El Paraiso to tell the contras of Laos. Sitting on the wooden porch of the shack, he shoved his street clothes into a plastic bag. Only his boots would go with him into Nicaragua. He took nothing else, no identification, no personal possessions, no camera or recorder. He laced his boots and watched the FDN fighters watching him.

Some men had the sun-weathered faces and scarred hands of farmers. Others looked like ex-National Guardsmen, tattoos on their arms and revolvers in holsters they wore on their belts. Many of the guerrillas had not yet turned eighteen. The teenagers and campesinos smiled, the ex-guardsmen maintained hard masks of arrogance.

"Where is your camera?" a teenager asked.

"Don't have one," Niles answered. Like the campesinos and guardsmen, the sun and exposure had scarred his face. The corners of his eyes crinkled from years of squinting into the distance. He looked older than his thirty-eight years.

"All the gringo journalists have cameras," a man with a scarred face said. "Why don't you have a camera?"

"I don't take photos. I remember what I see."

"You don't have a tape recorder," an ex-Guardsman said.

"I remember what I hear."

"Good shoes." A campesino with broken, decaying teeth smiled and pointed at Niles's boots. The campesino wore torn boots. String kept the soles of his boots and the canvas uppers together.

"I knew I would walk very far. So I brought my best."

"Where is your pencil and book of paper?" the campesino asked.

"I will write when I return."

"The other journalists," a teenager said, "don't wear our uniform. They are afraid."

Niles faked shock. He stared around at the contras and the pines and the night. "Is it dangerous? Commander Martillo said I should wear a uniform so my good clothes don't get dirty."

The crowd laughed. Niles knotted the plastic bag and went back to the door of the shack. A short, bull-necked man took the clothes. The man used the war name of El Martillo—meaning The Hammer. An ex-sergeant in the National

Guard, Martillo had a round belly and thick, vein-knotted forearms. The muscles of his shoulders stretched his shirt. Displaying macho vanity, Martillo wore a gold crucifix, a gold watch, and a nickle-plated Browning automatic in a black nylon shoulder holster.

Of all the men in the camp, only Martillo knew Niles had not come to report on the war for the newspapers. A colonel in Washington had spoken with a contra leader who described Martillo as a field commander worthy of American support. The colonel sent Niles to accompany Martillo on a cross-border raid. Knowing this, Martillo flashed a gold-toothed grin at the soldiers questioning Niles, then jerked a pack off the floor.

"Here is your equipment, reporter. Food, water, plastic sheet, hammock. And because we are going to fight, you will help carry our claymores and mortars. The weight will slow you down. So that you do not walk ahead of us on your long legs."

Nodding, Niles took the pack and almost dropped it. The crowd laughed again. Niles rubbed his hand across his face.

"Oh, yes," Martillo said. He passed Niles tubes of grease paint. "Your suntan lotion."

Niles squeezed out a dab on his fingers and smoothed the dark brown pigment onto his tanned face. With his other hand, he sorted through the contents of the pack. He took out a cardboard packing tube marked in Cyrillic letters, overmarked with stencilled Arabic code. On the other side, a label printed in English and Spanish identified the contents as: 82mm Mortar/High-Ex. The pack contained two of the heavy mortar rounds. He found two canvas cases with claymore mines and firing devices.

Stepping out of the storage shack, Comandante Martillo handed Niles a Kalashnikov rifle and a webbing set with ammunition pouches and a knife. Niles slipped the frayed suspenders over his shoulders and buckled the waist belt. Then he quickly stripped the Soviet rifle, examining the components for wear and corrosion.

"He is *Cia,*" a voice commented, using the common Latin American pronunciation of the initials of the Central Intelligence Agency—CIA.

Shouldering the pack, Niles tried the straps. "You see them carry a load? You see them carry a rifle? Or do they come in their cars with air-conditioning, bringing you their stories and promises and lies? I came in a truck. And I brought only my boots. Don't call me that name."

Sergeant Martillo shouted for his men to gather their packs and weapons. The crowd scattered, leaving Niles to check every detail of the issued equipment. Opening his ammo pouches, he examined the feed lips of the Soviet magazines, the head stamps of the Czechoslovakian 7.62mmComBloc cartridges, then thumbed down the cartridges to feel the pressure of the magazine spring. He adjusted the straps and tested the stitching of his pack. Finally, he put the contents in order, his hands moving with the ease of long, long experience.

Niles knew weapons and packs. He had served all his adult life in the United States Marine Corps, enlisting the morning of his seventeenth birthday in 1963 and taking a Greyhound bus from the poverty of Harlan County, Kentucky for the regimen of Perris Island, North Carolina—only the first of a series of camps as he progressed from recruit to private first class to combat meritorious sergeant in the I Corps of Vietnam, the squad leader of Recon units operating along the Demilitarized Zone and the Laotian border. After two tours of duty, he applied for Officer Candidate School. He returned to Vietnam as a very experienced 2nd lieutenant and led Recon patrols—wearing North Vietnamese or Khmer Rouge uniforms and carrying Soviet weapons—into Laos and Cambodia. Since then, he had served in the United States, the Caribbean, Central America, and Lebanon. He had transferred to Honduras five months before, joining the contingent of American servicemen training the Honduran and Salvadorian counterinsurgency battalions at Puerto Trujillo. But in fact, Niles—and a few other Marines under his personal command—took orders directly from a colonel in Washington, D.C. By telephone, the colonel had directed Niles to evaluate Martillo and his force of guerrillas. A pickup truck delivered Niles to this camp on the border of Nicaragua a few hours later—Niles knew no other way to

14

judge a combat unit except to accompany the soldiers and their commander into combat.

Sergeant Martillo assembled the contras in the center of the camp. The lines of men stood under the pines as Martillo waved a flashlight over the equipment and munitions carried by the fire teams. Two men bore the weight of heavy M-60 machine guns. Belts of cartridges criss-crossed their shoulders. A squad carried a Soviet 82mm mortar broken into tube, bipod, and base. Other men had RPG-7 rocket launchers. Niles waited in the center of the second platoon, watching the sergeant and looking at the men around him. Two men shifted their positions in line to stand close to him.

"I am Blanco," a thin contra told Niles. In the darkness, he could not see the young man's face, only the silhouette of his sharp features. He carried a folding stock Kalashnikov and an RPG, a rocket loaded in the launcher. "I was Sandinista. I fought in the revolution since I was twelve years old. First I carried messages, then I killed a Somoza policeman and took his rifle. An M-1 Garand. A good American rifle. I killed a guardsman from a kilometer away. I fight in mountains, I fight in the final offensive. But then the Cubans and the Soviets come and now I fight in the mountains again. Until victory. And this is Zutano—" Blanco put his arm over the shoulders of another man standing in the darkness. "He did not fight in the revolution, but I teach him how to be a guerrilla."

"And now I fight the communists who stole the revolution," Zutano added.

The lines of contras left the camp, following trails higher into the mountains. They walked by starlight and a fragment of moon, stumbling through the shadows of overhanging trees, men cursing, the noise of rattling equipment and scuffing boots loud in the night. Niles adjusted his webbing and pack straps as he walked. Letting his Kalashnikov hang by the sling, he rested his right hand on the receiver, the safety off and a finger hooked over the cocking handle, ready to jerk back the bolt and chamber the first cartridge.

After a few kilometers, the platoons reached the crest of

the mountains. Blanco whispered behind Niles. "This is Nicaragua."

The moonlit mountains extended into the distance. Though the map he had memorized showed towns and roads, Niles saw no lights—no farms, no towns, no headlights on the roads. The mountains and what he saw of the valley of Jalapa remained blacked-out.

Sergeant Martillo took point, leading the platoons along narrow trails overgrown with dry weeds. A brave man, Niles thought. Leads by example. But if a claymore or the first burst of an ambush takes him away, who leads these men out?

In Nicaragua, the contras moved more carefully, their rifles in their hands, their heads always turning as they watched the brush and trees around them. Their noise and voices went silent. They walked quietly along the trails, the sergeant halting from time to time.

They continued south until the sky blued with the rising sun. On a hill viewing the canyons and scrub for kilometers in three directions, Sergeant Martillo called a halt. Soldiers sprawled in groups, digging through their packs for food. The machine gun teams went to the perimeter and sentries watched the trails.

Niles scanned the expanse of mountains. Beneath the startling blue dome of the sky, cloudless and infinite, the ridgelines glowed with the horizontal light. The slopes and deep canyons remained black. Individual trees and outjutting rocks stood out like details in a stereoscopic viewer. Niles realized that no smoke stained the air. No cooking fires sent smoke drifting through the trees, no farmers burned the weeds and dry cornstalks from their fields, no trucks spewed out diesel soot—no one lived in these mountains.

Looking up through the trees, Niles scanned the sky for aircraft.

"Looking for the communists?" Sergeant Martillo asked. "You must wait until tomorrow. Tomorrow we hit them hard and you will see many, many dead ones."

"Don't they patrol the mountains?"

"They are too afraid. If they patrol, we kill them. The Cubans and Soviets can't get them out of the towns."

16

"And the helicopters?"

But Sergeant Martillo rushed away. His voice boomed as he shouted over the talk of his soldiers. A group of contras gathered around him as he unfolded a map. They looked out over the ridgelines and canyons, talking and consulting the map.

Niles backtracked up the trail. Finding a tangle of brush a few meters from a machine-gun team, Niles went flat. Behind him, he saw the contras littering the area with cans and papers and cigarette butts. He opened a can and spooned out beans as he watched the mountains.

Blanco and Zutano followed him and sprawled in the brush. The two young contras took turns eating, one watching the trail as the other ate. When Niles finished his beans, they watched as he used his knife to dig a hole. He buried the can, refilled the hole, then recreated the matting of dry grass and fallen leaves. Leaving his position, he used a stick to whisk away every mark of his presence. The two contras tried to erase their marks. Without speaking, Niles showed them how to comb the grass upright with a stick. Blanco nodded:

"Mister, you don't talk. But you know. My teacher in the Sandinistas, they trained him in Cuba and he fought in the mountains for five years. He did what you do. I know you are a soldier."

Niles shook his head, no.

"Then what? You say you are not *Cia*."

Niles leaned close to the young men and whispered, "Tourist."

3

A TWELVE-year-old boy zigzagged through lines of obstacles, a 9mm Beretta pistol in his hands. He wore a pistol belt, boots, and drab green fatigues. No insignia marked his uniform.

The obstacles simulated the doorways and windows of a street. A target—the form of a soldier painted with the camouflage green uniform of the Army of El Salvador—swung from a doorway and the boy snapped two quick shots into the chest of the target and a final shot into the target's face, the rapid shots reverberating in the walled firing range.

Another target appeared in a window behind the boy. Pivoting, his thin arms locked and steady, the boy fired at a blond-haired *norteamericano* wearing a gray suit, sunglasses, and holding an Uzi submachine gun. The boy scored two hits to the chest and a third hit on the blond man's forehead before sprinting away to the next confrontation.

Two soldiers watched from the back of the range. Both men wore the same dark green fatigues as the boy. One man, the instructor, sat at a panel of switches. He activated targets as the boy ran through the course.

The instructor flipped a switch and a bomb exploded only a step in front of the boy. The deafening blast staggered him but he did not stop. Coughing, wiping dirt from his eyes, the boy fired three quick shots at a target and ran, fired again at a pop-up target and reloaded.

At the last set of obstacles, five targets appeared simultaneously. The boy dove for cover and fired from the ground, hitting every target before firing his last cartridge.

The second man, Colonel Octavio Quezada, nodded his

approval. Colonel Quezada commanded the training camp. A veteran of eight years of struggle before the victory over the Somoza regime, he had lost his left arm and his left eye in the war. His injuries had ended his service as a fighter but did not end his fight for international revolution. With a staff of aides and instructors, he trained young men and women to strike at the other regimes in the Americas.

"Two months?" Quezada asked the instructor.

"Two months ago, he lived with his people in Guazapa. The bombs of their air force killed his family and our comrades sent him to us. He did not need any indoctrination. He says he lives only to kill."

"How is his English?"

"He learns but it is difficult. He cannot even read or write Spanish."

"Yes, the English will take more time than the guns and explosives. Run, boy! Run!" Quezada shouted. "Other comrades want to play here. You did very well. I am proud of you. Next month we will make you a teacher."

The boy ran back. His body streaming with muddy sweat, his chest heaving, he holstered the empty Beretta and gave the pistol belt to his teacher. Without a word, he started to the gate.

Quezada grabbed his shoulder. "What is this? Can you not say 'thank you' when your comandante praises you? Did that little firecracker kill your ears?"

Hard-eyed, the Salvadorian boy stared at Quezada, his mestizo face as impassive as a carved wooden mask—a mask that concealed nothing from Quezada. He had studied the reports on this boy. Agents loyal to Quezada—not to the Cubans, not to the Popular Liberation Front—had confirmed the details:

Born to a family of seasonal workers in Guazapa, the boy followed the harvests with his parents and brothers and sisters. The family picked coffee and cotton, existing from one harvest to the next. An infant sister died when the mother's breasts went dry, a brother died of pesticide poisoning. His oldest brother joined the guerrillas. An informer identified the family as communist sympathizers and the family fled into the mountains where the guerrillas ruled. But during a random bombing of the guerillas, an American-made phosphorus bomb fell through the branches concealing their shack. The boy had been a kilometer away, carrying water from a stream. Only ashes and bones remained of his family. He also found metal fragments of the bomb marked with manfacturing codes. A guerrilla who could read said the bomb came from the United States. The boy vowed to God to avenge his family.

Only years and national boundaries had made this boy different from Quezada. Like the boy, Quezada had a childhood in the fields. His family lived in fear of farm managers protected by soldiers and informers. His family never questioned why they lived in a rented shack and the landlord lived in a mansion, why they walked and the farm manager and his bodyguards rode in a Cadillac. Not even hoping for change, they only prayed for life to continue in unbroken cycles of rains and crops and work by the day.

But Quezada fought with the Sandinistas in the mountains, and after years of war, he and his comrades took Nicaragua from Somoza and his National Guard. Now he trained this boy, this boy who could be his little brother, to kill Yankees and Salvadorians.

Quezada brushed dirt from the boy's shirt and his sheared hair. "You did good. And that is no joke. You did very good."

The boy smiled, suddenly the child again. "But I missed. I missed targets two times. That is not good."

"You shot good. When I was a boy like you, I only dreamed of fighting. I did not have your courage—" And he punched the boy in the stomach, lightly, not hurting him, but doubling him and making him fall in the dirt. Startled by the blow, the boy stared at him. "Ha! You still have much to learn. Flattery and smooth words are as dangerous as bullets—even an old one-eyed, one-armed fighter like me has his tricks. Go! Why are you sitting down? Get out of here! You think you're a soldier already, go learn about rifles, go!"

The instructor followed his student out the exit gate. Quezada left by another gate in the high stone wall around the firing course. Stepping into the enclosed waiting area, he saw the next instructor and student, a lean young woman from San Salvador.

She glanced up as she thumbed cartridges into a pistol magazine. Scars from fists and boots marred her face. The bones of her fingers had mended in odd angles. Though Nicaraguan doctors had surgically corrected her smashed nose and the worst deformities of her hands, the night of interrogation—and torture and rape—in a basement somewhere in San Salvador had left her marked for life. She had survived because a drunken National Police sergeant had fired only one bullet at her head when they dumped her at the side of a road. Her hair covered the scar along the side of her skull.

"How goes it?" Quezada asked her.

"Good, I think." She smiled despite her broken teeth. "I always hit the targets. But I am not fast, not like the one who was in there—" She glanced toward the firing range. "I am slow, but I will try, I will keep trying. If you will keep giving me ammunition."

"Ammunition is nothing. You will shoot thousands and thousands of times before you return to your country. You must kill with every shot. Or you will die without advancing the—"

"Colonel!" An aide shouted. "The newspapers are here."

"Go. The range is yours now. Make every shot true. Speed will come with time. Does the recoil pain your hands?"

Looking down at her smashed and twisted hands, she nodded but said nothing.

"Don't let the pain stop you. In combat, you will use a rifle. But if your assignment requires a pistol, or if you must use a pistol in a fight, you will not feel the recoil and pain. Believe me, you will be very, very busy and you will have no thought of a little pain."

As the colonel approached, the aide opened a sheet-steel gate. The gate secured the training area and prevented the students from seeing the road leading to the administration complex—and whoever came to offices.

"Any messages from San Salvador?"

"Check-in codes. There is no problem."

As the aide locked the gate, Quezada hurried along the road to the top of the hill. Before the revolution, one of the old, wealthy families of Nicaragua had owned the hill and the surrounding mountains, growing coffee and grazing cattle. They ruled their domain from the spacious hacienda on the hilltop, entertaining visitors from Managua and León in their private movie theater, their children enjoying gardens, shaded lawns, and a swimming pool. Whitewashed walls three meters high and topped with broken bottles isolated the aristocrats from the campesinos who picked the coffee and herded the cattle. In 1979, when the Sandinistas took power, a chartered DC-3 landed at the airstrip and carried the family away to Miami.

When Quezada took the property for his school, his soldiers converted the barns to dormitories and classrooms. With high stone walls the corrals and stockyards became firing ranges. The walls also separated the buildings and training areas from the main house. Quezada did not allow his students to see his offices. Every student went through the courses of weapons, munitions, and communications alone, never meeting the other students or leaving the camp. They arrived at the airstrip in darkness, studied for months, then departed at night—without knowing the location of the camp or even the country that had provided the training.

Across the lawns and flowers, Quezada saw a van had parked at the entry to the hacienda. The stenciled white letters—TV—identified the van as a news vehicle. The colonel smiled at the cowardice of Emilio Pazos. The Cuban had the courage to torture and execute captured counterrevolutionaries, but he feared the roads north from Managua. He had painted TV on the sides and the roof of the van to guard against ambush. With the press credentials of a Mexican journalist, he braved roads untouched by fighting since 1979.

Quezada pushed through the flowering vines of the archway. In the courtyard, a fountain in the center shot a jet of water into the air. The splashing of the falling water almost covered the noise of typewriters and voices in the staff offices.

"Colonel!" A young man in jeans and a T-shirt left a

22

doorway. Raúl Condori served as an aide to Emilio Pazos, the Director of the Export Development Ministry. "Here are the newspapers from Managua. And Miami. I waited at the airport until they delivered the first copies."

"How dedicated you are."

"And here is a videotape of the scenes from the satellite news. I'm sorry it's in English—"

"Where is our distinguished comrade Pazos? Did they have a party to celebrate the killings?"

"No, Colonel. The victory came unexpectedly. But I am sure he will learn of the victory in San Salvador wherever he is. It is worldwide news."

"Yes, worldwide. We succeeded in shooting down four unarmed Marines, two unarmed businessmen, and six Salvadorians. A great victory for you Cubans."

"And Nicaragua! And Salvador! The Americans call it terrorism in their broadcasts, but the victory remains a triumph for the armed forces of the people. Now the Americans cannot deny they are in combat. In the mountains, in the fields, in the streets, we will find the Americans and shoot them down."

Quezada laughed. "Brave slogan, boy. Do you want to join an urban unit? I can fly you into Salvador tonight. You can murder Americans tomorrow."

The aide backed away. "I'm sorry, Colonel. But Commander Pazos left me in charge of the communications. And I must return. Immediately."

"When you tire of offices and typewriters and embassy parties, come to me. I'll make you a front-line fighter. . . ."

But Quezada talked to the empty archway. The engine of the van revved and the tires squealed as the Cuban lieutenant raced away.

"Brave slogan, you Cuban shit."

4

CONTRA soldiers walked along the trails in a long line, several meters between every man. Only a few pines provided concealment. Cutting of the pine and oak forests decades before had denuded the mountains. Now tangles of scrub trees and brush covered the slopes. In some areas, farmers had cleared the mountainsides for pastures. The line of contras zigzagged from thicket to thicket to exploit the cover, following cattle trails and weed-covered footpaths, sometimes climbing down eroded gullies.

Throughout the day, Niles watched the distant ridgelines and the sky. The contras continued their march in stops and starts. The line paused often as Sergeant Martillo checked tracks or sent out squads of scouts. No one risked talking as they crouched in the brush, watching the hillsides for ambushes. But as the men waited for the signal to move, Niles smelled cigarettes, the alien smells of tobacco and menthol drifting through the mountain air. And when the men moved again, cigarette butts littered the trail.

Twice, Niles saw planes. The first flew far to the south. Hours later, a second plane passed two thousand meters above the mountains. Niles dropped to a crouch and pointed to the plane overhead. At the same moment, a shout came from the platoon leader, telling the men to take cover. A minute passed before all the men found concealment. The platoons waited until the white speck disappeared behind the mountains, then continued their march.

They crossed an empty landscape, passing abandoned fields and burned-out farms. On a ridge overlooking the valley of Jalapa, the fire-gutted ruin of a mud brick house showed the marks of an assault—bullet pocks and a gaping hole blown through the thick wall by a rocket-propelled grenade. Slogans of the Sandinistas and the contras had been scratched into the walls.

Leaving his place in the line, Niles went flat on the highest point of the ridge. An afternoon haze grayed the details and colors of the long, flat valley. To the northeast, Niles saw the town of Jalapa. A river lined by trees wound down from the mountains, providing water for the town and a green checkerboard of small farms. West of the river, the fields turned yellow and dusty red. The areas without piped water could not be planted again until the rains came.

From Jalapa, the road angled southwest, cutting through dry fields and pastures. Fires had blackened sections of the roadside. To the west, where the mountains blocked his view, the road continued to Ocotal.

Martillo crouched beside him and pointed out a curve in the highway. "We hit them there."

The contras started down, following the contour of a wide canyon created by two long ridges. Almost a kilometer across at the highway, the triangle of flat, alluvial land narrowed to a point at the northern end where a gorge snaked into the mountains. Steep slopes walled both sides of the canyon.

A dirt road led from the highway to a cluster of burned-out houses surrounded by scorched trees. Unharvested corn stood dry and yellow in the fields. The plots of tobacco had died. Plots of tree-shaded coffee bushes lined the lower slopes of the mountains.

Following a weed-overgrown path, Martillo led the platoons into the shade of the coffee rows. Niles looked back and saw flat weeds and boot-broken earth marking their trail. Under the trees, smoking and talking, the contras rested while a squad went ahead to check the cornfields and road. Blanco joined Niles. He brought another friend with him, Omar, a hard-muscled, scarred teenager with curly hair and a spotless Fabrique National FAL rifle. Omar's eyes always moved, watching the fields, watching the brush for movement. He did not smoke or take off his pack. He never took his hand off the pistol-grip of his rifle.

"Why have we not seen patrols?" Niles whispered to the young men.

"Maybe they have seen us," Omar commented.

"They are four or five or six," Blanco explained. "Only a few. When they see forty men, fifty of us, they hide."

"They are not stupid." Omar nodded. "They hide and then they run and get a battalion."

Downslope, Sergeant Martillo paced and argued with his squad leaders, his voice carrying over the hillside.

"Think they've seen us?"

"Listen for helicopters." Omar watched the sergeant. "The Guard had helicopters and cannons and tanks and when they fought the Sandinistas, they lost. Now the Sandinistas have the helicopters and the Guard fights them again. . . ."

"He says"—Blanco glanced at the sergeant—"that we will be victorious, we will be in Managua in summer."

Omar laughed quietly, bitterly. "And maybe we will be in the dirt tomorrow."

The scout squad waved from the opposite ridgeline. Sergeant Martillo crossed first, all the others following in a ragged line. Head-high brush, vibrantly green despite the dry season, lined a dusty pathway. The greenery screened the contras from the highway and airborne observation. Wary of mines, Niles stepped in the bootprints of the men ahead of him. The platoons crossed quickly and rushed up the steep slopes to the ridgeline.

As his men spread out in the concealment of the brush, Martillo diagramed the action for Niles. "There, where the highway bends, we wait. They will send a bus first. If the bus hits a mine, it is an atrocity, so they always send a bus first. Then come the soldiers and supplies for the town. We know they come tomorrow. Our people tell us."

"And if they're wrong?"

"Then we wait. The trucks will come. There are many soldiers in Jalapa. There are many outposts on the road. A battalion or more. They must eat. When a truck comes or a convoy comes, we hit them."

"There are helicopters in Ocotal. What if—"

"Of course! That is why we came! Do you think I brought

26

forty-five men only to burn a few trucks? I can do that alone—"

A man hissed to Martillo, then pointed to the west. A line of Sandinistas walked along the road. All the talking and movement on the ridgeline stopped. Squinting into the setting sun, Niles studied the patrol. Twelve Sandinistas walked in two lines, six men on each side of the highway. From time to time, a man waved a metal detector over the road.

"Militia," Martillo told him. He passed his binoculars to Niles.

Teenagers and older men, the militiamen wore mismatched uniforms and carried only Kalashnikov rifles. Niles looked for an antenna or a radio-pack. None of the men carried a pack. As the militiamen passed the canyon, their faces turned, glancing at the fields and the hills, but they stayed on the road as they wandered toward Jalapa.

After dark, the contras shifted their positions. One platoon went down to the highway to set the ambush. The other men spread out on the ridgeline. Martillo told Niles to stay on the ridge.

"What if you are killed? Who would tell Washington of my victory?"

The platoon found positions in the brush and trees, then cut branches and lashed together camouflage. Niles watched as Blanco and Zutano set their position in an open patch of dry grass. They worked by starlight and a fragment of moon, using their knives to gouge fighting holes from the hard earth of the ridgeline.

"Why are you digging there?" Niles asked. "You have no cover. They will see you if they circle in a helicopter."

"That is why we are here. My rockets are for a helicopter. I cannot shoot from inside a tree."

"Have you shot at a helicopter before?"

"No. I have only seen them from far away. But the sergeant gave me instructions."

"If you are there, you will get killed."

Niles scanned the night landscape of the valley and ridgelines. He plotted the approximate orbit of an incoming helicopter. Then he found two tangles of brush growing close together.

"Here, come here and dig your holes."

As the teenagers worked, Niles carefully trimmed the downslope bushes to create a clear line of fire for a kneeling man. He wove the cut branches back into the bushes. Then he bent and broke other branches to overhang the position.

They worked for hours. When Niles finished, the teenagers had protection and a clear view of the canyon. They worked for another hour to dig a fighting hole for Niles a few steps away. As the young contras drifted to sleep, they whispered to him, telling him of the revolution and their hope for a free Nicaragua. Niles listened as he watched the valley.

From the lights of Jalapa, to the southwest where the mountains blocked his view, he saw only darkness. No cars or trucks traveled the highway. No lights showed from houses. After two years of fighting for the freedom of Nicaragua—contra raids, ambushes, and counterinsurgency sweeps by the Sandinista battalions—no one remained on the land between Jalapa and San Fernando. Two years of war had won only death and desolation.

As dawn paled the horizon, Niles scanned the valley and highway with the sergeant's binoculars. He swept the optics across the abandoned fields and along criss-crossing dirt roads, searching for the distinctive forms of walking soldiers. He watched the clusters of empty shacks. He saw no Sandinista patrols.

No traffic moved on the highway. He held the optics on the curve where the contra platoon waited in ambush, studying the area, looking for tracks, breaks in the roadside brush, any detail that might alert a truck driver or an airborne observer. He saw nothing that betrayed the unit.

On the ridgeline, the platoon of contras woke. They stretched under their tarps, talking, weapons and equipment clattering. The soldiers left their camouflaged positions and slid downslope to urinate in the brush. Others lit cigarettes. Niles heard the lookouts hiss warnings, telling the others to stay down, to be silent. Voices answered. Niles checked Blanco and Zutano. They remained silent within their screen of interwoven branches as they ate from cans and prepared their weapons.

He focused the binoculars on the canyon below him. In the still morning air, hundreds of tiny birds flitted through the cornfields. He watched the flocks for sudden flights caused by fright. The birds darted from row to row, feeding in nervous but undisturbed flocks. He swept the optics along the rutted dirt track and the pathways through the fields, searching for patrols. He scanned the triangle of the canyon from the mountain gorge to the highway—he saw only the birds moving.

The contras on the ridgeline talked and smoked. An empty bean can rattled down the hill. The noise brought Sergeant Martillo. He cursed and threatened until the soldiers went quiet. Niles saw the ex-sergeant pause beside the radio man, then continue along the line of hidden soldiers to Niles.

"You made that for them?" Martillo studied the position concealing Blanco and Zutano. "Very intelligent. I will remember that. You Marines can teach my soldiers many tricks."

"Vietnamese taught me that one."

"But if we had good missiles—Redeyes, Stinger missiles—we would not need these tricks. We could knock them down from high in the sky."

Niles scanned the western horizon. "Vietnamese knocked down hundreds of helicopters. They didn't need missiles."

"Don't sightsee. Watch that road."

"I think it's coming."

"I don't see it."

"If I were them, I'd send a spotter with a convoy."

In the west, a point of light flashed against the fading darkness—an observation plane. He focused the binoculars on the road and waited.

Kilometers away, a speck of yellow appeared.

"There it is. . . ."

Martillo scrambled back to the radio. The soldiers passed the word along the ridgeline. Niles saw the soldiers checking the tarps and branches concealing them. Blanco peered out of his position and gave Niles a clenched-fist salute.

Speeding over the dirt highway, the bus took form in the binoculars. Niles saw cargo on the roof. Two transport trucks followed. Dust clouded behind the bus, reducing the trucks to shadows. Niles followed the trucks with the binoculars but the distance and dust defeated the optics—he could not see what the trucks carried. He focused on the bus and saw what appeared to be men on the roof cargo rack.

The bus sped through the curve and continued east. Thirty seconds later, the first truck started the curve and the road exploded in a churning wave of dust as the ambush unit fired a series of claymore mines, thousands of high-velocity steel balls punching through tires and the sheet metal of the truck, instantly killing the driver, reducing the truck to a hulk rolling on the wheel rims.

The second truck stopped two hundred meters short of the curve. As the driver tried to turn the truck around, a machine gunner propped a weapon on the cab of the truck. Other Sandinistas jumped from the sides. Then a second series of mines exploded.

Dust and smoke obscured the action. Niles shifted the binoculars, following the road east. Hundreds of meters past the ambush, the bus stopped. Men with rifles climbed down from the roof. The bus continued to Jalapa as the Sandinistas ran into the fields behind the ambush, trying to attack the contras from behind. The faint popping of rifles drifted through the calm air.

Minutes passed as the contras annihilated the few survivors of the ambush. The teenagers on the ridge cheered on their compatriots. The riflefire died out and smoke rose from the wrecked trucks. As the dust cleared, Niles saw flames. The trucks and the dry roadside fields burned. Contras ran around the trucks, stripping weapons and equipment from bodies. Individual rifle shots popped. Then the contras left the road, groups of men running through the dry cornfields.

The few Sandinista militiamen from the bus stalled the retreat from the road. Contra squads maneuvered around the militiamen, killing the isolated and outnumbered men in firefights. But the elimination of the militiamen cost time. The spotter plane continued circling a thousand meters above the fields, watching as the contras retreated.

Niles heard the whine of the approaching helicopters. The contras on the ridge went quiet. No one moved as the two Soviet MI-8 troop transports banked into a steep turn. The pilots powered through a high circle, surveying the burning trucks, the fighting, and the ridgelines over the valley.

Mini-guns and rocket pods marked one helicopter as an assault version. The assault helicopter dropped and swept the far ridgeline with the mini-guns, the sound of the machine guns cutting through the rotor whine.

"No one move!" Niles shouted. "No one shoot! Get down!"

Pressing himself against the bottom of the narrow ditch, he heard the shriek of the helicopter and then the sound he remembered from Vietnam—the roar of mini-guns. Hundreds of heavy caliber slugs slashed through the brush and hammered the earth. The helicopter flashed overhead, brass cartridge casings showering down as the guns ripped trees higher in the mountains.

Martillo shouted, "Anyone hit? Report any casualties!"

Men answered with whistles and cheers. Niles looked up and saw the soldiers around him emerging from the holes. The storm of bullets had not killed or wounded any of the contras on the ridge.

The distant roar of the mini-guns cut off. Niles listened for the helicopter, trying to guess its position, but the rotor whine of the second helicopter covered the fading noise. The second helicopter descended into the canyon, dropping fast. The troop transport landed five hundred meters ahead of the contras retreating from the road.

The sergeant bellowed, "Now! Kill those Cuban sons of whores."

"No!" Niles shouted. "Don't! There's a—" Obeying the order, the contras fired, their rifles and machine guns overwhelming Niles's voice. He scrambled across the slope. As Blanco rose to one knee and aimed a rocket at the transport helicopter, Niles reached for the pistol grip of the launcher. "Wait—"

Blanco fired and the rocket flashed away. Before the first rocket hit, Zutano jerked the safety cap off the second rocket. Other teams fired rockets.

"Wait!" Niles grabbed the launcher.

Sandinista soldiers jumped from the side doors of the helicopter and ran through the rotor storm of dust and flying cornstalks. At that moment, the antiarmor rocket grenades hit. Men disappeared in flashes of high explosive. A mortar shell landed fifty meters past the helicopters.

"The sergeant ordered—"

"The other helicopter—"

The other rocket crews fired again and scored. The troopship cockpit exploded, fragments of metal and plexiglass spinning through the brilliant morning light, the helicopter tilting sideways, the main rotor blades slicing through running soldiers.

Turbines shrieking from behind the contras, the first helicopter returned from the east, screaming over the ridgeline and banking, turning to point its gun and rocket pods back at the contras. The two M-60 machine guns fired continuously, trying to track the gun-mounted troopship.

Niles took the loaded rocket launcher. Kneeling, he thumbed back the hammer and sighted through the 2.5X scope, setting the reticle lines on the hub of the five-bladed rotors. He waited. The pilot brought the helicopter around and started back, coming straight into the scope. Niles raised the reticle ahead and above the helicopter.

He squeezed back the trigger. The rocket shrieked away and at the same moment, the pilot fired his mini-guns, streams of slugs ripping apart the hillside hundreds of meters below Niles, dust and chopped wood churning, trees shuddering, a wave of dust racing up the slope as the pilot held down the trigger button.

The rocket went high, missing the fuselage but exploding in the tail blades. The helicopter spun out of control, the bullets from the mini-guns whipping to the side, 57mm air-to-ground rockets flashing from the pods but flying wild.

All the firing on the ridge stopped as the helicopter smashed into the steep slope, the rotors shattering. Impact reduced the fuselage to twisted metal. An instant later, the fuselage rolled down the hill, throwing junk and broken rotors as the wreck disintegrated.

RECON STRIKE

A mountainside kilometers away erupted in flame and dust as the volley of 57mm rockets hit.

The contras on the ridge shouted and raved. Cursing, Martillo ran along the ridge. He pointed at the road.

Two trucks crowded with militiamen came from Jalapa. The sergeant and the crew of the mortar jerked the legs and tube around and aimed at the road. The sergeant spun the elevation and traverse cranks, aimed, adjusted the gears again before dropping a shell down the tube. Seconds later, the shell burst at the roadside, a hundred meters west of the trucks. The trucks stopped, the militiamen jumping down. The sergeant adjusted the traverse. The next round hit fifty meters past the trucks. The Sandinistas scattered and the sergeant adjusted the aim again and sent the third round into the militiamen. The trucks left the highway, lurching over the fields to escape the mortars.

The contras on the ridge fired into the downed helicopters. Tracers touched off the fuel of the transport helicopter, flames rising from the wreck, ammunition popping, rockets exploding.

Niles focused the borrowed binoculars on the center of the valley. He saw Sandinista soldiers trying to rescue their comrades from the assault helicopter. Incoming rifle and machine gun rounds dropped men.

Hundreds of meters away, the contra ambush platoon ran for the mountain. A man fell and all the other contras went flat in the furrows. Searching the area, Niles found a line of Sandinista riflemen in a dry ditch, firing across the cornfields at the contras.

He saw dust puff around the Sandinista squad as full-auto bursts from the machine gunners found the range.

Two Sandinistas went still. Others ran. A stream of slugs from an M-60 spun a man, then a rocket splashed flame and left only torn corpses.

Niles looked for other Sandinistas still fighting. But smoke obscured the area as flames spread from the helicopters to the dry fields and brush. The smoke also hid the movement of the contras as they ran to the foot of the mountain and zigzagged up the slope.

Shouldering his pack, Niles rushed down the ridge to Martillo. The sergeant labored with the mortar gears, adjusting the aim to follow the Sandinista reaction force as they rushed through the fields. He grabbed the binoculars from Niles and watched the Sandinistas. Smoke rising from the canyon obscured his view. Only two 82mm high-explosive shells remained. Niles crouched with the crew and waited, exchanging grins with the teenagers.

Martillo cranked the gears. He took one of the shells and held it over the tube as he watched the Sandinistas in the distant fields. He dropped the shell and waited. Niles saw the explosion scatter the Sandinistas.

"Ha! I got the head dog." He raised the binoculars again. "Now they try to help him. . . ." The sergeant snatched up the last shell and dropped it down the tube. "Now we go. We are victorious."

As the crew disassembled the mortar, Martillo scanned the canyon, surveying the black hulks of the trucks, the burning fields, and the flaming wreckage of the Soviet helicopters.

"Did it not go as I told you?" Martillo asked him.

"You got them, no doubt about it." Niles squinted into the sky, watching the spotter plane circle. He scanned the horizon. "Question is, where are the gunships?"

"The gunships? Are you blind? It is burning down there—"

"That was not a gunship. It was a troopship. With guns and rockets."

But the sergeant had already rushed away, shouting at his soldiers, ordering the mortar and machine gun crews to move faster. Niles crouched there, his rifle in his hands, watching the contras assemble for their retreat to the Honduran border. He noted every detail: the men with the M-60 machine guns dragging the loose-swinging belts of cartridges through the dust, the teenagers firing their Kalashnikovs blind into the swirling smoke, the sergeant maintaining control over the platoon with shouts.

Gasping and coughing in the smoke, the ambush platoon staggered to the top of the ridge. Rifles popped a thousand meters away as the Sandinistas in the canyon tried to hit them, the spent slugs zipping through brush and skipping off the hard earth. Niles eased down prone, exposing only his face to the random fire as he waited.

He saw Omar emerge from the swirling gray smoke. He half carried a semiconscious teenage contra. A bloody bandage wrapped the wounded man's arm and a web belt cinched the flopping, broken arm to his torso. Another contra improvised a branch and rope stretcher.

The smoke reduced the men to a crowd of shadows. Martillo led the platoons north, the line of men running as fast as the weight of their weapons and packs allowed. Blanco and Zutano waited for the men carrying the stretcher. They alternated with the burden of the wounded man.

Last in the line, Niles watched the ridge behind him, expecting the Sandinistas to appear at any moment. But the contras reached the treeline without pursuit. There, Niles looked up, trying to see the observation plane. The column of smoke billowed high into the sky, blocking his sight—and the sight of the observer in the plane.

The turbine scream of the third helicopter came a minute later. The contras panicked and ran through the pines and oaks. Niles spotted a narrow, erosion-cut gully between two oaks. He called to the group struggling with the stretcher and helped them lower the wounded man into the narrow gully.

Like a long, tearing explosion, mini-guns ripped the ridgeline with a maelstrom of heavy caliber slugs. The guns went silent. Niles looked up and saw the belly and weapon pods of an MI-24 assault helicopter pass over him. The gunship circled and rockets tore into the section of the ridge the contras had occupied. Returning again, the gunship flew slowly along the ridge. They heard the turbine whine fade as the Soviet helicopter flew higher into the mountains, searching for the contras.

Niles and the others jerked the stretcher out of the gully and ran. They found the main force of contras leaving their concealment. Sergeant Martillo laughed when he saw Niles.

"Thought they got you. Who would have told my story in Washington? Who would have described my victory and asked them for antiaircraft rockets? I tell you, with a Stinger rocket, we could have killed three helicopters today."

"Yes, Comandante." Niles nodded. "It was a good trick. But I don't think you can ever try this again."

"Not again? I will do it many times! Tell them of the helicopters. Tell them I want missiles."

"I'll tell them. You can be sure I'll tell them about today."

5

EMILIO Pazos left the customs terminal of Damascus International Airport. A middle-aged, overweight Cuban, he dressed in a tropical-weight tan suit creased and wrinkled by the long flight from Havana to Madrid to Rome to Damascus. Though he claimed pure Castilian blood, he had thick Caribbean features and glossy black curly hair slicked back with pomade. His face glistened with smeared pomade. Shouldering through the chaos of passengers hurrying from the exit, he watched for the young man assigned to meet him.

Porters followed Pazos from the exit, grabbing for the suitcase and garment bag he carried, calling to him in Arabic and French. He ignored them as he scanned the sidewalk and traffic lanes. A group of Iranian women shrouded in chadors crowded from the exit doors and the porters left Pazos. The porters took the battered suitcases of the group, following the shouted instructions of a travel agent directing the women and the porters to a bus parked with the taxis and private cars in the lot.

Only official cars parked at the curbs of the traffic lanes. Here, in Syria, the nation that had invented and perfected the car bomb as a weapon of terror, police and soldiers enforced the laws prohibiting the parking of unauthorized vehicles at government buildings. At the entrance to the arrivals terminal, traffic police directed civilian traffic to the public lots. Police ordered even wealthy merchants to park their Mercedes sedans among the hotel vans and rusting taxis. Only the limousines of government and foreign officials stopped at the curb near the terminal buildings. Soldiers in green and rust camouflage fatigues watched a black Mercedes idling near the exits. Pazos looked through the tinted windows but saw only a silhouette. Then a voice called out in Spanish:

"¡Señor! ¡Señor! Su amigo está acá." A plainclothes security man rushed to him. Despite the young man's sunglasses and beard, Pazos recognized him as the young man he expected—a military aide he had contacted on previous stops in Syria.

"We'll speak English. Where is he?"

"Come." The young soldier walked Pazos to the Mercedes and opened the passenger-side front door. "He waits."

"Atallah?"

"Finally they release you from their pointless inspections. Please put your luggage in the back. Forgive me for not offering my assistance but it is better that I do not leave the car."

Colonel Nazim Atallah of Syrian military intelligence flicked his cigarette into the street and shook hands with his Cuban visitor. A gaunt, balding man, with a hooked Arabic nose, he displayed long, tobacco-yellowed teeth when he smiled. A livid scar hooded the corner of his right eye—a wound suffered in the Israeli retaliatory raids of November 1983 for the truck bombing of their headquarters in Tyre. The Israeli bombers had come within millimeters of killing the man responsible for delivering thousands of kilograms of explosives and detonators to the Shiite gangs of Baalbek, explosives which the Shiites then delivered by truck and suicide driver to the French and American Multinational Peacekeeping Forces in Beirut and the Israeli Headquarters in Tyre.

The colonel did not wear his uniform today. Instead, he wore a French-tailored gray suit highlighted with gold cuff links and a Rolex watch. The imported suit, the gold, the Mercedes, his apartment in France—though he used his image of wealth in his duties in Syria, Lebanon, and Europe, he did not buy the luxuries with his army salary. He avoided the Spartan life of a career officer by capitalizing on the socialist economy of Syria and the cargo capacity of his trucks returning from Lebanon. His trucks carried weapons and munitions to the allies of Syria operating in the Bekaa, and the trucks returned with consumer goods for the black market of Damascus—American cigarettes, Japanese electronics, French delicacies. He offered Pazos a smuggled Marlboro as he steered with one hand through the traffic.

"You of course know of the attack on the Americans in Salvador. It is in all the newspapers."

Pazos laughed. "Yankees!" He took a long drag on the cigarette and exhaled. "The stupidity and arrogance of the Yankees is beyond understanding. They prop up that puppet regime, they terrorize the masses of El Salvador, they strut and posture on the boulevards. And yet they react with indignation when the vanguard of the revolution strikes back."

"My congratulations to the vanguard." Atallah accelerated away from the confusion of the airport complex, following the highway northwest to Damascus. "But why only four soldiers? Why not the American ambassador? Why not the embassy?"

"Why do you ask me these questions?" Pazos smiled at Atallah. "The Ministry of International Development has no contact with the revolutionaries in El Salvador."

"Of course not. But I thought that you, as a man knowledgeable in that area of the world, might answer my questions. I cannot ask the television or talk to a newspaper."

"The embassy in San Salvador is impossible. It is a fortress. First, matters of visas and immigration are processed in a different area by Salvadorian hirelings. If fighters attacked that office, they would only kill other Salvadorians. Then, anyone who enters the area staffed by Yankees must have clearance, which is very difficult to receive. Even with clearance, there is an electronic search for weapons and explosives. I heard that a unit planned to pose as a news crew and take in a bomb—"

"As in the attempt on Pastora, in Costa Rica."

"That was a crime of contra against contra," Pazos said. And again he laughed. "But the Americans are not as stupid as Pastora. They used electronic sniffers and dogs to check the equipment. And after the bombings in Beirut, they prohibited all parking within a block."

"How unfortunate. Even Americans learn. That forces the fighters of the world to become inventive. But enough of this talk in the abstract. Tell me, how goes your work in Nicaragua? With the development of the export projects? What will be the price of the bananas?"

Both men laughed at the joke. Officially, Pazos had come to Syria with contracts detailing the sale and transshipment via Cuba of bananas and beef for Syrian and Iranian distribution. His briefcase contained the contracts—in Spanish, English, and Arabic, with schedules of shipments and deliveries. If a delay with his interconnecting flights had forced him to leave the transit lounge of an airline and pass through customs, a search and examination of his papers would reveal only a complicated commercial enterprise. The Americans had succeeded in intercepting couriers and photographing documents many times. Pazos had not risked the success of his future attacks by carrying a page of information or a photo of a target or the name of a fighter—all that stayed in his office in Managua. Only his memory and imagination traveled with him.

"The price will be acceptable to all parties. Less than the Americans paid Nicaragua, but more than enough to cover the additional shipping expenses. But that is a detail for the agents. Tell me of this product and this demonstration."

"Be patient. Tell me of your other development projects. I believe I will take a strong interest in that region in the future."

For the next hour, Pazos talked in generalities as Atallah drove through the dusty urban sprawl of Damascus. Pazos wanted the support of the Syrians in his actions but did not want to risk compromising the attacks. Atallah understood this. He listened and commented but did not demand details.

They reached the Syrian armed forces base at Daraiya, a high-security installation surrounded by concentric rings of barbed wire, minefields, bunkers, and antiaircraft guns. The perimeter protected office and barracks complexes of the elite units of the Syrian Army and Air Force.

At Daraiya, President Hafez al-Assad maintained battalions of Special Forces commandos on continuous alert. These troops—and their squadrons of helicopter transports and gunships—did not wait in expectation of an Israeli surprise attack. The elite airborne units guarded against any possible challenge to the rule of al-Assad by opposing Syrian political factions. In the event of a prolonged power struggle, runways four kilometers long allowed direct flights from the Soviet Union of Ilyushin cargo planes.

Atallah cleared the several guard posts and drove to a separate high-security compound. An eight-story building housed the offices and technical facilities of the intelligence services. A helipad served the needs of the officers, providing transportation to all units in Syria and Lebanon. Atallah parked his Mercedes at the helipad.

"To the Bekaa now."

A Soviet MI-8 troopship took them over Damascus to Beirut highway and through the mountains dividing Syria from Lebanon. Deafened by the noise of the turbines, Pazos watched as Atallah consulted with a crewman, looking from a map to the landscape below. The helicopter circled an area, then descended. Atallah opened a briefcase and motioned for Pazos to look inside.

"Examine it."

The briefcase contained a simple gray box. Pazos picked it up and turned it over in his hands. Lightweight, fabricated of sheet metal, the box remained open on one side. Inside, Pazos saw a rack of plastic circuit boards and heavy batteries. Wires ran to a simple switch marked ON-OFF.

"What is it?"

"You will see."

Atallah flipped the switch and closed the briefcase. The helicopter bumped down. A crewman slid back the side door. A storm of dust swirled inside the helicopter. Atallah stepped out and Pazos saw him set down the briefcase in the rocks and dry brush of a mountain ridge. The ridge viewed the expanse of the Bekaa Valley and the mountains beyond. Returning to the troopship, Atallah switched on a walkie-talkie. A shrill tone cut through the rotor noise.

"It is transmitting," Atallah shouted.

A short flight took them to a dirt road cutting through the foothills of the valley. Following Atallah, Pazos stepped down to the stones and rutted earth of the road. Sand blinded him as the helicopter lifted away. He felt grit clinging to the pomade in his hair.

"Now we drive again." Atallah opened the door of the Land Cruiser waiting at the side of the road.

The electronic tone droned from the walkie-talkie as Atallah drove west, following the dirt road west a few kilometers. He turned on a dirt track winding across hillsides of abandoned fields. Only concrete slabs and scattered bricks remained of a farmer's home. A heap of rusting metal with tank tracks and an out-jutting cannon barrel indicated a past battle in the area.

A kilometer downhill, another road cut across the fields. Pazos saw a diesel truck lurching across the ruts and holes, laboring to pull a trailer. A pickup truck followed the truck and trailer. Atallah switched channels on the droning walkie-talkie and spoke in a language Pazos guessed to be Farsi. A voice answered. He switched back to the electronic tone and parked the Land Cruiser. Passing a pair of binoculars to Pazos, he pointed to the truck and trailer:

"Watch the men."

Through the binoculars, Pazos saw that the diesel truck towed a flatbed trailer loaded with a cargo container. Both trucks stopped. Men in old fatigues and civilian shirts left the pickup truck. They opened the doors of the cargo container and took out tools linked with cords. In the quiet of the foothills, the faint noise of gasoline generators drifted across the fields.

"There, you see that mountain?" Atallah pointed to the east. "That peak. That is where we left the briefcase. About eighteen kilometers, more or less. And a thousand meters higher in elevation. If I challenged the finest Cuban artillery officer, the finest in your nation, do you believe he could hit that briefcase with his first shot? One and only one shell?"

"It would not be possible."

"With a rocket?"

"Impossible."

"Watch."

Pazos returned the binoculars to the truck and trailer. The men walked on top of the cargo container, the electric wrenches in their hands. They removed a line of bolts from the container. Dropping their tools, they climbed down the sides and stepped away from the trailer.

The panels of the container opened, one side falling, the roof and the other side slowly lifting away. The roof and side panel passed a balance point and fell, exposing a Soviet multiple-tube rocket launcher. Unlike the other Katyusha rocket launchers he had seen, this launcher did not ride on a truck. As Pazos watched, the launcher swiveled, the tubes rising.

Flame flashed and a rocket screamed overhead. Pazos turned and watched the distant mountain peak.

The electronic drone from the walkie-talkie cut off, dust and smoke churning upward from the peak.

"From eighteen kilometers," Atallah told him.

Disassembled 122mm rockets lay on wooden tables, the solid propellant fuel and the warheads removed. A wood and steel clamp held one rocket casing in position under a drill press. On another table, clear plastic wrapped a compact assembly of electronics. Four tiny fins stood out on shafts.

"This is the terminal guidance module," Atallah explained, lifting away the plastic. "Come, look at it closely. What do you read?"

Peering at the components, Pazos saw reorder codes and company trademarks. On one motor, he read, MADE IN USA. "This is American? How did you get it?"

"The parts are American. And Japanese and European. There is nothing Soviet."

"Except the rockets and the launcher."

"Of course. But the launchers are everywhere. Beirut. China. Africa. Nicaragua. Even the Israelis use them. What is significant is the guidance system. A very ingenious system, if I may say. Invented by an Iranian. . . ."

Pazos paced through the improvised factory as Atallah talked. A steel frame garage with a high ceiling, the interior of the building still smelled of diesel, and gasoline, and solvents. The front had rolling steel doors almost two stories high to allow trucks with trailers to drive from the highway into the service area. Though improvised, the factory looked organized and efficient.

"An Iranian who had been trained by the Americans to maintain the Shah's Hawk missiles. But for his system, he used only civilian electronic components. It is all very simple and very inexpensive. His system balances simplicity against cost and complexity to achieve very impressive accuracy—as you saw. A fighter places a transmitter at the target, then turns on the signal. The signal activates a small computer at the launcher. The computer calculates the direction and range, then aims the launcher and fires the salvo of forty rockets. As the rockets descend, each rocket homes on the signal of the transmitter, the steering fins on the nose guiding the rocket to the target."

Glancing out the back door of the garage, Pazos saw flatbed trailers loaded with containers. A welding kit stood beside a ladder. A long scorch line ran along the corner of a container where the side panels met the roof. He and Atallah had interrupted the conversion of another cargo container to conceal and transport rockets.

"An ingenious sytem," Atallah continued. "However, it disappointed the Iranians."

"Why?"

"It has no value on the Iraqi front. It requires a martyr to place the transmitter. And the minefields of the Iraqis do not make that possible. Also, the rockets do not have the range to avoid Iraqi artillery. Therefore, they decided to use this weapon on other fronts."

"Where?"

"Can you not," Atallah asked, "see the value of this weapon against an embassy? The transmitter is not a weapon or a bomb. We can conceal it within a video camera or a recorder. If a martyr can take a video camera to an interview, perhaps with the American ambassador. . . ."

Turbines screamed outside as a flight of helicopters passed over the office building. Atallah paused. He tapped another cigarette from the pack and lit it from the one he smoked. Pazos waited for the Syrian to speak again, watching Atallah stub out the butt, then looking away, his eyes scanning the hundreds of Arabic, English, and French books on the shelves. The noise faded, quiet returning to the office.

Typing continued in the outer office. Seconds passed. Pazos looked down at the intricate geometric and floral patterns of the Persian carpet—like the books, the Rolex, and the Mercedes, a display of the colonel's wealth.

"Can you provide a crew who speak English?"

The question surprised Pazos. "Why English?"

"Will your men speak Farsi?"

"No."

"And we do not have technicians who speak Spanish. Only English. The technicians will train the Salvadorians to maintain and prepare the launcher."

"But what of the Americans? When they find the launcher and the crew, they will know it is not a Salvadorian attack. They will strike out at who—"

"Strike out at who?" Atallah looked to the ceiling and clasped his hands together, praying. "Allah the Compassionate, the Merciful, shelter me from the revenge of the Americans, from the rage of their clown who is a president, for his rage, for his declarations of justice to come threatens me with death by my own laughter—Please, Emilio, no more jokes! Did you see him after the bombing in Beirut? Hundreds of their Marines dead. Hundreds! As I watched him speak his scripted lines on the television, I was racked by laughter. It threatened my heart. But let me tell you why I do not fear even my own laughter. Here—"

Atallah took a folder from his desk. "I anticipated your concern. There is the documentation on the launcher you saw today."

Pazos leafed through the pages. He saw photocopies bearing the seal of the Soviet Union. "I don't read Russian."

"Or Portuguese? Or Afrikaner? Or Ethiopian? The Soviets shipped a launcher and a truck to Angola. South Africa captured the launcher during one of their attacks. South Africa traded the truck, launcher, and rockets to Ethiopia for grain. Grain sent to feed the starving people of Ethiopia. Is that not interesting? This launcher will be used against Americans and American charity paid for the launcher? On the freighter, Palestinians dismantled the launcher and dumped the truck into the ocean. In the Port of Aseb, Ethiopia, they covered the launcher with sacks of coffee.

The freighter took the cargo to the Mediterranean. The Palestinians paid the captain to stop at Tripoli. They unloaded the launcher and it went to the Bekaa."

Atallah pointed his cigarette at the folder. "It is all there, far more information than their CIA or journalists will ever know. Who will the Americans accuse of supplying these rockets to the Salvadorians? The Islamic Jihad? The mysterious gang they cannot find. The Soviets? The super-power they will not attack. The South Africans? Or Ethiopia?"

"How will he transport the rockets to El Salvador?"

"Say the word and it will be done. You send a crew for training. We will provide the launcher, the rockets, and the transmitter. We will build the transmitter into the device of your choice—camera, recorder, whatever. You find the martyrs to carry the transmitter and decide the day. Those details of the victory will be your responsibility. Do you foresee any difficulties with the Nicaraguans and the Salvadorians? Will they possibly object to this?"

"I am their director. Who are they to object?" Pazos ran a hand over the pomade of his hair. "However, this question of martyrs . . . is there some other way to place the transmitter?"

"Perhaps 'martyr' is a poor choice of words," Atallah corrected himself. "My English is less than perfect. As is my understanding of Catholicism. Most Salvadorians are Catholics, yes? And Catholics do not rush to their paradise. Perhaps the word 'volunteer' is better. They might be told their responsibility is only to interview the ambassador. And martyrdom would come as a surprise."

Pazos laughed. "I can find volunteers."

6

A BUS roared past on the avenue, the wheels smashing down on the broken pavement, the cantina shuddering with the impacts. Black-and-white images of Salvadorian soldiers and United States Marines flashed on the television, music from the jukebox blasting away the voice of the narrator. Staring at the television, the old woman who owned the cantina ignored the loud talk and shouting of the two young men, her only customers that morning. The young men, dressed in new shirts and polyester slacks, drank and raved and waved their arms. Sometimes they leaned across their table and whispered. On the television, video stories from the hometowns of the dead Marines alternated with the somber faces of American politicians issuing statements from Washington, D.C.

The two young men shared a bottle of aguardiente, a tasteless, colorless liquor distilled from sugar cane. David Vargas poured more aguardiente into the glass of his brother, César. Already drunk, his eyes wide, César raised the glass toward the television and shouted out:

"Dead gringos! Kill them all! Revolutionary justice!"

Glancing at the two young men, the old woman almost smiled, her toothless mouth moving. But she said nothing. She turned back to the television and stared at a scene of teenager lovers running through a field of flowers. The singing and music from the jukebox paused. Outside, a sound truck blared a patriotic slogan, the amplified voice louder than the motorcycle and unmuffled engines.

"That shit," César cursed. Another record came on, the electric guitars and drums defeating the traffic and propaganda of the avenue. "I tell you, join us. We are killing gringos. Here in the capital. What does it count to fight in Chalatenango? Kill a soldier there? It is nothing! Nothing! Kill a gringo here and all the world knows!"

David shook his head, no. "The squads operate here. They took our brother, our cousin, our friends from school. If I had not gone to the hills, I would be dead."

"Then why am I safe?"

"You went to Nicaragua."

"Or Cuba. Wherever it was. They never told me. Fly there, fly back. But I tell you why. The unit gave me a new name and new papers. We operate alone. No other groups. And now, now in the capital, because the fascists are taking the orders of the gringos, there are no more death squads. And you, you still fight in the hills. Where they bomb, where they use the gunships, hundreds of soldiers. You starve and suffer. But here, here we stay in apartments and fuck our girlfriends and when the time is right, we hit the sons of bitches and all the world knows. Do I tell the truth? Would I lie to my own brother?"

"It is bad out there." David nodded. "We fight and run and the people tell the army and they send the gunships. Men died shooting their rifles at the sky."

"The war will not be won by preaching to the campesinos. They're too stupid. Give them a tortilla and you are the boss. The war will be won here in the capital. Come with me. I will take you to Paulino. We can use a man who's good with a rifle. Because the next time—"

César turned to look at the doorway and the other tables. No one else had entered the cantina. The old woman stared at the television and fanned flies from her hair. "Next time, we make a big hit. Paulino took pictures of the embassy and the mansion where the pig ambassador lives. I drove Paulino and that rich bitch Marianela around. Like tourists. They didn't tell me, but I know. Next time, it's big."

"What about money?"

"Good money! An apartment. Clothes. And I drive the taxi when I'm not with the unit. I always keep some of that money for me. I'll share with you. We can both drive the

48

taxi. We can make money and win the war! What do you say?"

"Can we talk with this Paulino? I don't want to—"

"Done! We go now—"

"I don't want to tell my commander I want to go unless it is for sure."

"We go now." César stood, the chair falling behind him. He held onto the table to steady himself. "Drink, finish it. The rich boy won't give us any shit. I want you in the unit and that is that. So we go. It is arranged."

David went to a mirror hanging on the back wall and smoothed his hair. He straightened his shirt collar. A new shirt, pale blue, long sleeved, yet cool, he had bought it the night before from a Chinese importer. "In a minute. I've got to go to the pisser."

Staggering out the back door of the cantina, he followed a pathway through trash and broken glass. Slat board fences and sheets of corrugated steel divided the lot from the other lots. He heard the banging of hammers on car fenders and the screech of a cutting wheel. At the back of the lot, four uprights of lumber, roofed with plywood and walled with sheets of plastic, served as an outhouse. Filth and black swarms of flies covered the concrete base of the toilet. Nauseated, he stepped behind the outhouse and urinated against the fence.

The midday sun glared down on him, but the alcohol put the tropical heat and the stink of the cesspool and the traffic chaos far away. He remembered years before, drinking beer at the beach and dancing and trying to kiss the high school girls and staggering home drunk in the darkness—like a different life.

Tables crashed in the cantina. Men shouted, "Police!"

David hit the fence, trying to climb but falling as the boards and sheets of plywood collapsed. Chickens squawked and flapped as he scrambled to his feet and ran through a winding courtyard of shacks. A woman washing clothes in a bucket looked at him and looked down, as if she had not seen him. He thrashed through wet clothes hanging on a line and came to a brick wall. A gate blocked the way to the street but he kicked it aside. A few more steps took him to the dirt street.

Walking—he forced himself to walk—along the narrow street, he passed trucks and vans. Cart men struggled to haul loads of fruit and vegetables from the trucks to the stalls of the market on the intersecting boulevard. David wove into the crowds of women carrying bags and zigzagged through the stalls. At a booth, he bought a fifteen-centavo plastic bag and a cheap soccer shirt with a white body and orange sleeves. Dodging into a doorway, he took off his good blue shirt and pulled on the cheap T-shirt. He concealed his dress shirt in the bag. He stood there thinking of his brother in the hands of the police—and he vomited, spewing out the aguardiente.

"Get out of here, you disgrace!" A woman cursed. "Take your sickness away. You should be working."

Turning his face away from the woman, David stumbled through the market. He bought sunglasses from a vendor. Then a bag of frozen juice. Biting off the corner, he sucked on the ice and wandered back to the avenue of the cantina. A crowd of teenagers and children stood on the sidewalk.

In the center of the block, National Police squad cars parked on the sidewalks. Shopkeepers stared from their doorways. Policemen searched his brother's taxi. He saw four policemen drag his brother—bleeding, his head rolling on his shoulders—from the cantina to a squad car.

They had taken his brother. He could do nothing to save him. But the capture of his brother meant danger to the other members of the urban unit. He owed those comrades a warning. Standing there a moment longer, the cheap sunglasses hiding his tears, David took a last look at his older brother, unconscious and bleeding, never again to walk free or to fight the regime.

For an hour, David took buses through San Salvador, walking from avenues to cross streets, then taking other buses before knocking on the door of his contact and telling of his brother's capture.

Then he left San Salvador, returning to the war in the Chalatenango.

*   *   *

50

In the mountains of Morazón province, a People's Revolutionary Army radio post received the coded message from San Salvador. The operator recognized the identification phrase and retransmitted the message to Nicaragua.

Machines in the offices of the Ministry of International Development in Managua automatically recorded the transmission. Raúl Condori returned from lunch and decoded the relayed message. Following the instructions of Pazos, he coded the information, added instructions, and keyed the message to Cuba.

In Cuba, the communications officer followed the instructions, typing one copy for the Directorate General of Intelligence, the Cuban equivalent of the American CIA, and a second copy for secure retransmission to Damascus where Emilio Pazos, the commander of the operation in San Salvador, met with Colonel Nazim Atallah.

Her blow dryer whirring in her hand, Lidia Rivas watched the evening news coverage of the ceremony at Ilopango Air Force Base. The television showed politicians and officers crowding a review stand set on one of the runways. An honor guard of Salvadorian air commandos in camouflage fatigues and berets slouched beside flag-draped caskets on wheeled stands. General Ochoa intoned a solemn statement in memory of the assassinated Marines, dedicating the armed forces and people of El Salvador to the continuing struggle for freedom. Security men in suits and black sunglasses faced outward from the review stand, watching the air force commandos and the crowd of onlookers.

The electronics of the television altered the colors of the assembled soldiers and dignitaries. The green of the camouflage uniforms, the red and blue of the flags, the sun-flashing gold of the officers' uniforms—the scene had the unreal look of a tourist postcard. The camera zoomed in on the General's sweating face to catch his final declaration: "Patriotism and liberty, or death!"

Rivas ran her hand through her scented hair and laughed. A band struck a funeral march and the air force commandos shoved the caskets to the waiting transport plane. At the cargo doors, a second honor guard of United States Marines stood at rigid attention.

Knocking startled Rivas. Dropping the hair dryer, she picked up her Beretta from the table and pointed the pistol at the apartment door. "Who is there?"

"Paulino."

"What is it?"

"An emergency."

Opening the locks with her left hand, she held the pistol ready. Paulino Rivera closed the door behind him. He wore tennis whites and carried an equipment bag. Rushing past her, he turned up the volume of the television. The funeral march covered his panicked whisper:

"They got César. The one that drove the taxi cab."

"How long ago?"

"This morning."

"What? Why wasn't I told?"

"I got it from the Party. They sent a messenger to me."

"Because they think you're the leader. Pretty Paulino, the leader. Wait outisde. I'll get ready. We'll go to Julio and use the radio."

"There are police watching his place. We've got to call him, warn him about—"

"Forget him. We'll go to Martín, use his radio. Get confirmation and instructions—"

"We don't need to. The Party got instructions from Managua to get us out through their network."

"That's not the procedure. We must radio our commander for instructions."

"Forget One-Eye! The Party will get us out tonight. It's all arranged. I can't go back to my place and César knows what you look like. The police are already looking for us. They'll be here next."

Rivas considered the risk of using the contacts of the Revolutionary Workers' Party. Cuban-financed, with hundreds of members throughout the country, with urban squads fighting in the cities and guerrilla units in the countryside, they had the organization to evacuate her group. But the security forces assigned agents to infiltrate known organizations. In Nicaragua, Quezada had told her not to use the

Cuban group. Yet if she waited for instructions, she risked capture.

"We go. And Paulino, until we return to our commander, your ambition is fulfilled. You will pretend to be the leader of our group. Now get out while I get ready."

Minutes later, they ran from the apartment house in matching tennis whites. Her sweater covered the Beretta stuck in the waist band of her shorts. Rivas wore an oversized purse over her right shoulder. She walked with her hand in the purse, gripping her Uzi submachine gun. She carried her tennis racket in her left hand. At the gate, Rivas stopped and scanned the quiet, tree-shadowed street.

A streetlamp shone on the corner, the amber light shattering through the trees. They saw no one walking. A few cars parked near one walled estate where a silhouette with a rifle paced at a gate. Lights shone from the guard positions of several estates.

"Walk slow. Laugh."

Rivera forced a laugh as he crossed the sidewalk to the parked Fiat and opened the door for her. Then they accelerated away, speeding through the residential streets. Rivera whipped through turns, studying the rear-view mirror for trailing surveillance. He turned onto a boulevard and wove through the traffic.

"Down," he told her.

"What?"

"Down! Put your head down. They said you are not to see where we go. It is security."

Pressing her face to her knees, she felt a coat go over her back. Then the little Fiat swerved through a series of turns to disorient her. Rivera switched on the radio. Blind, the music blasting into her ears, she rode doubled-over for several songs and commercials—perhaps fifteen minutes. The Fiat left the smooth boulevards of the central city and bucked and lurched, beating the back of her head against the dash, as Rivera continued into one of the slum districts. Despite the radio, she heard the roaring of diesel buses and smelled the particular rot and human filth stink of a *turgurio*—one of the cardboard-and-scrap-metal slums spilling down the steep ravines that cut through the city.

A final whipping right turn took the sports car into a building. Steel screeched as a roll-down door shut off the noise of the street. Finally Rivera clicked off the music and allowed Rivas to sit up.

"We are here!" The Peoples' Fortress!"

Laughter rang in the empty auto garage. Tools and junk parts lined the walls. Worklights hung from the high ceiling by cables. Squinting against the white glare, Rivas saw a second floor and walkway overlooking the work area. Forms with weapons looked down at the newcomers. Television voices and music came from a doorway.

A silhouette appeared in the doorway. The man leaned on the walkway railing and called down to her:

"Are you ready to go to Cuba?"

After she left the car, the man who talked of Cuba took her aside. Middle-aged, stinking of cologne, his gut straining at the sparkling sports shirt he wore, he introduced himself:

"I am Gonzalo Soto, the leader of the unit that will help you. I am organizing your trip to safety. What is your name, Comrade?"

"Marianela."

"Oh, Marianela the brave one. Come, come with me. I do not want to be overheard." He led her into an office stacked with boxes. He leaned close to Rivas and whispered, "I said Cuba for the others to hear. But you will go to another country. A country far more radical."

Rivas stepped back, eyeing this fat man who claimed to be a unit leader. Soto edged closer and whispered, "I do not want to be overheard by the others. We must always consider security. You have a future unlike all the others. And you must prepare for your role in the triumph of the revolution. I have received instructions from Cuba, from the director himself, and you will go far in the—"

"Who is this director? What is his name?"

Soto laughed. "A name would be a violation of security. But I can tell you that he is impressed by the little group you fight with. You will receive more training. A new identity. And a new role—I can say no more now. You will see."

Rivas reached under her sweater and touched the Beretta in her waistband. If this fat man tried to molest her in this filthy room, she intended to smash him with the pistol. He saw the grips of the Beretta jammed into the front of her shorts.

"A pistol! You are truly a dangerous one. But you will not need your weapons now. We will keep you very safe."

And he touched her, his hand stroking her hair, and she jerked away, her hand pulling the pistol free, but he had already stepped away. At the door, he turned and gave her a clenched fist salute.

Gonzalo Soto left by the basement door of the garage. A series of broken concrete blocks provided steps down to the path. The path ran between the foundations of the buildings facing the street and the *turgurio* shacks spilling down the ravine. Dim yellow glow from the papered-over windows above him lit his way through the trash and weeds.

Beautiful! He thought of the rich girl in her tennis uniform, her dark shining hair spilling over the white. Big ones. And those long, long legs. No wonder Rivera had her stop the gringos. Who wouldn't stop if she said a word?

But Rivera said she acts like a nun. A beautiful nun, but cold like one. Always talking about killing. Or looking in a mirror, like a revolutionary starlet.

Smoke, acrid with burning plastic, drifted up the ravine. Coughing, Soto staggered along the path. Music and voices and the cries of children came from the hundreds of shacks below him. A drunk wailed. The noise and the stink of poverty filled the night.

Why would she risk her beautiful life for the poor? Why didn't she go back to the north and marry a rich Yankee? Why didn't she forget the revolution?

Forget the questions! Once he got her away from the others, when he had her in hiding alone, then he'd put it to her. Run out on him in Tegucigalpa? And straight to a Honduran army barracks? Run out on him in Cuba? Yes, she could do that. Fidel himself would claim her. And then every Party functionary down the line until the post office clerks had her. Then they'd export her to Libya. Screw her in Honduras. Me or the Honduran army, rich girl. Then I'll give you to Fidel.

Soto had never joined the Communists. He managed signing groups and traveling entertainers. He never had time for politics. But his brother had been an active member of the Revolutionary Workers Party. The night Soto found his brother's headless corpse, he abandoned his wife and fled for the United States. Mexican immigration sent him back to Guatemala the first time. The second time, he paid a smuggler to take him to Chicago. U.S. immigration sent him back directly to San Salvador. His wife had moved in with a sergeant of the National Police. Soto saw his wife big-bellied with another man's child and fled, knowing the jealousy of a policeman would be fatal. The Party offered him false identification and a salary if he managed the business details— money, cars, apartments, jobs—of teenagers working in the city. He took the work. By skimming the money, he had saved almost enough money for an air ticket to Canada. Now he had this hurry-up job to get the killers of the Marines out of El Salvador. This job meant a chance to steal more money. With a ticket and a political persecution story, he had a chance to live in Canada. After this, he escaped his country for the last time.

At a rutted dirt lane, Soto cut uphill to the street. He dodged through the vendors crowding the corners and ran through the intersection. He hurried along the street of shops to another corner. There, women waited at a bus stop. He pressed back into a doorway and watched the street.

A pushcart vendor jingled a stick of bells. Running children taunted one another. Two mechanics worked on a car parked at the curb. Soto saw no one who looked like a surveillance agent but fear made him suspect everyone, even the children. No one had trained him to be a subversive and he knew he would not live to make two mistakes. He tried to look into the passing cars and trucks, but in the night and headlights, he could not see faces.

Screeching brakes and rattling sheet metal announced the arrival of a bus. Soto waited until the women boarded, then dashed across the sidewalk. He paid his centavos and squeezed through the standing passengers—his hand on his wallet—to the back door. The bus passed a line of waiting taxis and Soto stepped down.

A taxi took him to a café. He paid and rushed inside. Waiting until he saw the taxi pull away, he went out the café's back door. Running the length of the alley, he crossed a street and went into the office of a trucking company.

"Finally, you are here." Antonio Manos—the owner-manager of the company—flashed a gold-toothed grin and turned off a television. A bony, sixty-year old man with his thick, gray hair swept into a stiff pompadour, he glanced at Gonzalo's sweat-patterned shirt and sweat-streaming face. "Did you see the program about the Marines?"

Soto stepped back, his eyes fixing on the gray television screen. Then he took a jerking step toward the inner door that led to the garage area. "Where's the truck? When can I get the truck?"

"You said you needed a truck, a very special truck. And I have that truck ready. Come—" Opening the door for his compatriot, he motioned him into the garage.

A slat-sided flatbed truck carried a load of woven-plastic sacks. The hundred-pound sacks of fortified bulgar wheat bore the stenciled handshake and shield logo of the United States. "Look in the bags. Every bag has that shit rice they send."

"Every bag? If the soldiers open one and find rocks, they will search the truck—"

"Every bag. I bought it from the government at a good price. It is fit only to feed to campesinos and pigs so the soldiers will not want much of it. We will use it again when we must use the truck. Very convenient, I think."

"Where do they enter?"

"Here." Opening the driver's door, he reached behind the seat. A latch clicked and he pushed the seat forward. A second latch released a plywood sheet that covered a crawl hole.

Soto looked inside to see a wide, long compartment. "The soldiers will find this!"

"Pardon me, but no, they have not found it in all the times we used it. We have used the truck many times for rifles and ammunition."

"Into the liberated zones?"

"Everywhere. At the borders. At the department checkpoints. In the city. And that was with bananas and coffee and boxes in the back. With those bags from the United States, the soldiers will take their money and let the truck go through. Will you be inside?"

"No."

"Then what is your worry?"

"It is my life if they're caught."

"Oh . . ."

"How long can they stay in there?"

"To where?"

"The mountains."

"Chalatenango? Morazón?"

"The mountains. The border. Five or six hours."

"That is nothing. We have carried wounded men all the way to Nicaragua."

"Nothing can screw up, understand me? I will be waiting there and if they do not—"

"I am experienced in this, Gonzalo. Trust me." Throwing an arm over the shoulders of his compatriot, Manos escorted him to the alley door. "You call me when it must leave. And it is done, trust me."

After the sweating, overweight conspirator darted into the alley, Manos went to the telephone. Now Manos knew. Soto had responded to the Marine question with an abrupt jerk, as if Manos had slapped him. Then he said that his life depended on the fighters escaping—because he would not be in the truck, that implied he would be executed by the leadership. Finally, that he would be waiting in Morazón—that meant his entire cell would evacuate the capital.

The Marine assassins. Only the killers of the Marines would merit the expense and trouble.

Antonio Manos had worked for the gringos three years, helping them monitor the smuggling of weapons from Nicaragua to El Salvador. With the payments for information, he had already bought a house in Texas.

Dialing the number of his North American contact, Manos calculated the value of the information. The price of a swimming pool? Perhaps an American car?

7

IN the back booth of the Las Vegas, Niles leaned back against the wall and poured the third Cerveza Salva Vida down his throat. The wall vibrated with the bass of the Mexican ballads blasting from the jukebox. He put the empty beer bottle in the clutter of dishes on the table and signaled for another.

While he waited, he returned to his writing, slowly and exactly guiding the pen across the back of a tourist postcard, right to left, forming the sweeps and loops of the Arabic characters. He checked each line against his pencil copy before adding the card to the others inside an envelope.

Headlights flashed across the interior of the restaurant as a bus left the Danlí terminal. The engine noise overwhelmed the jukebox. Across the highway, buses and minivans parked at a curb. Passengers ran through the glare of headlights, the lights projecting their silhouettes through swirling dust and smoke. When the jukebox cycled records, the noise of the terminal came—bus helpers shouting out destinations, vendors whistling to get the attention of passengers, airhorns blaring, the low vibration of idling diesel engines.

The waitress brought his fourth bottle of beer. A teenager with curly hair and a moon face daubed with startling red lipstick, she wore a tight miniskirt over heavy thighs and a round belly. Her low-cut blouse exposed balloon breasts. Smiling to Niles, she levered the cap off the bottle and foam sprayed over her chest and face. Giggling, she wiped the foam off with her hand, her hand moving swells of breasts, leaving smears of dust and diesel soot.

"Where are you from?" she asked.

"Far away."

She put one knee on the bench seat opposite him and leaned on the table with her elbows. The angle revealed her breasts to him. "You look like a soldier."

"Me?"

"Only soldiers come here. And journalists. And bible workers. I don't think you teach the bible."

"I'm only a tourist," Niles lied.

She laughed, her pendulous breasts swaying within her blouse. "The last bus is gone."

"Last bus to where?"

"Back to the capital."

"The schedule said there is a bus at—"

"The schedule says. But no bus goes at that time. I think you must stay in Danlí. I know a good place for tourists."

Looking past her breasts, Niles saw Sergeant Jesús Alvarez in the doorway. The tall Marine from East Los Angeles wore a beret over his short-cut hair and a nylon jacket over his wide shoulders. Except for his sharp Mexican features, he looked like a Honduran. Niles slid out of the booth and put a twenty-lempira bill on the table—enough for the dinner, five beers, and a half-day's wage tip for the waitress. He smiled at her and took another beer from the cooler. "For the bus."

Alvarez waited in a battered Chevrolet pickup truck. Swinging open the door, Niles passed him the extra beer and got in. He glanced back at the Las Vegas and saw the moon-faced girl watching the truck pull away.

"Hey, zoot, I thought I'd die." Niles laughed, speaking English for the first time in days as the truck lurched over broken pavement. "That is the truth. I thought I'd die in those mountains."

"They get hit, sir?"

"No. But it was only luck and Sandinista incompetence that they didn't. The leader called himself *El Martillo*. Should've been *Carnicero*—the Butcher."

"He makes contact?"

"He's out there killing people. . . ." Niles drank his beer and watched the forested hills sparkle with the lights of houses and settlements. "Lot of women crying tonight, maybe a hundred kids without fathers. But you don't win a war by making martyrs for the revolution. And the first well-trained counterinsurgency unit he runs into, he is history."

"You hear the radio?"

"That that contra unit knocked down two of those new Soviet troop helicopters. That make the news?"

"No sir. A gang murdered four Marines in San Salvador. Embassy guards."

"Assault on the embassy?"

"Hit a sidewalk café. Four Marines dead, two other Americans, eight local people. This was two nights ago. The night I dropped you off."

"Embassy Marines . . . no weapons, right? Out on the town and they got shot?"

"A woman set them up."

"They know who did it?"

"Some gang."

"Guerrillas or death squads?"

"Guerrillas. Communists."

"They get the gang?"

"No, sir, not yet. But there's a jet coming down from Washington. I'm to take you to the airport. The restricted side."

"A jet from Washington? What time?"

"Lieutenant Stark called them after we got your call from Danlí."

Niles opened the glove compartment and found his watch and identification. "Where are Stark and Vatsek?"

"At the camp."

During the hour-and-a-half drive west, Niles told Alvarez the story of his days with the contras. He finished the story as they turned from the Carretera del Oriente to the chain-link and razor-wire gate of the military base. Honduran military police stepped out of the sandbagged bunkers, M-16 rifles in their right hands, the muzzles pointed straight up. On the roof of the bunker, two soldiers lounged beside a 50-caliber heavy machine gun—capable of stopping any vehicle not protected with armor plate. Niles and Alvarez showed the soldiers plastic-laminated cards identifying them as

61

American trainers. One soldier looked from Niles's face to the card, then shone a flashlight on his face and studied him. The soldier called out to the other:

"This one is a Marine?"

Niles laughed. Finally, the soldiers pushed the gate aside. Inside the camp, Alvarez drove past rows of wood-framed tents on raised plank platforms. The temporary barracks sheltered recruits from the sun and rain, the platforms raising the tents above the earth and allowing air to circulate under the floorboards. The framing supported the canvas covering throughout all the tropical rainstorms. Despite the air circulating through the nylon-mesh sidewalls, the tents became canvas sweat-boxes during the day. In the evening, as wind sweeping from the pine-forested mountains cooled the tents, soldiers sat on the steps, cleaning rifles, sewing up tears in their fatigues, and polishing their boots by the lights lining the gravel streets.

In the center of the camp, a cluster of tents served as housing and offices for the U.S. personnel. Niles left the truck and went to the door of one tent. He banged on the door—no answer. Through the mesh wall, he saw the personal possessions of Sergeant Leon Vatsek in semi-disarray—a Korean satin robe embroidered with dragons and lightning strikes, a weight bench improvised of welded steel pipes, a barbell set made of pipe and blocks of concrete. A near-naked Grace Jones, her lithe black limbs and torso polished with sweat, glared down from a color poster. With pen and ink, Vatsek had carefully placed a Soviet PKM machine gun in her hands.

Niles cut across the camp street to the light of a small prefab plywood office for the Recon training team. The fluorescent light inside the office drew hundreds of insects, the moths and beetles and mosquitos swarming on the screens.

Inside, he saw all the battalion papers in rectangular stacks, forms filed in labeled notebooks, the black plastic of the desk top gleaming, an eraser and pen in a precise position beside the typewriter.

Lieutenant Stark had quit for the night. Methodical and exacting, the lieutenant always left his office in perfect order. Nothing in the office detracted from the Spartan austerity. No photos of his family in Washington, D.C. No photos of girlfriends. No pinups. No ash trays. Only office equipment, materials, and his name plaque on the desk: 2nd Lieutenant Richard Stark, USMC.

Then Niles saw the note taped to the desk: *Soccer field until 22:00*.

"Strak-man's out kicking the ball around."

Three hundred meters from the office, past a line of old UH-1 troopships, Alvarez parked in a row of troop trucks alongside a lighted field. Two teams of soldiers ran across the field, their feet throwing dust with every step, dust exploding when they kicked the soccer ball. Niles spotted Lieutenant Stark immediately. In white shorts and a white shirt, the slim black man flashed through lines of opposing players as he led his team's offense for the striped 4 X 4 beams of the goal. A crowd of young men in green shorts and green T-shirts converged on him and the lieutenant kicked the ball over their heads to a soldier in a white T-shirt. With a sharp jerk of his head, the forward sent the ball through the rectangle of the goal.

Alvarez honked the truck's horn and flashed the lights. Stark left the game. A university graduate, 2nd Lieutenant Stark intended to serve six years in the Marines before going into the foreign service. A tall, slender black man with the good looks and grooming of a *Gentleman's Quarterly* model, he had the image the media demanded. He had served in Beirut from November 1983 to January 1984, then transferred with Captain Niles to Honduras.

"There's Vatsek . . ." Alvarez pointed to the other end of the improvised soccer field.

At the sidelines, Vatsek stood surrounded by a crowd of off-duty Honduran soldiers, his white blond hair and pale skin like a white flame under the lights. A dedicated bodybuilder, the muscles of his shoulders seemed to flow to his neck, the circumference of his neck almost equal to his head. One man shouted and the group of men laughed.

"What kind of trouble is he making now?" Not waiting for Lieutenant Stark, Niles walked quickly to the crowd of Hondurans. Vatsek stood in the center of the Hondurans. He wore dusty, sweat-muddied camouflage fatigues and dirt-plastered combat boots.

Taking a gulp from a can of beer, Vatsek surveyed the men around him, his almost-Asian eyes narrowing to slits, his lips twisting into a reptilian grin. His pale Slavic features looked evil.

Two young soldiers stood back from the crowd. Niles recognized the two teenagers from a class of trainees. He asked them, "What's the problem here?"

"They do not believe our teacher can fight all of them," one teenager started.

"All at once," the other added.

"But we believe . . ."

Joking to one another, some of the young men in the crowd put up their fists.

"Ready to go, pukes!" Vatsek declared, taking another gulp of beer. He held up his left hand—his wrist thicker than the arms of most of the men confronting him—and made a fist. Then he stepped back into a karate sparring stance and spat out the single word, "Attack!"

The Hondurans laughed. Some stepped forward. One young man shoved another into the circle.

Too fast for individual motions to be seen, Vatsek tore through the soldiers, kicking their feet from under them, throwing them down to the right and left. He did not use his right hand throughout the hand-to-hand combat demonstration—his right hand held the can of beer. One boy pulled back his fist to punch the rampaging American and Vatsek shoved him in the shoulder with his open left palm, the force of the blow spinning the soldier into the dust. Another soldier attacked him from behind. Vatsek jammed an elbow into the soldier's gut. The teenager staggered back and Vatsek snapped a classic back kick into his chest, throwing the soldier backward.

One of the downed teenagers tackled Vatsek. Falling forward, Vatsek executed a judo roll and came up in a crouch. The last standing soldier rushed him and Vatsek grabbed his jacket, jerking the teenager off his feet and throwing him down hard on the grass. Vatsek finished his beer, then raised his fists above his head and roared. On the ground, the Hondurans laughed.

"To the truck, Godzilla."

"Back in time for my demonstration. What did you think?"

"Why don't you pick on people your own size?"

"Hey, that was fair. Me against a platoon."

Lieutenant Stark waited at the truck, wiping the sweat from his face and arms with a towel. He snapped a salute. "Good evening, sir, I'm glad you returned so quickly. I assume it was successful?"

"Yeah, I got back."

"Colonel Devlin was very concerned that you might be unavailable for another week."

"What's going on?"

"The colonel did not inform me. But he is in-flight—" Stark looked at his watch. "In fact, he may already be waiting at Toncontín."

"Then it's time to go." Niles got into the pickup truck. "Didn't mean to break up your games tonight, gentlemen. But don't make any plans for tomorrow night. We could be working."

At the military gate to Toncontín International Airport, Honduran soldiers got in the back of the pickup truck. They directed Alvarez around the south end of the runways. Following the curving expanse of concrete away from the passenger terminal, Alvarez drove slowly toward the rows of planes and helicopters parked near the military hangers.

A soldier banged on the cab. "That is the airplane."

Alvarez stopped at a C-140 JetStar, a small commuter jet powered by four aft-mounted engines. Lights glowed inside the curtained ports. The soldiers in the truck called to the two soldiers standing at the ramp and the guards allowed Niles to pass.

Going up the steel stairs, Niles knocked at the port set in the door. A face looked out. Moments later, the door swung open.

Colonel Anthony Devlin wore the uniform of the executive—conservative blue suit, blue shirt, black tie. Beard stubble shadowed his severe, patrician features. Gray hair streaked back from his temples. A career officer in the Marine Corps, he had served with the Joint Chiefs of Staff as a spokesman before his recent transfer to the staff of the National Security Council. He welcomed Niles with a handshake.

"How did it go?"

"I'm lucky to be alive—"

At the front of the plane, a thin, pale bureaucrat in a gray suit and black bow tie waited at the jet's conference table—Richard Todd represented the CIA's Director of Special Operations. A second man, very young, with black hair cut in the severe Marine style, wore a sports coat and slacks. He sat at one of the side seats, clutching a briefcase.

Niles looked at his own clothes—his dusty nylon jacket, his dirty sports shirt, his wrinkled slacks, his dust-colored boots. Rubbing a hand across his beard stubble, Niles felt grease from his chicken dinner in Danlí.

"Alvarez didn't tell me this would be a conference."

Devlin lowered his voice. "What happened with Martillo?"

"A one-man disaster. I'll hire some of his men, but he's no one we want to work with."

"We'll work that out. Don't tell that to Todd. Or this man Montes when he shows up."

"Montes? Who's he?"

"Agency man with the embassy here. Delayed by a party. He thinks Martillo is on his way to Managua."

"Maybe in a body bag."

"Here's what we have as of now on the terrorists who murdered our men in San Salvador." Giving Niles a folder, he led him to the table. "Mr. Todd, you know Captain Niles, Recon. He has just returned from Nicaragua."

"It's a pleasure to meet with you again, Captain."

"Agency taking my one and only Farsi-speaking Marine?"

"The doctor says the corporal's ready for duty."

"How's your leg, Javenbach?"

"Very good, sir. One hundred per cent. I ran the Quantico course with a fifty-pound pack. I am ready."

"The corporal," Todd told Niles, "has been translating and keying the files you captured in the Bekaa. We now have every name, photo, and biography computerized and cross-indexed. I don't believe we could have interrogated that Iranian and gained the same volume of information."

Javenbach snapped open the briefcase and passed Niles a sheet showing a page of computer-generated photo and text.

"Looks good." Niles added, "But we lost Rajai."

"Unfortunate, but given the circumstances, perhaps unavoidable."

"And that means we lost the connections to Syria and Iran."

"True." Todd glanced from Javenbach to the senior officers. "Perhaps the corporal would like to speak to his friends outside—" Todd pointed out to the trucks.

Niles grinned. "He's telling you to get out."

"Yes, sir. Of course, sir," Javenbach saluted and pivoted to exit.

"Wait." Here—" Niles took the envelope from his pocket. He licked the flap and sealed the envelope. Checking the Arabic of the address a last time, he took his pen and block-printed BEYROUTH, LEBANON / PAR AVION. "I want this mailed from France. Nothing is to identify that letter as coming from the United States or an English-speaking country. Got it?"

"Yes, sir. I'll forward it tomorrow, sir."

"And don't cut your hair anymore, don't shave. You're no good to us if you look like a Marine. Now out."

The three men waited until the door closed.

"Isn't it perhaps dangerous," Todd asked, "to correspond through the mail with your sources in Lebanon?"

"She's not a source. But I still have to be careful. Not good for a Shia woman to be getting letters from an American."

"Of course. Mr. Devlin, can you explain the Salvadorian situation to the captain?"

"Before Alex Montes gets here," Devlin told Niles, "let

me say that your sources are producing. They are servicing the electronic scanners and forwarding the tapes to our technicians for analysis. They also report whatever they observe. In total, they provide the best street-level and small-unit information on the Revolutionary Guards in Baalbek that we are now receiving from any source."

"That's good, that's great." Niles nodded. "I knew they'd be dependable. And they're risking their lives—"

"They certainly are," Todd agreed.

"But it doesn't mean a thing if we don't act on the information. Five months now I've waited in Honduras and no action. The murderers of hundreds of United States Marines are still out there killing more Americans. The government that sent the Marines to Beirut to die may have forgotten, but I haven't. The only way to stop those gangs is to hit them, and we're still waiting here in Honduras."

"Your point is taken." Todd glanced at Devlin. "I have heard much the same quite often from Colonel Devlin. But we cannot send Americans into that area—"

"Why didn't anyone say that when the politicos sent the battalions to the Beirut Airport? Two hundred forty-one men dead for nothing—"

Devlin cut him off. "Mr. Todd doesn't make policy. But we've got action for you if you want to hear about it."

"Yeah? Tell me."

"First, the killers were Salvadorian but the command was Cuban. With links to Syria—"

"Syria?"

"Agents report a meeting between a Cuban intelligence chief now working in Managua and a Syrian army intelligence officer. The Syrian, a colonel named Atallah, appears in the files you captured in the Bekaa in January. He worked with Rajai. Interception of communications link the guerrillas in San Salvador to the DGI in Managua to the Cuban in Damascus—"

"¿Qué pasa?" A voice boomed. "Am I late? Looks like a Marine convention out there."

"The Cuba to Syrian link must wait," Devlin told Niles. "This is Alex Montes. . . ."

A tall, wide-shouldered man strode down the center aisle

of the jet. Square-jawed, his back-combed hair only one tone short of blond, Montes looked like a tan, athletic Anglo. But his voice had the rich Latin undertone of a lifelong Spanish speaker:

"Captain Niles, I am honored to meet you. The colonel speaks very highly of you. Thinks you are a brave and dangerous man. He said he saw you in action."

"We go way back."

"The colonel told me of your adventures in Nam."

"And Laos and Cambodia," Colonel Devlin added. "The captain is no stranger to cross-border operations."

"Southeast Asia and now Central America," Montes continued. "And always a volunteer. I only wish we had battalions of men like you."

"This man does get around," Niles admitted.

"Action in Nicaragua?"

"Mr. Montes," Devlin explained to Niles, "works closely with Sergeant Martillo and many of the other commanders."

"Well," Niles hesitated, thinking of what to say. "Martillo got his body count. Wiped out two or three militia squads. And he got two of those Soviet MI-8 troopships. Only one man wounded in his unit that I saw."

"Martillo does it again!" Montes laughed. "He's one of my most aggressive commanders. Always in the thick of it."

"Two helicopters?" Todd asked, incredulous. "Did you see any of the gunships? The MI-24?"

"Yeah, but they didn't see us, so I'm here to tell you about it."

"Watch the headlines, Captain Niles," Montes continued. "We're putting a lot of support behind Martillo and the other guys. In a few months, we'll have a completely different situation down here. They'll be taking a piece of Nicaragua and keeping it."

"A successful mission," Devlin commented, ending the conversation by opening his folder of photos and telex printouts. "We will need a report when it is possible—let us go on to the Salvadorian gang of terrorists."

The colonel spread out several eight-by-ten black-and-white photos on the conference table. Niles saw stark, flash-lit scenes of a sidewalk strewn with corpses, broken dishes, and overturned tables. Black pools of blood spread over the concrete. Salvadorian police held back crowds of onlookers.

"A street café. Didn't those Marines think they could get shot? How often did they go out?"

"Quite frequently. And it seems, often to the restaurants and nightclubs in that particular part of the city."

"Yeah, I've been there. El Paseo General Escalón. La Zona Rosa. It's the place to meet girls."

"One of the Marines happened to leave the table just before the attack. He said a young woman called them to the table. They talked and she left. She promised to come back."

"So they waited. . . ."

Devlin described the killing by the gunmen in the uniforms of the Salvadorian Army. "A call came to a local radio station only a minute later, claiming responsibility for the attack for the Mardoqueo Cruz Combat Unit of the Revolutionary Workers' Party. There had not yet been a news release at the time the station received the call. Information received since that time confirms they are in fact responsible."

"Responsible for straight-out murder. . . ." Opening his folder, Niles saw a topographic map of the Salvadorian-Honduran border. A series of high-resolution satellite photos showed roads and trails. "Morazón."

"The territory is dominated by the Peoples' Revolutionary Army. We have information that the unit responsible for the murders will be taken out of El Salvador. They will be smuggled by truck to Perquín. Then, via this road—" Devlin pointed to a satellite photo. From the rooftops of the remote town, he traced a line through the mountains to a dry river. "At this point, they will then meet another unit which will escort them into Honduras, with the eventual destination of Cuba or the Middle East."

"This information is positive?"

"The Salvadorians captured four members of the urban unit," Todd explained. "Our analysts are working closely with the interrogators. The information on the transportation, route, and destination comes from our sources in Salvador and Honduras."

Niles studies the lines and whorls of the mountains, comparing the topographic maps to the satellite photos. He waited for the next question.

"If we provide helicopters and equipment," Devlin asked, "can you intercept the unit?"

Niles nodded.

After Niles left the JetStar, Todd turned to Montes. "What is the procedure if the guerrillas kill or capture those men?"

"I know Niles," Devlin protested. "There is no enemy who is his equal. He will not be killed. His men won't be killed and no one will be captured. I would not have suggested sending him in to make this interception if there was a chance of failure."

"No one in history has been invulnerable," Todd answered. "Not even Achilles. There are always casualties. If not in action, then by accident. I'll rephrase my question to Mr. Montes. What is the procedure if we lose those men?"

Montes laughed. "Only four grunts? We can write them off as killed in a training flight."

8

QUEZADA watched and listened for movement. He lay flat in a tangle of brush, his eye scanning the gray-on-black forms of the bare hillsides. For an hour, he waited. Nothing moved. He heard only the occasional sound of an insect or the falling of a leaf through the branches.

This night challenged his student, a wiry and athletic teenager from Mejicanos, a slum district of San Salvador. The boy had taken the brave and vain name of Lobo, the Wolf. Tonight, Lobo had the task of slipping past the two instructors playing the roles of soldiers. And the boy had, so far, done very well.

Despite the months-dry earth and the brilliant stars and moon, no one had seen or heard Lobo on the hillside. He somehow moved through the dry brush and grass without noise and without revealing himself to his instructors or his commander on the ridge.

The stars and moon defined the brush and slopes of the hillside, denying Lobo the easy concealment of darkness. Moonlight glinted on the shifting leaves. The grass and dying ferns looked pale blue, every dry blade and stem reflecting the moon. If Lobo exposed his dark-clothed form as he bellied up the mountain, he failed the test.

Quezada looked at the luminous dial of his watch. He watched the dial as the second hand completed an exact hour, then he whistled to the gun crew.

A hundred meters away, metal scraped against metal and a mortar tube popped. Quezada shaded his eye. An instant later, the white magnesium light of a flare seared away the night, the glare creating an abstract landscape of white and

grays and shadows. Like scratches on glass, the monofilament lines of trip-flares and black-power bobby traps ran
across the slopes, sticks holding the lines at knee-height
above the earth. The parachute flare drifted down from the
infinite dome of the night sky, swinging from side to side on
its parachute. The scene swayed and wavered.

Only the shadows moved. Quezada studied the hillsides,
trying to discover the boy in the grass and rocks, mentally
comparing what he saw now to what he remembered.

The machine gun hammered the silence. A tracer streaked
through the glare as an instructor fired a burst into the black
splotch of a pine. Erosion had undercut the roots and
dropped the tree sideways but the pine continued growing
across the gullies, the low branches fanning over the hillside.

If Lobo had trusted his life to the protection of that tree,
the bursts of machine gun fire had taught him a sudden
lesson in the power of high-velocity, heavy-caliber bullets.
The firing continued and tracers passed through the pine and
streaked into the distance.

The flare sputtered out. Playing the roles of government
soldiers, the instructors launched another flare. Quezada
tried to guess the route of Lobo up the slope. The erosion-
cut gullies offered concealment. But booby traps made the
gullies difficult. The open slopes had tangles of brush for
concealment. But would the teenager have the nerve to
advance in the open?

Thumbing a cigarette lighter, Quezada touched the flame
to the long fuse of a paper-wrapped bomb. The absence of
his left arm made the throw awkward. He had to drop the
lighter, then pick up the bomb as the fuse sparked and
hissed. The National Guard torturers who had years before
clubbed and twisted his bullet-shattered arm had not made
him betray his unit, but they had ended his dream of playing
baseball after the revolution. Without the natural counter-
balance of his left arm, he threw wild and short, the bomb
going only thirty meters and landing two meters to the side
of the gully. He repeated his awkward light-and-throw routine, this time managing to bounce the oversized firecracker
into the gully.

The dull booms came seconds later. Balls of smoke and dust floated upward as he watched for movement in the swaying shadows. The flare dropped low in the sky, shadows stretching across the hillsides in long, swaying lines. Then he saw the form of shoulders and a head. A crease in the dry grass—created by a crawling man—led to the form. Light glinted off what appeared to be a grease-blackened hand. In the last seconds of illumination, Quezada threw another black-power bomb, scoring a hit on the form. Then the night went black.

Fire streaked through the air. Quezada saw the sparking bomb bounce two steps away. He did not waste time or risk his fingers to match the boy's trick. Rolling away through the leaves and mud, he put his arm around his head to cover his ears as the explosion slammed him.

The instructors fired—they had seen the boy throw back the bomb. Unlike the soldiers the young man would face in the future, they aimed high, keeping the bursts of slugs a meter above the ground. But, Quezada knew, the sound of the bullets ripping through the air would be a sound Lobo would not forget.

"That was a very good trick," Quezada called down to the unseen student. "But a firecracker is not a grenade. If you try that trick in combat, the dogs will eat the wolf. And all our time invested in your training will be wasted. You failed this test tonight. Lay there until morning and think of your error." He shouted out to the instructors manning the machine gun. "Gunners! If he moves before dawn, kill him."

A squawk came from his walkie-talkie. "What is it?"

"A message."

"Check-in?"

"No. There is an emergency."

"I am coming now."

Quezada scrambled out of the brush. He crossed the ridgeline and went down the opposite hillside. His technician had finally received a radio transmission from El Salvador. The radio operators of the unit had maintained their schedule of morning and evening coded transmissions—always at the exact time, always transmitting the exact code—until that night. No codes came at six in the evening and the operators did not respond to the quick messages from the base. If only one radio man had missed his time, Quezada would not have initiated an alert. But both radio men failed to report and both did not respond. Quezada immediately directed his communications technician to alert their other contacts. And now a message had come from the unit or one of the contacts—an emergency.

By memory, he followed the trail through the coffee rows and orange trees. He saw the lights on in both the communications room and the file room. The soldiers guarding the hacienda passed him through the high chain-link outer fence. He crossed the mined zone on the concrete walkway and entered the hacienda through a side gate, then rushed the last few steps to the radio room.

Antonio Salazar worked at the table, translating the coded message into text. Of all the technicians and clerks and instructors at the camp, Quezada trusted only Salazar with the codes. A veteran of both the revolution and the war against the contras, the young man came from a family of Sandinistas. His father and older brother had died in the revolution—killed in the National Guard's bombing of Estelí—and his mother and sisters served as couriers and nurses. After the triumph, Salazar volunteered for two years of service in the Sandinista Army. He learned radio operation and maintenance from Cuban and East German technicians. He reenlisted after completing his two years and applied to become a member of the Sandinista Party. His battalion's political cadre referred Salazar to Quezada. Salazar proved to be a very efficient young man. In the few minutes since he received the transmission, he had finished decoding and typing the message.

"Why did they not report?"

"The police took them."

Taking the typed page, Quezada read that Salvadorian police had captured one of the drivers early in the day. Interrogation got the names and addresses of two other young men. The police seized those members later. But the others had managed to evade capture. The army and police now searched the city. The source could not learn the names of the prisoners.

"Any messages from our support people? Did you radio them?"

"Yes, of course. But nothing. Only this one knew anything about what happened."

Rushing to his office, he dialed the number of the Ministry of Exports. No answer. He dialed the number of the mansion where Pazos stayed. The Cuban occupied a home abandoned by a National Guard general in 1979. Only a few kilometers south of the capital, with palatial rooms, a swimming pool, and expansive lawns, Pazos maintained a second office there. His aide Condori answered:

"Where is he? I want to talk to him now."

"The director is not available. I will have him call you when he can."

"Don't give me that excuse. You know who I am. Put him on the phone."

"He's not in the country."

"There's an emergency. Is there anyone manning the radios in the office?"

"We can't discuss what has happened on this telephone line. It is not secure. But we've consulted the director and the ministry is taking appropriate steps."

"What? You know about it? Why wasn't I told?"

"I had no instructions to inform you. It was unnecessary to inform you of—"

"Unnecessary? Boy, those are my fighters. They report to me."

"We have channels to get the product out."

"You what?"

"The emergency is over. We are moving the product out through our own channels."

"I want it stopped! You are not to endanger my fighters by—"

"It is already done. Speak with the director when he returns."

Holding her Uzi submachine gun, Lidia Rivas peered through the papered-over second-floor windows, watching the street and early morning traffic for police surveillance. The traffic slowed to a stop in front of the garage. Horns sounded as a trash truck clashed gears but did not move. Diesel smoke clouded from its exhaust stack and the grinding of the gears continued. Two helpers stood on the truck's back bumper, their clothing black with filth. The driver of a Fiat behind the truck leaned on his horn. Looking back at the Fiat, one of the helpers motioned for the driver to cut his horn. The driver shouted an obscenity. The blare of his horn and the horns of the taxis and pickups continued.

"When will that truck come?" Paulino Rivera complained from another window. Rivas did not answer.

The horns continued even after the trash truck lurched into motion. As the truck went around the corner, one of the helpers gave a backhand toss and a newspaper bundle arched through the morning light. Garbage splashed across the windshield of the Fiat. Swerving, but too late to turn and pursue the trash truck, the Fiat continued straight through the intersection.

Rivera laughed. Rivas did not take her eyes from the street. Her eyes ached with the strain as she watched every movement on the street and the narrow lane intersecting the street. She now wore her French T-shirt and only pair of designer jeans. Though the long sleeved T-shirt accentuated her breasts and small waist, she knew the dark blue of the shirt and the denim blue of her jeans presented a more revolutionary appearance than tennis whites. She had also wrapped her hair with a black cloth, in the style of a campesino woman, the cloth like a black helmet across her forehead. With her sunglasses, she thought she looked very much like the terrorists she had seen in magazines and films. But she needed combat boots. She had only her low-cut tennis shoes—now ruined by splotches of oil and filth.

"Soldiers!"

"Where?"

"In the shacks!" Two fighters watched the *turgurio* in the ravine behind the garage.

Throwing his chair back, Rivera ran along the walkway.

"Stay at your position!" Rivas hissed.

"There're soldiers back there. You're watching the—"

"Stay there!"

Rivera went back to his window. In the rear of the garage,

the lookouts scuttled from window to window to peer at the soldiers. Rivas saw only workers and traffic on the street. Then a police squad car appeared. Rivas watched the squad car cruise the block. The traffic jamming behind the police did not sound their horns.

The squad car—a black-and-white late-model four-door Dodge donated by the United States Agency for International Development—carried four policemen. Three pointed M-1 carbines out the windows. The fourth drove. Rivas saw the driver speak into a microphone.

"What are the soldiers doing?" Rivas asked.

"It's a patrol. Only a patrol."

"A police car!" Rivera's voice went high-pitched with panic.

"Quiet!" Rivas hissed. "Shut up."

Pressing her head against the crumbling paper pasted to the window, she managed to watch the police car cruise down the block. The car swerved into a driveway. Rivas watched the traffic surge past the parked car. The police remained inside the Dodge.

"Are they gone?" Rivera called.

Rivas did not answer him. She saw a soldier lean against the car and talk with the police. A line of soldiers walked down the street toward the garage. She called to the lookouts at the back. "Are there soldiers back there?"

"No, they're gone. It was only a patrol. Fascist dogs on a patrol, terrorizing the poor of the—"

"Shut up!"

"Shut your own mouth, you Castilian rich bitch."

"Louder," Rivas hissed. "The soldiers out front cannot hear you."

"What?"

"They're coming!" Rivera's voice cracked.

Honking sounded in the street. Rivas saw a flatbed cargo truck loaded with white sacks. Three people sat in the cab— from her angle she could not see their faces. Blocking traffic, the truck honked and the line of stopping cars behind it sounded a hundred horns.

"Roll up the door," Rivas shouted. "The truck is here."

"Oh, Jesus, no!" one of the back lookouts whined. "The soldiers—"

"You shits!" Rivas checked the safety of her Uzi, then put it on the planks of the walkway. She rushed to the chain and pulley assembly of the roll-gate. Loathing the feel of the oily links, she pulled the chain hand-over-hand to raise the door.

A soldier ran past the garage entrance. Rivas looked down at the rifle in his hands and she jerked back against the wall. Waiting, motionless, she heard a shout. She went back to her position and picked up her Uzi.

Looking outside, she saw a soldier stopping traffic in the street. The truck engine gunned. She saw the driver make the wide turn into the garage. Rivas set down her Uzi again and ran back to the chain and lowered the door.

They all heard the boots and clanking of equipment as the soldiers passed.

Anna and two young men got out of the truck cab. One man helped Anna to a crate. She sat there and shook, sucking down ragged gasps of air. The driver took a plastic sack of red pills out of his pocket and gave one to Anna. Rivas recognized the pills as one-hundred-milligram capsules of Seconal.

The driver looked up at the fighters on the walkway. "In the truck!"

In a hanger on the civilian side of Toncontín International Airport, Niles sorted through boxes of military equipment marked with the insignias and inventory numbers of the Salvadorian Army.

Throughout the morning, he carefully checked the equipment, examining every detail, discarding what failed his inspection—leaking canteens, expired antibiotics in the first-aid kits, fraying straps, corroded batteries. He had expected defects. The night before, when he prepared the list for Todd of the CIA, he had requested weapons and supplies for eight men, not four. The boxes of spare equipment provided replacements.

Only the camouflage fatigues for the Americans—marked with the insignia of the Atlacatl Battalion—came new.

Nothing that Niles and his men carried would identify them as American Marines.

Niles assembled sets of fatigues and web gear. On the concrete floor of the hanger, he laid out four rows of camouflage fatigues and packs, complete with boxes of rations, canteens, rope, compasses, flashlights—all the miscellaneous items required by his team.

A few minutes after noon, fists banged on the hanger door. "You inside! There is an American here."

Stepping into the glare, he saw Honduran soldiers standing with Alvarez. "He is with me. Also, I am expecting two other men. A white man and a black man. Bring them here when they come."

They waited as the soldiers walked away from the hanger. Alvarez took off the straw *ranchero* hat he wore and shaded his eyes as he studied the distant mountains. At the north end of the runway, turbines roared as a commercial airliner accelerated for takeoff. Alvarez pointed to the west, to a horizon churning with clouds. He shouted: "A storm."

"Looks that way—drive your truck in." Niles pushed the rolling door aside.

Inside, Alvarez took a heavy cardboard case from the cab of the pickup. "Where's King Kong?"

"At the range. Putting rounds through the rifles. He's already late. All the radios working?"

"Like magic," Alvarez told him. He opened the box, pulling aside sheets of foam padding. He held up a small radio in each hand and clicked the transmits. The hand radios showed no brand name or place of manufacture. Designed by the National Security Agency, the radios employed encoding circuits to scramble the transmissions. Without one of the four radios, a technician scanning the bands would intercept only bursts of electronic noise. "I ran the micro-vac over the boards. Checked them all with a microscope and put in new ni-cads. Ready to make spacenoise."

"And this one? Enhancements check out?" Niles picked up the telephone-style handset of the Salvadorian Army radio.

"*Perfecto.* Same routine, then tested the spook bands.

That set is set. Scanner, too—" Alvarez brought another electronic unit from the box. "I tell you, sir, the agency does have fine electronics. The Corps will never have technology this fine."

"The agency? What agency?"

"The travel agency that sends us to all these fantastic places. Colombia, the Bekaa—"

"Don't know what you're talking about, Sergeant. But I do happen to have here satellite photos of another exotic locale—which you may wish to study. Lieutenant Stark will be coming—" Niles checked his watch. "—any minute. With maps for all of us. With weather info."

"What about the storm? Any problem with that?"

"Not for us. There're your camos and gear."

"Atlacatl?"

Tires screeched outside. A drum beat and bass line thudded through the sheet steel walls of the hanger.

"Must be Vatsek," Alvarez guessed.

They rolled the doors open and a leased minivan pulled into the hanger, the screaming voices and wailing guitars of heavy-metal rock-and-roll booming from a stereo. In the front, Vatsek nodded with the beat, grinning to the captain and Alvarez.

Stark left the van. Though he held a briefcase, he tried to cover his ears with his hands. He rushed to the far side of the hanger and stood there with his hands over his ears, his eyes closed. In his white, tropical-weight suit and slacks, he looked like an international entrepreneur—tormented by the screaming guitars and voices.

Jerking and bopping with the music, Vatsek jumped out and slammed opened the side door. Music exploded from the van. With a final howl, the tape ended and Vatsek brought out an M-16/M-203 over-and-under assault rifle/grenade launcher.

"Finally . . ." Stark commented.

"Finally!" Vatsek shouted, raising the M-16/M-203 in his fist. "Months in this country and finally! No more training these Hondo-vatos to clean their rifles. No more. We're out of it. We are out to take heads and lay waste."

"Did you brief the sergeant?" Niles asked Stark.

"Sir, I attempted to. But there was a noise problem. Communication was not possible."

"Brief?" Vatsek asked. "What is there to tell me? We got action! We're on our way out, right?"

"It's just an in and out, Godzilla," Alvarez told him. "Walk in, make an arrest and—"

"Arrest?"

"You know, like cops," Alvarez added.

Niles leaned into the van and took out a short Colt Commando rifle. He jerked the charging handle to lock back the bolt. "Not quite. . . ."

Darkness and heat. The stink of diesel smoke and sweating bodies.

The gears clashed and the noise of the highway faded as the truck slowed to a stop. Soldiers shouted. Lidia Rivas lay in darkness, her hands gripping the sweat-slick steel of the Uzi. The driver jerked the manual brake and she heard the engine slow to an idle: a checkpoint.

If the soldiers discovered the compartment under the sacks, if they checked behind the driver's seat, she died. But not before she killed the soldiers who found her and the others.

The others slept the dreamless sleep of barbiturates. Only Rivas lay awake—she had not swallowed the capsules of Seconal the driver distributed to all the comrades. In the stinking, fetid darkness of the compartment jammed with her sleeping comrades, she listened to horns and the engine noise of other trucks. Staring into the darkness, she waited, listening, feeling streams of sweat flowing over her body.

Only a few more hours, she told herself. Only a few more hours and then they hid for the night. The driver had told them they would not risk the road into the mountains today. He would first send a car north on the Perquin road to look for army checkpoints. Tomorrow they traveled again. Then another night before they walked through the mountains to Honduras.

Only a few more days. . . .

9

ROTOR-THROWN rain hammering his face, Captain Niles leaned from the side door of the old Huey troopship. To the north, he saw predawn violet sky and stars and the graying forms of churning thunderheads. But ahead, the absolute black of the storm obscured the western horizon. He could see nothing of the ridges and peaks of the mountains of Morazón.

The storm would conceal their insertion into El Salvador.

Above him, the amber navigation light flashed, illuminating the rain streaking past him, reflecting from the rotor blades in instants of stroboscopic stop-motion.

Gray forest and shadowy folds of mountains continued into the distance. He could not see the roads indicated on his topographical map. The clustered lights of a town—La Estancia? San Antonio? Juniguara?—shone out of the night for a moment, then disappeared.

A hundred meters to starboard, Niles saw the navigation and anticollision lights of another troopship flashing against the darkness. The flashing lights gleamed on the plexiglass and enamel of the rain-polished fuselage.

Then the amber light above him quit. They had crossed into El Salvador—or more correctly, territory appearing on maps as part of El Salvador but also claimed by Honduras.

As he turned back to his men, he felt the helicopter slow and heard the turbine's whine change. The crew chief passed him the intercom headset. The Alabama voice of the copilot told him:

"Two minutes."

"Any problem with visibility?"

"We're locked in with terrain-following-radar."

"That radar see trees?"

"No, sir. That's why I'm wearing my night-vision goggles."

"Well, you watch out. We can walk home. Don't know about you."

Switching off, Niles questioned the others with a shout, "Ready?"

He heard Sergeant Vatsek answer, then Sergeant Alvarez.

For the last time, the captain checked the Salvadorian Army load-carrying-equipment he wore. The obsolete U.S./Army surplus pistol belt had an antique brass interlocking buckle. The old o.d. canvas rucksack had stamped-metal buckles on the straps. Hours before, as he had prepped for the mission in the hanger at Toncontín, he had wrapped every steel D-ring and belt-tip with black plastic tape. The same tape secured the rattling front handguard of the Colt Commando rifle he carried—a short-barreled version of the standard M-16A1 with a telescoping buttstock. With a slap, he confirmed the seating of the thirty-round magazine.

A luminous circle appeared beside his wrist. Lieutenant Stark tapped the captain's watch. Stripping off the velcro cover, Captain Niles held his arm steady while the two radium points of the second hands swept in sync.

The lieutenant thanked the captain with a crisp, "To the second, sir."

Rotors flaring, the helicopter angled down. The four Marines leaned from the side doors and scanned the darkness around and below the troopship. The black shapes of trees emerged, then the pale splotch of a ridge. Captain Niles heard the voices of the pilots through the headphones as they corrected the drift and angle of their descent.

"Okay, Marines. This is—"

Throwing his headset off, Niles unsnapped his safety harness. A swirling gray mist smelling of earth and rain enveloped the helicopter. When the skids touched the ridge, the Marines leapt out and rushed into the predawn storm. They went flat in the mud, forming a security X, facing in four directions, their boots touching, each man watching the darkness and rain in front of him.

The troopship lifted away, the rotor storm showering their backs with mud and leaves. Captain Niles waited as the rotors faded into the distance. Seconds later, another helicopter passed overhead, the noise beating through the graying sky.

Two other troopships had accompanied their Huey. American and Salvadorian helicopters often flew between the military bases in Honduras and El Salvador. Unless someone within a few hundred meters had heard the insertion, the passing of the three helicopters would be only one more early morning overflight of the mountains.

A minute later, they heard only the sound of the rain. Intermittent gusts of wind brought momentary downpours that hissed on the mud and drummed on their equipment. Niles kept his head low and his Colt Commando above the mud and rain-matted grass. Behind him in the weeds, his men remained silent and motionless, their prone forms invisible. They waited, listening, watching the darkness under the wind-swayed trees.

The eastern sky grayed, a gray-on-black panorama of clouds and the forested ridgelines of the Cordillera Nahuacaterique emerging from the night. Niles kicked the boot of Alvarez. The sergeant flicked the radio key-set to send a predetermined code. A coded reply confirmed their communications link.

Wordlessly, Niles led the men from the ridge. He moved a step at a time, almost blind in the darkness and downpour. He eased down the slope, testing each step on the slick grasses before committing his weight. His boots sank into the soggy earth with every step. With his left hand, he gently pushed aside branches and slipped sideways through the brush and tangled pines, moving, pausing to listen for pursuit, then continuing. He held the Commando in his right hand, the muzzle pointed at chest level, his thumb on the safety/fire selector.

The satellite-generated contour map showed a steep ridgeline sloping down to gentle hillsides that gradually descended to a small river. The captain maintained a southern bearing as he zigzagged down the slope. He accelerated the pace as the storm clouds glowed with dawn. The three men of his team followed silently, seeming to float through the lush foliage, their rifles ready, their eyes scanning the trees and brush around them.

A drop-off stopped the captain. Crouching at the edge of the sheer fall, the captain looked down at the gray, storm-swept valley. He glanced back. His men faced outward in three directions.

"Stark," he whispered.

As the lieutenant joined him, the sergeants shifted to watch the area, watching the random patterns of the tangled growth for the forms of men pursuing them. In the rain and gusting wind, they could not listen for movement—they depended on their eyes.

"Cartography error," Stark commented, looking down the fifty-meter drop. Rainwater poured off the canvas of his floppy gray-and-green patterned bush hat, a downdraft spraying the stream of water into the void. The cliff continued a hundred meters to the north, where it intersected another ridge. To the south, the cliff gradually descended to the rolling hills of the valley.

"Good reason not to wander around in the dark—there, the river will be there," the captain pointed at a crease in the valley as he whispered. "The bridge will be down around that bend. I want to cross there—"

As Niles indicated their route, the lieutenant squeezed out a dab of olive drab grease and streaked it down the glossy black of his face. He added dabs to the backs of his hands. He finally wiped his fingers clean on the Atlacatl Battalion insignia on his left shoulder.

"—where that creek comes down, then follow that ridge around. We'll come around behind anyone watching the road. Make sense to you?"

"Yes, sir. They will expect long-range patrols to come from Perquin, not Honduras."

"Not exactly a tourist road anymore . . ."

The Soccer War of 1969 had closed the north-south Route Seven to traffic between Honduras and El Salvador. In the later years of the next decade, war again closed the highway as insurgency took most of Morazón Province out of government control. Salvadorian Army units in the town of Perquin blocked all travel into the area, halting vehicles and seizing guerrilla suspects. Guerrillas controlled the section of road continuing to the Honduran border. No one traveled safely.

North of the disputed international border, Honduran counterinsurgency battalions harassed Salvadorian guerrillas carrying supplies to the war and arrested Salvadorian refugees fleeing the fighting.

Satellite photos had shown a weed-overgrown track cut by washouts and downed bridges. Except for infrequent airborne and infantry operations mounted by the Salvadorian Army, the guerrillas of the People's Revolutionary Army held and governed the isolated region.

Moving again, Niles veered south. He paused and signaled Vatsek, pointing north, then cocking his thumb back to point in the route of march.

The sergeant nodded and rushed away. Using his two hundred and twenty pounds of body weight and the forty pounds of equipment load, he stomped his boots into the soft red clay to create indelible prints. He followed the cliff to the north. At the intersecting ridge, he came to a sheet of naked stone. The stone continued in a band across the mountain, appearing and disappearing at irregular intervals. Despite the weight of the equipment he carried—M-16/203 combination automatic rifle and grenade launcher, 5.6mm and 40mm ammunition, fifty meters of nylon rope, rations for three days—the sergeant stopped and jogged backward up the mountainside, leaving a second set of bootprints marking his return.

Niles continued. Now, with daylight, they could walk without leaving a trail, placing their feet carefully, skirting stretches of mud or delicate ferns. Walking last in line, Vatsek corrected any missteps, brushing away bootprints and rearranging crushed leaves. The rain completed his task, erasing all marks of their passing.

For an hour, they followed a weaving course down the hillsides, exploiting the concealment of the pines and scrub oak. Rain continued to fall. Winds parted the cloud cover from time to time, brilliant tropical light illuminating the hillsides in moments of vibrant, multitoned green, the flowing reds and yellows of the soil abstract contrasts. In these moments, the squad went to ground, staying low and motionless until the light passed, until the gray shadows and rain returned.

The hills sloped into abandoned cornfields. The Marines could not avoid crossing the fields. Staying within the cover of tangled bamboo and bananas and flowering morning glory, the captain led his squad to within a few steps of a low wall.

For generations, farmers had piled rocks from their fields to create boundary walls. Now, after years of war, weeds and brush choked the fields. Corn and bean vines gone wild grew in clumps everywhere, the corn stalks dried and yellow. Niles noted that the ears of wild corn had been harvested.

Sections of walls and paths had disappeared under the growth. Leaving the bamboo, the captain crawled through the tall grass to an overgrown wall. He crouched there for minutes, watching the abandoned fields and listening. Misting rain continued, limiting his vision to a kilometer. Past that, the distance became gray and diffuse, the mountains lost in clouds.

When he signaled, his men followed. They crept cautiously from field to field, staying low behind the rock walls, never using the pathways—both the Salvadorian Army and the guerrillas used mines to inhibit the movement of their enemies.

A few meters from the remains of a burned-out adobe shack, the captain paused. A crater filled with stagnant water and shattered trees indicated that the shack had been a bombing target. Now morning glory vines and broad-leafed *chocón* covered pressed-mud walls eroding back to the earth.

Niles studied the muddy earth, advancing a step at a time, then stopped at a stand of banana trees.

Peasants in Central America often grow banana trees in their gardens. Each tree eventually produces a single stalk of bananas. As the fruit matures, bananas can be cut individually to feed the family or the stalk harvested to be sold in the village market. Niles pointed out the freshly severed center stem of a tree. Milky fluid still dripped from the cut.

Someone had harvested a stalk of bananas that morning. And only guerrillas occupied this area. Faint mismatched bootprints—some with the sole pattern of army boots, others with commercial tread—led from the banana tree to the field. By the rain-erosion of the tracks, Niles guessed the guerrillas had passed at dawn.

For the next several hundred meters, the Marines moved more slowly, more cautiously, staying below the level of the piled-stone walls, using the wild corn for concealment. They heard the stream before they saw it. A cornfield dropped off into a streambed. Churning brown water tore through the narrow channel, the roots of trees exposed on both sides. Captain Niles motioned Vatsek forward and pointed at the rope he carried. Vatsek nodded.

Studying the banks of the streambed, the sergeant moved upstream a few meters. There, bamboo and overhanging trees offered concealment.

As Stark and Alvarez watched the fields and Niles the opposite bank, Vatsek wound his rope into a cowboy coil. Then he knotted one end around a fist-sized rock.

His first throw sent the rock over an overhanging branch of a *ceiba* tree. Playing out enough rope to allow the rock to fall almost to the water, he jerked the rope taut. The rock swung like a pendulum and Sergeant Vatsek caught it on a backswing.

Niles looked up at the branch and hissed over the roar of the water, "What are you doing?"

Knotting the lines together, Sergeant Vatsek stepped on the knot and swung into space. He gave his chest two thumps with his fist as he flew over the rushing water, then dropped onto the opposite streambank.

"Tarzan . . ." Alvarez said, laughing quietly. He pushed through the bamboo and caught the returning rope. He crossed the stream, followed by the lieutenant. Captain Niles crossed last.

"California crazies . . ."

The bull-necked sergeant thumped his chest again as he re-coiled his rope. Niles crept up the bank and peered through the trees. He saw only a slope shaded by the *ceiba*. Matted leaves covered ground littered with plastic bags and rags.

The trash heap of a town? He checked his compass bearing and glanced at his plastic-coated contour map. An ink circle marked a bombed-out and deserted village hundreds of meters upstream. A line traced a winding dirt road. Past the road, they would begin the climb of the next mountain. The captain continued, his boots sinking deep into the matted leaves.

A hand clawed at his leg. He started, pointing his rifle, not firing, not believing what had touched him, staring at the skeletal hand reaching up from the leaves and trash.

"Mother of God!" Alvarez whispered, unconsciously crossing himself.

Niles took a step toward the arm and his boot crushed through the trash—an old smell hit him, the wave of stink so foul and nauseating that he staggered, kicking through the matting, scattering debris as he tripped to one knee.

A rotting face stared up at him, the eyelids half-closed over empty eye sockets. Framed by swirling black hair, the lips and face of the girl had drawn back to reveal teeth and the hole of her gaping mouth. Skin had also puckered back from a second hole in her face, a tiny, perfect bullet hole in her forehead. A flap of skull and hair hinged away from the side of her head where the high-velocity bullet had exited.

He clenched his jaw and stood, looking around at what he had thought to be trash: knees and elbows still clothed in rags, the pale and withered skin of hands and faces, the fragments of bullet-shattered skulls.

Watching from the stream bank, Stark held his bush hat over his mouth and nose. Motioning the others to follow, Niles forced himself to walk among the corpses, his boots causing arms and legs to move, leathery skin to crack and release putrefaction.

At the road, he went prone. He crabbed to the side to avoid the bones of a child—apparently killed by a machete, one side of the small skull sliced away—and looked out at the gullied and overgrown track. No vehicle had used the road in months. Rain-beaded grass showed no tire tracks or footprints. He waited until the others joined him, then dashed across.

They charged straight up the mountain, leaving the horror and stink of the murdered families far behind, gaining five hundred meters of altitude in a half hour. Short of the crest, the four Marines paused.

As the others faced outward, their rifles leveled, Alvarez keyed his handset again, tapping out a coded message to check in with their communications interlink. When the response came, he reported their approximate position. Before he clicked off, he leaned close to the captain and whispered a question:

"Do I report the massacre?"

Captain Niles shook his head.

"Little children . . ." Alvarez whispered as he switched off the transmitter and secured his key-set. "Sir, who do you think did it?"

Glancing at Alvarez, Niles saw the Chicano sergeant watching him, waiting to see how he reacted to the question. Niles looked away, focusing on the ferns and pines surrounding them, his eyes scanning the mountainside for movement. Clouds swept over the ridgeline, wind shaking heavy drops of rainwater from trees overarching the Marines.

"Not us," he finally answered, his voice only a hiss in his throat.

Paralleling the ridgeline, they avoided crossing the crest of the mountain. Overflight photos had shown networks of trails there, where the wide, flat terrain of the crest allowed the guerrillas to move quickly. The forested mountaintop also provided some concealment from gunships and bombers for the lines of guerrilla supporters transporting weapons and supplies.

Good trails merited security details to warn fighters and support personnel of counterinsurgency ambushes. Or the placement of booby traps to maim outsiders and alert the guerrillas.

A sentry or a mine could end their mission. And perhaps their lives.

They stayed a hundred meters below the ridge, moving

slowly, silently around the mountain. Bombs had shattered trees and cratered the mountainside. But the Marines saw no evidence of guerrilla casualties: no bones, no shredded clothing, no discarded bandages.

Above them, near the crest, they saw much more damage from the bombing. Fallen trees lay at all angles, branches thrown by the blast hung in other trees, and where the Salvadorian Air Force had employed napalm, skeletal trees stood black against the storm clouds.

An hour passed before they saw the red dirt gash of Route Seven emerging from the south. A flooding river ran west. But they could not see where the road crossed the downed bridge that marked their objective. They continued around the curve of the mountain very slowly, expecting to encounter guerrilla positions overlooking the road and bridge. Crawling from cover to cover, they stayed below the level of the ferns and grasses and brush, pausing to listen, moving, then pausing again, taking every meter of mountainside slowly.

The clink of a bottle betrayed the lookouts on the crest. The captain heard snatches of Spanish. Concealed from the ridgeline by a line of granite, he shifted slightly, angling up between the moss-covered rocks. He listened for minutes before he heard the laughter. He eased higher.

Low, shrapnel-chopped trees blocked his view of the ridge. But the tangle also screened the Marines from the sentries.

A hundred meters farther on, ten meters past a faint path, he found a position viewing the road and shattered bridge. Pines screened the position from the guerrilla lookouts above them and the twisted branches of a fallen—but still living—tree would provide a place to wait and to sleep.

Vatsek provided security while Stark and Alvarez silently deployed their equipment. Words unnecessary, the soggy matting of leaves on the mountainside producing no sounds, the two Marine technical specialists unpacked monopods, camera mounts, lenses, and microphones.

Lining up with the downed bridge, Stark drove two monopods into the soaked clay of the mountainside. Each monopod—an aluminum shaft fitted with a pan/tilt head—created a stable camera mount only a hand's width above the mud. The night before in Tegucigalpa, Lieutenant Stark had first wrapped his Nikon cameras and telephoto lenses in water-proofed soft plastic, then packed the delicate equipment in foam and soft vinyl protective cases, finally sealing the cases with tape. Now, under the protection of a green plastic sheet, the cases opened without a sound, the lenses locking into the camera bodies with almost inaudible clicks. He assembled the cameras, then secured the cameras to the monopods by touch.

Alvarez pushed another monopod into the mountainside, then mounted the long foam-shrouded tube of an ultradirec-tional condenser microphone. Utilizing internal amplifiers and electronic filter circuits, the microphone could monitor a whispered conversation from a hundred meters. A cable linked the microphone's amplifier output to a multitrack cassette recorder. He wrapped all the electronics and cables with plastic as protection from the rain. Slipping on head-phones, he tested the assembly by listening to the sounds of rain splattering on the concrete of the dynamite-shattered bridge.

Niles prepared for another duty. He removed the maga-zine from his Colt rifle, then slowly pulled back the charging handle to clear the chamber. He reloaded the short rifle with a magazine of twenty reduced-charge 5.56mm Interdynamic cartridges. The Interdynamic silencer locked over the muz-zle to make the Colt Commando a silent rifle, capable of killing at a distance of up to two hundred meters.

Finally he clipped a plastic device over the ejection port to hold the spent Interdynamics casings. Nothing would remain in El Salvador to betray their action.

With his converted rifle, he left the others and inched his way up the mountainside to the lookout position. He heard two sentries—one a low, guttural voice and the other a higher voice, the voice of a teenager. As the raspy voice talked, the teenager laughed.

Niles crept to within a few meters of the crest—gently pushing through the bottle and can litter below the posi-tion—but could not get a view of the lookouts.

A plastic tarp flapped and snapped in the wind. He listened as the older man talked of "taxing" foreign reporters:

"I tell them, they want my picture, they pay to the struggle. They tried to give me money. Money! What can I do with money in the mountains? They had no food. So I take their batteries and a cassette of music. . . ."

The conversation shifted to other techniques for maintaining the flow of necessary supplies into the war zone, the veteran guerrilla instructing the teenager with an endless string of stories and boasts.

Waiting for a mention of the urban unit of the PRT, Niles listened throughout the last hours of the afternoon and into the night. Rain fell, other guerrillas replaced the first two, empty cans clanked down the mountainside—but the guerrillas said nothing of the assassins from San Salvador.

A very patient man, Niles waited all night.

10

WHEN the rain paused, Lidia Rivas heard the far-off hammering of machine guns and the dull thudding of mortars. She sat up from the rotting car seat and pulled the sheet of plastic tight around her body. Around her, she saw that her comrades still slept—aguardiente and capsules of Seconal taking them far away from the cold and rain of this shack on the roof of a garage in Perquin.

She sat in near-darkness, listening. Lantern light came from the stairwell, the faint yellow light gleaming on the salvaged fenders, windshields, and crates of used auto parts cluttering the rooftop. Beyond the junk, the rain streaked down from the dead black of the night sky. No lights came from the houses and shops. The guerrillas had cut the power lines in 1979, leaving the town in the mountains without electricity, telephones, or a telegraph.

The sounds of fighting seemed to come from the south. She looked into the night, thinking she might see the distant flashes of mortars. Nothing broke the absolute black.

Then the rain returned in a sudden downpour, beating down on the corrugated steel roofing of the shack. A curtain of water ran from the corrugated sheets, splattering on the concrete. Sitting in the darkness, cold, fleas crawling through her clothes, her body stinking of sweat and diesel, she waited for the rain to pause again.

This would be her last night in El Salvador. Tomorrow, Honduras and—

Light appeared in the street. Frantic, she found her Uzi submachine gun on the car seat and clutched the pistol grip, her eyes scanning the rooftop for the black silhouettes of commandos. An engine roared, metal rattled. The noise could only be soldiers in a truck. The all-night curfew allowed only the army on the streets—any civilian risked execution on sight. Then the concrete roof shook twice as the tires of a heavy truck hit a pothole in the stone pavement. She relaxed as the troop truck passed.

The lantern in the garage went out. More lights passed in the street, the tires of trucks crashing into the pothole. Rivas listened as the noise of the engines faded. Finally, she heard only the sound of the rain.

Holding the plastic above her head, she stepped into the downpour. Cold water soaked her shirt. She felt her way through the darkness with the tips of her soaked tennis shoes. Flashlights waved inside the garage, the weak light allowing her to start down the stairs.

"Who's there?" Someone whispered.

"Marianela."

"Come down and listen to the radio." She recognized the hoarse voice of the truck driver. "It is a very interesting program."

A candle lit the garage. She saw a local teenager named Roman at a table with the driver. By the light of a candle, they adjusted the dial of a radio and passed headphones back and forth. Roman wore the coveralls of a mechanic but held an M-16 rifle. In the cab of the truck, another man snored.

The middle-aged driver, a pale, thin man with an alcohol-ravaged face and red, bleary eyes, gulped from a bottle of aguardiente. As she stepped itno the light, the eyes of both men fixed on her chest. She looked down and saw that her soaked shirt revealed the form of her breasts. Ignoring their stares, she took a chair at the table and casually crossed her arms to cover herself.

Finally raising his eyes from her breasts, the driver tore off the headphones. "Listen, girl. The army fights against the night."

She slipped the headphones over her ears but she heard only static. But after a moment, a voice spoke in a quick code of letters and numbers. Rifles and machine guns fired in the background. Another voice repeated the message to confirm reception and a third voice cut in, the young man speaking quickly, almost in panic. Rifles fired in long, full-automatic bursts. Men shouted and cursed.

"A battle!" The driver laughed. "All those soldiers shooting thousands of communists from Nicaragua."

"Be quiet," Roman hissed. "They can hear you in the street."

"Was that where the trucks went?" she asked.

"Reinforcements! They expect a grand battle, a world war!"

"There are only four," Roman told her. "We sent them to make trouble. Three rifles and a grenade launcher and listen to the trouble they made. Tomorrow, the soldiers will be searching the mountains for the brigade—"

Laughing, the driver offered the bottle of aguardiente to Roman. The teenager shook his head. The driver offered the bottle to Rivas. She pushed the bottle away and he caught her hand and tried to pull her to him.

Rivas pointed the stubby barrel of the Uzi at the driver's face. He released her hand. "I bring you to safety and now you threaten me? What kind of thanks is that?"

"You were paid," Roman told him, looking at the drunken driver with disdain. In the candlelight, the teenager's face had the calm, stoic expression of a man many years older.

The driver turned to the wall and lifted the bottle high. "My darling gringa, do you want a drink?" he asked a calendar hanging above the workbench. On the calendar, a blond Anglo in a cheerleader skirt posed with her red-nippled breasts outthrust. The calendar date read 1973. "Will you drink with a man who has lost everything to the war? Who exists now only in melancholy and loneliness?"

"You have not lost it all." Roman shoved the old man. He tottered back in his chair, then fell forward. "But if the soldiers hear you, you will. Be quiet and sleep!"

"The hero and the beautiful girl." The driver sneered. "Without the old man to chaperone. So romantic, Roman and his Juliet—"

"Shut up and sleep." The teenager glanced at his watch, then turned to Rivas. "In an hour, it is light and a truck comes. You and the others must be ready. Go, go now, wake them."

As Rivas hurried up the stairs, the driver shouted: "My lovely little rich girl! Come back, I—"

A rifle clattered and Rivas heard a groan. Glass broke. She looked back and saw Roman with his rifle in his hands, standing over the driver. The driver tried to rise. Roman raised the butt of the rifle, threatening to smash the bleeding man in the head again. Rivas continued to the roof and stumbled into the rain.

Rich girl. She had heard it before. Always the comrades thought of her as the beautiful rich girl. Never as a fighter, never as a woman who had abandoned the comfort and privileges of the elite to take up the rifle, to throw her destiny into the revolutionary struggle. Yet she had risked her life night after night to lure the Marines into the trap on the Paseo Escalón—more than her life if the police had captured her and taken her into the horrors of the torture cells where death came as a mercy.

Looking to the south, hearing the faint sounds of the fighting, she wished she could have joined the squad of fighters who alone attacked the army, gambling their lives to throw panic into the outposts and divert the soldiers from the road to the north—no, she would not fight like that, crawling through the darkness with a rifle, perhaps dying unseen and unknown, only one more corpse in the war. If she must, yes. But she thought of all the actions possible in the capital, with the cameras of news teams there to flash the blood and horror of revolutionary justice to all the televisions of the world—

Then the rain came down and she stood in the cold rain cursing—not her beauty, for her beauty had trapped the Marines and her beauty would again serve the struggle. She cursed the stupidity and arrogance of the pretenders who called themselves fighters and denied a rightful place in the struggle for women of imagination and daring. Men fought in the revolution and declared their alliance to all the other comrades of the world—but their Soviet ideology changed nothing: they remained chained to hundreds of years of male arrogance. They thought only they could fight, as if aiming and firing a rifle or a pistol required a man's strength. Castro, the Sandinista comandantes, the Salvadorian leaders, the individual guerrillas—all of them.

To strike the fascists of her country she must first prove herself to the leadership of the struggle. Prove herself to be more than a beautiful girl from a wealthy family. Only then would she win a place in the future of the revolution.

Loud laughter woke Niles. Through the falling rain, he heard voices a few steps above him on the crest of the hill. One voice talked over the others. The man mimicked the sound of an automatic rifle and then parodied, "Don't kill me! Please, no, no, no—"

The man made the sound of the machine gun again, then pronounced, "That is how we killed the gringos."

Dead Marines.

Niles listened as the loudmouth continued his entertainment of the guerrillas. He told them the action had won the attention of the media everywhere in the world and the action had cost only one—and here he used an odd word—of his *pollolitos,* meaning 'little chickens' or 'little boys.' But no matter. Now they would all be movie stars in Europe.

After a few minutes, the voice drifted away, the loudmouth and other guerrillas walking north on the ridgeline.

The sentries speculated on the easy duty of a Zona Rosa action. "That's the war to fight. Attack in a truck. Sit in a dry house and watch the news on television. Be a big man to all the world."

"They won't be stupid like that anymore," another guerrilla countered. "Now they will stay in their embassy. They will never come out."

"Don't they have airplanes? Shoot down the airplanes at the airport. Don't they have a country? Attack in their country. They attack us. Attack them. . . ."

An hour passed. The rain died away. Niles saw the eastern horizon graying with dawn. Then, in the silence and calm, he heard movement on the road one hundred meters below him. Brush blocked his sight but he heard boots splashing through the mud and metal clinking against metal. He recognized the sound of a belt of cartridges clacking against the receiver of a squad automatic weapon. A squad leader issued a command in a low voice and he heard the soldiers thrashing into the roadside brush.

Above him, a silhouette appeared against the graying sky. One of the sentries looked down at the road, then turned away. The sentries resumed their conversation. Silently, slowly, Niles slid backward through the mud, following the same path he had taken up the hill. He paused every few seconds and rearranged the trash and leaves, erasing all trace of his passing as he snaked back to the other Marines.

Before dawn, a battered pickup truck left the garage and lurched a few hundred meters through the streets to a rutted dirt lane. Lidia Rivas lay flat in the back of the truck, a black plastic tarp over her back. She peered through a rusted hole in the side of the truck. Chickens fluttered and a dog barked as the old man driving the truck backed into a garage made of warped boards and scraps of sheet metal. The old man dragged the double doors of the garage closed, then limped to the back of the shack and eased aside a sheet of rusted corrugated steel.

Rivas went first. She checked the pouch holding two spare magazines of 9mm cartridges for her Uzi, then crawled out the hole and slid down a muddy hillside to the half-darkness of a ravine choked with mud and trash. She heard the others cursing as they thrashed through brush.

Splashing into water stinking of excrement, she crouched and waited, her eyes searching the tangled brush. Behind her, she heard kicking through the trash and breaking branches. A shadow moved. She pivoted and pointed her Uzi.

"Don't," a young man told her. He seemed to wear mud. Mud plastered his clothing and equipment. Only his Galil rifle remained clean. "I'm your contact."

"Where now?"

"This is shit!" Rivera called.

"Be quiet!" the guerrilla hissed. "Are all of you here?"

Rivas counted and nodded. "All six of us. Where do we go now?"

"Now you walk." The guerrilla pushed through branches,

following the flowing mud and trash. In some places, they dropped into holes chest deep. Rivas kept her Uzi above the water. Above the ravine, she saw steep hillsides strewn with trash. Smoke drifted from cooking fires. She heard the voices of children and women calling to one another. On the other side, she saw white-washed walls and tile roofs.

The ravine opened to a fast-flowing brown river. Across the churning water, Rivas saw hills and open fields. Retreating, she pushed into the concealment of the brush and trees along the river bank. But the guide hissed to her:

"Here." He pointed to a rope. "Move fast."

Knots secured the rope to the exposed roots of trees along the water. Cinching the sling of her Uzi tight, Rivas pulled herself hand-over-hand through the current, using all her strength. The force of the current and the harsh fiber of the rope hurt her soft hands, but she moved fast—any army patrol had a clear view of them.

A hundred meters ahead, another guerrilla waited. Without speaking, he motioned her into the brush. They crouched there in silence as the others came.

"I lost my pistol," Rivera complained. "That was a good Browning—"

"Shut up," Rivas told him.

The mud-smeared guerrilla came last. With a knife, he cut the rope away from the roots, letting the current carry away the short lengths. Then, holding his Galil above his head, he crouched in the water, letting the water sweep over his head, washing all the filth from his hair and uniform and equipment. Clean, he grinned at his comrade and Rivas. He avoided looking at the others from the city as he pointed to a trail running parallel to the river.

They pushed through the rain-heavy overhanging branches and walked to the north. Rivas took second in line, ten meters behind the point man.

LOUDMOUTH LEADER AT 500—NOISE ON ROAD 515—WHAT YOU HEAR/SEE?

A shatterwork-design of shadow and brilliant dawnlight patterned the pad of paper. Printing out the words, Niles questioned Stark. They sprawled in the mud under the branches of the fallen tree. They could not chance whispers with the sentries positioned above and guerrillas below on the road.

APPRX PLATOON DEPLOYED, the lieutenant answered in his precise hand-lettering. OVERHEAR ZERO VOICE.

BOZO JOKED OF KILLING MARINES—THINK WE GOT GANG!

The lieutenant nodded. He pointed outside. An arm's distance away, Vatsek and Alvarez maintained their watch of Route Seven. The lieutenant motioned, passing the field note outside for the noncoms to read. Niles nodded and started out with the note.

A hiss from Vatsek stopped him. Seconds passed. Two shots popped in the distance. Two shots answered from the ridge above them. One of the sentries shouted. Shots sounded somewhere to the north.

"G's coming up the road," the sergeant whispered.

Niles snaked into the glaring light. A clear eastern horizon allowed the rising sun to illuminate the landscape, creating a vista like a tourist postcard: undulating lines of green and brown mountains, shadowy mist-filled canyons, the trees and brush around the Marines glittering with millions of hanging raindrops. But banks of clouds remained overhead. The black western horizon indicated the approach of another storm.

Squinting into the glare, he saw a line of men and women struggling through the mud of the road. Two carried rifles and wore camouflage fatigues. He counted six others in street clothes—four young men, two women. A woman leading the line carried an Uzi submachine gun. He could not see what weapons the others carried.

Captain Niles grinned, scabs of mud flaking off his face. He pointed to the printing on the field note:

THINK WE GOT GANG.

Passing the note to Alvarez, he handsigned for a radio report and whispered, "Alert airborne."

Stark took his position behind the Nikons. After keying the coded alert and receiving the confirmation, Alvarez slipped on headphones and switched on the ultradirectional microphone. He and the Stark would man the technical equipment while Niles and Vatsek provided security.

On the road, the line of young men and women stopped at the edge of the surging river. The two guerrillas stayed apart from the six others. A young woman—perhaps older than the others, wearing tight designer jeans, a mud-soaked shirt, and a scarf drawing back her hair from her fine-boned features—stepped out onto an outjutting fragment of bridge and shouted. She raised her Uzi over her head.

"Comrades!" she declared. "I am Marianela of the Annihilation Unit. We are the ones who executed the gringo Marines!"

A middle-aged, overweight guerrilla in new camouflage fatigues stepped from concealment. "It's them. Get them across."

Captain Niles recognized the voice of the loudmouth braggart from the night before.

Guerrillas appeared on the road, some with ropes. In the next few minutes, the urban group struggled through the river. The braggart embraced the teenagers as they emerged from the river, kissing Marianela. She twisted away from his embrace and scrambled up the embankment to the other guerrillas. Niles saw the young woman stand several steps away as the braggart introduced the teenagers to the mountain guerrillas.

The cameras and microphone recorded the introductions—every face, every name.

With his arm around the second girl, the braggart pointed up the slope. The teenage comrades gathered together.

"Down!" Alvarez whispered to the other Marines as the first guerrilla started up the mountainside. As one, the Marines went to the earth, covering their equipment, shifting to aim their weapons.

Thrashing through the brush, using their rifles to part branches, the guerrillas followed the switchbacking path up the steep mountainside. The local guerrillas divided their attention between the muddy trail and the sky, glancing up through the trees every few steps.

The overweight braggart led the teenagers. The teenagers stared around at the undergrowth, slipping and lurching, grabbing branches for support. Talking loud, pointing like a tour guide, the braggart told them they would be in Honduras today, Cuba tomorrow, Europe very soon.

As the groups passed, Niles studied their feet and pants, contrasting the faded, stone-washed fatigues and fraying boots of the older guerrillas to the jeans and tennis shoes of the teenagers. The teenagers had not come prepared for a long-distance march. Either they did not have the equipment or did not know what to expect.

Amateurs, Niles thought. Student radicals gone terrorist. Teenage murderers of teenage Marines. Commanded by a loudmouth with the hots for the prettiest girl.

When the guerrillas passed the lookout position, silence returned. Niles nodded to Alvarez and the sergeant keyed his radio handset. Stark disassembled his equipment in a rush, first removing the film from the cameras and triple-sealing the rolls in plastic bags. On the radio, Alvarez received a confirmation code and signaled Niles.

Airborne.

Waiting until the others had repacked their equipment and shouldered the loads, Niles led the pursuit of the guerrillas. Vatsek remained behind for a moment to police the area, searching for bits of paper or forgotten gear, sweeping away marks in the mud and grass, rebending branches that had served as living camouflage. The touch-up took only seconds.

Niles followed the path toward the crest, then cut to the east, signaling Stark to continue straight up. Snaking into his position of the night before, Niles put the aluminum stock of the silenced Commando to his shoulder and rose to a crouch.

He heard boots pacing on the crest, the soles sucking from the mud with every step. To his left, the captain saw Stark—his M-16 fitted with an Interdynamics silencer—prone on the pathway. Niles crept forward, searching for clear ground in the litter of plastic and cans, sliding his boots through the grass and mud.

A few steps short of the top, Niles stopped. He saw a straw hat. He went prone and continued forward.

Two sentries watched the highway. One man had the weathered face and the sinewy, knotted-vein arms of a campesino. With his old G-3 rifle slung across his body, he stood with his scarred, blunt-fingered hands crossed over the receiver. The other man—actually a boy—had only one eye, his left profile a mass of keloid scars, the eye socket covered by a band of black cloth. They wore camouflage shirts, patched polyester pants, and military gear captured from the Army of El Salvador.

The one-eyed boy had his hand on the grip of his M-16 rifle. Niles shot him first, the 5.3gram bullet punching into the boy's temple. Dying on his feet, he took one step and fell.

Startled, the older man spun as he heard the mechanical clack of Niles jerking back the charging handle of his Commando to chamber the next Interdynamics round. Niles rushed forward, pushing the silencer against the campesino's chest and firing the silent bullet through his heart. Simultaneously, he grabbed the heavy rifle and pulled it from the man's hands. The Salvadorian fell backward, his eyes fluttering, his mouth opening to cry out, then he died with his shout in his throat as Stark jammed the muzzle of his rifle in the Salvadorian's right eye and fired a second point-blank round.

They moved fast, following in the footprints of the guerrillas. Rain fell again, the first drops rattling through the overhanging trees, then a downpour coming in a steady roar. But the low sun lit the ridge brilliantly, the trees glowing, the rain streaking silver as the Marines rushed north.

Niles saw the back of the last guerrilla and went down flat. Behind him, the other Marines stopped. They advanced in alternating dashes, the captain covering Lieutenant Stark until he received the signal, then sprinting past the lieutenant, the falling rain covering the sound of their boots.

A kilometer later, they heard the distant rotor throb. Guerrillas shouted to one another. Niles crept forward and watched the guerrillas scattering to cover. The teenagers from the capital remained together.

On a signal from Niles, the Marines shifted forward and formed a line blocking the retreat of the guerrillas. Alvarez radio-keyed the code of their position.

Helicopters appeared from the clouds. Circling the mountain, the troopships followed the ridgeline from the south to the north as gunners tried to spot the guerrillas. A doorgunner raked the trees with blind auto-fire, the heavy 7.62mm NATO slugs tearing through the branches and hammering the earth.

No one moved. The machine gun fire continued a few hundred meters to the north. Unseen beyond the trees, a helicopter circled, the doorgunners firing wildly into the mountain.

The Marines and guerrillas heard the rotor flare of a landing. The turbine shrieked as the helicopter lifted off, then another helicopter descended. Alvarez radioed the exact position of the guerrillas to the south of the landings.

Two rifle squads of Atlacatl airborne troopers blocked the trail to Honduras.

The leader of the Morazón guerrillas went to the urban squad. Niles watched the leader direct the braggart to take another route. Confused, his mouth shut, the braggart thrashed from the trail, blundering down the steep slope. The teenagers followed.

Niles crept to Alvarez. With the rotor throb and machine gun fire to hide his voice, he whispered, "Tell them to keep all fire off the west side of the ridge. The gang's going west. We will follow and disable. We will radio again for the soldiers to make the capture."

The Marines paralleled the descent of the teenage guerrillas. Rain continued, the mountainside flowing with runoff. Trying to lead the group, the braggart fell again and again. He rose covered with mud and cursing.

"The soldiers will hear!" a young man cautioned him.

A firefight on the ridge silenced them. Bullets zipped overhead, cutting through the treetops. The braggart dropped to his hands and knees on the slope. Niles saw the pretty girl named Marianela jerk at his collar:

"Get up!" she spat out. One-handed, she pointed her Uzi at the distant firefight, her eyes searching for a target.

Maneuvering ahead of the teenagers, Niles crawled under a low bush. He watched the braggart over the sights of his Commando and waited. Firing continued on the ridge. The girl forced the overweight man to his feet. Another burst of stray fire startled the braggart and Niles squeezed off the shot.

The silent bullet smashed through the man's left knee. Screaming, he rolled in the mud, clutching his shattered kneecap. The teenagers took cover in the mud, crawling sideways behind the shelter of rocks. But no more bullets came. Marianela helped their leader to his feet.

"Alfaro, come here. I can't carry this fat man alone. Shut up, Gonzalo! Stop crying!"

A boy rushed to the man's side. Staggering, they helped him down the mountainside.

Stark signaled Niles and continued downhill. As the teenagers lurched toward Niles, he went flat, molding himself to the roots and uneven ground under the bush. He watched the three urban guerrillas walk past him, their legs brushing past the branches of the bush concealing him. Turning, the soaked leaves under him making no noise, he aimed at the girl's leg.

Marianela paused, one foot up, the other downslope to brace her as she helped the wounded man down. The bullet punched through her ankle.

Screaming, falling back, she sprawled against a tree. The boy dropped the fat leader and went to help the young woman. She waved him away as she struggled to her feet: "Take him! I can still walk. If they get him, he'll betray all of us."

Niles waited. He watched as the young woman braced herself behind a pine and looked for the sniper who had shot her. But her eyes scanned the slope high above him.

Riflefire continued on the ridge, the doorgunners of the orbiting troopships strafing the guerrillas as they retreated from the Atlacatl squads.

One of the teenagers screamed, his voice trembling with pain as he cried out for help. "My leg! Marianela, help. I've been shot, there're soldiers here somewhere—"

"Quiet!" she shouted back. Walking on her wounded ankle, gasping with each step, she managed to stumble after the others.

Niles moved again, this time at an angle to the mountainside. He crawled, sometimes slid, letting gravity pull him through the mud and rotting leaves, circling to the left of the teenagers as they struggled down the mountain. Their wounds had slowed them to a painful stumble.

The second girl cried out as an Interdynamics bullet wounded her.

"I'll kill you!" Marianela shouted, firing wildly, trying to kill the unseen sniper. The 9mm slugs tore through the branches and whined off rocks as Niles joined his sergeants.

"Where's Alfaro?" A boy called out. "Alfaro!"

Vatsek pushed Alfaro's face into the mud while Alvarez looped green nylon rope—of the same type used by the Salvadorian army—around the boy's ankles, then his wrists. Strips of tape—purchased in San Salvador—went over the boy's eyes and mouth. They left him there.

The three Marines closed on their targets, immediately immobilizing and taping the braggart, then another young man, then the other girl. But Marianela and the last boy eluded them.

Dragging her wounded foot, Lidia Rivas clawed through the mud. Rocks scraped across her ankle and she shuddered with the pain but she continued down the slope until a ledge of rock sheltered her. There, she stopped and listened. Automatic rifles fired on the hill above her and helicopters continued circling above the trees.

Someone gasped and slid through the brush. She saw Tonio—the boy who had driven the pickup truck of riflemen on the Escalón—struggling through a tangle of brush. Blood poured from a wound to his right knee.

A bullet had punched into his knee, making running or walking—even crawling—impossible. A bullet had broken Gonzalo's knee. And a bullet had punched into her ankle. All nonlethal wounds—that made escape through the mountains impossible.

The army wanted them alive. When she had heard the helicopters, she had feared death. Now she realized they would not allow her to die. Rivas felt terror seizing her, overcoming her anger and adrenaline paralyzing her mind as images of corpses disfigured and mutilated by torture flashed through her imagination—capture meant hell.

Pressing her body to the earth, holding the Uzi ahead of her to keep the barrel out of the mud, she slid downhill. If she could reach the bottom of the hill, if she could hide . . .

Tonio thrashed through brush as he slid and fell down the slope, gasping, crying out every time he jarred his wounded leg. He stared around him at the hillside. Bullets cut through the trees above him and he cringed, covering his head with his arms and rolling down the hillside. He cried out, "Marianela! Help me! I can't walk. Please . . ."

Let the army take him. Rivas stayed low and moved away from him. Looking back, she saw him pushing himself upright with a stick, trying to use the stick as a crutch.

A shadow moved in the grass. She saw the line of a weapon and an arm. Almost invisible in the mud and leaves, the soldier crawled from the brush, a weapon in his hands. She recognized the black tube of a silencer on an M-16 rifle.

Rivas shifted, slowly turning, ignoring the pain in her ankle, forcing herself to breathe slowly and evenly even as the pain seared through her legs and back. The soldier pointed his rifle at Tonio and Rivas saw his black hands and face—not black with camouflage face paint, but black by African heritage.

An American. The fascists had sent Americans to hunt down the killers of the Marines in San Salvador. On the Paseo General Escalón, she had not used a weapon. Now she would kill her first American—and any other American soldier blocking her escape.

Slowly, she brought up her Uzi—but too late. The falling rain covered the sound of the rifle as the American shot Tonio, her comrade screaming and falling, rolling through the brush. She jerked up her Uzi to aim and the magazine scraped on a rock. The American turned as she fired.

Firing betrayed the position of the assassins. Niles spotted Marianela prone in the mud, her Uzi's metal stock unfolded and shouldered. Blood flowed from her bullet wound. Less than twenty meters away, the last teenager boy cried and pleaded, dragging himself through the brush on his elbows. Both of his legs glistened with blood.

Marianela tried to kill Stark. The Marine lay flat behind

the shelter of a low rock, trapped. Aiming two and three shot bursts at the lieutenant, the young woman skipped bullets off the rock protecting him, bullets tearing through his backpack, smashing cameras and lenses.

If the lieutenant moved, if he raised his rifle or tried to withdraw, she would kill him.

Niles passed his weapon to Vatsek with the one-word instruction, "Wait."

Shrugging out of his light pack and web gear, Niles crawled fast to the side, gouging his legs on rocks and dead sticks as he slid down the slick mountainside. But Marianela moved, rolling down the slope, her Uzi locked in her hands. She hit a tree and gasped, but did not stop moving, crawling behind the tree for cover.

His speed down the slope made noise. Marianela looked back at Stark, then her head whipped toward Niles, her eyes locking on him as she brought up the Uzi. Throwing himself to the side, he heard the simultaneous blasts of the submachine gun and the rip of the bullets tearing past him—and the firing stopped. The submachine gun empty, she jerked another thirty-round magazine from the pouch on her belt—

And Niles lunged at her, one hand going for her eyes, to cover her eyes, to protect the fiction that Salvadorians pursued her, but she battered his arm with the Uzi, hitting him once in the side of the head, and their eyes met for a long instant as he grabbed her wrist and wrenched the weapon aside and drove his fist into her gut, doubling her. In seconds, the Marines had bound and taped her.

The Marines left the Salvadorians for the Atlacatl troopers to find.

11

A FIST ended her struggle. The Americans bound her, one man pressing her face into the mud and grass while other hands looped ropes around her wrists and ankles. A hand jerked her head up and she saw an instant of a camouflage uniform and then tape covered her eyes, the tape going around her head, then over her eyes again.

Blind, her hands tied behind her, her feet tied, Rivas felt the hands withdraw and she kicked out, ignoring the pain of her ankle, trying to find the Americans, to strike out a last time before they took her. Her kicking only sent her rolling down the slope.

Brush scraped her and she stopped. Leaves and branches pressed her. She heard no voices or movement around her— only her own breathing and the sound of the falling rain. In the distance, the noise of the fighting continued on the ridge. Rotor throb came from helicopters.

Why had the Americans left her? To capture the others?

She jerked at the ropes on her hands, trying to tear her hands free, trying to do the impossible and break the ropes. Pain stopped her. She tried to find the knots with her fingers, bending her hands back until her wrists ached, but she could not touch the rope.

Desperate, she felt for rocks in the mud and grass. Her fingers found the long, jagged edge of a rock. Turning, shifting her position, she felt branches hooking at her, leaves scratching her face as she laid back and sawed her wrists against the rock. She worked frantically, ignoring the pain of rock scraping away her flesh.

111

Rifles fired random bursts in the distance, the firefights ending. Voices called out—in Spanish. She felt blood flowing over her hands and she twisted her wrists. The rope did not part. But when she put the rope against the stone again, she felt the edge catch at a place—she had frayed a notch in the nylon. Working harder, straining outward with her arms to hold the rope taut as she dragged the frayed section along the edge of stone, she forced the pain of her wrists and the ache in her shoulders out of her mind.

Men crashed through the brush. Weapons and equipment clattered. A voice called out—in Spanish. "There's another one."

She did not move. Boots knocked rocks free to roll down the slope. Then the soldiers stopped a distance above and away from her. A boy screamed in pain and the soldiers laughed.

Slowly, silently, she wrenched her hands apart, the sawed rope giving, long fibers stretching and snapping, the coils falling away. She lay still, slowly, silently easing her bleeding hands to her face.

The adhesive tape tore, giving her vision—but she saw only broken darkness. She lay inside heavy brush, the tangle of branches and leaves concealing her. Rain fell, water dripping through the leaves. She turned and she looked up the slope.

A trail of plowed leaves and red mud led directly to her. In the gray brush and rain, she saw soldiers criss-crossing the hillside. One soldier picked up her Uzi. He slung the submachine gun over his shoulder and continued kicking through the brush, searching for her.

Bending, she untied the knots of the ropes binding her ankles. Her wound still bled. She wiped it off with rainwater, grinding her teeth against the pain. Just above her ankle, a small-caliber bullet had entered behind the bone of her leg, passed between the bone and the tendons and muscles, and exited on the opposite side. She felt her ankle and leg, her body flashing with pain, but she did not find shattered bones.

Boots approached. She waited, listening. She had no weapons, her Uzi gone, her Beretta gone, not even a knife. The soldiers followed the marks of her slide. She looped the cords around her ankles, then patted the adhesive tape down on her face. A space allowed her to peer out. She found a rock the size of a fist and put her hands behind her, waiting, faking unconsciousness.

"There!" one soldier said to the other. "A white shoe! One of the *capitalinos*."

"And blood."

Two soldiers scrambled to the brush concealing her. Not moving, she peered under the tape, seeing the boots and camouflage pants of the soldiers as they thrashed into the branches. A hand grabbed her foot and dragged her out.

"Got another one."

"Quiet! Keep quiet. She's ours. Look at her. She's a beautiful one. Even under all that mud and shit she looks like a princess."

"Look at that, tied up and her pants on. And no one's fucked her yet."

Hands pulled up her shirt. She did not move, controlling her panic, forcing herself to breathe slowly. They pulled up her bra and she felt the rain on her breasts. The two soldiers went quiet.

"Anyone else?" one whispered to the other. "You see anyone?"

"They're all up there."

"We'll fuck her. To hell with the lieutenant and the colonel. This time we get first fuck on one of the girls. No one will know. Hold her down."

Plastic clattered. She saw the boots and camouflage of one soldier. The soldier propped his rifle against the rocks, then crouched and opened her pants. Hands took her shoulders. She faked a semiconscious moan, turning her body.

"Hold her!"

The hands on her shoulders gripped her hard. Grinning, glancing up to her, the soldier between her legs stroked the curve of her waist. He tried to pull down her tight jeans. She moaned and turned, as if regaining consciousness.

Swinging with all her strength, she smashed the rock into the soldier's skull and twisted as the soldier fell sideways, clawing at the hands of the second soldier, hitting his face with the rock, hearing him gasp and curse. He punched her but she blocked the blow with her left shoulder. The soldier fell forward, off balance on the steep slope, falling over her as she hit him again and rolled backward under his body.

They crashed through brush and saplings, his rifle barrel slamming into her head, rocks gouging her back. But she kept her left hand knotted in his rifle sling and shirt, holding him against her as she hit him again and again.

A tree stopped them. He slammed sideways into the trunk and momentum jammed her against him, her naked breasts scraping against the equipment on his fatigues. She hit him again with the rock but he did not move.

Blood bubbled as the soldier struggled to breathe through his smashed face. Rivas held onto his shirt and dragged him farther down the slope, finding shelter beneath a ledge of rocks. No one could see her. She closed her pants and pulled down her bra and shirt. Her right hand throbbed, a fingernail somehow torn away, her fingers and knuckles cut and torn from the soldier's shattered teeth. Blood welled from the gouges on her wrists.

She found his bayonet. Putting the point against his throat, she threw her weight down on the handle, driving the blade full depth into his neck as he convulsed and choked. She held on with both hands until his body went still.

Blood and mud and filth covered her. She worked quietly, quickly, stripping his body. She took his web gear and shirt, then his boots, bundling it all together. Slinging his rifle over her shoulder, she continued down the ridge, sliding and limping, until she came to the overgrown road.

In the ruins of an abandoned house, she washed herself in the falling rain. She cleaned the mud from the barrel of the dead soldier's M-16 with a rusty wire and a bit of rag. Then she laced the boots on.

With a branch as a crutch, she continued higher into the mountains of Morazón.

Minutes later, in the Managua office of the Ministry of Exports, Raúl Condori heard an incoming code sequence on the radio monitor. He played back the recording, decoding and transcribing an urgent message from a transmitter in the Honduran town of Cabañas. He keyed the confirmation code, then called the mansion in the suburbs south of Managua.

Pazos did not answer. He had returned late the preceding evening from Cuba. Thinking his superior still slept, Condori let the phone ring for minutes. Finally, one of the Cuban soldiers who guarded the residence answered.

"Who is this?"

"Condori. From the office. Where is he?"

"With the girls."

"Which place?"

"This an emergency? He said only if—"

"What's the number?"

"No telephone . . ."

Condori took the panel van and sped through the rain-flooded streets of Managua to the failing shops and beach clubs along the lake shore. After the earthquake destroyed the factories and commercial buildings in the center of the capital in 1972, the tourist businesses enjoyed a brief boom as international relief organizations sent experts and workers. But Somoza's plundering of the foreign aid and fears of communist revolution halted the economic recovery. In the years of the civil war, no tourists came to Nicaragua—only journalists. Most of the resort owners left after the Sandinista victory. Whoever remained did not waste their few dollars on imported paint to brighten their motels and hotels and discos for European hippies and East European military advisers.

The apartment house dated from the 1930s. Two-story, with neo-colonial ironwork on the balconies, the building stood alone on a muddy street of broken concrete and vine-overgrown lots—most of the other apartments and shops on the block had not survived the earthquake. A faded sign offered rooms in Spanish, English, and French. Now the old proprietress offered more than rooms. Condori parked on the sidewalk and rang the entrance bell.

A square window in the door opened. The old woman's yellowed eyes peered through a mask of powder, mascara, and lipstick. A Hermes scarf bound her hair, the patterns and brilliant colors framing the pastels of her face. Her perfume overwhelmed the smells of garbage and diesel.

"Who are you?"

"I want Díaz, the Mexican."

"Sir, I do not know of whom you speak."

"He's here. He's a regular. There's an emergency at the office and if I don't get him, he'll be fired for sure."

Looking past him, she glanced at the panel van marked with the letters, TV. "If it is a matter of urgency, I will allow you to disturb my guest."

She unbolted the heavy door. In the entry, Condori saw the Ministry of Exports Mercedes and a Soviet WAS jeep parked bumper to bumper, their rain-polished paint splotched by sodden leaves and flowers from the *copa de oro* vines. Tropical plants filled the central courtyard, the original garden lost in tangles of fronds and glistening leaves, vines advancing over the paving stones. *Copa de oro* covered the interior walls, twining through the wrought iron of the second-floor walkways. Under the heavy rain clouds, the courtyard remained in semidarkness, the air cool and scented with the old woman's perfume. She led him up a flight of tiled steps to a second-floor room.

"You wake the gentleman. The responsibility for this intrusion is yours."

Pazos heard her voice. "Who is it?"

"There is a message at the office."

"What?"

"I can't shout it."

Seconds later, the door opened. A girl in a nightgown slipped out. As thin as a child, her breasts only points on her chest, she looked no more than twelve or thirteen years old. Condori stepped into the darkness of the room. Pazos sat against the ornately carved headboard, the sheets tangled over him.

"So what is so important that you must tell me now?"

"The army wiped out the unit."

"What? All of them?"

"Helicopters attacked them in the mountains. A few of the guerrillas escaped. But on one in the unit."

"What of Lidia Rivas? Any word of her?"

"It is not known if they are dead or captured. But none of them made it to the meeting place."

Outside the door, the old woman listened to Pazos cursing. Then she heard him say:

"What a loss! She was so beautiful. We killed some Marines, but no Marine was worth losing her. Not a hundred Marines."

Maps of the action covered one wall of the wood-paneled office, tape joining topographic printouts of the town, the river, and the mountains. Green ink indicated the path of the Marine squad to the observation point. Other maps showed the route of Highway 8 through the mountains of Salvador, then north through the lines and whorls of the disputed national border to the towns of Cabañas and Marcala in Honduras. A tourist map of Honduras showed the road continuing north to the department of Intibuca.

In his office in the Old Executive Office Building, Devlin studied satellite photos of Highway 8 between the border and Cabañas. That section of the highway had deteriorated to a rutted, one-lane road serving only a few scattered farms. The fields and pastures of the farms spread through the narrow valleys. Corn rows curved along steep hillsides. Foot trails scarred the ridges. Beyond the road and farms, the trails continued through the mountains, winding along ridges and slopes to remote shacks. Some of the trails ran to the road, others paralleled the road and continued to the town.

A few kilometers north of the Salvadorian border, the roof tops of Cabañas lined the intersection of Highway 8 and the Carreterra de la Paz. The dirt track of the carreterra snaked east through the mountains, linking villages and logging camps to the department capital of La Paz. In the 1960s, truck traffic from the departments of La Paz and Intibuca had passed through Cabañas with loads of lumber and cattle and coffee en route to the cities of El Salvador. Then the wars had stopped all cross-border trade, isolating and impoverishing the town.

However, Cabañas continued to be a market town for the surrounding area. In the satellite photos, Devlin saw foot trails radiating from the town, following ridgelines and hillsides to patchworks of fields and pastures of the small farms.

A few of the trails joined the trails cutting through the mountains. Devlin traced several zigzagging footpaths from El Salvador to the trails converging on Cabañas.

A folder contained photos of a coffee farm south of the town. The photographer had parked across the road and snapped photos of the adobe house, the slat-board and barbed-wire gate, and the trees and barbed-wire fence enclosing scrap cars and trucks. Behind the house, tree-shaded rows of coffee bushes covered the hillsides and merged with the pine forest.

Another series of photos showed the farm as seen from a hill. The back of the house opened to a work yard. Heaps of coffee beans dried on concrete slabs. Rusting cars and trucks lined the fences.

Comparing the snapshots to the satellite photos, Devlin found the road and the rectangle of the farm house. A north-south trail to the Salvadorian border ran along a ridge overlooking the road. A faint footpath cut through the pines and trees to the back fence of the work yard.

A report from agency sources in Honduras identified the coffee farmer as a contact for the Workers' Army. The operator had been assigned to transport the gang from the mountains to their transportation out of Honduras. This farm and the contact men waiting there would be the next target for the Marines.

A call interrupted Devlin. The hiss of electronic encoding circuits denatured the voice speaking from San Salvador:

"Colonel?"

"Here."

"The army reports six prisoners. Five identified as teenagers from the capital. The sixth prisoner is a co-conspirator from the capital, a middle-aged man. He is already talking."

"Casualties?"

"All wounded. Bullet wounds to the knees and ankles."

"No other casualties?"

"The army reports a few men dead and wounded. But the guerrillas got wiped out."

"Any extraordinary elements? Cubans, foreigners?"

"Not that the army reported."

"Keep me informed—" Breaking the connection, Devlin keyed an extension in the basement of the White House West Wing.

"Intelligence Coordination."

"This is Colonel Devlin calling for Phil Carpio."

"Colonel, please call the third-floor conference room."

Devlin keyed another number, this time an extension on the floor above him in the Old Executive Office Building.

"Carpio speaking."

"This is Devlin. I just got a call from down south. The army made the pick-up. Complete success."

"What about your men?"

"Not a word. I'm leaving the office now. I'll fly down there to debrief them and give them the next assignment."

"Don't. We've got a problem."

"Is this my problem? A problem with my men?"

"No, but it'll be your problem to solve."

"I'll be there in five minutes."

Stripping the sheets of paper from the walls, Devlin rolled the photos and computer-generated maps into a tube and locked the materials in the closet of the office. The maps and photos of Cabañas went in his briefcase. He rushed from his office and hurried through the turn-of-the-century rococo decor of corridors. A guard at the stairs checked his pass and allowed him to run up the fire stairs to the third floor.

Phil Carpio answered the door. Richard Todd paced the room as he spoke into a telephone. He nodded to Devlin and motioned him to the conference table.

"State," Carpio whispered. A balding, retirement-aged administrator who had flown combat missions as a young pilot in the Korean War, Carpio worked in the bureaucracy of the CIA, specializing in the coordination and confirmation of information from foreign sources. He had worked closely with Devlin on the contingency planning for a counterstrike after the 23 October terror bombing of the Marine barracks in Beirut. The Administration had never authorized the air strike on the Iranian-sponsored gangs of Baalbek, but Carpio had continued working informally with Devlin, managing the assembly of information from various U.S.-government and foreign agencies. This allowed Devlin to exploit many sources of intelligence material without exposing himself to questions.

Todd nodded to Devlin. Devlin and Carpio waited as the slight, gray man paced the room. His jaw clenched with anger as he listened to the handset but he spoke very calmly:

"Of course, I realize the importance of this opportunity. That is why I believe this operation must continue in complete secrecy. . . . No, the correct time for that is after the Salvadorians seize all the other members of the terrorist organization. The Salvadorians not only must conduct exhaustive interrogations in complete secrecy, they must also continue the interrogations until the security forces seize . . . I must object . . . Yes, of course . . . to present the Salvadorian armed forces to the world . . . in the best possible light. However, it would also somewhat diminish the success of the operation. . . . Yes, of course. . . . I have complete confidence in the Salvadorian security forces. . . . Yes, of course. Keep me informed."

Slamming the phone down, Todd did not speak for a moment. He finally turned to Devlin. "Good morning, Colonel. We've received word that your men performed exactly as expected. A perfect operation. However, as Mr. Carpio told you on the telephone, we have a problem. A problem in El Salvador. It seems that the capture of the gang presents a media opportunity that the Salvadorians—and the state department and the embassy—cannot allow to pass."

"A what? A media opportunity?"

"Your men in Honduras did as we asked and delivered the prisoners to the Salvadorians. When we agreed to that delivery, the Salvadorians told us their interrogators and security men, with the assistance of a special investigative team from the FBI, would continue the operation against the organization in complete secrecy. However, the ambassador and the state department demand that we allow the Salvadorians to manage the publication of the capture of the murderers of the embassy Marines. We cannot stop it. They assure us that the investigation will continue, however—"

"There is no point in continuing," Devlin told him. "The organization will disband and scatter."

"That is already occurring."

"Our sources in Honduras . . ." Carpio glanced at a telex page. "In Cabañas. The sources report trucks leaving the farm where the gang would meet their drivers. We've got to assume the organization got word of the captures and sent out the alarm to all the other contacts along the line."

"Then we've lost the chance to pursue the network back to the leaders."

"No," Todd answered. "The technicians salvaged this for us. The NSC monitored the gang radio transmissions and identified one transmission location."

"We think it's the training base." Laying out satellite photos, Carpio pointed to a hill topped by a complex of buildings and security perimeters. An airstrip cut across flat pasture land. "Interrogators in San Salvador can't get a definite place of training from the killers. The killers don't know. Cuba or Nicaragua, they don't know. Planes flew them there in the night. But they did describe the camp where they trained. Matches with this camp. NSC got a fix on the radio messages going out to the guerrilla radios. It's here. Near Palacaguina, small town on the Pan American Highway, north of Estelí and Managua. Information's still coming in, but the Cuban who runs this gang out of Managua—we've got a fix on his transmitter, too—this Cuban named Pazos travels in and out of the country as Emilio Díaz, a Mexican journalist. In Nicaragua, he has an office called the Ministry of Export Development. He drives up to the camp in a truck marked with white letters, TV. So he doesn't get shot or kidnapped by contras. What do you think, Colonel?"

"Can your men capture this Cuban?" Todd asked.

Devlin poured a cup of lukewarm coffee from a thermos on the table. "And give him to the Salvadorians? What is the point?"

"This time it will be our operation. State is out, the embassy is out, the Salvadorians are out. We'll run this operation from the council. No cooperation with allies or other departments. The operation will not exist except as actions. When your men capture this man, or anyone else in his organization, our personnel will conduct the interrogations."

"Like the operation into Colombia and the Bekaa?"

"Exactly. Except that this will not be a one-shot action. This will be the continuing operation you have wanted since we brought you on staff. Your men will not be reacting to attacks. They will be following the chain to its source. They will neutralize the terrorist organization before they kill Americans again."

"They will have authorization to do whatever is necessary?"

Todd nodded.

"And back-up?"

"Covert support—information, money, transportation, specialists. Whatever they request. But nothing that involves documentation. Nothing will be in writing. Your men will operate on their own whenever possible. This will be a tight operation, an operation that officially does not exist."

"That is exactly what they want."

12

THE intercom buzzed. Quezada picked up the telephone and heard dot-dash code in the background—he knew Salazar was calling from the radio room before he heard the young man's voice. He splashed across the courtyard to the small office where Salazar leaned over the table, penciling down the sequences as the monitor blared the scratchy dot-dash staccato of the coded transmission.

Quezada understood a line about Americans. The transmission ended and Salazar replayed the tape, correcting his rough copy. Then he tapped out the confirmation to the distant radio.

"What is it about the Americans?"

"There was an attack. What it was, I am not sure—one moment, sir. One moment and I will make sense of this."

Waiting as Salazar worked with the message and the code books, Quezada tried to think of nothing. He turned and stared out the office window to the rain flowing over the stones of the courtyard. In times like this, when he remained in the safety of the school while his fighters risked their lives in action, he cursed his injuries. The loss of his arm and his eye made him an old man at only thirty-one years old. Ten years before, wounded by the bullets of the National Guard—his arm smashed, a bullet fracture in his skull, a hole through his leg—they took him alive and tortured him until he prayed for death. He served the revolution by remaining silent. Months later, after the amputation of his arm, an exchange of captured diplomats for prisoners freed him. He went to Cuba as an emaciated, one-armed wreck of a man worth nothing in a battle. Refusing to abandon the struggle, he studied radios and learned to encrypt communications. East Germans taught him to organize networks of agents. The Cubans taught him the tricks of discovering government informers. He went to Tegucigalpa and ran intelligence operations in northern Nicaragua, bus drivers collecting information from sources in towns along their routes, Quezada typing coded reports with one hand, then dispatching the summaries to the Sandinista forces in the mountains.

In the last days of the revolution, the National Guard executed an intelligence director in Managua and the Sandinistas sent for Quezada. He sped south with a staff of clerks and radio operators, the trucks loaded with equipment—and Somoza's air force hit the convoy on the flat, exposed highway outside of Guapinol. A fleck of steel shrapnel destroyed his eye.

No more combat for him. He had fought and lost twice. Now he taught teenagers to fight in the wars of liberation. They fought in El Salvador and Guatemala while he waited to hear of their victories—or deaths.

"I cannot decipher all of it—"

"What? Who sent it?"

"Marianela—"

Lidia.

"—but I cannot make sense of the last name. I think she has confused the codes—".

"She was not one of the technicians. What is it she sent?"

"That she fought the Americans. That she is free. In the mountains."

"Americans?"

"That word is positive. She repeated it."

"And what of the others? The others in her unit?"

"No word. Or no words that I can understand."

The telephone rang. Salazar took the call, then told the colonel, "It is the gate. The two Cubans are here."

"Radio back. Tell her to recheck her coding and repeat the message. Call me immediately when you have the information."

Outside, the rain had paused. Streams of water still poured from the roof tiles. Quezada went to the entry and watched as Pazos left the van. Condori waited at the steering wheel.

"Where are my fighters?" he called.

"Octavio, I bring you grief. I would have called you the moment I received the reports, but you know the telephones are not secure. I do not want the CIA to hear what I say. So I came myself to tell you of this tragedy. The army attacked the comrades escorting your fighters from Salvador. What reports we have, and they are incomplete—I understand it is maddening not to know the fate of those brave young men and women—but the report is that they did not escape the attack."

The round face of the Cuban twisted into a theatrical expression of grief, his jowls quivering, his eyes downcast as he continued. "What terrible sacrifices the struggle takes. I hope that coming generations read of the wars of liberation with awe and reverence, knowing that uncounted millions of brave fighters suffered unimaginable hardship and death to break the chains of imperialism and capitalism, so that the peoples of the world would live in freedom and know the—"

"I want to know. Are my fighters alive or dead?"

"That, I do not know."

"Were they killed? Are they scattered in the mountains? Is the army hunting them?"

"That is possible! Our information was that they had been attacked by the Atlacatl and that they had failed to reach the meeting place. Of course it is possible they are separated from the others. There may be hope yet."

"Pazos, they had some training, some experience. But I trained them to work only in San Salvador. They had no equipment for the mountains. They know no one there. If they are pursued in the mountains, I don't believe they have hope."

"But some may return. We can hope. And if they are gone, that is the cost of war. We must make sacrifices and look to the future. Some of us will be martyred. It cannot be avoided if—"

"Some of us make sacrifices, others make slogans. Come back when you have information on my fighters—"

The Cuban quit his act. "You, Octavio, do not issue the

orders. I realize that the loss of this group of young people may be difficult for you, but do not risk losing this—" Pazos gestured around to the courtyard and offices of the hacienda "—for a stupid outburst of anger. If you remember your role in the organization, you will remain a commander. If not, look for a position in Managua. Hundreds of veterans with disabilities work in the government. You can work in the bureaucracy. You can direct secretaries. You can charm the girls with stories of the war. You will not be lonely. Or you can hear of your new assignment, the next project to kill Americans, to strike terror against the fascist—"

"You do not order me, Pazos. No assignments. No orders."

"No orders? Then no money. Or do you believe your government could somehow find the money to finance this camp? And if they are to proovide the money, they will review the political implications of your camp. Are you willing to face that? You and I and your friend Borge are in agreement—" Pazos meant Tomás Borge, Minister of the Interior and chief of the secret police. Borge also oversaw the various expatriate revolutionary groups headquartered in Nicaragua. "—but will everyone in the junta agree that assassination and terror is the path to revolution?"

Quezada realized that the Cuban had won this confrontation. The DGI financed his school. Their money—actually Soviet money—paid his salary and the salaries of every clerk and instructor. Their money bought the weapons and the ammunition, the houses and cars for the units, the commuter planes that shuttled recruits between their countries and the school. Comandante Borge had agreed to the school if the financing came from Cuba. If Quezada rejected the money, then he must go to the Sandinista leadership for approval and money. Most of the junta members had no knowledge of his school. When they traveled to other nations, they could truthfully deny any involvement in Central American terror.

"Your money," Quezada told him, "does not buy the lives of my fighters. I do not send them out to death. So stop the stupid slogans."

"Octavio, my friend." Pazos grasped his shoulder. "Forgive me, this is a difficult moment for both of us. I tried to honor the dead and I only offended you. You knew those young people. I know you were very close to the girl—"

"That has nothing to do with this—"

"You think I only make slogans and go to parties? You are wrong. I also take my chances for the cause. When I travel to Europe, when I meet with our comrades in the Middle East, I risk my life. The CIA is everywhere. If we can forget our differences, if we can forget our losses in this disaster, we can fight together. Of course I do not think I buy your fighters. It is my pleasure—and my duty—to contribute to the international struggle. Please, let us end this argument. I bring you a new weapon. A weapon that will kill one hundred Americans at once, destroy their entire embassy, leave it only a ruin."

"What is this? A missile?"

"Forty rockets. A Soviet BM-21 rocket launcher."

"And will the Soviets send an artillery officer to aim the launcher?"

"This launcher is different. There is a transmitter and a computer to aim the launcher. First the crew positions the launcher. Then an advance team will go to the embassy with the transmitter. The transmitter sends the electronic signal and the computer aims the launcher. The advance team withdraws to safety."

"There is no need for a spotter to correct the fire?"

"Every rocket is perfect. When the time is right, they radio or telephone the launcher crew to fire the rockets. Before the army can even start searching for the fighters, they will be gone."

"How do we know that the electronics and the computer work?"

"The technology is proven. I saw it work. In recognition of our victory over the Marines, the Islamic Jihad will send this gift to Salvador. Say the word, provide a crew to man the weapon, it is yours."

"Why do they not use their own fighters?"

"Mohammedans in San Salvador? Octavio, you joke."

"Colonel!" Salazar called.

Rushing back to the communications room, Quezada heard another coded message on the monitor. "Is it her?"

"Yes, Colonel. She is transmitting. But another message came in. From an agent in San Salvador. They have information on the . . ."

"Where are they?"

"In prison."

Salazar gave him a typed page. The Salvadorian airborne troops had attacked the *capitalinos* and the escort group only a few kilometers south of the Honduran border. The soldiers had captured all of the urban squad. The agent reported a total of six prisoners. A courier would follow with additional information.

All of the squad taken prisoner—how could that happen? They had carried weapons. The soldiers would shoot to kill. Had they surrendered? Impossible. They had executed American Marines. They knew the regime would make an example of them. Had the army somehow caught them sleeping? But even when they slept, they held weapons. Quezada had taught all of them that a pistol meant the difference between quick death in combat and a slow, miserable death in a cell.

But the army took them alive.

The dispatch of a courier meant information that could not be radioed. Without a doubt, the American spy agencies had recorded the coded transmission from San Salvador. Perhaps they had already broken the code. But the courier could not be scanned and decoded. In a few days, Quezada would know the details behind the capture of the *capitalinos*.

Only Lidia Rivas had escaped. She had radioed of Americans. What did the Americans do in this?

"Marianela is repeating the message," Salazar told him. "She is free. She is with a force in the mountains. The Americans captured the others. The contact in Cabañas does not respond to her calls."

"That is because," Pazos said from the doorway, "we alerted all the contacts. The contacts in Cabañas are already gone. Why should they wait for the death squad?"

128

"Radio the code for a plane. We will get her out immediately."

"So Marianela escaped?"

"Somehow." Quezada left the communications room and closed the door behind him.

Pazos put an arm over Quezada's shoulders. "It was not a complete disaster. You did not lose your beautiful Lidia Rivas. That would have been a tragedy for any man with blood in his veins. Come, let me tell you of this rocket launcher. Forty rockets, electronically guided, each with a warhead of fifty kilos of explosive . . ."

Shacks and red mud streets blurred beneath the troopship. Niles pressed his face against the rain-streaked plexiglass and looked ahead. Against the gray sky and the hills of the *colonias* south of Tegucigalpa, he saw beacon lights flashing on the terminal of Toncontín International. He took his pack from the floor and slipped the straps over his shoulders. Stark and Alvarez followed his signal and assembled their equipment and weapons. Vatsek slept with his pack on, his M-16/203 in his hands, his head against the bulkhead housing the transmission, oblivious to the turbine noise.

The pilot spoke through the intercom. "There's transportation waiting at the airport."

"Imagine that, limousine service."

"It's a truck." The pilot ignored Niles's attempt at a joke. Unlike the Alabama pilot who had flown the insertion flight, this pilot spoke without an accent, his words correct and neutral. "They want you out of this aircraft and into that truck immediately."

The horizon tilted as the Huey cranked through a half-turn and flared, then dropped to the asphalt in a high-angle descent. Niles saw headlights leave one of the Honduran army hangers. A panel van sped across the rain-slick asphalt and stopped outside the rotor circle of the helicopter.

The pilot clicked on the intercom but Niles threw the headset off and stepped out the side door. Running to the van, he threw open the double doors and shouted back to the others, "Move it! You want to make the cover of *Time?*"

"No journalists here . . ." A voice commented.

Niles turned to see Colonel Devlin—dressed in sunglasses, a Hawaiian print shirt, denims, and running shoes—waiting in the van. A camera in a case hung by a strap over his shoulder.

"It is Mr. Marvel." Niles used the colonel's code name from their Vietnam operations. "You look like a journalist. I wouldn't have known you."

"This is my tourist disguise. Just talked with the Salvadorian commander. He told me it was a perfect operation."

"My opinion exactly. We put them down, one through seven. They don't know what happened to them—and neither does *el comandante*."

The other Marines stepped into the van, rain dripping from their boonie hats. Behind them, the helicopter lifted away, the rotors throwing a horizontal spray of rainwater against the van.

"Gentlemen," Niles shouted, "you all know our distinguished visitor."

Vatsek—his fatigues plastered with mud, his face and hair and hands smeared with green and black grease paint—raised his hand in a slow salute, but the colonel extended his hand, shaking hands with Vatsek, then Alvarez.

The van sped away with the Marines. The colonel waited until the rotor noise faded, then reached into a plastic bag under the van's bench seat. "Brought the squad a reward. For service beyond the call of duty—"

"Air express beer!" Vatsek took a can and jerked the tab. He gulped, foam running over his face and throat. Emptying the first can, he took another. "Four six packs . . . why didn't you bring enough for the other guys?"

Devlin laughed as he distributed cans. "In Washington, they cater the meetings, but this is the best I could do for this conference. The Salvadorians made the pickup. Not a single serious injury to the prisoners. How did the monitoring go?"

"Pictures and tapes," Niles answered.

Setting down their weapons, Stark and Alvarez shrugged out of their packs. Devlin noticed the bullet holes in Stark's pack. He examined the tears, slashes, and holes. "What happened to this equipment, lieutenant? Looks like you encountered a chainsaw."

"A submachine gun, sir."

"An Uzi in the hands of a beautiful girl," Alvarez added.

"A girl did this? You were wearing this pack at the time this damage occurred?"

"Yes, sir."

"You are very fortunate not to be a casualty."

"Not luck." Niles laughed.

"A rock," Vatsek added.

"However," Stark explained, embarrassed, "my Nikons were not so fortunate—" Smashed cameras and lenses spilled out of plastic bags. He pulled a smaller bag out and took out four canisters of film. "Group shots and individual portraits."

"And I got all their talk." Alvarez handed a cassette to the colonel. "They brag about shooting our men."

"Excellent."

The roar of a descending jet overwhelmed their voices. Tires shrieked as the airliner landed. The van continued along a straight road, then slowed. They heard a soldier shout out, *"¡Alto!"* The van stopped. The Marines did not speak until the van lurched into motion. Through the small windows in the double doors, Niles saw the beacon light and orange control tower of the Toncontín terminal—they had not left the military side of the airfield.

"We're not going back to that hangar?" Niles asked.

"No. Nor will you return to the base. As far as the base records go, you are reassigned."

"To where?"

"You'll be operating from . . . a hotel here on the airfield. Our men took all your personal gear to the rooms."

"A hotel?" Niles asked. "We just walk in like this? Weapons and Atlacatl uniforms?"

"Maids and room service?" Vatsek took another beer. "Satellite TV? A disco on the roof? A weight-training room?"

Devlin laughed. "Not quite. I should have said, 'a transit facility.' Rooms, beds, showers. The most attractive feature is the high security. There are three guarded gates between you and the street. Also, there is a telephone with a scrambler. I can call you direct."

The van whipped through a half turn and then reversed. Steel rattled against steel as an automatic door raised. The van backed into a garage. Devlin stepped out first, then motioned the others to follow. Niles saw only the blank walls of other buildings outside before the van pulled away and the door came down.

Inside the garage, Niles saw Vatsek's four-wheel-drive van and Alvarez's old pickup truck. Tools and spare tires hung on the walls. A gas pump provided fuel.

"We operate out of here? What's the operation?"

"Against that gang's headquarters in Nicaragua—"

"All right!" Vatsek laughed. "We're on them. Search and destroy."

"The U.S. of A. gets serious!" Alvarez added.

"When will we hear what the gang knows?" Niles asked.

Unlocking a steel door, Devlin led them into a hallway. He pointed through doorways. "Put your equipment anywhere. All the rooms are the same. And all the rooms have televisions. The Salvadorians intend to hold a press conference and show the gang to the world."

"What? They're going to broadcast this? Look, Colonel, as far as—"

"It was not my decision."

"I didn't think it was. But hear me. As far as the leaders and the organization know, that gang is dead. Wiped out by an airborne assault. But if they know we took that gang alive, they'll break up their organization and scatter their people. We'll never track it back to the headquarters—"

"It was a political decision . . ."

Niles looked at the other Marines. Stark turned away and put his rifle and pack of shattered cameras in a room. Alvarez shook his head. Vatsek curled his lip in a sneer and silently mouthed the words "Fuck politicians."

A political decision. A political decision gave the murderers to the Salvadorians for a press conference—instead of a long and exacting interrogation to expose every member of the organization. Niles had no confidence in the value of Salvadorian police or military interrogation of the gang—the Salvadorians had a reputation for torture. A prisoner suffering a beating or burning or shock treatment said anything to stop the pain. And if information came from whatever suffering the Salvadorians inflicted on the killers, action on the information required another political decision from Washington.

Devlin continued into a lounge. He set his briefcase on a table and snapped open the locks. "We could do nothing to stop it. All I can tell you is that it was decided at the highest level. However—"

"You told me yourself that they had a network going from San Salvador to Cuba. Put us on it. Call north on that direct line and get that authorization. We'll take who we can before the Salvadorians put the gang on television. Give us the information you have and we'll track it back to the head man."

"Exactly!" Devlin took several folders from his briefcase. "I didn't fly two thousand miles to deliver that beer. Here are maps of Nicaragua and Palacaguina. Photos of the camp. Background information on a Cuban named Pazos. We think he's the director of the gang. Ten thousand dollars, ten thousand lempiras. Don't get caught, but if you do, bribe your way out. There will be more money when you need it. Also, there will be back-up personnel available to you. Specialists, security personnel on contract to the agency." He pushed the folders of information and the stacks of cash across to Niles. "This will be exactly the action you wanted. You go into Nicaragua, you take that Cuban, and we close down his gang."

13

L IGHT blazed from the west as the sun passed through a clear band of horizon, the red disc above the mountains and below the gray storm clouds. The slanting light illuminated the hills and forest overlooking the pastures. Leaning against a tree for support, Lidia Rivas watched the plane descending from the gray sky. Red sunset light flashed from the windshield.

A guerrilla spoke into the radio handset. "It is clear. Our squads checked both sides of the field."

"Any wind there?" the pilot asked.

"Almost none."

"Coming in. Get him out there."

The guerrilla signaled two men. Rivas put her arms over their shoulders and they rushed from the trees, splashing through soaked grass. Engine noise tore the silence of the valley and the plane's oversized wheels touched the pasture, spraying water and mud.

Lurching across the pasture between the two men, Rivas reached the slowing plane. The pilot turned the plane around and a man ran ahead and jerked open the door. Rivas limped the last few steps, the pilot reached out to her, the hands of the guerrillas grasped her leg—and she hit the seat.

The door shut. Revving the engine, the pilot grinned to her. "What a lovely surprise . . . so this is why this is a very special flight."

As the plane soared away, Rivas pulled out the rusty revolver she had taken in trade for the dead soldier's M-16 rifle.

"Why the gun?" the pilot asked.

134

"I will not be a prisoner."

"May I be your prisoner?"

"Fly. There is nothing to say."

The pilot followed the contours of the mountains until the sky went black. Gaining altitude, he watched his instruments, slowly changing his compass heading from west to southwest as they flew blind through darkness and storms. Rain beat at the windshields, winds battered the plane. The pilot made no more jokes—he kept his hands on the control yoke, his eyes constantly scanning the darkness and the glowing instruments. Voices and static came from the radio. Rivas forced herself not to sleep, holding the pistol at her side, between her body and the door, ready.

After an hour, the pilot switched radio frequencies. He listened to a conversation. "I think we're in Nicaragua."

"How much longer?"

"Minutes. If we can find the camp. You are very lucky. The head man said to bring you straight. No visits to the islands. No run around. There! That's Ocotal." He pointed to a pattern of lights to his left. "A few more minutes."

"How can you be sure that is Ocotal?"

"I know these mountains. There is nothing else out here . . ." He recited a series of numbers into the microphone and waited. A voice answered in numbers. The pilot watched the distance. "There!"

Magnesium flares guided the pilot to the camp. Only after she identified the familiar lights of the hacienda and the barracks did she jam the revolver into her waistband. Headlights appeared on the gravel airstrip. The pilot brought the plane down and bounced across the ruts to a truck with drums of gasoline.

Rivas left the plane without a word, limping, pain jolting through her leg, trying to run to the one-armed figure standing away from the others. He reached out as she neared and she embraced him, her arms closing around the strength of his body, the smell of his uniform and sweat meaning strength to her, and for a minute she did not speak or move—she only held him.

The others refueled the plane. Quezada took her to a car, his arm around her, bracing her as she limped.

"I thought I'd lost you," he told her. "And I have lost all the others. When the check-in messages didn't come that night, I couldn't believe there was trouble. I refused to believe it. I went out and taught students. I curse myself for that. I could have flown all of the others out. If I had used our contacts and our transportation, instead of the shits the Cubans hire, there would have been no informers and no betrayal and the army could not have been waiting for your group there in the mountains—"

"It was Americans," she told him. "Without the Americans, the army could not have caught us. The Americans waited for us and then the army came in helicopters. Because we killed their Marines, they sent their special forces into Salvador."

"The Americans. And Pázos."

"Pázos came here, his mouth running with words of sorrow . . ." In the darkness of his rooms on the second floor of the hacienda, Quezada talked as he paced the bare wooden floor. "I did not know yet if the unit had lived or died and Pázos already wanted another group of fighters for another attack. As if fighters were only bullets to load and shoot at the regime, worth only a few centavos apiece. What a loss . . . only you come back, only you out of ten—"

"Who was it that reported the police taking the driver?" Rivas sprawled on the bed, the bandages on her ankle and fingers startling white against the shadow of her body. "I know it was not one of the unit. I knew nothing of the police taking the driver, taking César until that night, when Paulino came. And when Paulino came, he told me police were around Julio and Martin. We could not go to the radios."

"It was the brother of César. His brother went to a contact in San Salvador and the alert went to the Cubans."

"To the Cubans? Why?"

"The message of the capture of César came through that network of shits the Cubans operate. Send a message for the Ministry of Exports, and the Salvadorian army command and army gets the word first. The little playboy bureaucrat at the Ministry—Condori—got the message and issued the orders to evacuate the unit. He said that he followed the instructions of Pazos. Instructions. Pazos did not even talk with me. He was out of the country, unavailable. I had no chance to radio you. And now the Salvadorian army has my fighters. I lose nine fighters. And the Americans lose only four. There was no victory in that."

"They were the first Americans killed in the war. Everyone in the world knows of the dead Americans. And it was our victory. Ours. No one else in the struggle can claim it."

"Except for the Cubans. Pazos."

"What was the other attack? The other attack Pazos wanted?"

"Again on the Americans. Again he wants us to attack Americans and not the regime. Not the National Palace. Not Ilopango. This time, the American embassy. And if I refuse, I lose his money."

"But how? We looked at the embassy. And the house of the ambassador. It will be impossible. Even a truck bomb is impossible, the embassy is like a bunker—"

"Rockets."

"There are high walls. There are steel plates in front of the windows. There are wire screens. The rockets and grenades will never touch the—"

"Artillery rockets. A Soviet rocket launcher and forty artillery rockets, each one with fifty kilos of explosive. The launcher will be concealed in a truck and driven into San Salvador. Then they will be aimed at the embassy by electronic devices. Every rocket will hit the embassy, he says."

Rivas did not speak for a moment. "Finally. Finally, the Soviets give us the weapons we need. Now we can drive the Americans out. With this, with more launchers—"

"No. Not the Soviets. It comes from the Iranians. The Islamic Jihad. He went to Lebanon and they gave him the rockets and the launcher. Because of the killing of the Marines."

"Why not us?"

"Because the Cubans told the Iranians that Pazos is the leader."

"That pig! A leader? He does nothing."

"He brings the money from Cuba. Now he offers me the rocket launcher. Without him, no money. No rockets."

"Can you not speak directly with the Iranians?"

"It will be possible . . . Pazos wants a crew of four men to go in the truck with the launcher. I must send them to Lebanon for training."

"Why men? Is it technical? Who can you send?"

"There is no problem with the crew that goes with the truck. I have four men here who can go. Lobo who speaks very good English. The others a little. They know cars and trucks. I can send them to Lebanon immediately. They know nothing of electronics but Pazos told me that was unnecessary. After they return, I will talk with them. I will have a chance of going directly to the Iranians."

"What if they go directly to Salvador? There is a chance they will be killed or captured, that they will never come back here."

"If they go direct, I will tell them to speak with a contact in Salvador. They must have secure contacts if they hope to escape. I do not think Pazos cares if my men live or die after they fire the rockets."

"Tell them to talk with the Iranians. To tell them the truth about Pazos. That you are the real leader."

"And what if the Iranians report to Pazos what my men say? It will not be so simple to cut out the Cuban. There will also be a second team. They will have the responsibility of the guidance electronics. My men will know nothing of that."

"What are the guidance electronics?"

"He did not explain."

"Octavio, do you have any loyalty to this Cuban?"

"Why do you even ask?"

"Send the men to Lebanon. Let the Iranians train them. They can also watch and learn about the other team with the electronics. If we can learn of the others, we can take them and the attack will be ours and Pazos will be unnecessary. After the victory, the Iranians must come directly to you. Because the pig Pazos will be gone. We will kill him."

14

SHAFFIK Hijazi manuevered the truck through the traffic of Baalbek. The design of the street—a civic project of French colonial administrators fifty years before—had failed to anticipate the commerce and the vehicles of the future. Too narrow to allow parking and the free flow of traffic, the one lane of pavement forced drivers to stop and start as they wove past cars and trucks parked sometimes on the asphalt, sometimes on the sidewalk. Only motorcycles and bicycles moved quickly. But Hijazi drove a loaded truck.

Horns blared. Motorcycles whipped around him. The buildings on both sides of the street rose three floors, the street level shops, the second and third stories offices and apartments. In the narrow vertical space between the opposing buildings, the noise of cars and motorcycles and the blaring music from the shops reverberated in an unending cacophony. The line of cars eased forward meter by meter, exhaust clouding up from the traffic to create a noxious, gray pall.

Hijazi felt sweat running through his beard. Sweat coursed under his long-sleeved shirt. The two-hour drive from Jounieh had left his clothing soaked. He thought of the truckers in New York driving in undershirts and swim trunks during the summer. Here, in the areas controlled by the Iranians and the Party of God, short sleeves and bare legs meant an interrogation and a warning. For only comfort, Hijazi would not risk a confrontation with the Islamic radicals. His documents identified him as a Sunni Moslem with an address in West Beirut. But his business required travel

139

between Jounieh, East Beirut, and the Bekaa Valley towns of Shtaura and Baalbek—a route very suspicious to the Iranians, who questioned every contact with the Christians and foreigners of non-Moslem Lebanon. If the Iranians held him and requested a Syrian check on his background—though he had manufactured a believable past and a legitimate import company, the facts of his training at Fort Benning, Georgia, in the United States, and his liaison work with the Marines the year before in Beirut meant death if discovered. He avoided all contacts with the Iranians and Syrians—even if he must wear a beard and long-sleeved shirts in the Lebanese summer.

As he strained against the steering wheel, easing the truck around a Syrian army staff car, Hijazi saw an officer in camouflage fatigues leave a shop. A clerk followed the Syrian with a wheeled cart stacked head-high with boxes of American cigarettes. Hijazi glanced in the rear-view mirror and calculated the profit of the shop on the cigarettes. He guessed at the profit for the Syrian when the officer resold the cigarettes in a souk—one of the open marketplaces in Damascus where merchants displayed goods smuggled from Lebanon.

A good profit for the shop. A good profit for the officer. Perhaps a month's army pay.

Sounding the air horns, Hijazi slowed at the shop of his cousin. A shop boy ran out. Hijazi endured the heat and exhaust and the blaring horns of the traffic as the boy moved cars from the curb in front of the shop. He finally steered the truck into the space and eased the wheels over the curb.

A group of cousins left the shop. Hijazi unlocked the rolling steel door of the truck and searched through the cargo of cardboard boxes and shipping crates. He found a box marked FRAGILE and went into the shop as the cousins formed a line to unload the cases of Japanese tapes and electronic units.

In the shop, floor-to-ceiling racks featured stereos, speakers, videotape players, wide-screen projection televisions, and home video cameras. Locked, glass-covered bookshelves displayed the titles of hundreds of videotapes, thousands of stereo cassette tapes. A rhythm and blues tape played on the shop sound system, Mississippi voices singing in an American dialect incomprehensible to the teenage Revolutionary Guard militiaman buying a cassette-to-cassette duping deck.

"Here are the recordings from Europe!" Hijazi called.

"Good, good." Raman directed a clerk to count the piles of cash the Iranian spread on the display case. "Go direct to the office." Raman unlocked the stairwell leading to the second floor. "Did it come through Jounieh or the airport?"

"The airport is closed again." Hijazi went up the narrow stairs as Raman locked the door behind them. "I had these couriered through Cyprus."

At the top of the stairs, Raman unlocked another door. "The taping is going quickly and without problems." He closed the door and locked it. Dropping his voice to a whisper, he asked, "Did the Americans make the payments?"

"Always." Hijazi set the box of record albums on a work bench. "They were not late with the money. It was the fighting. With the telephones not operating, I could not call the bank and confirm the deposit. It took time to cable and receive an answer."

"The bank sent the money to the university?"

"Of course. The next time you come to Beirut, I will show you the bank forms. Why don't you transfer the money to Ali's account? He can write checks for his expenses. And for the school of Hussein."

"Trust a boy of his age with that amount of money?"

Though actually cousins, Shaffik Hijazi thought of his cousin Raman Hijazi as an uncle. Twenty years older than Shaffik, Raman had many years of experience as a merchant and the respect of his extended family of cousins, brothers, uncles, and sons. But when he spoke of Ali as "a boy," Shaffik laughed:

"He is in the United States. He is twenty-one years old. If you cannot trust him with money, you sent him to the wrong country for his education. With money, you can buy anything in America. Anything."

"I do not want to hear that. For him and his brother, I am a spy, and now you tell me that the money will only lead them into error. Do not tell me that. Leave me in my ignorance."

"You are not a spy—"

"Then what?"

"A technician. Do not say it. Do not think it. And no one will ever know."

"Then let us stop talking of it. Come check the machines."

Rows of machines for the duplication of cassettes—both music and video—lined the walls of the second floor. Here, above his shop, Raman operated a recording center furnishing imported entertainment to Baalbek, the Bekaa, Syria, and Iran. For music, Raman ordered new albums of American and European releases. Hijazi delivered the air-couriered albums to the shop. He and his sons recorded a master reel-to-reel tape of the album, conformed the tape to the cassette format, then used a high-speed gang recorder to make as many as ten cassettes at a time. A local printer supplied Arabic labels for the cassettes. Without the expense of foreign attorneys and licensing fees to the European and American companies, Raman made a good profit.

Videocassettes required a more complex international organization. As soon as the Hollywood studios released a film in the United States, entrepreneurs copied the film onto one-inch reel-to-reel videotape and sent the tape to a Beirut processing center offering computer-generated subtitling. Translators prepared Arabic subtitles. Technicians electronically superimposed the subtitles on the master tape, then recorded several high-quality cassettes. Those cassettes—complete with Arabic subtitles—went to distributors who owned duplicating machines. Within the month of the release of the American film, Lebanese and Egyptian and Kuwaiti merchants distributed thousands of copies to Arabs with videotape players—without paying a cent to the Hollywood studio for licensing. Raman operated two of the videocassette duplicating machines.

Raman took his cousin to the third floor. In a back storeroom stacked with albums and tapes, two other duplicating machines stood against a wall. The power lights remained dark. Hijazi flipped open a service panel. He saw a footage counter advance one number. The cassette in the right-hand machine had recorded an entire cassette and automatically transferred the incoming signals to the left-hand machine. That machine still had tape remaining in the cassette.

The machines did not duplicate films. Though the machines looked identical to the duplicating decks in the other room, these machines recorded radio signals. American electronics engineers had added masses of circuitry to the consoles. Though the machines could duplicate videocassettes, the new circuitry scanned the low-power communication frequencies used by the Syrian army and the several Iranian and Lebanese militias, the machines digitally encoding, then recording the many transmissions on standard videocassettes. The wide, high-density magnetic tape allowed the machines to record days of walkie-talkie and radio talk on every cassette. When a machine completed a cassette, circuits switched to the other machine and a new cassette. Raman checked the machines every day, changing the videocassettes when necessary, then passing the recorded videocassettes to his cousin Shaffik for transportation to the Americans. For this, he received a monthly deposit in a New York account and student visas for his sons and daughter to attend universities in the United States.

Shaffik reloaded the machines. "Did you see any special units? Is there any talk in the town?"

"Only of the Israelis. And they Syrians. There is talk of war."

"There will be no war. The Israelis want out of this country. Unless the Syrians attack the Israelis, they will be gone. What of the Iranians?"

"Those dogs. They turn the youth against their parents, against their teachers. They are taking disturbed young men into their gangs. You have heard of the car bombings. The Iranians are involved in that."

"Do you have names?"

"There is only the talk. I have no names. I risk my life to ask names."

"There is no need. You are doing enough—"

A telephone rang. Raman rushed out. Hijazi stacked the

recorded cassettes and reset the counters. Flipping down the access panels, he checked the fuses, then pressed the button activating the diagnostic programs—no problem.

"An Iranian speaks no Arabic and he wants tapes that are not English or French. Will you talk with him?"

"Of course." Dumping out the imported albums and video masters, Hijazi filled the box with the unmarked videocassettes and went down the stairs to the showroom. A clerk from another shop waited there.

"Come, this Iranian is waiting at the shop of Reyal."

As they walked through the traffic to the business of his uncle on the opposite side of the street, Hijazi asked, "What does this Iranian want?"

"Music from Spain."

"Tell him to go to there."

"He is Pasdaran. And he has been drinking alcohol."

"An Iranian drinking?"

"Please. Talk with him. Get him to go away and not bring trouble down on us."

They entered the narrow shop as the Iranian shouted in English:

"It's Spanish. It's a language, you know? The language the people speak in Spain. Most of the people south of the Rio Grande speak Spanish. So what's the big problem? You got tapes here from Denmark. Why can't I get what I want? I need a court order? A decree from the Ayatollah? You want to see my money?"

The Iranian wore the uniform of the Revolutionary Guard—beard, short-cut hair, mismatched fatigues. Though he did not carry a rifle, he wore a pistol in an old Lebanese army holster. He looked perhaps forty years old, white hair streaking his hair and beard, his eyes red and bloodshot. Except for his age, he looked like any of the other Iranians occupying Baalbek. But the idiomatic English meant he had lived in the United States.

"Sir, the clerks do not quite understand you." Hijazi affected the British English of his high school. "Their English, unfortunately, is not as excellent as your own. Is it possible I may help you? What is it that you wish to purchase?"

144

"Tapes. Disco, rock-and-roll, folksongs, songs—in Spanish. Like maybe a hundred tapes."

Making a note on an order pad, Hijazi smelled the alcohol on his breath. "Music? Or video?"

"You got them? Music and video in Spanish?"

"No, sir. But I am the foreign buyer for a number of concerns. I can order and deliver whatever you desire."

"How about a blow-up love-doll?"

Hijazi pretended not to understand. "Is that a title or a group?"

"Can I order a selection? And a catalogue?"

"Certainly. However, because this is an extraordinary purchase, we will require payment in advance. Would that be too much to ask?"

"You take dollars?"

"American dollars? We would, in fact, prefer dollars. I will give you—" He turned to Sayed, a thin, stoop-shouldered bookkeeper who had married into the Hijazi clan. In Arabic, he negotiated buying Sayed out of this deal. "I want his dollars. I'll pay you ten percent in Lebanese if I can take this business for myself."

"And you may keep the ten percent if you will take him away without violence. I will not sorrow when this strange foreigner is gone."

Speaking in English again, Hijazi told the Iranian, "Thirty-five Lebanese pounds a tape. Plus fifty American dollars for the air shipping cost from Europe."

Using a hand-held scientific calculator, the graying Iranian computed the exchange rate, then took a roll of American currency from his fatigue pants and pulled off four bills. "I want three hundred and fifty dollars worth of tapes. Get all kinds. And I want a catalogue of what music they've got. And get me a catalogue of Spanish movies."

"Do you read Spanish? Or should I request this catalogue in English?"

"Fuck no. I won't be watching that shit. Get it in Spanish. So you order this stuff from Europe? How long will it take?"

"I must order all the cassettes from Europe, sir. There is no recording industry in Lebanon. As to time, expect your order within a week. I will telex the instructions to my

European suppliers this afternoon. And I will of course instruct the suppliers to purchase what you order only from the companies of nations other than the United State—"

"I couldn't care less where you buy this shit. Buy it from old Ronald McDonald himself. Listen, if I give you company names and addresses and parts numbers, can you get some tools and parts for me?"

"Exactly what would these tools and parts be?"

"It's too technical. But any computer maintenance supply would have it all. You know, like for personal computers. But I want it fast. A week."

"There will again be a fee for special air handling."

"I'll pay it. I'll put together my list. If you come through with all that Spanish shit, maybe I can send some more business your way. What's your name? You speak great English."

"I am Shaffik. I was fortunate to have British teachers throughout my education. Is there a number where I may call you when the merchandise arrives?"

"Yeah, here." He wrote a number on one of the hundred dollar bills. "But give up the telephones. I'm working in town here. I'll stop by the shop. One more thing. Can you get me a tape of *Deep Throat?*"

"Pornography?"

"A shitty movie. But a classic. I saw it in LA, years ago. Can you get it?"

"It would be a fearful risk. You know that the Pasdaran will lash anyone who deals in pornography."

"Won't whip me. You can, get me a cassette of it. I'll pay the going price. Later, Shaffik."

"And, sir! What is your name?"

"Muhammed Ali. Like the fighter."

The Iranian stepped into the gray smoke of the street and walked away, glancing at the windows of the other shops he passed. Hijazi spoke quickly with the teenage shop clerk. "Take your bicycle. Follow him. Don't let him see you but follow him until you know where he goes."

"Why do you send the boy out?" Sayed asked. The gray, stooping old man stood at the shop's door, looking out at the Iranian. "I think that foreigner is only trouble."

146

"Trouble he is. But he pays with one-hundred-dollar bills and he has many more to spend. I want to know more of that foreigner."

In the afternoon, Hijazi returned to Jdaide, a commercial sector on the highway to Jounieh where he had an office overlooking the Bay of St. George and the Mediterranean. He operated his company alone, working without a secretary or clerks, an answering machine taking telephone messages and an IBM personal computer managing his inventory and orders. A telex machine maintained his contacts with foreign suppliers.

He switched the telephone to replay and listened to the calls of the day as he taped a box together. A shipping agent in Tripoli offered him a pallet load of Kalashnikov rifles from Hungary. A militia captain wanted a video camera and recording deck. A shopkeeper finally had money to pay a bill. Odd calls separated the messages as the failing circuits of the Beirut telephone system switched random calls to his telephone. He smiled at the confused questions of the strangers as he packed the bubble-wrap protected videotapes in the box.

Turning on his mini-computer, he printed a mailing label for the box and a series of customs forms for the enclosed videocassettes, which he described as blank, defective cassettes returned for credit.

Then he typed a report of his meeting with the Iranian named Muhammed Ali, describing the Iranian in detail—his request for the Spanish-language tapes, his idiomatic English, the money, the scientific calculator, his mention of Los Angeles, and his request for computer parts and tools. He added that the Iranian worked in a sprawling trucking yard two kilometers south of Baalbek. Until recently, a company had repaired and sold trucks from the fenced lot and garage. Now, Revolutionary Guards seemed to be rebuilding diesel trucks and trailers for heavy transport.

Finished, he plugged a cable into the back of the computer, then ran the cable to a modified stereo cassette recorder.

He transferred the report to a music cassette. The label of the cassette listed a group and songs in French, but the narrow band of oxide between the A and B tracks now carried the report on Muhammed Ali. Hijazi taped the cassette to the inside of the box, then closed the box for shipment.

Calling a courier service, Hijazi sent the box to the air freight office at Beirut International Airport for shipment to Germany, where Americans would forward the tapes to Fort Meade, Maryland, and the technicians of the National Security Agency.

15

HEADLIGHTS streaking through the darkness and swirling rain, the panel truck sped across the rain-polished airfield to the Antonov transport and braked to a stop at the tail. The four young men stepped from the truck and rushed up the loading ramp. In seconds, the ramp closed and the ground technicians signaled the pilot with flashlights. Turbo-prop roar penetrated the quiet and comfort of the limousine as the transport slowly taxied to the takeoff strip.

In the back of the Mercedes limousine, Pazos turned to Quezada and Rivas. "Your boys will be in Baalbek tomorrow. Cuba, France, Libya, Lebanon, then Baalbek. Their rooms and comforts are ready. They will begin their instruction immediately. It is all arranged."

"They are good men," Quezada told him. "Very young, but intelligent and cunning. They are all from San Salvador, all experienced at fighting. They trained at my school three months."

"I read through your folder on them. I have no doubt of their ability. Now we need only to discuss the embassy."

"The American embassy," Rivas stressed.

"Why can it not be the National Palace?" Quezada asked. "A successful attack on the palace would kill all the leadership of the government."

"Why not, indeed?" Pazos knocked on the glass partition and the car accelerated away. "I think our friends in Lebanon wanted an attack on Americans. That is what we discussed." He glanced at his watch. "In time for the reception. I hope you will join me. It will be a relief from the isolation and hardship of your school in the mountains—"

"I am watching every report from San Salvador," Quezada told him. "From every agent, every informer. Even the newspapers for important events. Big events, where all of them will be in one place at one time. What if we get a chance to hit them all at once?"

"It is possible we could choose such an opportunity," Pazos nodded. "A time when one attack will satisfy all of our revolutionary aspirations. Perhaps the night of a diplomatic event at the Palace. Or a ceremony. The Americans could not fail to attend if the—"

"The Americans own Salvador," Rivas interrupted. "To bomb the embassy is to attack the true leaders of the regime. Kill the generals, kill Duarte—who in the world will care? The masses of the world know nothing of the gangsters of Salvador. But kill an American and every radio will tell the story, every newspaper will display his photo, every television will show the blood."

Pazos laughed. "Who is the student and who is the teacher? Octavio, you watch this girl, she will some day command both of us. But I did not invite you to Managua to flatter your beautiful student. The training of the launcher team will not be difficult and in a few weeks they will be ready. So, we have a month to arrange for another team of men to enter the embassy."

"What? Into the embassy? That is impossible!"

"It is possible. The Americans still speak with journalists, do they not? And journalists carry recorders and video cameras, correct?"

"The electronics will be inside a camera?"

"Correct. Do you have a man with the education and appearance to pass as a journalist? I can supply the documents and the false background and the equipment. A second and third man will accompany him as the cameraman and sound recorder. They will be a news crew."

Lurching over speed barriers, the limousine entered the lights of a checkpoint. A Sandinista officer spoke with the driver. Soldiers in slick plastic raincoats shone flashlights through the tinted windows, the beams pausing on Rivas for several seconds. Then the officer motioned the driver to continue. The limousine passed through two chain-link gates woven with barbed wire. Soldiers in a concrete bunker powered up a steel crossbar, allowing the limousine to turn onto the highway to Managua.

"I can find the men. But I will need time to check their backgrounds, then train—"

"A month. Is that sufficient?"

"Only a month to find and check these men and then train them? No. All my contact is with young fighters. From the villages. From the slums of San Salvador. You are asking for men who already have technical training. The launcher crew was no problem, but this news crew is different. I will need more time."

"I anticipated the problem. I will find other comrades to do this duty—"

"Who?" Quezada demanded. "Who will you recruit? You risk the lives of my men if you use any of the shits from your organization in—"

Rivas stopped him. "I can do it. I speak English. I look like one of those goddamned starlet journalists. I can walk in there and—"

"You cannot risk returning." Quezada told her. "The danger is too—"

"Why?" she demanded. "Why is it dangerous?"

"My dear Lidia." Pazos smiled at her. "You are so brave. Only last week you were wounded and already you volunteer for yet another attack on the Americans. But, please, let me find someone else for the attack on the Americans. You cannot take all the glory for yourself."

"What risk will there be? Will the four with the launcher know who I am? Will the Americans detect the transmission from the camera? When we get the camera, we will check that. But what risk will there be? If my identification is good, I will walk in, talk with the fascist, and walk out. If they will not give me time to talk with the ambassador, I will stand at the gate and talk. I saw journalists do that. When the launcher is ready, I will make the call from far away and watch the rockets come down from the sky. It will be safe, much safer than the attack at the café."

"No," Quezada told her. "No. They have your description now. If you apply for an interview with the ambassador, you will walk into a trap. It is not brave what you are saying, it is foolish."

Pazos spoke calmly. "We will hire, through a company we create, a known journalist and his news crew and send them to conduct the interview. We will exchange their camera for a camera containing the transmitter. In that way, we can—"

"You don't think they know their own equipment?" Rivas asked, incredulous.

"Their camera will be damaged beyond repair. Our camera will be the replacement."

Quezada shook his head. "I cannot accept that. What if they turn the camera on to check it? The rockets will destroy a hotel. What if they use it in the city? The rockets will destroy a slum. Only the innocent will die. No, we cannot trust anyone but one of us to do this correctly. It must be one of us, with a proven background and some training with cameras. It will take time, but I will find someone. And it will not be you, Lidia."

"Who else can do it? I look the part. I already know the area of the embassy, the security and the routines. The soldiers will only look at my body, not at my face."

"Not you, Lidia," Quezada repeated.

"Listen. Forget the interview. It is not important that we get clearance to talk with the ambassador. When the launcher is ready, I can fly into Salvador and go directly to the embassy with the transmitter. I can talk at the gate. We can videotape the visa office. The Americans have no photographs of me. With a new hairstyle and makeup and identification, they will never recognize me."

Pazos laughed. "You are so determined. But I do not believe you are correct about the risk. The danger is extreme. The Salvadorian army knows you were the leader of the unit. They know you killed two soldiers and escaped." Opening his briefcase, he took out a photocopy. He snapped on the overhead light. "Keep this for yourself, a souvenir.

Read it. It is a bulletin they distributed to their officers. Your description, even a guess at your background. Perhaps they will discover your true identity and then they will have photos."

"Old photos. From high school. Because I speak English, they guessed I was in the United States. Me and a million others. Let them search the visa files."

"Nevertheless, if you return, it could go very badly for you. Stay here, in Nicaragua. You have done your duty as a front-line fighter. But, Octavio, you are right. To control the camera, we must have a team in whom we have absolute confidence. Two men who are not linked to any other organization. But that does not mean we cannot employ an outside news man. The man we hire—as a commentator, as an interviewer—can request the appointment with the ambassador. I will give this some thought. Will you both accompany me to the reception?" He glanced at their fatigues. "Do not be self-conscious of your uniforms. The president often comes to these affairs in uniform, much in the manner of my esteemed President Castro. I can even introduce you as Cubans, which would explain everything and anything, if that would be amusing."

Quezada said only, "No." Looking through his own reflection, he stared out at the shacks and businesses lining the highway. Fluorescent tubes illuminated the crowded interiors of corrugated tin cafés, smoke drifting from wood fires. People took shelter from the rain in the cafés and in doorways. They stared at the passing limousine. Quezada reached up and switched off the reading light. "No, we won't be going to that reception."

"You do not wish to attend. But what do you say, Lidia? Do you share the revolutionary disdain of Octavio for the decadence of the foreign community? If you hesitate because of your uniform, you may change at the Las Colinas house. We have a stock of clothing there for women—formal wear, casual clothing, shoes, everything. For the event of women operatives needing the correct clothing for an operation."

"And what will I do for transportation back to—"

153

"It would be better for you to avoid returning tonight. Stay at the Intercontinental. We have an open account there. Return in the morning when the roads are safe."

"Why not?" Lidia asked. "I'll—"

"Borge forbids it."

"Why does the interior minister concern himself with whether Lidia goes to a party or not?"

"Because she is involved in foreign actions. In the Salvador killings. If she is recognized of photographed, there would be trouble for Nicaragua."

"His secret police will not be at the—"

"His men are everywhere. We cannot risk trouble with Borge, do you understand?"

Pazos turned to Rivas. "Colonel Quezada has spoken. He dictates your answer. How unfortunate. You escaped the regime in Salvador, only to surrender to a regime in Nicaragua. When was the last time you had the pleasure of a film? Or a gathering of friends? But then, those pleasures conflict with the discipline of the revolution. Ah, here is the office. Last chance to reconsider. The barracks or the—"

"No, Pazos," Quezada stated. "We won't go against Borge. What if he threw us out of Nicaragua? Where would we go? Cuba? Miami?"

The limousine slowed to a stop behind their parked truck. Quezada stepped out, rushing through the rain and knocking at the driver's window. He looked inside. Standing in the rain, he looked in all directions—the streets, the isolated office building, the grass-overgrown lots of buildings destroyed by the earthquake. At the end of the street, light came from the windows of a restaurant. He jogged away, his one arm swinging in stride. Pazos laughed.

"The colonel is not so cunning. He leaves me here alone with you to whisper promises of night life and gaiety. Do you really accept the joyless life of the soldier?"

"Yes. No. It is what I must accept. What choice is there? Borge writes the law. Go against him and I go. But forget that. I want to carry that transmitter."

"Must we continue to argue that? No. Octavio says no. And I say no. The risk—"

"The risk is acceptable."

154

"What a lovely young woman—and so ruthless. Even with your own life. What I said about you becoming a commander was not flattery. Though your liaison with Octavio is unfortunate—you must realize that—with your intelligence and daring, I know you will somehow—"

"I work only with Octavio."

"Your loyalty is commendable, but misplaced. True, Octavio was a hero. He suffered grievous wounds for the cause of the revolution. But he is already a character of the romantic past. He thinks he can fight the Americans as he fought Somoza, with rifles and pistols and the courage of a few dedicated, courageous fighters. Noble warriors of the people against the evil soldiers. He is wrong. The Americans are not Somoza. Their weapons and their CIA can defeat any heroism. But they cannot defeat what they cannot fight. The world saw the defeats of the Americans in Lebanon. Defeats inflicted by the mysterious Jihad. Marines, businessmen, tourists, teachers, whatever—the war of the future is to drive all Americans out of our lands. By any means. Are we not in agreement, you and I?"

Rivas nodded.

"Then forgive me if I suggest that your blind loyalty to Octavio is blocking your advancement in the struggle. You heard him tonight. He would not risk the bombardment of a hotel. Who would be in the hotel but Americans and their bourgeois lackeys? Kill them all—as you did with the so-called innocent bystanders at the café."

"My loyalty is not blind. I recognize his strength. And I know it would be easier to persuade him to change his strategy than to find another commander of his training and experience."

"I can replace him with a telephone call." Pazos glanced toward the restaurant. A block away, the silhouettes of the one-armed Quezada and four soldiers crossed the lighted windows. Leaning toward Rivas, he touched her thigh, running his hand up the inside of her thigh. "But you, you are—"

Slapping his hand away, she grabbed for the door. He clutched her arm and she turned, her other hand reaching out to claw him. "Take your hand off me. Do not touch—"

155

"You? Who fucks a one-eyed cripple? You reject me? Listen, pretty girl. You are smart. Think about it. If you want glory, if you want the world to recognize you as the enemy of the Americans, you must work with me. I give the assignments. I work with the sponsors of this war—"

"Octavio will not always work for you. He will—"

"He is nothing. That slum cripple, with his noble ideas of revolution and victory. He has never left Nicaragua—only for a year or two for a camp in Cuba. He knows nothing of the world. Does he speak Arabic? Or even English? You girl, you come to me when you want to be a leader—now go! Go to your pathetic hero—"

Pazos shoved her away. Throwing open the door, she stepped into the rain. She walked to the truck and stood there waiting for Quezada and the soldiers. Keeping her back to the limousine, she laughed, knowing that Pazos watched her back and lusted for her. Quezada and the soldiers ran the last few steps to the truck. The limousine sped away as the joking, shoving men fought for the window seats. Quezada waited for her to tell him:

"He did it," she whispered. "The pig wants me. Promised me the leadership of the world revolution if I fuck him. But also, he—"

"Only of the world? Not the moon and the stars?" Quezada hugged her against him. "Soon we will be done with him. Soon."

"It must be soon," she added. "Because he hates you. Because you are what he will never be. I fear for you if we do not hit him soon."

Quezada smiled and nodded, rain running off the black nylon oval of his eye patch. "When it is possible. Until then, we play his game."

Pazos went to the walled and guarded Cuban embassy compound on the Camino del Sur. The Cuban DGI men at the gate passed the limousine immediately, directing the driver to park with the other cars at the end of the circular drive. But when Pazos walked to the entry, he veered away from the crowd of guests and presented his identification to the soldier at the stairway to the offices.

Rushing upstairs, he nodded to the clerks and technicians on duty as he continued to the room outside the communications rooms. A young man in a loose white *guayabera*—the Caribbean equivalent of the sports coat—typed at a desk. His close-cut hair and wide shoulders identified him as a soldier—assigned to the coding office. The young man recognized Pazos and passed him a pad of lined paper.

Using a numerical identification to route the message to Colonel Atallah in Syria, Pazos confirmed the dispatch of the four Salvadorians. Then he added: VOLUNTEER FOUND/INTERVIEW IMPOSSIBLE/WILL COME DAMASCUS/DISCUSS CHANGE.

16

A CRESCENT moon lit the mountains. Outside the truck, after hours of highway noise and the voices of the other men, Niles heard only the wind surging through the trees. His eyes searched the trees and brush. Light came and went as clouds swept across the moon. He crouched a few steps from the truck, listening to the wind, feeling the wind on his face, the wind cool and fragrant with rain and life, the river-rushing sound of the wind a vast chord of night moving through the forest and the mountains as the atmosphere flowed over the planet.

For weeks he had worked in the stink and chaos of Tegucigalpa, interviewing Nicaraguan contras, cross-checking their stories against agency background records, judging whether they bragged or lied or told the truth as they knew it. Now the others waited in the truck a minute longer while he enjoyed a long moment of peace—

Sheet metal scraped. The truck driver hawked spit and stepped out in the road with a short-barreled shotgun in his hands.

Old man, Niles thought, you ain't here to meditate. He waited for a moment of darkness, then pulled open the cargo doors of the truck. The Marines and Nicaraguan contras stepped down, the soft rasping of the fatigues against their canvas packs seeming loud, the steel-on-steel clatter of weapons like hammer strikes.

Niles waved his blue-lensed penlight across the cargo floor. Nothing remained but the stacks of cardboard boxes. The boxes—the plastic liners stapled, the flaps taped shut—contained all their street clothes and identification: the eight

158

North Americans and Nicaraguans crossed the border as anonymous soldiers without names or countries, wearing Soviet-made Sandinista uniforms, Soviet boots, and carrying ComBloc weapons.

Walking straight east, Niles left the ruts of the dirt road and angled up the slope. The weight of his pack forced him to lean forward, straining against gravity—Niles and all the other men carried a combat load of weapons and ammunition, equipment, and freeze-dried rations for ten days. The line of men followed him, their boots making no noise on the rain-soft earth.

Aerial photos had shown two ranges of mountains between the Honduran border and the terrorist camp outside of the Nicaraguan town of Palacaguina. Pine and oak forest covered the mountains. Decades of logging operations had stripped the lower hills, leaving the land eroded and covered with scrub brush. Where farmers had worked the land, the satellite photos showed small fields of corn and vegetables and coffee. Cattle grazed in pastures. Informers reported Sandinista patrols. But the contras had not exploited this section of the border—so close to the Pan American Highway and the Sandinista garrison in Somoto—as an infiltration route. With no contras in the area, the Sandinistas had limited their defenses to casual patrolling and the posting of squads of militia in the villages. They had not mined the mountain trails, as the contras operating around Jalapa reported.

A few kilometers from the truck, before crossing the border, Niles veered up the mountainside. He walked until he came to a ridgeline knoll he recognized from satellite maps. In the lowlands, he saw the lights of San Marcos de Colón and El Espino. Hills blocked his view of Somoto. Waiting for the other men, he found a line of sight through the trees and counted two knobby forested ridgelines to the west. He continued a hundred meters to the east, then broke sound discipline with a quick whisper to every man:

"We're in Nicaragua."

Blanco—the fighter who had joined the war against Somoza as a boy of twelve, then turned against the Sandinistas after the revolution—took point. He led the contras and

Marines into Nicaragua, along foot-worn trails soft with mud and mule droppings. He knew these mountains. Born in a shack south of Ocotal, he had smuggled weapons, food, medicine, and messages from the villages to the Sandinista units hiding in the mountains. Blanco claimed not only to know the mountains but to even know many of the people by name. Niles had questioned him intensely during the interviews in Tegucigalpa, testing the loyalty of the young man to the anticommunist cause, then using agency technicians to question him while wired to a polygraph machine and drugged with pentathol and methamphetamine. Niles had interrogated all the contras in the same way—and they had all convinced him of their loyalty.

Zutano—meaning, What's-his-name—had not fought on either side in the revolution. But the Sandinistas had persecuted his family because of an uncle in the National Guard. After a political cadre from Managua invalidated their land title and forced the family into a resettlement cooperative, Zutano joined his friend Blanco in the resistance. Zutano spoke some English, learned during his years in a Peace Corps school.

Vibora—meaning Rattlesnake—had operated radios for the Sandinistas in the last year of the revolution. After the overthrow, his officers recommended him for advanced training in Cuba. But Vibora had married his sweetheart and did not want to leave for the year in Cuba. He lost the chance for the training in the Cuban and Soviet schools. Then his teenage wife ran off with one of his officers, flying to Mexico to live in the capital of Spanish-speaking America while her new lover worked with other Central American revolutionaries. Vibora went by bus to Mexico to bring back his wife, and Sandinista security men beat him bloody and threw him into the streets. He never returned to Nicaragua. Taking the bus to Honduras, he joined the contras.

Omar had fought in the National Guard. Enlisting in the last months of the regime, he had never completed his course at the Elite Infantry Training School. The war had forced every soldier into combat. When Niles checked the record of the intense and brooding young man, some officers in the contras reported doubts on the loyalty of Omar. They reported that he often slandered National Guard officers. Niles had questioned him on this and Omar told of the last desperate struggle for Managua, officers already gone to Salvador or Guatemala or Miami, the soldiers and noncoms fighting to the end as the officers issued pompous declarations from asylum. Since then, Omar had hated the rich officers and politicos even more than the Sandinistas—at least the communists fought their own wars, Omar told Niles. After interrogation under drugs, Niles had accepted Omar.

However, for Omar and the three other contras, the real test of loyalty came now, in Nicaragua.

Throughout the night, Blanco stayed on the trails high on the ridgelines, far from the isolated settlements and the Sandinista outposts. Families still lived in the mountains despite the dangers of the war, working the abandoned coffee plantations, grazing a few cattle, laboring at fields of corn and beans. The line of men maintained a quick and even pace, never pausing for more than a few seconds as dogs occasionally barked in the distance.

Five hours after leaving the truck at the Honduran border, Blanco dropped to a crouch at the side of the trail and waited for Niles. He whispered, "The highway."

They had reached a north-south road running between Somoto and the high mountains. As Niles went forward with Blanco, the men formed into an outward-facing security line—each man a few steps from the next, every other man pointing his weapon in the opposite direction.

Road work crews had cleared the brush and trees on the hillsides to deny concealment to contra ambush units. Niles looked down on the road. The setting moon cast long shadows over the ruts and mud, the hillside below Niles in complete darkness, the far side glowing in soft blue light. To the north and the south, bends in the road limited the view of any lookouts to this one short section of road. Niles cupped his hand over his watch and pressed the light button—only an hour remained until dawn.

"Wait," Niles told Blanco. "Watch." Snaking backward, he returned to the others. "Hey-zoot?"

"Here."

"Scanner?"

"They are out here. I got listening posts talking, platoon leaders checking in."

"Distance?"

"Within a few clicks."

"We're crossing the road, then taking a break." Moving along the line, he told the other men. "Strak-man. You and me first. King Kong back up."

Cloth brushed cloth, branches scratched across weapons. The two Marines and the other three Nicaraguans took positions over the road. Blanco led Niles and Stark down the embankment. The young contra crept down slowly, his rifle ready in his hands, his head pivoting.

Walking silently but quickly, Niles stepped beside Blanco and whispered. "Act like a Sandinista. There are no contras here. You are tired. This is a long patrol."

With his Kalashnikov swinging in one hand, Niles continued to the road. He kept moving—denying any militia rifleman an easy target—as he strolled across the road. He checked the ruts and mud for bootprints. He saw only tire tracks. Water pooled in the tracks—Niles judged that rain had fallen during the preceding day, no later than the afternoon. Stooping, he ran his fingers across a track cutting across the ruts and felt a thin brittle crust of mud intricately textured with the patterns of the tire.

The truck had passed since the rain in the late afternoon—sometime during the night, the wind drying the track.

Blanco scrambled up the slope, followed by Stark and Niles. Using the last minutes of moonlight, Niles slipped through the brush and trees, searching the area for any marks of patrols or outposts. He found only cow trails. Going higher on the ridge, he came to a trail patterned with hoof marks. His fingers found grass sprouts standing in the tracks—days had passed since the horses left the hoofprints. Above the trail, at the ridgeline, gnarled pines and oaks twisted through up-jutting rocks. He went to the top of the rocks. The rocks viewed the twisting line of the road, moonlit pastures, and a cluster of yellow lantern lights in the distance. Niles returned to the men and led them up the mountain to the rocks. There, concealed by the stunted trees, they slept in turns as shifts of two men maintained a watch.

Omar watched the American who called himself *Viejo*, the Old Man. He studied his movements in the darkness, his easy walk that made no noise and left no bootprints on the trails, how he carried his rifle, how he wore his equipment. Omar had recognized the American as a soldier that first night more than a month before, when the scarred, hard-muscled stranger put on the FDN fatigues and stripped a Kalashnikov by touch—the American had not needed the kerosene light, his hands moving quickly to open the cover, pull out the springs and bolt, then reassemble the Soviet rifle as easily as breathing. Unlike the pasty white journalists and phony mercenaries, the old soldier carried a pack for a night and a day without a complaint, not even a complaint about the shitty beans and the greasy meat from cans. Friends in the second platoon of the gas-bag sergeant told Omar how the American helped Blanco make a tricky place for firing rockets, working half the night, cutting branches with his knife and digging in the dirt like a peon. Then the rocket hit on the helicopter. Some of the loudmouths said they hit it, Blanco and Zutano said the old man hit it. But Omar had seen himself how the American moved when the gunship came, no stupid macho heroism, no whining-dog shaking and shitting with fear, just cunning and experience and motion, finding the gully and getting shelter for wounded Luis, finally going flat himself—and the whole time not panicking, always watching the smoke for the Sandinistas and keeping his Kalashnikov ready.

This American knew war. If only the United States would send more men like him. Instead of the fat shits from the *Cia* who could not speak Spanish and did not know the story of Nicaragua but only talked of Cubans and Russians. Or the ones who spoke Spanish like professors and wore suits and watches and carried briefcases, making a man in a uniform and old boots feel like a begger.

In the capital, when *Viejo* interrogated him, Omar knew why. He respected the suspicions of the American. Had not the Sandinistas put spies in all the contra units? Omar answered with the truth to every question, telling him of his brother dying in service with the National Guard, of his other brother refusing to surrender his farm to the cooperatives and dying when the masked assassins came in the night with machetes and pistols. He told the American the truth about hating Somoza even as he trained in the Guard. Like his brother had said, defeat the communists, then march on the Palace. Then Americans questioned him with the machine and the injections. No problem.

He wanted to learn from the Americans—and he did. Hundreds of small things. Like the little bending of his Kalashnikov selector lever. Viejo showed him how to spring the lever away from the receiver, then put a piece of plastic plumbing tape in the hinge of the lever—and suddenly, the selector moved silently, without clacking. Then, with a drill from a jewelry shop, the American who looked like a son-of-a-bitch Russian and even talked Russian drilled tiny holes in the backsight of the Kalashnikov and one in the front. The Russian fixed a tiny bead in each hole with a drop of super-glue—and the beads glowed in the dark, so that he could aim in the blackest night. And then the Mexican one showed him how to repair boots with the same super-glue. And the black one who talked Spanish like a Frenchman changed the straps on the packs and changed the metal rings for plastic and suddenly the pack did not cut his shoulders and made no noise when he walked.

And now he went into Nicaragua with the four Americans, moving like shadows along the trail, no talking, no noise, no smoking, no trash. The old man had all the trails in his head and walked through the night without making a wrong turn, knowing the way almost like Blanco.

After walking all night, they slept for a time and ate—and all their trash, even their piss and shit went in a hole where no patrol would ever find it.

In the day, Omar and Blanco went out with Viejo, searching for the Sandinistas. They walked slowly and quietly across the steep hills, never stepping on a trail. The old man showed him how to ease his boots through the grass and ferns and leafy *chocón* covering the ground, parting the cover with his boot, then putting his weight down so the boot made its print in the dirt under the cover of the leaves and could not be seen. Where the bootprints showed, *Viejo* used a stick to brush a footprint out of green grass. With a pine branch, he wiped footprints out of dirt—and then scratched the dirt so that it looked right. No prints remained where they walked.

They took a place overlooking a line of shacks along the road. Sandinistas sat in the shade of a truck, talking with the local people and demanding the documents of whoever traveled on the road. The hours passed and the American did not move, he only watched.

A platoon of Sandinistas stumbled down the other side of the road. The soldiers sprawled on the roadside while their officer talked with soldiers at the checkpoint. Omar watched the Sandinistas. He saw the American writing in a little book.

Calling his soldiers together, the Sandinista officer sent them east. The officer walked in the center of the line, a radio man a few steps behind him.

Viejo signaled Blanco and Omar. Crawling backward on their bellies, they rubbed out the marks of their watch and scattered dry leaves. Then they walked east, paralleling the trail the Sandinistas walked. Omar felt his hair rise with what they did—the three of them following a twenty-man platoon of Sandinistas in their own territory. Only three against twenty if it came to a fight. But the American walked along the side of the mountain, weaving through the brush, stopping and listening before walking from cover to cover.

This one had balls. Blanco looked to Omar with a wide, nervous grin, his eyes moving side-to-side like Cantinflas about to panic. Omar had to nod. Who would not be afraid?

Omar prayed to God the American did not make all of them meat for the dogs.

The American dropped. Blanco tripped a step and did the same. Omar went flat in the rotting weeds and leaves and wondered what—

Soldiers came up the mountain. He heard the squeaking of packs and the rattling of metal. Omar put his face into the weeds, forced his body to the ground, trying to force his whole body into the dirt and disappear like a mole.

Jesus, Omar prayed, I am one of your faithful. I will prove it. I will buy a carved likeness of you and spend months painting it, I will use the finest brush and make your blue eyes as transparent and as deep as the morning sky if you will grant me some drafted soldiers from the city who know nothing of the hills and only look at their feet as they walk—

He heard their boots scuffing the dirt and rocks. They walked quickly, cloth rubbing, equipment in their packs rattling with every step. Omar held his breath, they seemed so close, but he knew the American lay up there even closer.

The gang of them seemed to take all day to walk past. Ants crawled over his hands and he felt a fly sucking on his neck—Omar let it suck. Finally he heard the sounds of the platoon going away and he raised his head.

The old man motioned for him and Blanco to come on. For the first time the American used the walkie-talkie he carried, whispering into it and waiting, then whispering again. He put away the radio and he went to the trail. Looking at all the bootprints left by the Sandinistas, he stepped on the soft dirt and made his own bootprint. It matched the prints made by the communist boots. Grinning at Omar and Blanco, he started after the Sandinistas, walking fast and silent on the trail.

Blanco looked at Omar with fear on his face but they said nothing and they followed the crazy American—and Omar knew the American had gone crazy. To walk on the heels of a platoon? What if one of the communists stopped to piss? It would be a shitload of bullets in all directions. But he followed.

Your likeness, Jesus. And a likeness of the Blessed Mary, Omar promised. Painted with the finest enamel in a church in a free Nicaragua. If only I can live through these lessons from the old man . . .

17

IN the air-conditioned darkness of the bar of the Damascus Sheraton, Pazos sipped Cuban rum mixed with American Coca-Cola. A musician played quiet jazz on an electric piano, improvising melodies and syncopated duets with an electronic synthesizer. Women talked in French at the next table. Blond, their faces masks of makeup, the women touched and stroked the Saudi sitting between them. Rings flashed on their hands. Ignoring the chatter of his women, the Saudi drank and stared at the entry, waiting. Pazos waited also, but he waited alone, drinking his rum and Coke, his eyes watching the faces of the travelers and Syrians in the bar.

Languages identified some of the foreigners as Europeans—some spoke English, others French. A group of several men argued the future of the America's Cup in both languages, a tanned Frenchman lapsing into French as his English failed, but intermixing "Aussie" and "jib" and "winged keel" as he explained the ideal design of a new racing yacht. His friends continued the argument in English. At the table past the Europeans, two men in sports coats and slacks, their dark hair military short and their faces creased with scowls, leaned close together and spoke in whispers.

A young man in sunglasses stopped in the entry. Bearded, wearing a suit tailored in Europe, he took off his sunglasses and scanned the tables. He saw Pazos. Pazos nodded and finished his drink, leaving an American five-dollar bill as a tip.

In the lobby, journalists crowded around a Lebanese politician and a militia leader. Video cameramen stood on tables, focusing over the heads of reporters. Sound men held out microphones on long aluminium handles. Photographers elbowed one another as their flash units splashed the scene with instants of white light. Reporters shouted questions and held out miniature recorders to the two men.

A group of Iranian Revolutionary Guards watched from the sides. Awkward without weapons, they folded their arms across their chests and glared at women in skirts and thin summer dresses. Four Syrians in dark suits provided security for the Lebanese, their hands on the pistol grips of their folded Kalashnikovs as their eyes swept the crowd of foreigners and the people waiting in the lobby. Other security men stood at intervals in the lobby, watching the doors and the elevators over their newspapers.

Pazos noted the video cameras with a smile—even the Syrian secret police, obsessed with security, allowed television crews into the privileged domain of the Sheraton.

The young man led him out a side door. In the parking lot, he saw the black Mercedes sedan in the rows of limousines and private cars. He went straight to the car. Attallah welcomed him with a handshake and a Marlboro:

"So, I see you again so soon, my friend Emilio. Perhaps we should truly start a business. With you flying endlessly this way and that, we should put your travel to a profit. What has Nicaragua—other than bananas—that we here in Syria would pay high prices for?"

"Nothing. The country is a disease."

"You say that?" Attallah did not start the car. They sat in the parking lot and talked. "You who are devoting your expertise to the development of its exports?"

"Why don't you come and see? Sample their tasteless food, their shoddy goods, their stupid women. To think that there is talk of a war for that country is a joke. There is nothing there which deserves a fight."

"Then you are wasting your talents. Why do you not come to Syria and manage our exports? We need—"

"I am, am I not?"

Attallah laughed. "True. Except, of course, that I will always deny any part in our export venture. I will let the

Jihad take the profit. And, of course, the Salvadorians. So you have the volunteers? But what must be this change?"

"The volunteer cannot expect an interview with the ambassador. To even request an interview would be suicidal."

"Suicidal? An ironic objection."

"Suicidal before the interview."

"Oh, I see. Why then do you choose to accept this particular volunteer?"

"Because she will not allow any other volunteer. She is the leader of the unit that killed the Marines in San Salvador. She is also the only one of the killers who escaped from Salvador. And it is a proof of her intelligence and her . . ." He searched for the word in English. "It is hatrèd. She is a very strange one, a killer but intelligent. If she was not she would not have escaped."

"How is it that she escaped and the others did not?"

"Two soldiers tried to fuck her. And she fucked them."

Choking on smoke, Atallah gasped and laughed, the scars on the side of his face going white. "An interesting illustration of two meanings of that Anglo-Saxon verb. One literal. One figurative, I believe."

"Killed them with a stone. Took a rifle and escaped."

"Very exceptional."

"Oh, Nazim. You cannot know how exceptional. This woman is so beautiful, like a lovely flower. Her loveliness moves me to poetry, I think of only touching her, of caressing the delicate bloom of her youth. And I can't. She fucks this Nicaraguan cripple. He is her hero. He took her from the luxury of the Colonia Escalón and made her into a revolutionary in boots and camouflage. It is a sacrilege. A Madonna in camouflage."

"Are you confident of her background?"

"The Nicaraguan checked her. I checked her. She does not work for the Americans. Her father was some fool who talked about revolution in the university and the squads killed him. They sent her to Los Angeles, to the University of California. She came back a radical. She tried to join the guerrillas. She wanted to buy a pistol and kill Americans."

"Did she?"

"The cripple got her first. He ran her through his training camp. And she hooked him! Now she is with him in everything. His disciple. She thinks he will make her a leader of the struggle. It is so disgusting. What a waste of a beautiful woman. That beauty embraced by that mutilated wreck, that peon in a uniform. It makes me sick to imagine. But now this beautiful woman and her cripple challenge my authority. They will not accept their positions as subordinates in the organization and I am sure they will eventually look for another sponsor. They already undercut my authority at every opportunity. It is very difficult. This matter with the camera—they would not accept my guidance. As they have with so many other matters, they contested every detail. The Nicaraguan with his bourgeois concern for civilians. And her. She would not allow us to consider anyone else for the task of the camera. A thousand objections. Therefore, I decided to accept her as the volunteer, even though—"

"And because," Atallah commented, "of the killing of the Marines, she is hunted by the Americans? That is why she cannot risk applying for an interview? And why she cannot enter the embassy?"

"That is it. But against that is her hatred and her ambition. She will not stop. Nothing will stop her. She will take the transmitter to the embassy. I have no doubt of this. She will die. That beauty will be lost. But the embassy will also be gone."

"What does she know of the transmitter?"

"I told her that it allows the launcher to find the target. She thinks she will go to safety and then signal for the launch of the rockets. The idea of watching the rockets fall excites her."

"But she will not enter the compound."

"That will be impossible. And, in truth, it may be impossible for any journalist we hire to enter. The Americans are becoming extreme in their security precautions. At a press conference with the ambassador only a few days ago, they allowed no journalist whom they did not invite. And all the journalists were Americans."

"And what is it that you suggest?"

"Me? I know nothing of the electronics of your launcher

170

and rockets. What can your technicians devise to make this possible? I will convey the instructions to my insubordinate subordinates."

"And that is actually the difficulty? Your subordinates are insubordinate? Rebellious rebels?"

"Exactly. The cripple would fight the war by his obsolete bourgeois concepts of insurrection and armed struggle. She would share the glory of the attack with no one."

"I will speak with my Iranian. Your beautiful revolutionary will have the glory she is so determined to take."

18

VATSEK stared over the sights of his RPK machine gun, watching the four Sandinista soldiers scan the distance with binoculars.

You pukes. Make a revolution, then give it to the Stalinists. I joined the Corps to kill you.

The soldiers manned an outpost on the end of a ridgeline overlooking the valley of Somoto. Deliberate fires had scorched away the brush on the hillsides and along the ridgeline. Only ashes, mud, and twisted black sticks remained, denying any cover to anyone trying to approach the position.

Sandbags formed a square. Sheets of olive drab plastic on poles sheltered the soldiers from the sun and the rain. The metallic tape of an antenna hung from the bare, fire-scorched branches of a tree. The soldiers relaxed in the shade, their rifles on the sandbags. They watched the hills and the distant fields with binoculars. An officer scanned the valley with tripod-braced high-power binoculars.

From the elevation of the ridge, the soldiers viewed an expanse of the valley, the hills, and four highways. Vatsek saw the streets and rooftops of Somoto several kilometers to the northwest. The asphalt line of the Pan American Highway ran east-to-west, curving from Somoto in the west and disappearing behind hills to the east. Two other paved roads angled out into the mottled green and yellow and black landscape of the river valley. The lines of other dirt tracks twisted between the major roads.

The soldiers observed every car and truck on the roads. Their binoculars would discover any daylight movement of men in the open or any action during the night. With the flights of observer planes and patrols along the roads, this outpost—and the other outposts on the hills overlooking Somoto and Ocotal—denied the southeast end of the valley to the contras.

At the edge of the perimeter of ashes and mud, Vatsek lay in the brush, watching the soldiers. Zutano sprawled an arm's distance away. Five paces back, Alvarez and Vibora monitored the Sandinista radio traffic on the frequency scanner.

Vatsek marked the position of the outpost and area viewed by the soldiers on a map. A penciled line represented the trail leading downhill from the outpost to a village. From his position on the perimeter, he could only guess at the size of the village directly below the outpost, but satellite photos had shown shacks and gardens at the foot of the ridge. Vatsek paused in his drawing as he saw one of the soldiers speaking into their radio.

"Patrol . . ." Alvarez whispered. "Lay cool."

Easing down low, Vatsek put his right hand on the grip of the RPK machine gun. He kept his eyes on the soldiers. His left hand swept leaves from the few exposed cartridges of the belt between the closed drum magazine and the port.

The wind brought the voices of the soldiers. Insects flitted through the leaves but repellent kept the flies off his exposed skin. He glanced over at Zutano and almost did not see the contra, flat in the weeds and branches, the metal of his rifle covered by his body. Only his eyes and the grease-painted mask of his face showed.

What's-his-name, that's what Zutano means. Righteous kid. Gives up his country, his family, even his name to join the contras. He wants to fight. For Nicaragua and democracy, he says. Said he wanted to learn and he did. The Old Man picked some winners with these four commie-killers.

Looking out at the expanse of the hills, the valley, the distance-paled mountains of the border, Vatsek thought of Fontana. We fought and bled just for thrills. Racing cars and fighting and popping off revolvers at each other, sometimes scoring a hit, sometimes a guy dying—and for nothing. Dead end life out in the desert. Steel mill and bored teenagers, killing each other, fucking each other, starting the cycle of life in the desert town again.

But what if his grandfather had sided with General Secretary Stalin instead of Trotsky? Would have been a steel mill in Russia, with no way out but vodka. A great-uncle got the family into America as Ukrainian fugitives from communism instead of fugitives from a purge of party dissenters. Not that anyone in the U.S. knew the difference between a Stalinist or Trotskyite, a Menshevik or a Bolshevik.

From the gulag of Stalin's Russia to Fontana. Two hours inland from Los Angeles. The Kaiser steel mill on the edge of the desert. Zeroland.

A family that talked Russian in a town of Pollacks and Mexicans and Oakies. A joke of history and politics put his grandfather, a communist labor commissar from the Soviet steel mills into an American steel mill. Commissar Vatsek escaped the Russian civil wars for America, his sons escaped to the Korean War, translating Soviet weapons manuals for the army. But after the truce, they went back to Fontana and the steel mill.

After the Vietnam War, Vatsek heard all the stories of fighting communists from his brothers and he started his training for his turn in the next war. He rode his bicycle into the foothills and perfected his sniping with a .22 rifle on Peoples' Army of Vietnam rabbits and lizards. His brothers started him with karate and weaponsmithing. But no war came. Twenty years old and tired of waiting, Vatsek decided to join the Marines and look for a war.

Never even thought of going back. After Fontana, anywhere became a place of wonders. Camp Pendleton, the green hills to the east, the unlimited horizon of the Pacific to the west. The stark gray streets of East Berlin. The boring bourgeois streets of Bonn. Beirut. A fly-buzzed cantina in Honduras.

Anywhere but Fontana. The Corps took him away. But with Captain Niles, it got interesting. Niles got the authorization to make wars. Killing the Shiite gangs of Beirut, offing Palestinians in the dope-forests of Guajira, chasing down Iranians in the Bekaa. Find and kill. A cool adventure.

But this studying the Sandinistas has got to quit. Time to do it. Get a meat count. Take heads.

Soldiers came up the trail, their rifles loose in the hands or slung over the shoulders. One man carried a radio pack. The others only wore web gear and canteens—a short-range patrol. Vatsek counted eight—an officer with a pistol, one with the radio, all of them with rifles, no squad-automatic weapons or rocket launchers. The officer talked with the men at the lookout, then led the patrol south along the ridgeline trail.

Vatsek listened to the voices of the Sandinistas. He looked over at Zutano. The contra grinned and Vatsek grinned back. These contras caught on quick. If the enemy don't know you're there, then you ain't.

After the last man passed, Vatsek hand-signed Zutano to shift back. The contra snaked back silently, brushing up the crushed ferns and leaves with his hands. At the Sandinista outpost, the soldiers kept their binoculars on the highways. Vatsek went back to the others. Alvarez tapped the earphone he wore and whispered:

"Captain got his section checked. Now it's straight to the camp."

"Finally . . ."

Zutano took point, following the Sandinista patrol, staying several hundred meters behind the last man. Footprints and gum wrappers marked the trail. But the pace of the Sandinistas slowed after a kilometer. Vatsek and Alvarez studied the map the recon squad had prepared of the mountain trails and found a route higher on the mountain. Angling away from the Sandinistas, they zigzagged through the trees and brush until they found the trail winding along the ridgelines. Zutano set a quick pace, breaking into a run to dash ahead and check curves in trail, then doubling back to signal the others to continue. He watched for any sign of soldiers or local people, sometimes pausing for minutes to listen or examine traces he found along the trail.

A stack of cut wood warned them before they heard the sound of the ax. In a whisper, Alvarez told the contras to continue ahead. "You are Sandinistas, separated from your platoon . . ." He and Vatsek went straight up the hillside. A hundred meters above the trail, they heard the ax stop. A dog barked. The scattered trees and brush screened the Marines as they worked their way across the steep hillside. Descending, they stopped above the trail and waited. A few minutes later, they saw Zutano and Vibora.

"That man," Zutano explained. "He hates us. We ask him questions and he says nothing. He spits on the ground. If we do not have our rifles, I think he would have killed us with his ax."

They added the detail of the woodcutter and his dog to their map of the mountains. Continuing, Zutano and Vibora alternated on point, watching for patrols, reading the trail for tracks. Litter lay in the dirt—cigarette butts, a plastic wrapper, even a pink wad of gum—but no cartridge casings or ration cans. Thirty minutes later, they came to the ravine where the trail divided, the wider, mule-traveled trail switchbacking down the side of a ravine, a second path following the west side of the ravine up to the gap in the ridge.

The other Marines and contras waited at the top, in a gully over-arched by scrub oak. The green cave had sheltered the men during the night—the third night since they crossed the border. Captain Niles questioned Vatsek and Alvarez quickly, adding their sketches to his own map. Then they studied his map, transferring the webwork of trails he scouted that morning to their own maps. If separated during the withdrawal from the Cuban camp, every American had a map of the trails back to the border, marked with villages, possible ambushes, and Sandinista outposts.

Niles signaled the others to assemble their equipment. "Now we get that Cuban."

Fifteen kilometers to the north, Comandante Martillo scanned the Ocotal Highway with binoculars. The asphalt line of the road wound through low hills covered with grass and brush. He crouched on a low ridge paralleling the highway. Martillo saw no concealment for his men near the highway. The Sandinistas had stripped the roadsides of cover, reducing the growth to stubble, leaving the bare earth exposed. But he saw no problem with placing his riflemen and machine gunners on this ridge, two hundred meters away from the highway.

Martillo turned and focused on the hills behind his column of men. His men rested in groups, sprawled in the brush along the rutted mud track, only their boots showing. They had marched hard for two days, dawn to dusk, to reach this zone south of Ocotal.

Squad leaders waited for his instructions as he studied the hills. What he saw confirmed all the CIA maps and photographs. Almost a kilometer from the road, the hills had a few low trees to provide cover for his squads with the missile launchers. A pasture overgrown with chest-high weeds separated the hills from the ridge overlooking the road. Martillo glanced at the road and the sky, calculating the distances. His plan would work.

Here, the communists did not expect attack. His informers had told him the militia patrols never left the roads. The informers described the truck convoys moving in long lines, at a slow and easy speed, without any fear of ambush. Only after Ocotal did the convoys accelerate, trying to race past the contra ambushes along the road to Jalapa. Martillo had paid American dollars for the information—but tomorrow morning, his investment repaid him a hundred times. Following the maps prepared by the informers, he led fifty men past the Sandinista garrisons to this stretch of road on the north-south highway.

The CIA had finally supplied the antiaircraft missiles. With four men trained to fire the Soviet SAM-7 rockets and eight of the rockets, Martillo planned a defeat that would make his name feared all through the province. And with yet another victory to his credit, he could expect a doubling of the money and weapons channeled to his command. More money and weapons meant more men and more men meant more victories, until Martillo marched into Managua and put all those communist sons-of-bitches against the wall and washed their revolution away with blood.

As he anticipated his victory, he heard the rasping of diesel engines. He dropped flat in the weeds and fixed the binoculars on the road. A troop truck appeared, followed by a bus and a transport truck. Soldiers stood in the trucks, rifles slung on their backs. People crowded the bus. Through the binoculars, Martillo saw the soldiers in the trucks talking to one another, their backs to the roadsides.

Martillo laughed. The Sandinistas thought nothing could happen here. He would show them. Turning to his squad leaders, he pointed out the positions, detailing the placement of the weapons squads.

A storm gathered in the afternoon, the sky graying with clouds, the vibrant greens and yellows of the hills darkening to smears of drab on gray. Niles saw the coming storm and knew that he had only three hours remaining before sunset and the rain brought a storm-black night. He accelerated the pace, alternating the contras on point as security as he drove the squad without pause along the trails he had scouted at dawn that day.

But they stopped three times—twice when the pointmen encountered woodcutters, once when a herdsman guiding a cow and a bull blocked the trail. None of the local people saw the foreigners, the Marines taking cover and waiting for the trail to clear, then continuing their rush to the east.

Rain came, hammering down on their sweat-soaked fatigues and making the hillsides run with mud. But the rain provided concealment, dimming the afternoon light and limiting visibility to a few hundred meters. In the gray half-light of the storm, Niles took the point himself and led the line of men off the trail and higher into the ridges, following a route he plotted from satellite maps.

The gray light faded to darkness. Niles found a patch of brush that offered shelter from the wind. In the night, by touch, the men found food in their packs and ate. Then they rested in the warm rain, water flowing over and under them. Niles took the first watch, sitting in a clearing a few steps away from the others, watching the black-on-black darkness of the storm.

Surges of wind shifted the unseen brush, thrashing black walls of branches, rain splattering down on the leaves and mud. Niles swept his eyes across the black, searching for changes in the darkness, his ears taking in hundreds of simultaneous sounds—the wind, the swaying and thrashing brush, the beating rain.

And a point of light blinked. He stared. The infinitesimal point came and went with the shifts in the gusting wind, the light jumping and flickering. He realized that the light remained motionless and the brush moved.

Slipping out his compass, he took a bearing. East-southeast. He compared his memorized map of the mountains between Somoto and the Pan American Highway to his approximate position.

A voice hissed. "Captain!"

He crabbed back to the brush concealing the squad. "What?"

"Coded radio communications," Alvarez whispered. "Strong signal. And some walkie-talkie static. Guards checking in."

"Looks like we're there."

A burst of riflefire exploded. Martillo thrashed free of his plastic poncho and looked down on the road. But he saw nothing. The storm blocked all the light from the sunset and the sky, the road and the hills only a black void loud with wind and beating rain. Then he heard the faint screaming, a high-pitched shriek like the sound of an animal. His radio man scrambled through the mud to him, holding out the handset.

"Did they radio?"

"No, comandante."

"Maintain the radio silence. I'll shoot anyone who screws up this operation."

The red lens of a flashlight zigzagged through the black. Martillo put his fingers over the lens of his own flashlight and blinked several times. The red point veered to him, a soaked and gasping soldier staggering out of the darkness.

"This dumb-shit peon was walking along the road and he found us setting the claymores."

"You shot him?"

"Only hit him once. He's still alive—"

Rushing down the hillside, Martillo kicked through the

grass and brush. He did not need his flashlight. He had memorized the ground between the hillcrest and the road. Tripping over a tangle of sticks, he fell and rolled through soggy grass, but jumped to his feet, not falling again until he stumbled over the road. Several red flashlights clustered around two forms.

A child cried. A man coughed and choked. In the red light of flashlights, the blood spraying from his mouth looked the same as the mud and blood smeared everywhere on his body. Papers lay on the roadside, the sheets glowing red in the waving lights. A few steps away, the red light streaked the spokes of a bicycle.

The man raised his hands as if in prayer, begging the armed men crouching around him, "Please, a doctor. Give me the help of a doctor. I am one of you. I must take my little daughter to the doctor and the communists and the gringos at the clinic will not help us. I had to take her to the pharmacist and now this rain and the people along the road know I am one of you and they will not give us a dry place out of the night—"

A kick stopped his pleading. He put an arm around the girl clutching him, wiping the blood away from his mouth with his other hand. The girl bled also. Martillo saw a coil of intestines hanging from her dress—a bullet had torn open her body. Her father opened his mouth to talk but he coughed blood and a contra kicked him again. The girl cried, holding her father, the rain pouring down on her thin dress and ghastly wound, her hair a black, rain-soaked mass covering her face and her father's shoulder.

Martillo stepped past the prisoners and picked up one of the papers. A soldier put a light on the page—a communist ration form. Another sheet prescribed a drug for Anna Esperanza Gallegos. Then Martillo jerked a machete from the web belt of a soldier and brought the heavy blade down on the neck of the wounded man, severing his spine, killing him instantly. The girl screamed and Martillo brought the blade down on her skull. Her body continued to thrash with dying nerves as he told the soldiers:

"Clear this shit off the road."

19

DISCO rhythms boomed from the dance floor. At a pay phone near the rear exit, Lidia Rivas dialed the number and listened as the circuits clicked. Laughter and voices came from the tables, a woman shrieking, glasses breaking. Rivas turned her back to the nightclub and leaned against the wall, trying to block the music and noise. She listened as the number rang.

Hands touched her, caressing the flow of her back to her pants and touching the inside of her thigh. She spun, knocking her temple against the pay phone. A blond foreigner spoke to her, his words lost in the noise. He wore blue jeans and a shirt of gaudy polyester, the buttons open to expose his muscled and sweat-glistening chest. The foreigner smiled and spoke again, loud, almost shouting incomprehensible Spanish and another language. She understood only the East European gutturals. Motioning him back, she held the receiver to her ear and listened to the telephone ringing.

Still shouting his gibberish, the foreigner tried to grab her hand. She twisted her hand free as he pressed closer and then slammed him with her palm, staggering him back. His lip curled up in a sneer.

The ringing stopped as Pazos answered. Rivas spoke over his greeting. "This is Marianela. Can I talk with you tonight?"

"Who?"

"Marianela. You know me by another name. We talked in your office—get away from me!" She shouted at the for-

eigner as he reached for her. She cursed him in English.
"You Russian clown! Get away!"

"Oh, yes. Now I know . . ."

"No, not you. I am talking from a disco. Will you meet me at—"

"I will come there. Which disco? Are you with our friend Octavio?"

"No, meet me at—"

The foreigner called. Two other men joined him. Like him, they wore European clothes. But their short-cropped hair and hard-muscled torsos identified the foreigners as Eastern European sailors or ComBloc advisers. They stood eyeing her, discussing her in their language.

Rivas had heard the stories of the rapes and the beatings of Nicaraguan girls by East German advisers. Comandante Borge of the interior ministry did not allow the police even to question the advisers. When Soviets or East Germans or Bulgarians presented their identification, the police had instructions to stop the questioning. None of the foreigners ever faced prosecution for their crimes.

Pulling her new Browning from under her jacket, she casually held the pistol in her hand while she gave Pazos directions to a hotel on the highway north. The foreigners disappeared into the nightclub, suddenly uninterested.

"I cannot be seen with you. We can talk there. We have much to discuss."

"I will be there, my lovely."

"And I will be waiting."

Hanging up, she rushed away from the telephone. The exit doors opened directly to the parking lot. She held the pistol concealed under her jacket until she got in the car with Quezada.

"The pig is coming."

Pazos immediately dialed the apartment of his assistant, Raúl Condori. No answer. He dialed the ministry office. Condori answered. A teletype hammered in the background.

"I am meeting with the girl Lidia Rivas at the Hotel Las Palmas. I may be there an hour or I may be there all night.

Stay in the office and wait for my call. I will call in an hour, more or less."

Then he dressed for the occasion, putting on a white silk shirt and a suit of pale raw silk, shoes hand-crafted of alligator hide. He brushed rose-scented pomade through his hair, shaking his head to give his curls the wild look of an American rock-and-roll star. He studied his image in the full-length mirror.

"You devil! Screwing a woman and then sending her to die. Maybe if she is a good fuck, I will show her mercy. But then, maybe not—"

After a last handful of cologne, Pazos rushed to his Mercedes and drove from the estate, speeding north on the highway to the old lakeshore road. He saw the plywood sign of the hotel and followed the long, palm-lined driveway to the line of stucco bungalows.

He saw only two other cars. A Volkswagen parked at the main building and a Toyota rental agency van parked at the bungalow where the woman waited. Pazos drove to the end of the property and parked there, then walked back. He fought his excitement and anticipation glancing at the windows and shadows even as he dismissed his suspicion.

Blackmail? How could this woman blackmail him? Let her go to her cripple and tell him of meeting his superior in a hotel. Rivas had much more to gain by winning the affection and influence of Pazos. He knew exactly why she wanted to talk—she had finally realized he held the key to her future.

Of course, she had no future, but she did not know that.

Slapping aside the moths circling in the lighted entry, he carefully adjusted the collar of his shirt and jacket, then knocked.

The fading jeans and the simple blue cotton blouse Rivas wore somehow made her more lovely. A rubber band pulled back her shining hair. She wore no makeup and did not smile. Looking at her, Pazos thought of a schoolgirl. Only the shoulder-holstered pistol she wore spoiled the illusion. The straps of the holster pulled the front of her blouse tight, revealing the forms of her breasts. His eyes watched her breasts sway against the thin cloth as she turned, and he forgot the cautious, formal offer he had prepared.

Reaching out, taking her slight body in his hands, he felt an instant of struggle, then she accepted the obvious and allowed him to pull her against him, surrendering to his embrace. The soft scent of her hair intoxicated him and for a time he only held her against him, enjoying the warmth of her body against him. Then his hands caressed the curves of her body, touching her breasts, a hand taking the weight of a breast and crushing against the nipple, feeling her gasp—pain? pleasure? He did not care. Tonight he had her, tonight he used her like a two-dollar whore, tonight he gave her his cock every way he wanted—and if she refused, she got nothing, no advancement, no introductions, no future. Perhaps if she proved herself as a good whore, a very pleasing whore, he would delay the delivery of the rockets and let her live a few more months—

Pain crashed through his body and his knees hit the hard tile of the floor. He tried to cry out as he fell forward and a hand jerked his head back by the hair, then smashed his face into the tile again and again. He heard a high whining scream, his own scream, as he lost consciousness . . .

"Don't kill him!" Quezada pushed Rivas away from the bleeding, groaning Pazos. "We cannot question a dead man."

The other two comrades came from the closets. Instructors at the school and loyal only to Quezada, Moya and Barrios looped straps around the ankles and wrists of their prisoner, then rolled him into a canvas tarp.

Quezada and Rivas went out the door first. A match flared in the darkness of the palms—the signal—and she opened the doors of the van. Moya and Barrios brought out the long canvas bundle.

As the van left the bungalows, the three men assigned to security casually stepped from their positions. Quezada passed the men the keys Pazos had carried. Two of the men went to the Volkswagen, the third took the Mercedes.

They drove south a kilometer to a rented house. Walls and maguey cactus surrounded the property. The guard posted there opened the door of a concrete-block garage and they dragged Pazos inside, dropping him on the bare springs of a bed. The second car came from the hotel and all the men found concealment. In the house, a stereo blasted a rock-and-roll concert tape, the music almost overwhelmed by the noise and cheering and screaming of a crowd.

Moya and Barrios strapped the Cuban to the steel springs. Quezada prepared the generator cables, turning on the voltage and sparking the cable jaws together. Pazos stared at the flashes of electric fire. For seconds, he did not understand what he saw—and then he screamed, twisting and thrashing on the springs, pleading, begging the men to release him. Urine ran from his pants. Rivas laughed.

Clamping one copper jaw to the Cuban's ankle, the other to the soft flesh of rubbery belly, Quezada switched on the generator.

Throughout the eternity of the questions, Pazos kept the secret. Not because his will defied the pain coursing through his body, but because Quezada did not ask. Pazos surrendered every other detail the Nicaraguan demanded—the combination of the code safe, the names of his agents and couriers in Salvador, the name of his superior in Cuba. And he told him of Atallah in Syria.

Yet Quezada never asked the series of questions that would save the woman.

Finally, the questions stopped. They gagged him and tied him and wrapped him in canvas. He knew he had no hope now. They had the answers to their questions and now he must disappear.

Even as he went to his death, he knew he had his revenge. The cripple and the woman had conspired to seize the rockets, to take the glory of murdering the Americans. When she fulfilled her mission, rockets would scream from the sky—and in murdering Americans, avenge the murder of Emilio Pazos.

Teletype clatter covered the click of the lock. They eased the office door open and entered, Moya moving to the left, Barrios to the right, their boots silent on the carpet. Quezada followed, a suppressor-fitted Skorpion 7.65mm pistol in his hand, the wire stock extended and pressed between his arm and his ribs, steadying the automatic pistol.

Raúl Condori walked from the communications room with teletype paper in his hands. He saw the men and started, the papers spilling as he grabbed for the door. Barrios grabbed Condori's arm and spun him across the office. Condori slapped a karate backfist into Moya's face, then drove a punch into his gut, not dropping him but sending him backward into the wall. One more step took him to his desk and he snatched a pistol from under a clutter of papers, pivoting to point at Quezada.

Quezada put a burst into the young man's chest, the small bullets striking without shock but gouging away pieces of his knuckles, whining off the steel of the pistol. Small caliber holes appeared in his white shirt. Despite the hits on his hands, Condori tried to aim. Quezada held back the trigger, raising the Skorpion to punch a pattern of holes in the young man's throat and face, a hit to the eye finally killing him. Quezada went to Condori and fired a last burst through his skull.

With the combination, they opened the office safe and took the code books. A ledger listed the names of Salvadorian agents, the backgrounds, their pay, their radio frequencies, and contact times. Quezada searched through the drawers of the desks as Moya and Barrios systematically looted the file cabinets, tying folders closed and dropping them into burlap bags. A relay of men in the hallway carried the bags to the back stairs.

They emptied the office of materials. Quezada watched his men place glass three-liter bottles of gasoline in the outer office, in the private office of Pazos, and in the communications room. They wrapped loops of explosive det-cord around the bottles, then ran the lengths of det-cord to the center of the floor. Following their commander's instructions, they set duplicate battery-powered timers and blasting fuses.

"Done."

20

STARING through the wind-driven rain, Niles watched the lights of the old hacienda. He lay in the grass and broadleaf weeds under coffee bushes tangled with vines. In front of him, the ground dropped away in a vertical fall of perhaps ten meters to a slope of coffee rows shaded by the spreading branches of trees. The rain alternated with starlight, the coffee rows and trees on the slopes emerging from the darkness for a few minutes, allowing Niles to survey the pale band of a trail at the bottom of the bluff and the pattern of other trails cutting through the rows. The coffee bushes and the trees whipped in the wind but he saw no movement on the trails. When the storm clouds blocked the night sky, the three hundred meters of slopes and trees went black.

A wire fence topped by strings of bare light bulbs circled the grounds and buildings. Inside the perimeter fence, he saw the black splotches of trees and the gray blocks of the buildings. Lights showed in a few windows. He focused the binoculars on the windows and watched for a moment—but nothing moved inside the main buildings of the hacienda. Shifting the optics to the windows of the converted stables, he saw a silhouette pass across a wall. Then the room went dark.

At the gate, two sentries talked in the shelter of a shed, their faces moving under the light, their hands gesturing. Niles searched the cleared ground outside the high chain-link fence. Rain-beaten grass rippled with the gusts of wind. He saw no tangle-foot wire or spikes, only the short grass.

187

Beyond the grass, a second wire fence circled the area. A footpath ran outside the second fence.

He scanned the asphalt road. Beyond the lights of the camp perimeter, the road disappeared into darkness. The satellite photos showed the road winding through gentle hills covered with coffee rows and shade trees. A long, flat pasture, bulldozed across the hillsides served as an airstrip. Niles stared at the darkness, watching for flashlights, lanterns, any sign of a patrol. He saw nothing. Even when the wind swept the clouds past and allowed a moment of starlight on the landscape, the hillsides near the camp remained black-on-black.

Blanco shifted, his quiet breathing becoming a snore. Niles shook him awake and passed him the binoculars. Behind him, Stark and Omar faced upslope. Niles snaked back.

"We divide today," he whispered in Spanish. "From here, one of us will watch them. And four of us move down to the road. And we wait."

"And if he does not come?" Omar asked.

"We keep waiting. Strak-man"—Niles switched to English to avoid any misunderstandings—"go back to the others, bring them up. Spread them out along this slope. First light, I send you out."

Stark and Omar slipped away. Niles watched the camp, looking for patterns in the movement of the sentries. In the times when the rain faded, he listened, trying to hear patrols. But the sounds of the immediate area—wind rattling branches, rain dripping through the coffee bushes, rivulets of water trickling down the eroded hillside—covered any distant sounds.

"There!" Blanco pointed.

Light silhouetted a ridge. Headlights flared on the road. Niles took the binoculars and watched the gate. The sentries left the shack, rifles gripped in their hands. Then they recognized the cars and rolled the gate open.

Cloth brushed cloth, branches dragged across wet canvas as the other Marines and contras carried the packs into the cover. Niles kept the binoculars on the camp. Though he lost sight of the cars, he saw lights go on in the buildings—in the converted stables, in the offices, and on the second floor above the offices.

"Strak-man!" Niles hissed. "Camera up. Max telephoto." As Stark found the sealed cases and assembled the camera and lens, Niles shifted his position for a better view of a second-floor window and braced his elbows in the mud to steady the binoculars, holding the optics steady. The angle of the hillside to the window allowed Niles to look into the room.

A woman appeared. She stood near a lamp and combed her hands through her hair. Her body type and general appearance looked the same as the woman the Marines had captured in El Salvador—and who had then escaped from the Atlacatl. But the optics of the binoculars did not define her features. Niles studied her mannerisms. By her movements and hair style, he guessed her to be very young. She stripped off her shirt and pants. By the look of her full, out-jutting breasts, she had never had a child. He noted her thin waist, her shapely thighs and buttocks—indicating a low-starch diet combined with light sports. That girl had not endured the hard life of a campesina with only corn and beans to eat.

"Oh, beautiful . . ." Stark whispered.

"That's Marianela. The one who escaped. Can you get a picture of her?"

"Can't. Not enough light for an exposure."

"Stay ready. We got daylight in . . . thirty minutes."

A man walked through the room, passing the almost naked young woman with the casual disregard of familiarity. He passed the window so quickly that Niles could not see his features. Niles kept the binoculars steady on the window. The young woman stepped out of sight.

Minutes later, the man returned to the window and looked out. Silhouetted by the light, his form showed an odd asymmetry. Then, stepping back, he gestured with his right hand. The man wore white cotton pajamas. The left sleeve of his shirt hung empty—the man had only one arm. And Niles saw a deep shadow in his left eye. The shadow did not shift. Watching through the binoculars, Niles realized that the man wore an eyepatch.

The prisoners interrogated in San Salvador had described the commander of the training camp as one-eyed and one-armed. One of the prisoners claimed that Marianela, the leader of the assassination squad, had a romantic relationship with the commander.

"Stark . . ."

"Yes, sir."

"If we can't take the Cuban, we take that man and the woman."

In the darkness of the room, Quezada stared at the ceiling. "Now we wait. We cannot contact the Syrians because Pazos never told us who supplied the rockets. If we are not to betray ourselves as the killers of those Cuban dogs, we must wait."

"How long?" Rivas asked him.

"Many things can happen now. The Syrians and the Iranians are training the fighters. When they return, perhaps they will bring information. Or the Syrian colonel Atallah will come to us—"

"Because he cannot place the transmitter. That is when we will talk with him."

"If the Cubans assign another functionary to replace Pazos, that will be a complication. But we will work around him, if we can—"

"Or we will kill him like Pazos."

Quezada laughed. "No, Lidia. We cannot do that again. We would betray ourselves. Borge and the Cubans will guess it was we who killed Pazos and that will be the end of all of this."

"No! Borge needs you."

"As Pazos said, there are many more veterans of the revolution. With my experience. And without my injuries. Borge needs the Cubans and the Soviets more than he needs this one old comrade."

"You created a strong organization. You gave him victories in El Salvador. He will remember that."

"When a fighter strikes as I did tonight, he prepares in secrecy, he acts in secrecy, but there is the fact that his opponents may break that secret. That fact is the risk."

"Then why did you risk killing the Cubans?"

"My Lidia, let me teach you this. There is always risk. We prepare, we plan, but when we act, there is still risk. There are a million things that cannot be anticipated. To accept the risk and still step into the fight is courage. To wait for when there is no risk, to wait for the perfect time and the perfect place, that is the way of the coward. If I had not eliminated Pazos, he would have continued losing my fighters—giving my fighters to the enemy as prisoners and as corpses to be counted for North American television. And in time, Borge and the Cubans would see me as a fool and they would be done with me. So I did not wait. Now, if they learn of what I did and I die, I will die for my action. But I will not die for the stupid mistakes of that perfumed dog Pazos."

"What can you do? If they try to—"

"What can I do? What do you think? Go to Cuba? Go to Russia? Or Libya? No, this is my country. And who knows? Perhaps Borge will approve of what I did, if he ever learns. He was no friend of Pazos."

Lying beside him in the bed, Rivas listened to what he said. She believed what he told her of the risk. But she had no loyalty to Nicaragua. She would not resign her life to the odds of secrecy or discovery.

"You are talking like a hero. Would you wait until they close the door of a cell on you? Or put a bullet in the back of your head? Can we not prepare to contact the Syrians?"

"Be patient. We must wait—"

"No. We can take action—"

"We will be patient. When the crew returns—"

"No. We know they are in Lebanon with the Iranians. Pazos told us that. If the interior ministry goons come for us, we will go to Lebanon. We will find—"

"And how do we find them? The American *Cia* cannot find the Iranians—"

"The Syrians control Lebanon. They control the Iranians. They will see us. We are the ones who will place the transmitter. They need this organization. They need you—"

"And you. You will be the one who goes into Salvador—"

"I am only one of many in the organization. Your organization. Without that, their rockets are nothing. Their scheme

191

against the Americans stops. Pazos is gone. The Syrians have no contact with us. If the Cubans move too slowly to replace Pazos, then of course we will be concerned. We will go to Lebanon. That will not surprise the Syrians."

"And what will Borge think?"

"We do not leave Nicaragua until we see his goons coming to take us."

"Then you mean, if we run, we run to Lebanon."

"Not run. Leave. We must prepare—in secret. We will get dollars, we will get new passports. If we must leave, then we leave quickly."

"Borge will know."

"We only run if the goons come. We murdered a brother in the revolution. If they take us to a People's Tribunal, we can expect thirty years. If Borge does not want to embarrass the revolution, it is a bullet and a ditch. Right?"

"True. That is the risk I accepted."

"Then we prepare. In secret. Perhaps the Cubans will believe the contras killed Pazos and they will send another functionary—I hope we do not endure that again. If the Syrians come to us, good. But if time passes and there is nothing, if the crew does not return from Lebanon, if we think Borge and the Cubans are conspiring against us, or if they send the goons, we go to Lebanon. Are we agreed?"

"Agreed."

In the last hour of the night, a Sandinista outpost east of Palacaguina reported a burning car. Four soldiers walked south from their position on the Yali-San Fernando road and found the smoking hulk of a Mercedes with diplomatic license plates.

A dead man lay in the road. Point-blank pistol shots had stained the white silk of his coat with powder. But he had died of a rifle burst to the head. Ragged scraps of bone and scalp and face littered the mud.

Bootprints surrounded the car. The soldiers checked the tracks with their flashlights and saw the treads of several different types of boots—contras.

Apparently, a contra gang had kidnapped the man in the white suit and forced him to drive the Mercedes here. When he tried to run from the car, the contras shot him in the back. They finished him with a rifle burst. Bootprints led from the road. The soldiers followed the bootprints up a trail into the hills.

After only a few hundred meters, the soldiers stopped. The trail led into the mountains controlled by the contras. The murderers had escaped to Honduras.

The Sandinista soldiers returned to the road and searched the area. They found Kalashnikov cartridge casings stamped with the factory codes of Portugal—where the contras bought the ammunition for their Kalashnikov rifles.

By radio, the patrol reported the burning of the Mercedes with diplomatic plates and the murder of the unknown man in the white suit. The night duty officer in Palacaguina forwarded the report directly to the Ministry of the Interior. Within minutes, the clerks found the license number of the Mercedes registered to the Cuban embassy.

The office director sent Lieutenant Rene Sanchez to the Cuban embassy. A young army officer assigned to the Ministry of the Interior while his bullet-shattered arm healed, Sanchez drove a battered and smoking Lada to the walled estate in the suburb of Las Colonias. Despite the ministry numbers on the Lada and his identification, the guards at the steel gates ordered him out of the car for a search.

Standing at the gates, Sanchez leaned against the steel and tried for a few minutes of sleep. The ministry scheduled him for all-night duty in the offices—sorting telexes and delivering messages to foreign advisers throughout the country. During the day, he tried to continue his architecture studies. He carried his books in the Lada because he often had to wait for hours for a return message to the ministry.

In 1982, the Sandinista draft had interrupted his last semester in the university. They refused to delay his service until after his graduation. However, because of his education and his action with street units during the revolution, they trained him as a second lieutenant. Then he went into the mountains of Jalapa—and got a bullet because he wore the insignia of an officer.

"You! Soldier!" A guard motioned Sanchez to the gatehouse and handed him a telephone.

The voice asked, "What do you want?"

"I am Lieutenant Sanchez," he explained. "I am with the Ministry of the Interior. There has been a killing in the north. The man had no identification but one of your embassy cars was found very near to his body. It was a Mercedes sedan, with the license number—"

"Wait in your car."

The guards did not open the gate. Parked in the driveway, Sanchez drank bitter coffee from a made-in-Hungary thermos. He glanced at the lines of the mansion the Cubans occupied and wondered why the structure had survived the earthquake. A transnational bank had once owned the mansion and the walled estate. Sanchez speculated that the foreigners had employed European or American architects to design the structure and supervise the construction—rather than accepting the work of a Somoza company. This structure survived the earthquake. Most of the other buildings in Managua—built by Somoza companies—did not. But Somoza still profited. After the earthquake, one of the Somoza banks had bought the property for almost nothing. Then, after the revolution, the junta seized the property and transferred the walled grounds and mansion to the Cubans.

Sandinista slogans raved against the history of American exploitation of Nicaragua. Only a communist with a third-rate Cuban education could twist the reality that far. Exploitation? Foreigners exploit us, we exploit the foreigners. Somoza used the Americans and the Europeans. Now the junta uses the Eastern Europeans and the Russians.

Revolution meant nothing without development. And revenge and socialism and war meant destruction, not development. Until the junta forgot about Sandino murals and Sandino slogans and Sandino celebrations and learned to make a country, Nicaraguans would continue as always—speaking the language of Spain, aping the styles of North America, buying cars and trucks and weapons from developed nations, and selling their products to whatever foreign power supported the regime in power. Somocista or Sandinista—it made no difference.

But Sanchez hoped he did not sleep in a Russian building the night of the next earthquake.

Passing helicopters interrupted his thoughts. Wind had swept away the rain clouds and the dawn silhouetted two helicopters in flight. Sanchez watched the helicopters cross the sky—probably, he thought, taking some directorate comandante or a Soviet boss to the airport. In the past, American bosses. Now, Russian and Cuban bosses. What did the revolution mean? Why did Nicaraguan fight Nicaraguan? To change bosses? Of the two—North American and Russian—Sanchez preferred the Americans. He had studied English since his first days of school. He could speak English. Now, for politics, did the Sandinistas expect him to study Russian?

The glass-blue of the sky reminded him of the morning five months ago. In his naivety and vanity, he wore his lieutenant's insignia on his shirt collar and a pistol taken from a dead contra on his belt. He walked in the center of the platoon. The sniper had watched all the other soldiers pass, then chose Sanchez—because of his pistol and his insignia. The bullet dropped him. Deflected by the humerus of his left arm, the bullet missed his heart, tearing through the pectoral muscles of his chest. Enduring a series of operations and casts, he spent three months in the hospital as his shattered arm healed. After that morning in the mountains, he had vowed never to wear his insignia again.

The memory made his arm and chest ache. He took an American aspirin and drank the bitter lukewarm coffee. When would the fighting end?

A fat Cuban in a wrinkled suit came out the gate—then Sanchez realized the bulk stretching his coat meant muscles. "I am Felix. Let us go look at this Mercedes."

"But—it is not in Managua. It is in the north, near Palacaguina."

Felix laughed, the sound sharp and vicious, like the barking of a dog. "Boy, drive to the air base. A helicopter will be ready."

21

GRAY streaked the eastern horizon. Martillo checked his watch—dawn came soon. He scanned the sky for observer planes or helicopters. Intermittent rain fell, gusts of wind bringing downpours, then minutes passing with only scattered drops. As the day came, the rain stopped. Bands of blue sky appeared. Black storm clouds covered the mountains to the east. But above the valley, the foothills, and the mountains to the west the clouds thinned, promising a clear day.

A soaked platoon leader crawled through the grass. "No rain, no clouds. The goddamned communists will have good visibility today."

"That will change nothing," Martillo told him. "Let them see us. We have the missiles. Check the machine guns, keep all the men under cover. And no one uses the radios until the fight."

The squad leader watched the highway. "Comandante, I think that is now . . ."

Headlights came from the south. As the squad leader alerted the men with a shrill whistle, Martillo focused his binoculars on the lights and counted the pairs of headlights winding over the hills. Ten trucks and cars. A major convoy. Exactly as his spies in Managua and Estelí had reported. Truck after truck of soldiers and supplies. Maybe the Sandinistas even transported their political workers and their clerks in this convoy.

Martillo crawled forward to the crest of the ridge and looked at the hillside. The first gray light of day showed no

196

marks of his explosives squad on the grass and earth. The rain had beat down the grass into tangled masses and washed the earth clean of bootprints. He saw the electrical-detonator wires leading from the ridge to the claymores concealed at the side of the highway. Drops of water beaded the wires.

But the Sandinista drivers would not see the wires, Martillo reasoned. Driving fast, watching the road, they had no time to stare at the hillsides—Martillo had no worries of the Sandinistas spotting the wires.

What a slaughter this would be. None of the FDN units had hit this stretch of road in a year. Today this highway became a major problem for the communists. Patrols, lookouts, observer planes, a battalion of soldiers—all taken from the border.

And today the Cubans and Russians flying the helicopters did their share of the dying . . .

He called to the men with, "This is it! Ready?"

Voices and whistles answered him.

The noise of the trucks came first, the diesel trucks laboring up the incline, the engines roaring as the drivers down-shifted and revved. Martillo watched the headlights of the first truck in the line appear on the straightaway. In the gray light, he could not see the colors or phrases painted on the truck, but he saw the high stake-side cargo walls—a cattle truck. Did it carry livestock or troops? Another cattle truck came second, behind that, a pickup truck, then a bus. Too bad if any civilians rode in the Sandinista convoy.

Martillo went to the squad leader with the first claymore firing handle. The man watched the road intently, his head moving slightly as he looked from the truck to the claymore, then back to the onrushing truck. Martillo reached to the device and checked the safety wire—off. The man looked at the handle, then Martillo, then back to the road, saying nothing as he watched the truck speed into the kill zone.

The other men with firing handles looked at their squad leader. As the truck passed a gullied slope, he squeezed the handle down.

Nothing. Looking at the firing lever in his hand, he pulled up the lever and tried again.

A flash lit the truck as the windshield disintegrated, the sheet metal of the fenders and doors and hood suddenly torn by hundreds of impacts, the cargo side boards splintering.

An instant later, the other claymores fired in a ragged series of blasts, the roadside flashing, smoke obscuring the road, flame coming seconds later as the gasoline-fueled pickup truck exploded, the cloud of orange fire engulfing the pickup and the bus tailgating the pickup.

But the long line of interconnected claymores had not hit all the vehicles of the convoy. Almost a kilometer away, the last trucks skidded to a stop, one truck crashing into another, a truck going off the highway. Soldiers jumped from a troop carrier.

Up and running, Martillo shouted for the mortar crews, the hammering of machine guns and automatic rifles drowning out his shouts. The men worked with the tubes and tripods of two Soviet mortars, sighting on the trucks and soldiers at the end of the convoy.

Martillo rushed back to the leader of the explosives squad and pointed at the distant Sandinista troops. "Down there. There! We need claymores down there. Booby traps to kill those commie shits. Or they will come up behind us and shoot us when we pull out."

"We only have the claymores for the march back."

"Fuck the march back! Do what I said! Go!"

On the highway, wrecks in the kill zone burned. The drivers and passengers of the first four trucks had died instantly, the cabs and cargo backs destroyed by thousands of lead balls. The machine gunners and riflemen on the ridge directed their fire down at the flaming bus and the damaged trucks in the last half of the convoy. Drivers careened over the embankments, trying to turn their trucks, trying to escape the ambush as the contras followed the trucks in the sights of their weapons.

Windshields shattered, tires popped, soldiers and campesinos fell from the backs of the slat-side cattle trucks. Hundreds of high-velocity bullets rained down on the trucks. A rocket-propelled grenade flashed from the ridge, arching across the hundreds of meters of distance. Falling short of a truck, the rocket skipped across the asphalt and exploded in the packed earth of the embankment.

But the mortars scored. The first 82mm shells hit a hundred meters past the last truck. The crews adjusted the range and walked the mortars along the highway, shrapnel tearing the tires off the last truck, a near-miss killing the driver of the next truck.

In the wreckage and flames, soldiers threw families from the trucks, campesinos and their wives carrying children, wounded sprawled on the asphalt. Martillo watched the panic through his binoculars, the scenes wavering with the heat of burning trucks. Families scrambled over the embankment, bullets finding the people at random—a man dropping, a child spinning, a woman's leg suddenly flexing wrong. He laughed as he watched. Let the Sandinistas call this an atrocity. If they evicted families from their farms in Jalapa, then tried to replace those farmers with crowds of loyal communists, all the communists—male and female, old and young—deserved the bullet. After this, after the Sandinista newspapers showed the pictures of the dead on the highway, who would volunteer to work the stolen land? Let every dead communist—man, woman, child, baby—shout the warning to the people of Nicaragua.

Rifles flashed on the highway as the few soldiers tried to fire back at the contras. A rocket-propelled grenade tore into the hillside, throwing a splash of mud and wet grass. Martillo ignored the few bullets zipping past him as he ran along the ridgeline, shouting out the orders to start the withdrawal.

The men threw off the branches and black plastic serving as camouflage. Crawling backward from the crest of the ridge to the safety of the backslope, the men assembled their gear and shouldered their packs before running to the northeast. Martillo put his binoculars on the brush-covered hills, searching for any sign of the missile squads. Nothing betrayed the men concealed there.

At the south end of the ridge, the explosives squad placed claymores and stretched tripwires. Martillo crouched beside two teenagers with a Soviet RPK machine gun, one boy firing the machine gun, the other searching for targets with binoculars. Empty cartridge and lengths of steel-belt links littered the grass.

"Move!" Martillo pointed to the claymores. "Down there! Cover the pull out."

Deafened by the noise, the teenagers only stared at their commander. Martillo jerked the gunner to his feet and shouted into his face. Finally understanding, the teenager nodded. The two boys ran to cover the explosives squad.

The squad leaders took over the shifting of the men, most of the contras retreating from the ridge in a long, widely spaced line while a few men maintained the fire on the Sandinistas, blocking any effort to follow the retreating column. Martillo found his radio man and joined the men on the south end of the ridge.

Only wreckage and corpses remained on the road. Acrid black smoke clouded from the flaming trucks, the smoke drifting over the hillsides and rising black against the dawn. All the survivors had taken cover in the gullies and ditches on the other side of the highway. The smoke screened the Sandinistas from the contra weapons.

Martillo cursed as he saw the survivors in the safety of the ditches. Why hadn't the Americans granted him all the munitions he requested? If they had supplied the Prima-cord, his demolition squad could have laced the ditches with the ropes of high explosive, killing or cutting the legs off the communist shits who survived the ambush. Now his men wasted ammunition trying to kill Sandinistas sheltered by meters of earth—

Rotor throb stopped the firing. His men, the Sandinistas— all the rifles and machine guns stopped, his men all looking to the north.

"Move!" he shouted. "Move! Scatter and run. Set those booby traps and get out of here."

Helicopters came from the north. The contras pulled the safeties on the claymore tripwires, the machine gunners covering the men with long, sweeping bursts of heavy caliber fire into the Sandinista riflemen, then jerking the RPK guns from the ridge and running down the backslope of the ridge. Martillo took a last look at the destruction and flames and corpses. Against the losses of the communists, he had not suffered a single man killed—if he had only brought a news team to videotape this victory. Then Martillo followed his men.

A shallow valley divided the hill overlooking the highway from the foothills to the northeast. Years of cattle grazing had flattened and smoothed the ground. After the revolution, the landowners had slaughtered and sold their herds. No cattle had grazed on the land in years, allowing weeds and broadleaf shrubs to grow chest-high. New grass and vines intertwined with yellow weeds.

The retreating contras did not angle south and follow the old dirt road curving into the foothills. They thrashed straight through the weeds, only their heads and arms and packs showing, every man leaving a path through the growth. Last off the ridge, Martillo followed his men, running, falling and running again, hacking through the weeds with his folded Kalashnikov.

Turbine roar came like an unending explosion, the combined sound of the turbines and rotors a machine thunder overwhelming all other sounds. The contras dropped in the growth and watched the Soviet helicopters. The troopships stayed high, out of range of the machine guns and rocket-propelled grenades. But the pilots of the armored MI-24 gunships had no fear of the weapons they saw on the ground.

Rotors like a silver disc, the lead gunship turned back, the contras screaming and running as they looked into the rocket pods and mini-guns. A man stood up and fired his RPK from the shoulder, his body shuddering with the recoil of the machine gun—but for nothing. The 7.62mm slugs skipped off the titanium of the fuselage without even marking the metal. The contras scattered, sprinting away as the gunship came in low, the rocket pods almost skimming the brush.

The teenager who carried the radio stayed at the side of his commander. Reaching out for the handset, Martillo saw the boy shaking with fear, his dark *indigena* skin suddenly the color of ashes. Martillo forced a laugh.

"Watch this. This you will never forget."

Before Martillo spoke into the handset, the first missile

flashed from the hilltop and shot across the hundreds of meters of sky to the gunship—and hit behind the turbine exhaust with a spray of flame—

Without effect.

Mini-guns firing in a long tearing explosion, the gunship strafed the pasture, hundreds of bullets chopping the earth and weeds, the ground blurring in the spray of debris and low-angle ricochets, running men suddenly tangles of guts and bloody rags. Martillo felt the wind of the rotors pass and then the gunship soared away.

Parachutes opened in the sky and flares descended slowly—decoys for the infrared sensors of the missiles. Another missile shot from the hilltop, streaked past an incandescent flare, and continued into the distance.

On the ground, a ten-meter wide swath of death remained, the weeds flattened, men laying where they died, their bullet-torn corpses, surrounded by shredded equipment and bent weapons. Screams came from a wounded man dragging himself by his arms, a leg torn away by a hit from a 12.7mm slug. None of the running contras risked their lives to turn back for him as they ran again, shrugging off their packs, carrying only their rifles as the second gunship fired rockets.

Chains of explosions took men in midstride, their bodies disintegrating, flesh and limbs and rifles flying. One man lost both legs to scything shrapnel, blast shock knocking him down. Not yet knowing of his terrible wounds, panicked, he tried to run, lurching along on the stumps, his blood leaving a trail behind him.

Another SAM-7 streaked from the concealed launchers—and hit one of the flares, the warhead exploding in the air as the gunship soared away.

Martillo screamed into the radio. "Hit the helicopters! Fire them all! Or we'll all die down here!"

But the first gunship had seen the missiles launched from the hilltop. Roaring over the dead and wounded and panicked contras, the pilot sighted on the hilltop and fired his mini-guns and rockets.

At that instant, another missile shot out from the trees, the booster burning away in a line of white fire—and the warhead splashed flame on the armored side of the gunship as Soviet rockets and bullets destroyed the top of the hill, the trees and brush disappearing in the rolling flame of explosions, the mini-guns pouring in hundreds of bullets on an area only a few meters in circumference.

As Martillo stared at the smoking devastation of the hilltop, his missile squad with their useless SAM-7 launchers gone, he heard the gunships returning.

22

AS the headphones went from Alvarez to Vatsek, Niles heard Russian voices laughing.

The three Marines sprawled in a mass of coffee bushes and vines. Years of neglect had allowed the morning glory vines to interweave with the coffee branches, the weight of the vines bending down the branches and creating caves inside the row. The vines grew over the drop-off and flowed down the eroded slope like a green wave. On the other sides, the vines spread over the earth, threatening to cover to the next row of coffee bushes.

Reaching past Niles, Alvarez had to weave his arm through the maze of branches. Vatsek twisted against the branches and slipped on the headphone. Alvarez explained to Niles in a whisper:

"I had some back and forth Spanish on field radios. But this is on the aircraft frequencies."

"Tape on?"

Alvarez nodded. They waited as Vatsek listened. He concentrated on the transmissions he followed, his lip curling back in a sneer, mouthing obscenities as he stared into space. Finally he passed the headphones back.

"Wipe out of a contra unit. Body count of hundreds. Big joke for pilots. Good times."

"Where?"

"On the highway to the Ocotal—" Alvarez answered. "Ten, twelve kilometers north of here."

Turbine noise came from the south. The Marines listened as the simultaneously whining/roaring sound approached,

204

passed overhead, and faded into the north. Unlike American helicopters with two or four blades, Soviet helicopter troopships and gunships employed a five-blade rotor. Five-bladed rotors did not produce the distinctive throb associated with the older American helicopters, the sound of the Soviet rotors lower and continuous, a bass vibration dominated by the high-frequency whine of the twin turbines powering the aircraft. By the sound, Niles guessed three or four helicopters in the flight.

Tuning the scanner, Alvarez sketched a map as he listened to the transmissions. He scribbled notes on the pad, then passed the drawing to Niles.

Another flight of helicopters passed. The noise divided as one of the helicopters left the flight, turbines shrieking as the helicopter landed—somewhere to the east, no more than a kilometer away.

Niles glanced to the east—as if he could see through the matted branches and vines—then studied the sketch. Alvarez had drawn the highways between Estelí, Palacaguina, and Ocotal. He pointed to a series of marks along the highway.

"Troops. They think there's infinite contras out here. And they want to find them."

"Not good . . ." Niles compared his topographic map to the sketch, trying to imagine the retreat of the contras through the mountains and valleys to the Honduran border. To the east, the mountains of the Cordillera Isabella—with no sanctuary until the Atlantic coast, four hundred kilometers away. To the south, the garrison of Palacaguina. To the north, the garrison of Ocotal and the counterinsurgency battalions patrolling the Jalapa highway.

To the east, only Somoto, a few militia outposts, and thirty kilometers of rolling hills to the Honduran border and safety. A young soldier could run the distance before dark—

Through the escape route scouted by Niles and his squad.

And the Sandinistas would pursue the contras, soldiers and militiamen sweeping the foothills while airborne platoons of counterinsurgency troops deployed in the Somoto mountains to ambush escaping contras.

When the Marines and contras of Niles's squad tried to escape with their prisoner, instead of a few isolated outposts manned by bored draftees, they now faced highly trained and experienced counterinsurgency hunter/killer units.

"Out-foxed myself on this one . . ."

Waving aside flies, Felix followed the clerk into the whitewashed morgue. Lieutenant Sanchez stopped in the office—he had seen corpses. He sat on one of the benches and tried to sleep. But the combined stink of the morgue—the disinfectant, the blood, the shit, the cigarettes of the attendants—drove him out to the street.

On the instructions of the interior ministry, a helicopter had taken Sanchez and the Cuban north from Managua to Palacaguina. At the landing field, two soldiers waited with an old National Guard jeep—the Guardia insignia painted over with a stencil of Sandino—to drive the five kilometers to the burned car. Sanchez had slept in the jeep while the soldiers and the Cuban hiked the muddy trails, taking photos and collecting cartridge casings. Now the soldiers waited in the jeep, listening to the radio exchanges of a major action against the contras somewhere near Ocotal. They laughed and cheered as if they followed the plays of a soccer game. Sanchez left the soldiers to their radio war and crossed the muddy street.

Flies from the garbage in the gutter—and the morgue—orbited the interior of a one-room café. A woman with a toothless narrow face, her dark skin stretched over sinews and frail bones, glanced at his uniform and said nothing as he entered and asked for coffee. Sanchez sloshed the steaming coffee around in the cup to scald away the fly-spots, then stirred in grainy brown cane sugar.

Sleeping for a moment with the cup in his hand, the woman's whisper startled him.

"What?"

"Pardon me for disturbing you. But please—did the contras attack the morning trucks?"

Airborne in the helicopter, he had seen columns of black smoke rising from the highway. He had overheard the soldiers in the jeep talking about a massacre. But who killed who? "I know nothing. There is fighting. But I know nothing about whatever trucks. I came from the capital."

The old woman—old? Sanchez saw no gray in her hair, she might be only forty or forty-five—looked from him to the soldiers in the jeep. Her hands twisted a dishrag. She went back to the counter and wiped the old wooden planks, her arm moving with the habit of a lifetime, her face impassive. Sanchez regretted his abrupt answer. He asked:

"Who in your family went with the trucks?"

"My son. His wife. The comandante offered them land near Ocotal. We are not political but—" She watched him for his reaction. "Land is land."

"Is there a telephone to Ocotal?"

"The contras cut the wire."

Sanchez gulped his coffee and put money on the table. "I will ask them. They have a radio."

Two troop trucks rattled along the street, one truck shuddering to a stop behind the jeep, the other continuing past the morgue to park. In the back of the second truck, Sanchez saw faces and limbs and pink dresses with vast stains of blood. Men and women and children lay in a filthy fly-swarming load. Blood drained from the corpses. Sanchez looked back to the café. The old woman stood in the doorway, waiting. He did not want to know who had died on the highway. Rushing to the morgue, he saw Felix examining the identification cards inside a wallet. A wristwatch and money lay on the table.

"Is he your man?"

The Cuban nodded.

"Then we go back to the helicopters?"

"Not yet . . ." He signed a printed form.

A woman wailed. Voices cried out. Boots scuffed on the dirt and stones of the street, men cursing and shouting to one another as they ran.

In the street, townspeople stared at the dead. The crowd blocked the jeep. The driver gunned the engine and leaned on the horn, forcing the crying women and stunned men to move aside. Sanchez looked into the faces of people—shocked, staring without seeing, streaming with tears, impassive, twisted with anger—and he turned away, the images of suffering people shaming and angering him. Ten years of war and still the people died. What did the revolution mean if the killing did not stop?

The radio squawked numbers and the soldiers in the front seats laughed.

"You hear that? The helicopters wiped out the contras. Killed them all. Not one of those sons of bitches left to put against the wall—Lieutenant, now where? The helicopters?"

"No." The Cuban passed a map to the driver. "First I must talk with a colonel."

Shooting stopped Niles. He listened to the distant rifles and pistols—training had started at the camp. Continuing through the coffee rows, advancing one slow step at a time, Niles scanned the shadows and sunlit hillsides. Wind rustled through the trees and brush, covering the faint sound of his steps as he carefully placed his boots on the rain-damp leaves, his boots leaving no marks on the earth of the trail.

Niles walked to the end of the ridgeline, where the trail curved around the hill. There, he hand-signaled the three men behind him and dropped to a crouch. Taking slow, silent breaths, he slowly turned his head to sweep the area with his hearing. He heard the shooting and the wind. He heard a bird's wings cut the air. In the far distance, he heard the whine of the Soviet helicopters—but nothing moved near him.

On the trail, the rain had erased every mark, leaving the dirt with a natural texture impossible to fake. No patrols had passed on this trail this morning. Niles looked back to the other men. Concealed in coffee branches, Blanco and Omar faced in opposite directions, watching for lookouts or patrols. Alvarez watched the trail behind them.

Crossing the trail, Niles pushed through the coffee bushes and angled down the slope, accepting the noise of his boots and the sounds of the others following him. He counted his strides. At eighty-five, he slowed. The satellite photos showed a curve in the winding dirt road—

The slope dropped away and he saw the ruts and stones of the road a few meters below him. Niles hand-signaled the others and they waited, listening for minutes to all the motion and life of the coffee plantation.

At one time, the owners of the hacienda had paved the road. Now, only a few patches of asphalt remained. The road appeared several hundred meters to the east, then curved past Niles, the curve continuing to the west. The condition of the road—the potholes and ruts, the broken asphalt—would not allow a vehicle to speed.

Niles arranged his gear for a long wait, setting out his binoculars and note pad, his hand radio. He placed his pack under him and lay down. He used a few stems of grass to tie twigs aside, giving him a clear field of view of the road. Sometime in the next three days, if Pazos came to the training camp—

Rocks clanged against sheet metal. A jeep appeared. Niles snapped up the binoculars and focused on the four men in the jeep. His pulse raced as he saw the round-faced, curly-haired Latin in the back. Three Sandinista soldiers rode with him, the men in the front seat wearing old fatigues and web gear, the Sandinista in back with new pressed fatigues, without insignia or unit identification. Niles saw the driver mouthing curses as he strained against the steering wheel, weaving across the road to avoid the holes, the old jeep lurching and swaying and crashing down on its springs.

The Cuban fit the description of Pazos—overweight, with a mustache, wearing a sports coat. Niles made a snap decision—

"Hey-zoot!" Niles hissed, breaking his silence. "This is it! Ready?"

Alvarez grinned, nodded, taking a last glance at the men with his own binoculars. "That's the man!"

"Quick and dirty. I kill the two men in the front and we drop down on them. Tell Blanco and Omar. Thirty seconds—"

Niles found two earplugs in his front shirt pocket. Valved, they protected his ears from the nerve damage of gunshot noise. Then he shouldered his Kalashnikov.

Bumping and swaying, the jeep weaved across the road. Niles followed the driver's head in the sights of the rifle and waited, watching the angle change. The driver cursed and laughed, turning in the seat to joke with the Sandinista officer in the back seat. Niles waited until the jeep passed directly below him, the sights centered on the head of the driver and including the soldier in the right-hand seat—

The driver died instantly, a burst of high-velocity 7.62mm bullets smashing through his skull, the bullets continuing and punching into the chest of the other soldier, a second burst raking the front seats again, the corpses jerking and shaking as the bullets tore through their bodies.

As the second burst of bullets struck the dead men, Alvarez and the contras dropped from the hillside and rushed the jeep. The Cuban reached for a pistol under his jacket and Omar slammed the butt of his rifle into his arm as Blanco dragged him backward from the jeep. The Sandinista punched at Alvarez until Omar rammed the muzzle of his rifle into his gut, doubling him.

The Cuban hit the road and rolled away. He tried to reach for his pistol—but his arm did not function. Omar kicked him in the stomach and hit him with the rifle butt again. With one arm paralyzed, with blood flowing into his eyes, the Cuban came up in a fighting stance and snapped a kick into Omar's gut, dropping him to one knee. The Cuban grabbed for the Kalashnikov Omar carried, but Alvarez moved too quickly, sweeping the Cuban's left foot and smashing an elbow into the back of his head, stunning him. Omar and Blanco hammered the Cuban with their rifle butts. The Cuban fought, punching, kicking. Alvarez stepped back, waiting for the exact moment, then stepped in fast and kicked the Cuban in the groin.

Niles watched the road as the others looped plastic handcuffs around the wrists of the prisoners, then tied ropes around their necks. The Cuban continued to struggle as Alvarez urged him up the embankment. Finally losing patience, Alvarez dragged him by the rope leash, the Cuban losing consciousness and going slack. Omar grabbed him by his coat and jerked him to the top.

The Sandinista ran. Blanco sprinted after him and caught the rope, jerking him back, the Sandinista falling, gasping and choking. Omar and Blanco dragged him up the embankment as Niles cranked the steering wheel of the jeep to the side and pushed the jeep and the two dead men off the road, the jeep crashing through the brush for twenty or thirty meters and disappearing. Niles swept away the tire tracks with a branch.

Only a minute had passed. Niles searched the road for any trace of the capture. He kicked dirt over blood, brushed away bootprints, then scrambled up the embankment after the others.

The Cuban still fought. Even with his hands secured behind his back, a rope around his neck, blood pouring from cuts to his face and head, he fought, trying to twist away, kicking at the contras. The Sandinista officer stood against a tree, the rope around his neck tied to the tree, immobilizing him—he could not move without strangling. Alvarez looked at Niles and held up a syringe. Niles nodded.

Using his hand radio for the first time since they reached the camp, Niles alerted Stark and Vatsek. "Gentlemen, be advised, we made our pick-up. We will depart immediately."

"Repeat, please."

"We did it. Got him. Get ready to go. Any reaction by opponents to the firing of weapons?"

"What firing?"

"Any opponents in motion?"

"Clear in this area."

After the injection of the sedative, the Cuban stopped struggling. But still conscious, he cried out until Alvarez slapped a length of tape over his mouth. Using cable saws—flexible cables with teeth like saw blades—Blanco and Omar cut long saplings, trimmed the saplings with their knives, then used rope to make a stretcher. Niles scattered all the twigs and leaves trimmed from the poles, then buried the stumps in dead leaves.

The Sandinista officer stayed silent, immobilized by the rope around his neck, watching the men who had captured him. Niles saw that he did not wear a pistol belt. He searched the Nicaraguan carefully for hidden weapons—and found only a ring of keys. He went through his pockets, finding identification in the name of Lieutenant Rene Sanchez of the Third Battalion. A second card identified him as assigned to the Ministry of the Interior. Some scraps of paper had what looked like a license number on one, a list of book titles on another, a drawing on a third. The drawing seemed to diagram the placement of reinforcing rods in a pillar.

"We got our Cuban." Alvarez passed Niles a passport with an identity photo of a round-faced Latin. The passport identified Emilio Pazos Ruiz as a citizen of Mexico, listing his birth date, the dates of application and expiration, and an address in Cuernavaca.

"Are you Americans?" Sanchez asked him in English.

Niles did not answer him. Signaling Blanco and Omar, he pointed up the hillside. They took the stretcher and labored up the slope. Alvarez took the lieutenant. Niles checked his watch—five minutes. He carefully brushed the leaves and dirt of the area clear of bootprints, then followed the others, using a branch to erase the marks of their climb.

No sign remained of the capture.

23

TROOPSHIPS landed on the hill to the west. Martillo stepped into the ferns at the side of the trail and found the ridge with his binoculars. Sandinista soldiers rushed from the tail doors and formed squads. He tried to fine-focus the binoculars on the soldiers and their weapons but the distance defeated the optics. Draftees? Or the highly trained and experienced volunteers of the Irregular Warfare Battalions? Draftees or hard-core communists, those twenty soldiers blocked the escape of Martillo and his surviving men.

Only ten men followed him, two of them wounded. All the other men of his command had died in the attack of the gunships or disappeared in the panic.

The communists had destroyed his force—because the Americans gave him junk missiles and then sent him out to die.

Martillo squinted into the distance, searching the line of hills for an escape. Flights of troopships and spotter planes blocked any retreat to the north—going north meant fighting against battalions. And now they blocked the west. He must do the unexpected and retreat to the south, through the unfamiliar areas where the FDN forces had not operated.

The trail ahead followed the curves of the mountain ridge into the west. Signaling his men, he veered off the trail, leading his men straight downhill. He hacked through the brush and ferns with his folded Kalashnikov, his boots sliding on the wet grass of the near vertical hillside and gouging long scars into the mud. Dropping through a screen of branches, he splashed into a stream.

Muddy water flowed knee-deep, the stream snaking a winding course to the east. Trees and brush blocked the sky. Martillo followed the stream, pushing through tangles of debris, rushing ahead and doubling back, ignoring his fatigue, always finding a way through the mud and branches for his men.

Hatred and revenge drove Martillo. He had asked that grinning dog Montes for antiaircraft missiles to knock down the Soviet helicopters and gunships. And what had the Americans given him? Trash. Trusting the shit missiles, he took his men into the attack, executing a perfect ambush and then retreating and drawing the Sandinista pilots into a trap—and the victory became a slaughter of his men. For that, Montes of the CIA got a bullet in the head. No, in the gut. Forty bullets in the gut, one bullet for every one of the men in the force who died because of those shit missiles.

The ruts of a road cut through the water. Grass grew in the ruts—no trucks had used the road in weeks. But fresh cow dung and rain-filled hoofprints indicated that local farmers grazed their cattle here.

Martillo waited until the wounded men stumbled up. One man had suffered a rifle wound across the ribs during the ambush. The pain from the wound forced him to walk bent over, with his left arm clutched against his ribs. The other man had survived a rocket blast by some miracle. The blast had only burst an eardrum and gashed his left arm and leg with bits of shrapnel. In a normal march, neither man would be counted as seriously wounded. But on this retreat, any wound that slowed a man meant death.

Falling in the stream had covered the men with mud. Giving their rifles to other men to clean, he checked the rags and bandages covering their wounds. Joking with them, he gave them a melted candy bar from his own field kit. Then tablets of benzedrine to keep them moving despite their pain and blood loss.

"Tomorrow, we're out. Then we rest for a month in camp. Women and beer and a hammock. Think of that."

But he did not assign men to help them. He could not sacrifice all the others if those two men fell behind.

The revving of a motor alerted them. Martillo pointed out positions for his men, the men silently taking cover on the embankments and in the shadows of the brush overhanging the stream. Waiting, they heard voices. Martillo hand-signaled his men to wait for him to fire.

A militiaman ran from the east. A boy no older than sixteen, he carried a new Kalashnikov and wore new web gear over a ragged work shirt and patched polyester pants. He shouted:

"There is water here!"

Other men ran to the stream. Like the boy, they carried new rifles and equipment but wore their own field clothes and sandals instead of uniforms. A battered and rusting pickup truck rattled to a stop, steam clouding from under the hood. Several men jumped from the back of the truck and filled plastic jugs in the stream. They poured the muddy water over the radiator while other men checked the dirt road for signs of the contras.

"No Guardia here."

The contras watched as the militiamen refilled the radiator of the old truck. The militiamen continued west on the road. Martillo waited until all sounds of the patrol faded away before scrambling up the embankment to the hillside above the road, a gentle slope of grass and rocks alternating with brush. Cattle trails criss-crossed the hillsides. Walking quickly, concealed by the pines and oak trees from airborne observation, Martillo led his men southwest, gaining altitude as they follwoed the cow trails. They heard helicopters but saw no sign of patrols.

At midday, they came upon the Pan American Highway. He signaled for a rest and they lay in the shade of pines, wind cooling their sweat as they watched Sandinistas patroling the highway in jeeps and troop trucks. The men with canteens rationed out water to the others. Martillo went from man to man, whispering a few words of encouragement. All the men—even the wounded—looked strong, their spirit unbroken.

They had a chance to survive this defeat. They had already entered the mountains of Somoto. Past the highway, only thirty kilometers of easy hills and cool forest remained to the Honduran border.

Then on to Tegucigalpa, to execute Montes.

A gunship flew low along the ridgeline, the rotor storm tearing at the pines. Niles crouched in a tangle of ferns and pine seedlings and watched the Soviet helicopter pass. Faces looked out from the cockpits and the troop windows, searching the mountainsides with binoculars. He watched the gunship disappear to the west, the turbine whine finally fading to nothing, lost in the sound of the wind sweeping through the pines. Only then did he move, signaling Blanco and Omar with a hiss.

The young men scrambled up the rocks. Niles touched his chest and pointed up to the ridge, then signaled for the young men to continue straight through the pines. They nodded. Alone, his boots leaving no marks, he wove across the rocks to the top and dropped flat, minimizing his silhouette as he scanned the distance.

Only a few kilometers away, he saw Honduras. But between him and the truck back to Tegucigalpa, the gunship zigzagged along the ridgelines, searching for the contras. Niles looked at the sky and saw, a thousand meters above the mountains, the wings of a plane. Niles shifted his position and scanned the ridgelines and mountainsides. A smear of smoke rose from a fold in the mountains. He noted the fire on his map.

Then, directly to the west, in their line of march, light flashed on glass. He checked the angle of the sunlight before raising his binoculars—he didn't want reflections from the lenses to betray his position. He found the point of light. A gray green speck floated away from a hillside. Rotors created a gray, shimmering disc as the helicopter banked away, staying treetop low as it flew north. Niles fixed the binoculars on the distant hillside, studying the features of the area. Then he tried to find the exact hillside on his map. He could only circle the approximate area. But even as his pencil touched the plastic of the map, he plotted a route around the ambush.

Wait all day, wait all night, won't see me.

Sliding down the rocks a few meters, he moved along the slope, paralleling the ridgeline without silhouetting himself, as he looked for traces of Sandinista units. He had scouted this section of the mountains on the way into Nicaragua—he knew the possible helicopter LZs, the best observation points, and where the trails met. The several days of preparation had paid off. Now, with the unforeseen Sandinista operation against the contras complicating the exit of his unit, his maps and notes and memory of the route meant the difference between a dangerous escape attempt and a careful exfiltration.

In fact, Niles realized, the counterinsurgency operation had succeeded in making this mission almost dangerous—

Green moved against green in his peripheral vision and he dropped flat, his reflexes concealing him before he recognized Blanco in motion thirty meters away. He watched the young man visually search the mountainside, looking for him. Niles flicked a rock and waved. Blanco pantomimed—using hand-signs Niles had taught him: Four men. Hidden.

An ambush. Niles keyed his hand radio, clicking a code to halt the other men, then eased down the slope to Blanco. Lower on the mountainside, Omar crept through the brush, moving only one arm at a time, one leg, picking up dry sticks and setting the sticks aside before advancing. Finally, he stood and carefully walked the last fifty meters to Niles and Omar.

"Four of them," he whispered. "Irregular warfare. With a radio. They are waiting at a perfect place, where the pathways come together and they can see anyone. We can kill them, but it must be with rifles—"

Niles shook his head. "We will go around them."

Sending Blanco back to guide the men with the prisoners, Niles went ahead, Omar leading him to a position overlooking the Sandinista squad. Niles saw the intersecting trails and the line of men walking into the ambush. He recognized Comandante Martillo an instant before the claymore fired.

Light flashed. Flame passed and the sky turned—and then Martillo hit the earth. A metallic whine shrieked through his mind, all other sounds gone. Not questioning his senses, not

217

thinking, he reacted, clawing at the earth with one hand, his other hand locking around the pistol grip of the Kalashnikov as he scrambled off the trail and pushed his way into the brush.

Sounds came through the whine in his ears. He heard the full-automatic popping of rifles. Men shouted. A rocket screamed overhead and exploded somewhere behind him.

Turning in the weeds, he tried to stand, to rush the source of the riflefire killing his men—

Pain slammed through him and he fell back, his breathing coming in ragged gasps. The shooting continued. Some of his hearing had returned and he heard bullets ripping through leaves, the sound of bullets hitting trees. Easing himself over on his back, he reached for his legs and felt blood.

Blood poured from wounds in his legs. For a long moment, he stared at the ragged cloth of his pants, the blood, the exposed bones of his left leg and the dangling boot—then he jerked out his knife and cut the sling from his rifle and knotted the strip of webbing around his left leg. The bleeding slowed. He used his pants belt around his other leg.

Though he would not bleed to death, the Sandinistas had killed him. He had no hope now.

God, he prayed, turning, pulling himself by his arms, looking up the hillside and seeing the muzzles of rifles flashing. Give me strength now, only a few more minutes of life and strength, to kill the men who killed me . . .

Sighting on the back of the Sandinista twenty-five meters away, Niles fired a quick burst. Dust puffed from the man's uniform as three bullets punched through his back and a fourth bullet slammed his head forward, killing him instantly. A few steps away, Omar fired two long bursts.

The last Sandinista soldier whipped around, spraying full-automatic bursts, the bullets tearing through the brush concealing Niles and Omar as the Sandinista jerked the empty magazine out of his rifle and scrambled for a new position. Rifle fire from the contras hit the soldier, then Niles and Omar fired simultaneously, the impacts of their bullets throwing the soldier back. Struggling to rise, he pointed his rifle again and Niles aimed a last burst.

Contras continued firing, men rushing through the trees and snapping bursts at the positions of the dead Sandinistas. Very aware of the Sandinista Popular Army uniform he wore, Niles stayed low as he shouted:

"They are dead! We killed them! Martillo, where are you?" The mountainside went silent. But no answer came. "Martillo! You alive?"

A man sprinted from the brush. Pointing his rifle with one hand, he checked two dead men sprawled on the trail. He veered to the other side. Niles waited. Finally a contra called out.

"Who are you?"

"No shooting! I am one of you but I am wearing an enemy uniform."

Niles rushed down the slope. Beside one of the dead Sandinistas, a teenager no more than eighteen years old, the squad radio lay in a carefully prepared hole gouged into the earth and rocks. Niles took the handset of the radio and heard static. Had the boy reported the sighting of the contra unit? If the dead boy had radioed, that meant a helicopter and reaction platoon in flight.

Holding his rifle raised above his head, Niles crossed the open ground. Dead men lay where they died. The claymore had killed the men in the center of the squad instantly, hundreds of explosive-driven lead balls punching through their bodies. They lay twenty meters away, their blood staining the trail. Walking point, Martillo had only taken the side of the blast. Niles found a contra crouched over the leader, wads of blood-soaked bandages in his hands.

Tourniquets bound both of Martillo's legs. The shrapnel of the Sandinista claymore had destroyed his left leg, the long white shafts of bone exposed, his foot hanging by only strands of flesh. When Martillo recognized Niles, he reached out and grabbed Niles's shirt, pulling him down to face him.

"You, Marine," he said in English. "You are a soldier. You are like us. I want a promise from you."

"What promise?"

"Kill Montes, that *Cia pocho*. Put your Kalashnikov into his belly and cut that *puto* in half."

"What are you saying?"

Martillo lapsed into Spanish. The contras gathered around him, listening as their commander explained the disaster on the highway. "I told Montes I wanted antiaircraft missiles. I begged him. Without missiles, we had no hope against the Cubans and the Russians. And finally, he gave me some Russian missiles. They were shit! We hit the helicopters but the missiles did nothing and the helicopters wiped out my force."

"Sam-Seven missiles? You tried to knock down gunships with Sam-Sevens? Sometimes those missiles will down a jet, but a jet has no armor. And those gunships are built like a tank."

"Why did not Montes tell me that?"

"What does he know about anything? What would he know about those missiles? Talk with an Israeli pilot. Talk with me. Why did you not talk with me?"

"Montes said you were not part of the operation, not to be trusted." Martillo closed his eyes for a moment. His voice dropped to a hoarse whisper. "Kill him, American. I swore to God I would put a bullet in his gut for every man I lost. And now I will die here and he will live."

"Your men can carry you out."

Shaking his head, Martillo looked at his legs, then at his men. "I die here. There will be more fights before Honduras. If they carry me, they all die. And I would die here before I live as a cripple in another country. Tell me you will kill Montes and it will be enough."

Niles shook his head.

"You kill him! My men died because of him."

"But—" Niles looked at the men gathering around their wounded commander "—I will not warn him if some other man will take your order. But now we go. No more talk."

"Shoot me and go."

"Your men will carry you."

Martillo jerked the Browning out of his shoulder holster and put the pistol to his head. "All of you, go. Let me do this alone."

"Wait—" Niles turned to a contra. He pointed to the hillside where the dead Sandinistas lay. "There is an RPG there. Bring it. Comandante, you are willing to die? Will you die fighting? And give us more time?"

Only five of the contras walked away from the ambush, the two men already wounded, another man with a superficial bullet wound to a leg. Niles directed the men back over the trail, then up a rock slope. Zigzagging through the trees, they rushed into the cover of the pines along the ridgeline and broke into a run.

The rotor/turbine whine of a helicopter came from the north.

It all ended here, Martillo thought as he listened to the approaching helicopter. His life and all the years of service to Nicaragua ended here, alone, in the mud of this mountainside.

Since the day he enlisted in the National Guard, since that first day in the Elite Infantry Training School, he knew he risked death. Like other recruits, he gloried in the machismo of patriotism and death, offering their lives to Nicaragua, God, and Somoza. Instructors mocked boys who showed fear and the officers took the stage to rant in praise of the heroes of the past wars and revolutions and campaigns.

Later, in his first action, a sweep of the mountains for a band of guerrillas, he watched a hero die. Newspapers might print beautiful stories of patriotism and sacrifice, President Somoza himself might honor the hero with a medal, but Martillo remembered the soldier who had volunteered to lead a search screaming with the shock and terror of a hollow-point slug from a Sandinista rifle. The hero cried and moaned for hours, flies on his stinking guts, as the other soldiers tried to carry him back to the road. That day marked a change in the career of Martillo. He resolved, from that day on, never to risk his life for nothing. He wanted to live and fight as a soldier, not feed flies.

Of course, the officers never offered themselves on the altar of heroism. That remained the duty of the enlisted men. In the final months of the regime, officers disappeared after every defeat—and not into the unmarked pits where the

Guard buried their dead. The officers saw the end on the horizon and escaped to their foreign homes, to exile financed by their deposits in the banks of the United States and Europe. They left the enlisted men to fight heroically against the mobs and guerrillas.

In the long last months of the fight, the men trusted Martillo because he knew when to fight and when to "maneuver"—an honorable word for retreat. If the Sandinistas had snipers watching the mountain trails, Martillo took his men into the towns. If the communists had distributed rifles to the local teenagers, Martillo called for an air strike. He did not waste his men searching for hidden guerrillas.

And if the air strikes drove out the people, Martillo took the opportunity to put the young ones on the ground, their arms and legs spread, soldiers standing over them with rifles as Martillo checked their papers. When he caught a guerrilla without papers, the guerrilla—man or woman—went to Intelligence for questioning with electric shock and machetes. When he caught a sympathizer, they got a bullet in the head. The sweeps of neighborhoods and the checkpoints took more guerrillas and their teenage sympathizers than combat. And without the loss of soldiers. What did it matter if the enemy died in the mountains or the streets? Every dead enemy meant one less firefight to bleed his soldiers.

Forget the flowery eloquence of the white-uniform speeches from stages and radios and televisions. War meant killing the enemy. Victory meant living through the war. What if a soldier showed himself a hero and died? So what? Once, a lieutenant ordered Martillo to take his men down a street lined with guerrilla riflemen to recapture a Panhard armored car, an armored car the officer had lost through his cowardice. Martillo saved the lives of his men by shooting the lieutenant. For that, his men called Martillo a hero.

As the regime collapsed, the wealthy abandoned their estates. The last officers flew to Honduras in the air force planes. But the National Guard continued the fight, without their officers, without air support, without resupply, without communications—and then Somoza betrayed his soldiers and fled to Miami.

The communists took Managua. When the Sandinistas

sent out radio broadcasts demanding the surrender of all the National Guard units still fighting, Martillo did not waste time with talk of a suicidal assault to retake the palace. He looted what money he could from the banks and the homes of the rich, then seized trucks and drove his platoons north to the Honduran border. In that time of desperation and meaningless death, surviving the revolution meant victory.

Some of the Guardsmen gave up their rifles and became workers and farmers. Others continued the fight against the revolution, walking into Nicaragua and killing Sandinistas, then returning to their adopted towns on the border. Martillo took work as a policeman in El Salvador. For a year, he worked from lists of addresses, taking communist sympathizers—student radicals and union men and workers—from their houses, shooting them, dumping their bodies to be found by other sympathizers. His squads defeated the revolutionaries in the mountains of Morazón and Chalatenango by exterminating their support in the cities.

But his heart remained in the fight for his own country. Rich Nicaraguans had their condominiums and resorts, the middle class their new homes and work in the United States, but Martillo and the other soldiers who had fought for the privileges of the regime had only the privilege to fight the wars of other countries. Without money and influence, the ex-Guardsmen faced deportation at the whim of a clerk or politician. Only the liberation of Nicaragua offered an end to their exile.

Martillo supported the men still fighting. He arranged for donations to the counterrevolutionary units, transporting the money, supplies, and weapons from patrons in El Salvador to the Nicaraguans on the border. Often he found work for the fighters, arranging for a quick kill of communists in El Salvador or Guatemala that paid for weeks of fighting in Nicaragua.

Then the actions of the Sandinistas won all the support the ex-Guardsmen needed. In Nicaragua, for all the world to see, the revolutionaries revealed the truth: they had not fought to free the nation from dictatorship, they had fought to impose their own dictatorship. The common people revolted against the communist regime. Farmers walked north to Honduras and El Salvador and volunteered to fight. And in the other nations of the Americas, the rich and powerful decided to support the few men who still fought for freedom.

Salvadorian army officers introduced the Argentines to Martillo. Martillo gathered soldiers and the fight began again. When the defeat on the Malvinas Islands meant the overthrow of the generals in Buenos Aires, the North Americans replaced the Argentines. Month by month, more money and more weapons came, farmers and truckers and school teachers came to carry rifles, and the fight became a war.

But for Martillo, the war ended today. He had fought and killed the communists until they killed him. No one could expect more from him.

Patriot. Hero. Martyr to freedom. He laughed at the words. The teenagers that followed him into the war, they deserved the speeches and parades. They could have gone to California to work in the parking lots and restaurants. Instead they stayed and fought for their suffering country. And for them, he stayed here with the grenade launcher, to give them a chance to run to the safety of the border.

Rotors cut the sun, the helicopter passing low over the mountainside. Wind scoured away the dust and leaves, making the uniforms of the dead men on the trail flap like flags. He saw a machine gunner leaning out the side door of the troopship, looking down, pointing his heavy 12.7mm machine gun at the shadows. Sandinista soldiers crowded behind the gunner. As the helicopter passed, Martillo decided to die at that moment.

Trying to lift his arms, Martillo felt the weakness of his blood loss, his vision failing.

I will die now, but not before I fire the RPG, not before I knock this shit out of the sky and give my boys a chance to run, not before I give those brave young patriots who followed me into this war a chance to escape, to lead other units against the enemies of our suffering country, so that some day the world will remember us who died and know we died to free our country from the Soviets and Cubans . . .

He summoned all his strength and lurched upright, pointing the grenade launcher at the side door of the helicopter.

RECON STRIKE

The rocket flashed away as the gunner pivoted his heavy machine gun and fired, the stream of slugs slashing the earth, the impacts searching for Martillo.

But the rocket killed the gunner first. Martillo saw the man disappear and then the explosion tore through the turbines powering the rotors, the turbine fans disintegrating in a spray of shattered metal, flaming fuel showering the forest as the helicopter fell—

A kilometer away, the line of contras and Marines watched a churning ball of flame and black smoke rise from the trees. Niles paused a moment, then turned his back on the fire and continued west.

The water flickered against the blades of the idle
machine and fired, and the rotor uncurled, pushing the knife,
the machine's cutting jaw flexible...

...oil froze into one explosion core through the nuclear...
...the computer, the machine core disintegrating...
...sparked shattered metal, flaming fuel, sheet metal, the...
...the needle...inter scale...

...in fluorometer...wave...the line of contour and...inclines...
...which had a contrast beam of flame and black smoke that from

24

COLONEL Atallah recognized the Latin waiting in the
outer office. He had seen the young man driving the
limousines of Cuban delegations and serving as a
translator for diplomats at the late-night parties of United
Nations bureaucrats. Another time, the young man had
stood at the door of the ambassador's residence, checking
the names of reception guests against an official list. Now
the Cuban paced the office with an envelope in his hand.

"This courier," his clerk told Atallah, "insists on delivering his message only to you."

"Those are my instructions," the Cuban answered in
smooth Arabic.

Taking the unmarked envelope, Atallah continued into his
private office. He tore the seal and found only a sheet of
paper—without letterhead or signature—with several paragraphs typed in English:

> Unknown terrorists, believed to be counterrevolution-
> ary mercenaries, attacked the Office of Export Develop-
> ment in Managua. They murdered Secretary Raúl Con-
> dori and kidnapped the distinguished Director Emilio
> Pazos Ruiz.
>
> The terrorists looted the office, then destroyed what
> remained with fire bombs before forcing Señor Pazos to
> drive from the city in his own car. In the mountains,
> Pazos apparently tried to escape. Soldiers reported bul-
> lets fired into the car. The contras then took Señor Pazos
> from the car and cruelly executed him. The gang escaped
> into Honduras.

A doctor noted the marks of a beating on his body, but no evidence of torture.

There is no explanation for the attack on the Office of Export Development. Police believe the contras may have mistakenly assumed Señor Pazos served in some function as an adviser to the Sandinista Revolution. If the contras had succeeded in taking Pazos to Honduras, he would have undoubtedly suffered a long and terrible interrogation. However, when he attempted to escape, his wounds made his marching to Honduras impossible and the terrorists executed him—a sad end for a tireless friend of the People of Nicaragua.

It is hoped that this vicious crime will not disrupt the export enterprises already created by the Office. However, the threat of another attack by the mercenaries prevents the reopening of the Office at this time. The Governing Junta of Nicaragua and the Republic of Cuba are pledged to the concept of international cooperation outside of the conventional multinational corporate imperialism and will certainly reopen the Office after the threat is passed. In the memory of our dear comrades Secretary Raúl Condori and Director Emilio Pazos, let us maintain our existing enterprises and individually strive to open more foreign markets for the products of Nicaragua Libre.

Though the paragraphs read like an article from Barricada International, the official newspaper of the Sandinistas, Atallah realized that the page represented a coded message from the Cuban DGI.

The Americans had identified Pazos as the director of a guerrilla network in El Salvador. Perhaps they had suspected him of organizing the attack against the Marines in San Salvador. The Americans—or the Salvadorians—sent a force of ex-National Guardsmen to seize Pazos for interrogation. However, the mercenaries had blundered and killed Pazos.

The mercenaries escaped with documents from the office. This would inconvenience the guerrillas in Salvador as they shuffled their networks and changed their radio codes. But the information looted from the files detailed past actions, not the future.

Pazos had carried the details of the rocket launcher in his mind. Perhaps the mercenaries forced some information from their prisoner about the cargo container and the rockets before he attempted to escape. Perhaps he had betrayed his connections to Syria.

But Pazos had known nothing of the means of delivering the rockets to San Salvador. The date of the attack still remained uncertain. He knew only that the woman would carry the targeting device.

And what did that mean? A rumor. A prisoner telling the mercenaries of a wild conspiracy of Syrians, Iranians, Nicaraguans, and Salvadorians to attack the American embassy in San Salvador. The Americans had received many reports of Shia and Iranian plots against their Marines in Beirut. Did they respond? No.

In fact, if the contras had tortured the outline of the attack out of Pazos, the report of a rocket threat to the embassy would only add to the confusion. Rocket-propelled grenades? Katyushas? Long-range Scud missiles? An atomic missile? Would the Americans dispatch their fleets to patrol the oceans for Libyan submarines?

The last paragraph of the message instructed him to continue with the rocket attack, working directly with the Nicaraguans and Salvadorians. This also freed him to pursue other alliances with anti-American movements in the Americas.

After the destruction of the embassy, when the Americans searched through the thousands of filed threats and found a report correctly describing the attack to come, again, as in the months following the destruction of the barracks while hundreds of Marines slept, the American bureaucracy would wage war against itself. Departments would attack other departments through the media with critical statements credited to unnamed spokesmen. Commentators would analylze the resolve of the Administration to react to foreign provocations. Atallah had seen it repeated several times in the preceding year—after the bombing of the American embassy in West Beirut, the mass killing of the Marines, the bombing of the embassy in Kuwait, then the inevitable bombing of the American embassy annex in East Beirut.

And the Cubans now had the luxury of enjoying the spectacle of the attack without risk of retaliation. Only Pazos had known of the Nicaraguan and Cuban link to the Salvadorians manning the launcher. If by some chance the Americans took one of the Salvadorians prisoner, what could he tell his interrogators? Of his training at a camp somewhere in the mountains? Of a long flight in a closed aircraft to Europe? Of his training by fanatics in the Bekaa?

Any investigation ended in the Bekaa.

Atallah dialed the desk extension of his aide Ahmad Qaddam, the Spanish-speaking lieutenant who had dealt with the Cubans in the past. The young man rushed to the office of his commander.

"Our dear friend and associate Señor Pazos died in action. You are to go to Nicaragua and offer my heartfelt sympathies to his subordinates. Also, during your brief visit to that country, you are to speak with several other persons who may become our associates in the future. Here is a list of names . . ."

Only an hour later, the aide took a taxi west from Damascus. He had changed his name to Ahmad Madaya, a Lebanese representing a Middle Eastern oil company—which existed only on his business cards.

The identity papers listed Ahmad Madaya as a Shia Moslem born in Khodor, a village in the Bekaa.

Lidia Rivas knocked at the door marked 209. An electric lock buzzed. Pushing against the weight of the door, she saw only a small room of scuffed linoleum and dirty walls. When the door snapped shut behind her, a second door opened and a young man stepped out.

"Cash or money orders?"

"I want to buy dollars."

"Oh . . ." He searched her, quickly touching under her arms, the small of her back, then starting when he found the Browning under her belt. He checked the hammer with his fingers, then pulled out the pistol.

"High-power. You are a rich one."

"It is a good weapon."

"Not like the shit the Russians send. Want to sell it? I will pay in dollars."

Rivas shook her head. He confirmed the safety and put the pistol in his pocket, then resumed his search. Her tight jeans hid nothing. He went to one knee and checked her ankles. Opening her shopping bag, he looked through the stacks of córdobas.

Inside the second office, a middle-aged man worked behind a desk, totaling columns of figures with an old mechanical adding machine. Heavy iron safes stood at each side of the desk. Sunlight came through a window crossed by bars. The money-changer checked a total with a hand-held calculator and turned to her. "Good morning. How may I help you?"

"I need American one-hundred-dollar bills."

"How many?"

"Show me one."

His smile showed gold bridgework and mismatched teeth, some white, some yellowing. "You want to confirm the quality?"

"I was warned against counterfeits."

Behind her, the young man laughed. He sprawled on a couch and opened a comic book epic of kung-fu warriors. A folded Kalashnikov rifle lay on the floor.

The money-changer slid a hundred-dollar bill across the desk. Rivas held the bill up to the light of the window. Minute threads flecked the paper. She studied the scrolling of the borders and the lines of the engraving shading the face of Benjamin Franklin. All the thousands of lines appeared distinct, perfect.

"I have one of my own, I want to—"

"Compare the inks. It is your right to be careful."

She reached inside her shirt to her money belt and took out a worn banknote. Holding her own hundred-dollar bill against the other hundred, she saw that the colors of the gray and green inks matched—a counterfeiter had not printed the bills on an exotic photocopy machine.

"How much?"

The money-changer tapped numbers into the calculator. He showed the digit display to Rivas.

16,949.15. "That is," he stressed, "sixteen thousand nine hundred fifty for each one hundred."

"What?"

"That is the price."

"But fifty thousand will only buy . . ." Taking the calculator, she tried to key the number but her hand shook and she pressed the wrong numbers. Gently, the money-changer took the calculator from her hands and totaled the figures.

50,847.45. "Fifty thousand eight hundred fifty for three hundred."

"I have some American fives and tens and twenties. Can I pay some of it with those?"

"I will pay you—" He showed her the numbers: .0095.

"What is that?"

"Ten times the official rate."

"You are paying only ten thousand for every hundred but you want almost seventeen thousand to sell a hundred—no!"

His smile never failed. "Why do you want hundred dollar bills only?"

"Because I want them."

"Then go to the bank." His pale hands closed over the American bill.

"Forty thousand for the three hundreds."

"Fifty thousand."

"Forty-five."

"Forty, forty-five. There is no difference. Córdobas are worthless."

"Fifty." Replacing her U.S. bill in her money belt, she lifted her plastic shopping bag and spilled out the stacks of new currency. She broke a bank-band and counted out crisp one-hundred-córdoba notes.

"Please." Taking the stacks of bills, without tearing the bands, he thumbed through the counts, the money blurring with speed. He gave her three one-hundred-dollar bills. "Examine the money, please. Counterfeiting does occur. We must all be careful."

Again, she held the bills to the light, checking the threads in the composition of the paper, the engraving, even the serial numbers. Then the young man escorted her to the hallway and returned her pistol. "You want to sell that gun, you know—"

Rivas hurried away. Only three hundred dollars for fifty thousand córdobas. She ran down the stairs to the lobby, then out to the street. The ragged watchman who guarded the cars on the street followed her to the van. She passed him a córdoba and he took it without thanking her. Córdobas meant nothing even to beggars.

"What rate did you get?" Quezada asked her.

"You see anyone watching?"

Quezada laughed. "Only the young men watching you and the old men looking at that shopping bag of money."

"Only three one-hundreds for the fifty thousand."

"Oh, Mother of God . . . Why is it that Reagan does not buy this poor country? Fifty thousand córdobas—my father worked a day for five. For five little pesos. A day gone. And now a dollar buys . . . that's ten years of a man for every dollar."

"Forget that—" Rivas accelerated away. Looking in the rear-view mirror, she did not see any other cars leaving the curb to follow the van.

"Watch the street!"

Skidding and swerving, she avoided a military jeep speeding from a garage. Two soldiers riding in the back held up their hands. "Shit! They want to stop us! Are there soldiers behind us?"

"Watch the street. I watch the mirrors. They are not trying to stop us—" Quezada laughed. "Yes, they wanted you to stop. They wanted to live. Girl, watch your driving, your nerves are making you dangerous."

"How much more can we take out of the Cuban accounts?"

"The interior ministry manages those accounts. If we take all the money, the clerks would call for an audit—and there would be questions."

"Why can't we get the money in dollars?"

"We can. But we must go to the Cubans—"

She hit the steering wheel with her fists. "The Cubans, the ministry, the clerks. Who are we fighting? The Americans or Cubans? The guard wanted to buy my pistol. Offered me dollars. How many Brownings do we have at—what was the word at the camp? Anyone watching for us?"

"I could not find a telephone that worked. Contra sabotage, they say. Go to the Intercontinental. The telephones there are good. The ministry of communications would not allow foreigners who pay in dollars to be inconvenienced by counterrevolutionary telephones."

Gasoline rationing had taken much of the private traffic off the streets. She forced herself not to study the few cars behind her as she sped south, weaving around motorcycles and bicycles. At the Calle Colón, she stopped for a line of slow-moving military transports blocking the intersection. The trucks carried hundreds of campesinos and militiamen for a demonstration at the Presidential Palace. They waved plastic flags of Nicaragua and the Sandinista Front.

Whipping between two trucks, Rivas accelerated past the convoys, speeding for a block, then braking at a checkpoint. Quezada showed his Ministry of the Interior identification and the guards allowed the van to continue to a parking lot filled with rented cars. North Americans and Europeans— reporters, journalists, technicians—stood in groups, talking.

Quezada slid low in the seat to hide his face and eye patch. "Look at the cameras . . ."

"I will take you to the front entrance."

"Those cameras. Cameras, video cameras, film cameras, recorders. Show our pistols, load this truck until the springs go flat. Hijack a plane to—to where? Where could we sell all that shit?"

"What?"

"Hawaii. Sell it to the tourists. Forget the international revolution and live on the beach. Or we go to New York and start our own news network. Laugh, girl. I am joking. Let me joke when I can and let me hear you laugh sometimes. Inconvenience those journalists? And make the propaganda ministry angry? Then we would have problems—"

As she slowed at the front of the hotel, Quezada threw open the door and stepped out while the van rolled. He hurried through the lobby to the line of coin telephones. Rivas parked on the Calle Colón and watched for cars with two men in the front seat—the sign of the interior ministry. Groups of journalists walked past her. She heard English and French. In the rear-view mirror, she saw the parking lot, where technicians continued loading equipment into the rented cars. She moved the mirror and watched the checkpoint.

A form moved in her peripheral vision and she started, her hand going to the pistol as she turned in the seat. A sunburned Anglo with red veins in his face shouted through the window, "Taxi?"

After shaking her head, she ignored him. The foreigner slammed the door and rejoined his associates. Then she saw Quezada rushing back to the van.

"To the airport. There is a Lebanese coming."

Following the instructions relayed from the camp, Rivas met Ahmad Madaya at an airport car-rental agency. The young man seemed exhausted—his clothes wrinkled, his eyes red from fatigue, his face shadowed with a two-day growth of beard.

"Do you want to go to your hotel?"

"There is no time," he told her in his slow, limited Spanish. "We talk with your officer now."

"Would you prefer to speak English? I can translate to Colonel Quezada."

"I speak your language."

Rivas led him through the terminal. Hippies and chic radicals from arriving charter flights shouted to one another, exchanging room numbers and addresses as their Sandinistas tour guides tried to announce assignments. Wealthy Nicaraguans stood in long lines, struggling with suitcases and boxes. Rivas saw an interior ministry agent questioning a young man in a ticket line, demanding the young man's identity card while two soldiers approached—a draft evader. A woman cried out and clutched the arm of the agent.

Outside, she wove through the taxis and buses, staying several steps ahead of Madaya. Drivers called to her, announcing the names of hotels. Militiamen waited at trucks, banners on the sides of the trucks painted with the names of cooperatives in English, French, and German.

A line of battered transport buses blocked her sight of the van. Stopping between two buses, she scanned the parking lot. Cars bumped over the broken asphalt, men and women talked at trucks, families loaded luggage—anyone could be maintaining surveillance. Quezada signaled her and she continued to the van.

"Where is the Arab?"

"There." Rivas threw open the side door. "He wants to talk with you now. No hotel, no—"

"Drive out to the highway." Quezada turned and introduced himself as Madaya got into the back seat. "I am Colonel Quezada. What business brings you to Nicaragua?"

"The export. The Cuban is gone. The time of export comes soon. I come to talk of the export."

Quezada spoke slowly and distinctly. "My men are finished with the school?"

"Yes, soon. Soon finish."

"The Cuban promised a demonstration. I sent my men to Lebanon but there was no demonstration. I want a demonstration."

"Here? Impossible!"

"In Lebanon!" Rivas shouted back to Madaya. Turning to face him, she allowed the van to drift to the shoulder of the airport access lanes. "We will go to Lebanon to see the demonstration of—"

Quezada shoved the steering wheel on line. "Watch the road! Drive!"

"Tell him Lebanon—"

"Not here. We will go to Lebanon to see the rockets."

"You go to Lebanon? You and woman? Why woman?"

"She speaks English. And the export goes to her. There will be a radio, correct? She will work the radio. She wants to see the demonstration."

"Lebanon, why not?" Madaya shrugged. "You and woman will see the rockets. Then we export."

25

AT a table in the back room of Reyal Entertainment, Hijazi watched as Muhammed Ali Foruhar inspected the components. The Iranian checked the French and German invoices against his list, then compared the shipping lists to the identification numbers of every part. He took the computer circuit boards out of the padded boxes and eyed each assembly. He pulled over another lamp and switched on the bulb, bathing the circuit boards in stark light.

"Is not the quality equal to the other electronics?" Hijazi asked.

"Oh, yeah. Looks okay. Won't know nothing until I test it all. But I know I got what I paid for."

"Did you, sir, have any doubt?"

Foruhar laughed. "Whip your ass if I did."

"I personally confirmed every invoice."

"Yeah. And I pay for you personally confirming it, too."

"This is very extraordinary merchandise. Do you realize a United States of America Customs agent inquired as to the destination of those . . . I forget the name of the part. It was fortunate that I had ordered the part from Germany for shipment to my French air cargo agent. My agent offered a suitable, though false, explanation. Mr. Foruhar, please understand, I am required to invest considerable—"

"Hey, I pay, right? I complain but I pay. And I pay cash so it's not like I can stop payment on the check if you rip me off."

"I have no such intention."

"Hey, I know. You like my money. And you know it is not good to rip off some dude who's got a gang of crazy Pasdaran on line."

"My first concern is always the satisfaction of the customer, regardless of—"

"Okay, okay, all this looks straight. I won't hassle you no more. I got another list. Get it, drop it off here. But I don't want problems, understand?"

"It is only necessary to say a word to my dear associate Reyal, and I will immediately come to your apartment or workshop and discuss—"

"I come here. Got it? I come here."

"But may I call you?"

"From Beirut? Waste of time. I tried to call you, took hours, got some bitch who talked French. Next time, I'll radio Damascus, tell them to telex—" Foruhar cut off in mid-sentence, reconsidering what he said. He brought out a typed sheet. "Here's the new list, here's the money I owe you, here's front money on this order—"

Foruhar counted out a stack of one-hundred-dollar bills. As Hijazi recounted the money and prepared a receipt, the Iranian walked through the shop to the street. He returned with other Revolutionary Guards. Hijazi kept his face down, writing, as the young men gathered armloads of the boxes and returned to the truck parked on the street.

"In a week?" Foruhar called.

"If not sooner, sir."

The clerks watched the Land Rover drive away. Reyal came down the stairs from the second-floor office. He closed the door to the shop before he told Hijazi:

"This is the last time that Iranian brought fear to my shop."

"Reyal, there is no reason to—"

"Then there is no reason you cannot take this business to your cousin Raman. Whatever your business is with that strange creature—"

Hijazi held out a one-hundred-dollar bill. Reyal shook his head.

"I want nothing to do with that business."

"Will you direct him to Raman?"

"After today, we will direct the Iranian to your cousin."

Leaving the shop, Hijazi stopped in the doorway and squinted into the midday glare, his eyes scanning the street. Few people risked shopping today. The Islamic radio station had reported a series of Hezbollah victories against the Zionists in the south. In the past, the Israelis had retaliated for terror bombings with air strikes. Hijazi saw only shop-keepers and Syrian soldiers on the sidewalks.

Loudspeakers blared music into the street, electronic rock, Arabic voices, and the sultry crooning of American women singers competing for the attention of the few possible customers. At the shop next to Hijazi, a traditional Arabic melody wove through the noise of passing cars and motorcycles. A group of off-duty soldiers passed Hijazi. They glanced in the window at a display of videocassettes. As they went to the next window, the shopkeeper ejected the Arabic cassette and dropped in another. The loud-speaker blasted a French disco song. One of the soldiers asked the price of the tape. Past the soldiers, a taxi parked on the sidewalk. The driver and a clerk talked in a door-way.

Looking past the traffic, Hijazi searched the shadowed doorways on the opposite side of the street. Clerks arranged displays in windows. Shopkeepers paced from the counters to the sidewalk, waiting for customers. He had parked his truck on the sidewalk in front of the shop of his cousin—where a teenage cousin washed the truck with a soapy rag.

Hijazi saw no one watching Reyal Entertainment.

Crossing the street, he went back to the shop of his elder cousin Raman. He scanned the other shopfronts, seeing only the faces of competitors and associates. The rhythm of business continued despite the threat of air strikes. He saw nothing extraordinary—but then, if he worked for Syrian counterintelligence, he would not send agents to watch a suspicious shop, he would hire one of the shopkeeper's envious competitors. For that reason, he must not vary the pattern of his business. In fact, Reyal forcing him to meet the strange, American-speaking Iranian at the shop of Raman eliminated a deviation in his routine. Now he would conduct all his business as usual, delivering—

"That is him." A clerk pointed at Hijazi.

Two Syrians in suits turned from the counter. All his cousins watched as Hijazi faltered a step, then continued into the shop, forcing himself not to turn and run from the men he recognized as Syrian agents. Of what intelligence branch, who knows? In addition to the several competing departments of the secret police protecting the regime of Hafez al-Assad, the three branches of the armed forces each had intelligence and counterintelligence units. The efficiency and rivalry of the services kept the cells of Mezze Prison always occupied and the interrogators continuously employed.

Hijazi felt his pulse beating at his temples, his throat going dry as he approached the Syrians. Sunglasses hid their eyes. Very young, perhaps only thirty, they wore cheap off-the-rack suits of inferior ComBloc cloth. The suit coats stretched over the muscles of their shoulders. Barbers had cut their hair, not stylists. Hijazi guessed they served in one of the intelligence units of the Syrian army, where commanders promoted intelligent and experienced officers directly from the field.

"You are the importer?"

"Mine is a small and insignificant company. However, if there is any way that I may be of any service to the esteemed gentlemen—"

"Come."

They did not seize him or point a pistol, but the pulsing in his temples became a crashing. When he had served in the Lebanese army, he had fought the various militias, he had heard bullets rip past his head—once he had felt a bullet flick his uniform. When Captain Niles and the Marines flew into the Bekaa in a captured Soviet MI-8 helicopter troopship, Hijazi accompanied the Americans into the territory of the Islamic gangs. In all those actions, he felt the inevitable fear, yet he had a weapon and his training and exhilaration carried him through the combat. But now he felt terror as they escorted him to the sidewalk. Did they somehow know of the recording machines? Or did this involve the Iranian?

"We want what that shopkeeper sells. But we object to his prices."

Hijazi smiled. "Oh, of course . . ."

They had sought him out for profit. Like many other Syrian soldiers stationed in the Bekaa, they wanted to buy foreign products available in Lebanon for resale in Syria. The special relationship of the armed forces to the Assad regime allowed soldiers returning to Syria on leave to avoid the formalities of import restrictions or customs taxes. However, the orders they discussed—American and European luxury foods, Japanese electronics, an eclectic selection of Arabic, European, and American music and films—indicated they had ambitions to become major importers.

As Hijazi returned to his office in East Beirut, he marveled at the diversity of his company—electronic intelligence to the United States, free market luxuries to the socialist dictatorship of Syria, and restricted American electronics to the Iranian Revolutionary Guard. And he owed his success to Captain Niles and the Central Intelligence Agency. The Marine had introduced him to the CIA. The CIA had financed the opening of his company. His CIA-financed company had undercut the prices of other importers and therefore won the good will of his cousins. The good will of his cousin Raman had led to the electronic surveillance of the Syrians and Iranians for the National Security Agency. The continued trade in consumer electronics and entertainment had led Muhammed Ali Foruhar to him. Now he began another enterprise forwarding tons of luxury goods direct to Syria.

The time had come to find a warehouse in the Bekaa. Reyal had demanded that he take his business with the Iranian elsewhere. The Syrian intelligence officers had unnerved Raman and his cousins—soon Raman would ask him to remove the scanners. Though he had not yet received a deposit from the Syrians on their first shipment, those two officers did not represent a minority in the army. Despite their socialist government and their Communist Bloc allies, many of the Syrians stationed in Lebanon looked for opportunities to make money.

A warehouse in the Bekaa would allow him to exploit business opportunities without involving his hesitant cousins and associates. His competitors maintained shops and warehouses in Shtaura, on the main highway between Beirut and Damascus. However, with his rented warehouse in Jounieh and his contacts in Baalbek, he needed a location near the junction of the Jounieh-to-Baalbek road.

But that would be difficult. A warehouse in the town of Baalbek meant all his cargos would be subject to Syrian and militia inspection. He needed a building outside of the checkpoints. At one time, several manufacturing companies had operated on the north-south highway to Zahle. However, the Israelis had destroyed one complex of buildings and the Revolutionary Guards working with Foruhar had taken the other. What shops and small garages remained would be inadequate—there must be space for a guard, for the merchandise, and the American scanning equipment.

At his office in Jdaide, messages waited on his answering machine. He retyped the list of components ordered by Foruhar as he listened to the playback. When he heard the precise, university French of one caller, he recognized the voice before he heard the name. Hijazi wrote down the address of the nightclub and left without reviewing his other calls and telexes. This business took priority.

Weaving through the crowd on the patio, Hijazi entered the smoke and noise of the cabaret. A Lebanese band faked American top-forty songs, a girl with wild black hair posturing on the stage as the musicians mechanically played the chords and bass line, the music and beat a physical force. Stylish men and women stood in groups at the bar, drinking and shouting over the band. Hijazi searched the faces. He walked to the back of the cabaret, scanning the bar and the tables and the dance floor, twice seeing the black man before he recognized the handsome foreigner dancing with the sleek young blonde as Lieutenant Stark.

Hijazi sat alone at the bar and waited, casually sipping a drink and watching the dance floor. He had never seen the

American in civilian clothes—only the uniforms of the United States and Syria. Tonight he wore expensive fashions straight out of a New York magazine. A stylist had trimmed his short, tightly curled hair. When the band paused, Stark talked with the blond woman—then he saw Hijazi waiting at the bar. He exchanged notes with the woman and left her.

"We talk here?" Hijazi asked.

"We leave. She's a Swede with the United Nations. Palestinian relief."

"How did you meet her?"

"No one else would dance with me."

"You did not come to dance. What is our business?"

They left, Stark walking out first, Hijazi following after he finished his iced tea. A cool wind came from the Mediterranean, the smell of the ocean refreshing after the alcohol and tobacco stink of the cabaret. Hijazi watched the traffic. One car flashed its headlights, then veered to the curb. He talked with Stark as they followed the wide, sweeping boulevard from the metropolitan center of East Beirut to the coastal road leading north to Jounieh.

"The captain did not answer my letters or cables. Is not the captain stationed in Honduras?"

"We're still there, but the communications are not ideal. I brought a new address for you. Communicate via that address. We do get summaries of your material and the captain follows all that with extreme interest. I would have come sooner to talk with you about the Iranian but—but this is a very small operation. Underfunded and overexploited. Your work is very important, yet we cannot devote the time necessary to monitor and analyze your information. When the summaries come, we read them. The captain sends his apologies."

"I am not offended." He glanced at the slip of paper—a post office box in Alexandria, Virginia. "It is better you have little contact with me. My business in the Bekaa is extremely dangerous. If the Syrians or the Iranians or the Hezbollah thought I dealt with the Americans, it would be my end."

"Does the Iranian trust you?"

"No. But as he says, I can deliver."

"What did you see inside the factory?"

"He receives the components and tools he orders at a shop in Baalbek. I offered to deliver the merchandise directly to his workshop. He would not allow that. He thinks his factory is a secret from me."

"That factory is on the main north-south highway?"

"Do you not remember it? By chance, it is the very same concern where we asked to use a telephone. It was that night to capture the Iranian."

Stark laughed. "No wonder they didn't let you and Javenbach in."

"No, they were not there at that time. A truck company operated the enterprise. Then, only recently, the Pasdaran took the facility. It is a very large building. There are work areas outside. I see cargo trailers there. All the workers are Pasdaran. There is a wire fence with concertina. There are Pasdaran guarding the gates."

"You watched the factory?"

"Only for a few minutes. It would be very dangerous if the Pasdaran learned of my interest."

"Is it possible to take a house or a building near the Iranians? For observation?"

Hijazi considered the question for several seconds. "For observation only?"

"No. It must look like a legitimate business. Trucks and workers coming and going."

"A warehouse?"

"With a direct line of sight on the Iranians, if possible."

"There is a complex. Several buildings. Warehouses. But there is damage. It may be very costly to repair."

"Estimate what you need, the money will be deposited in your account."

"And one other thing. Very important. This complex was a place the Syrians used. They put antiaircraft guns there. And the Israelis bombed it. Please, for all of us, contact the Israelis and tell them that I am not working with the Syrians."

"I will definitely do that."

"Even if they observe Iranians and Syrians stopping at this warehouse."

"Iranians? Syrians? Why will—"

"Lieutenant, the circumstances do not allow the luxury of a legitimate business. A company establishing a legitimate business in the Bekaa would be immediately suspect. What is normal for the Bekaa is hashish and weapons and smuggled electronics. But is not a normal—" he stressed the word "—and accepted business equal to your requirements?"

26

NILES ran up the steel stairs and through the door of the JetStar, leaving the midday heat and kerosene stink of Toncontín for the air-conditioned interior of the Air Force commuter plane. Colonel Devlin closed the door, cutting the noise of the airfield. Niles saw no one else in the passenger cabin.

"Where are the pilots?"

"Taking a tour of the city."

Then Niles saw the stacks of boxes and shipping cases. "Why the equipment?"

"You and the men will leave Honduras immediately."

"To where?"

"Stand by. I'll brief you. I brought the transcripts of the interrogations."

"What did the man know?"

"The Cuban you brought back was not Pazos."

"What?"

"We understand the error. Fortunately, you brought back that second prisoner, the lieutenant. He is cooperating. He explained the circumstances."

"That was Pazos! We checked his identification."

"Pazos is dead . . ."

Devlin passed two photos to Niles. One of the black-and-white prints showed the Mexican passport of Emilio Pazos. The other photo showed the man Niles had brought back from Nicaragua a week before. Side to side, he instantly recognized the men as different. But their hair and the shape of the faces matched.

"Why did he have that passport? Why did he come down that road?"

"He is Felix Maruri, a DGI security man with the Cuban embassy in Managua. The morning of his capture, a report had come in of a dead Cuban found in the mountains. He and the other man, the Nicaraguan lieutenant, flew to Palaca-guina to identify the body. Maruri confirmed the dead man to be Pazos and took the miscellaneous personal effects found on the body—that is why he carried the identification of Pazos. Then he directed the driver to take them to the camp outside of the town. Under drug interrogation, he said he wanted to question the colonel in the murder of Pazos."

"He thought the Nicaraguans may have killed the Cuban? Why?"

"Maruri said only that the questions would have been routine. The interrogation specialists believe he is succeeding in withholding information despite the intensive questioning and drugs."

"They haven't broken him?"

"They are confident it will be only a matter of time, once he realizes his isolation and—"

"And that you've got him forever." Niles nodded. "A professional. They trained him to take it. Chances are, he won't break. Maybe he'll deal information for a chance to get traded to Cuba. But that will take time—"

"Months."

"We don't have months. When Stark gets back from Beirut, we'll go back into Nicaragua and get those other two, the colonel and the woman."

"No."

"They know what we need to know. There's no other way to get the information."

"The colonel and the woman are secondary."

"With Pazos gone, who else can we take?"

"We need to turn to the operation Pazos initiated with the Syrians. That operation is continuing—and I believe they may be preparing for an attack somewhere in the Americas. I sent Lieutenant Stark to Beirut because the scanners monitoring the low-power frequencies of the Revolutionary Guards picked up Spanish."

"Nicaraguans in the Bekaa?"

"Their nationality is unknown. But the intercepted transmissions confirm that a Revolutionary Guard unit is working with a group of Central Americans there. The leader of that unit is also buying electronic components."

"What type of electronics?"

"Civilian. Computer components, relays, sensors. There are no direct weapons applications for the components but it is a point of concern."

"Why wouldn't he get what he needs through Syria? Or Iran?"

"That is one of our questions. We also monitor telex traffic between Cuba and Syria. The DGI sent a telex to Colonel Nazim Atallah, the Syrian army intelligence colonel who has an office at the Darai base. He directs that end of the operation. The telex informed him of the death of their associate Pazos."

"This is the Syrian in Damascus? Pazos was there when his gang murdered the embassy Marines? The Syrian who worked with the Iranians on the twenty-three October bombing?"

"Correct. What was odd was that the message was in English and that it took the form of a news release. Here is a copy."

Niles skimmed the page. "Any chance that Montes sent a squad in to grab Pazos?"

"No."

"An independent unit? Out to hit Cubans?"

"Possible. But unlikely. The operation would have involved men operating in Managua. Vehicles, documents, surveillance of the office and personnel. Last year, the FDN sent a man into Managua. The Sandinistas took him the same day. If an organization of freedom fighters has the ability to operate in the capital, we don't know about them."

"Maybe the Nicaraguan colonel did kill the Cuban. But why?"

"Ideology. Ambition. Conflicts among conspirators are the rule rather than the exception. However, the death of Pazos did not break the link between the Syrian end of the operation and the Nicaraguans and Salvadorians."

Devlin took several eight-by-ten inch photos from his briefcase.

The first print, a black-and-white enlargement, showed the profiles of two men at a partially open car door. Motion blurred their features. In the background, a group of women in chadors crowded onto a bus marked with Arabic script.

In a second black-and-white photo, Niles recognized the profile of Pazos as he got into the car. The second man—sharp featured, thin—also appeared to be a Latin.

Devlin laid a third photo on the table. In color, with sharp focus and depth-of-field, the photo showed the young man again, this time with a young woman. They leaned against the counter of an Avis Rent-a-Car booth. All the signs had Spanish words and prices in U.S. dollars and córdobas.

With the quality of the color photo, Niles identified the young man as Middle Eastern, not Latin. Niles recognized the woman immediately—then he checked himself, taking a few seconds to study her. She leaned against the counter, her head turned, her features in profile, the curves of her body accentuated by her posture. He compared the woman in the photo to his memory of the woman in El Salvador and the training camp in Nicaragua.

"That's Marianela, the one that escaped in Morazón. That picture's taken in Nicaragua, right?"

"The first two photos are Pazos leaving the arrivals terminal at the Damascus airport and going to the car of Atallah. The second man is an aide to Atallah. Those photos are courtesy of the Mossad. They had no positive name on the aide, but he traveled to Nicaragua—via Madrid and Santa Domingo under the name of Madaya and he spoke Spanish. He sent a cablegram from Madrid to Managua giving his flight number and instructions for one of the export associates to meet him—a code number routed the cablegram to the group Pazos had commanded. The woman met him at the car rental counter of Sandino International. She took Madaya to the Nicaraguan colonel . . ."

Devlin laid other color photos on the table. One photo showed Madaya entering a passenger van. Another photo showed the van leaving the airport parking lot. Glare and shadow reduced the three passengers to silhouettes. But

Niles did see the suggestion of a man's face, his features sharp, one eye covered with a black oval—the commander of the camp in the mountains.

"That's him."

"We did not receive any information on their meeting. But this Syrian also met with a Guatemalan exile representing the Guerrilla Army of the Poor—a hard-core Marxist insurgent group. And later the same day with a Colombian of the M-19 movement."

"And with the Cubans?"

"Not that we observed. He left Nicaragua the next day, flying through Santo Domingo to Spain, not Havana. Which is significant because—"

"It looks like they cut out the Cubans. Send us to take him—and the woman. They know what's going on."

"No. My judgment is that they are secondary players in this. An unknown force takes Pazos? Then the colonel and his woman disappear? The Syrian will assume we are attacking his organization cell by cell. He will dispatch the unit of Central Americans to their target—with weapons and explosives for the attack. But before that attack, Atallah will disband his organization."

"So we go direct? We take the Syrian?"

"Not the Syrian. Damascus is impossible. The Daraiya base is more than impossible."

"Baalbek . . ."

Thousands of meters above the forested mountains of Honduras, Alvarez and Vatsek studied a computer-generated map of central Lebanon. The long, narrow map—actually several projections joined end-to-end by tape—showed roads, villages, and topography from the coast port of Jounieh to the Syrian border. Other maps, satellite photos, and color snapshots added details to the area. On the oversized map, symbols in various colors of ink marked the highway. The symbols formed a pattern around Baalbek. Colonel Devlin explained the marks:

"Red, the forces of the Syrian army. Green, the militias. The highway, the back roads."

Some of the photos showed checkpoints manned by Syrians and groups of Islamic militiamen—the Iranians and Hezbollah fanatics searching cars and trucks, interrogating individuals at the roadsides. Entire families stood with their hands in the air as the fanatics waved Kalashnikov rifles.

"And we're going in there?" Alvarez asked, incredulous.

"Closed trucks take us in. This shows where we go." Niles held up a satellite photo of the highway. "This was a factory and warehouse until the Syrians put antiaircraft guns in it. The Israelis wiped it out. But there's still a warehouse three stories high. From there, we can look out at the area without exposing ourselves. When we can make our move, we place electronic surveillance equipment. Check it, get out. Then our people there will service the machines. We won't be there more than two nights."

"Ah . . . yes, sir." Alvarez pointed to the photos of the checkpoints. "They won't stop our trucks?"

"We'll go through as cargo."

"Hijazi?"

Niles nodded. "He's been working there for months, setting this up. He has a going business now, importing from Europe and Japan and the United States, selling to Syrians and the Iranians. We go in as one more load."

"Actually," Devlin explained, "the route will not require that you cross the checkpoints around the town. The trucks will be exposed to cursory examinations only. Once you get to the warehouse, you will proceed as the situation dictates. In addition to the electronics the mission requires, you will have Syrian and militia uniforms—a Soviet uniform for you, Sergeant Vatsek. Civilian clothing purchased in Hungary. ComBloc weapons. Nothing of United States origin. Except the surveillance electronics, which were purchased on civilian market and modified by our technicians. Comments, Sergeants?"

"Javenbach going with us?" Vatsek asked.

"He is waiting in Washington. Lieutenant Stark is in Jounieh."

"Great. Sounds straight to me . . ." Vatsek glanced at the cardboard shipping cases that lay in the aisle of the JetStar. Some of the open boxes contained cameras and lenses, other boxes rifles and ammunition. Vatsek reached into a box and took out a PKM machine gun. He lounged back in the leather chair and hinged open the feed cover. "A straight-out recon in force."

At Andrews Air Force Base outside of Washington, D.C., Corporal Ali Akbar Javenbach waited in the limousine, staring through the tinted glass windows to the expanse of heat-shimmering concrete. The JetStar taxied to waiting technicians in orange uniforms. As the plane eased to a stop, the technicians rushed to their work, a supervisor with a radio and a clipboard directing the technicians through their duties.

For the past several months, since a Kalashnikov slug punched through his left leg, Javenbach had remained on light duty, limping to an office in the Old Executive Office Building. There, he studied the captured files of Fahkr Rajai, the Revolutionary Guard officer who had coordinated the arming of the Islamic militias in Lebanon. The thousands of typewritten and handwritten pages recorded more than a year of activity in Lebanon as Rajai developed his contacts with the militias of Beirut. The Iranian had recorded information on hundreds of fighters and gang leaders, detailing their backgrounds and skills, noting his contacts with each fighter. Many of the files contained photos. After Javenbach divided the files into levels of security clearance, Colonel Devlin then distributed the files to translators in the Central Intelligence Agency and the National Security Agency.

However, Colonel Devlin did not allow one group of files to leave the offices of the NSC. Those files detailed the day-by-day activities of Rajai with the gangs that had taken part in the murder of 241 Marines on 23 October, 1983. Devlin assigned Javenbach to the task of translating those pages. Working alone, Javenbach keyed those files into a word processor, then translated the Farsi into English. The information went to trusted analysts in the bureaucracies of the NSC, CIA, and Defense Intelligence Agency, the counter-terrorist specialists and academics who studied the threat of Iranian and Syrian terrorism against the democracies of the world.

Javenbach had met with a few of these analysts—though

they had talked intelligently and forcefully of the terrorist threat posed by Iran, they had qualified their comments by stressing the regional strategic importance of Iran. All the specialists said the Soviet Union, not Iran, presented the greatest threat to peace in the Middle East and Asia and that the United States must soon reestablish diplomatic relations with Iran to counter Soviet threats to the Persian Gulf.

The specialists ignored the threat of Khomeini. Only five years before, Javenbach had fought in the revolution. He saw mullahs urging their fanatics into the machine guns of the Shah's army. The fighters who survived the suicidal attacks dipped their hands in the blood of the dead and used the blood to scrawl verses across their own faces and chests. Then they rushed the guns again. In those battles, Iranians fought Iranians and the army surrendered after killing thousands of their countrymen.

His father and brother died in the struggle, his father executed in the prisons of the Shah, his brother murdered for speaking against the ravings of the mullahs. Javenbach saw a death-worshiping regime of fanatics rising out of the chaos and he took his extended family away from Iran, to the United States. He joined the Marines to demonstrate his gratitude to the nation that provided a home to his family. When Lieutenant Stark interviewed Javenbach for a covert mission, Javenbach volunteered without question. Captain Niles took him into combat against the Pasdaran.

In the months he recovered from his wound, Javenbach tried to explain the insane fervor of the Islamic Revolution. But the experts countered that Iran would someday return to the modern world and that the United States government must be waiting to talk with the new Iran.

Talk—the experts knew nothing. They deluded themselves with their talk of diplomacy. Diplomacy could not stop the Pasdaran—only death. Grant the fanatics the martyrdom they wanted. Assassinate their leaders, bomb their gangs, destroy their weapons—reduce the Pasdaran to only a mob of fanatics with no power outside of Iran.

Field workers finally pushed stairs to the cabin door of the JetStar. He waited until the door eased open, then left the limousine, his Air Force pass in his hand, the technicians staring at the slim young man in the shaggy black hair and black beard who ran up the stairs and slipped into the jet.

When the door opened again, the technicians saw a graying executive—sunglasses hiding his eyes, his face downturned—descend to the limousine. The JetStar left minutes later, for an unknown destination.

In the radio room of the hacienda in the mountains west of Palacaguina, Nicaragua, a coded message clicked from the monitor of the radio room. The lieutenant recorded the message and decoded the first line—then stopped and called across the courtyard for Quezada.

"It is only for you, Colonel."

The first line used the standard five-character mathematical code used for the radio traffic between the camp in Nicaragua and their agents in Salvador. That line authorized only the commander to proceed with the decoding. A name signed that line—El Lobo, one of the boys sent to Lebanon. At that point, the code shifted to a one-time code of nonrepeating numerical sequences—impossible to decipher even with supercomputers and a staff of mathematicians.

Ahmad Madaya had passed sheets of the one-time codes to Quezada three days before when they talked in the van. Now, the colonel peeled the plastic cover from the first sheet to reveal the codes and decoded the message letter by letter. Rivas came into the radio room as he worked.

"The demonstration is confirmed," he told her. "We are to fly to Madrid. Then we wait for their agents. They will arrange all the travel and papers from there to Lebanon."

"Finally! No longer do we work for the Cubans . . ."

27

ALUMINUM scraped sand. The headlights fanned across an expanse of beach, illuminating rocks and drifts of sand, long slashes of black stretching between the ridges. Behind the lights, the vehicle remained invisible within the predawn darkness. Niles jerked back the cocking handle of the Kalashnikov and stepped from the boat. Warm water swept over his shoes. He rushed to the beach and dropped flat, crawling from the wave-swept high-tide sand to the rocks. There, he stayed below the headlight beams and scanned the beach.

A few kilometers to the south, across the wide bay, the lights of the Maronite Christian city of Jounieh rose from the Mediterranean. In the spring of 1983, Niles had taken a weekend leave there, spending almost a month's pay on overpriced hotels and restaurants. Marinas and resorts lined the beaches. Villas spread up the mountainsides. After his months training soldiers in Beirut, the peace of the Maronite enclave, untouched by the war, seemed unreal. Teenagers crowded the beaches on weekends, the wealthy waterskiied in the bay or took their yachts into the Mediterranean.

Warlords operated the shipping docks, collecting taxes on the importers—like Shaffik Hijazi—who offloaded cargos of goods destined for all the nations of the Middle East. The Lebanese customs office did not receive the taxes. The authority of the government of Lebanon extended no farther than the checkpoints south of the city. Phalangist troops maintained other checkpoints closer to the commercial center and patrolled the streets. The importers, merchants, and residents paid their taxes and fees directly to the Phalange, the Phalange then paid the government officials to continue the pretense of civil government in the otherwise independent city.

Niles waited and listened. He heard only the hiss of the gentle shorebreak. Waves slapped the aluminum of the boat. Nothing moved. Niles signaled the other Marines with two clicks from his hand radio. They splashed from the boat, bolts clacking back to chamber cartridges in their rifles. Shoes ran through the sand, forms passed across the lights of the city. Then silence. The Americans waited, listening. Niles keyed his hand radio:

"El viejo está aquí."

The headlights went black. Flashlights waved through darkness as two figures came down from the road. Niles waited, watching the men. He recognized the tall, wide-shouldered form of Lieutenant Stark and the shorter, stocky Hijazi.

"Looking for us?"

"Yes, sir. Truck's waiting."

"Hey, Shaffik. Long time no see."

"Captain Niles. I am very glad you returned. It is a pleasure to assist you again."

"We'll see about that. How's business?"

"For me, excellent."

"Making money off the Iranians?"

"Yes, sir. I have been fortunate in my dealings. However, another merchant was not. This information is too recent for me to have reported. The Iranians approached a merchant by the name of Saada. They bought Soviet rockets from him—"

"Katyushas?"

"Yes, sir. And then this man Saada disappeared. His son went to various associates, inquiring as to his father, and he also disappeared."

"Interesting. But tell me about it later."

The Marines unloaded the boat and pushed the hull clear of the sand. The Israeli contract man took the boat back into the darkness of the Mediterranean, returning to the coastal freighter waiting a kilometer offshore. Staggering under the loads of weapons, equipment, and miscellaneous uniforms, the Americans followed Hijazi to the road.

There, Hijazi crouched under a semi-truck and trailer. A sheet of metal swung down, exposing a hatch in the bottom of the trailer. Niles stood and swept a penlight across the interior of the trailer. Crated motorcycles and cardboard shipping boxes walled off one end of the trailer. The forward half remained empty.

"You've taken this truck into their territory?" Niles asked.

"There is no problem with this. I traveled with this truck to Baalbek only two days ago."

Lifting the equipment through the trap door, they climbed into the trailer. The large area allowed the Americans to sprawl on the plank cargo deck.

"I have placed plywood on the sides to stop sound, but you must not speak when we stop. God willing, they will pass the truck again without examination."

Gray light came through air vents at the roofline as the truck lurched over the highway, the noise of the tires reverberating in the trailer. The Marines rode in silence. Alvarez switched on his scanner and listened to the frequencies, from time to time motioning for Niles to listen to an Arabic exchange.

A few minutes after leaving the beach, the truck stopped for the first checkpoint. They heard the voices of soldiers and drivers through the air vents. But the truck rolled again immediately. The engine labored as Hijazi low-geared up the steep grade of the mountain road. Time passed and the men slept in the half-darkness.

As the sun rose, the trailer warmed. They woke and stripped off their sea-damp civilian clothes, putting on their ComBloc fatigue pants and boots—then sat and sweated, the cool high-altitude air of the mountains no relief as the plywood walls of the trailer heated.

"Why couldn't He-jazz," Vatsek asked out loud, "smuggle ice cream? And cold Coors? And cool, cool women for the Arab sheiks? Take us into the desert righteously fucked."

Hours passed before the road angled down. As the truck gained speed, the trailer swayed from side to side as Hijazi swept through the turns, making good time as he descended into the Bekaa. Dry lowland air came through the vents. The plywood walls became hot. Their sweat flowed as they endured the claustrophobic semi-darkness and heat in silence, even Vatsek suffering without words. Niles glanced at his watch, estimating the distance remaining until—

The truck slowed. Niles told the others, "Sixth Battalion. Sunnis and Shias. Paid by Lebanon and Syria. Sometimes take orders from Syria, sometimes Beirut. But all the time, they're on their own. I've been there. They check identification and take their payoff. We'll slide through quick."

Brakes squealing, the trailer shuddering, the truck came to a complete stop. After hours of road noise and vibration, the silence seemed total. Then they heard cars and trucks passing in the opposite direction. Wind whistled through the vents but the air in the trailer heated. They smelled their sweat going rank. From time to time, the truck lurched forward, advancing in the line of waiting vehicles.

Outside, the voices of boys called, offering iced drinks to the drivers. Niles looked over to Alvarez. But the sergeant monitored the radio channels, wearing his headphones. Sweat streaming down his body, Niles laughed quietly to himself at the irony—if he had not studied Arabic, he would not know of the ice only an arm's reach away. Then again, if he had not learned Arabic, he would not be on the highway to Baalbek—

"Out of the truck!"

Niles forced himself not to react to the shout. The other Marines had heard the soldiers outside. Alvarez took off his headphones. Of the other men, only Javenbach reacted. Understanding some Arabic, his hand closed around the grip of his Kalashnikov. Niles shook his head.

They heard an argument. Hijazi stated again and again that he had legal documents for his cargo. A voice shouted him down. The argument continued, the voices leaving the area of the cab and passing the length of the trailer, fading away as the several men went to the cargo doors.

Metal clanked on metal and the hinges of doors shrieked.

Wood and metal creaked as someone climbed into the trailer. They heard the boxes shifting. Niles hand-signed for the Marines to wait. They did not move as boots sounded on the planks, soldiers calling. Niles understood and smiled. He scratched out a message on a note pad and passed it to the other Marines.

THEY ARE CONFISCATING THEIR PAYOFF.

Boxes shifted and fell. A slash of light appeared in the wall of crates and boxes, the voices suddenly loud. Hijazi protested the damage to his merchandise. Soldiers laughed and told him they wanted to see all the cargo.

"What are you hiding from us?"

Niles rose to a crouch and slowly, infinitely slowly, went to the boxes walling off the other end of the trailer. He whispered to Vatsek, "If they come through, we try to take the officer alive. Maybe we can get out of this."

"What is it that you want?" Hijazi asked the soldiers.

The search stopped. Waiting, Niles heard talk but could not make out the words. Minutes passed. Then the boxes shifted again. A crate scraped across the planks. He heard cardboard rip. Plastic clattered and the soldiers laughed.

Metal shrieked again, the doors closing, the trailer going dark again. The voices returned to the cab. Niles did not move until the motor started and the truck accelerated away from the checkpoint.

Harsh fluorescent light illuminated the interior. Niles blinked against the glare and felt the cool of the warehouse chilling the sweat on his body. Fire had scorched the concrete walls black. Shrapnel had pocked the walls. In places, gray concrete had filled gaping holes. Interior walls had disappeared, only stumps of steel beams and reinforcing bars remaining, the ends of the rusted metal rods gleaming from hacksaws or fused by cutting torches. The walls beside the truck showed the reinforcing rods of a second floor, cut away to create a two-story-high garage area.

Rolling doors of heavy lumber and salvaged corrugated sheet metal blocked the entry. Niles saw two other trucks in the garage—a battered Land Rover and a Soviet transport, painted the dull green of the Syrian army, the slat-side cargo area covered with canvas. Hijazi and the Marines had used the transport truck in January when they pursued Fahkr Rajai and his Pasdaran bodyguards.

"Does this meet the requirements, Captain?" Hijazi asked in a whisper.

"What's outside?"

"A wire fence with razor wire. Locked. And I installed an electric alarm."

Niles went back to the trap door. "Out of the box, gentlemen."

Vatsek came out first. He wiped splashes of sweat from his torso and glanced around at the shattered building. "Baalbek Hilton?"

"There was an Israeli air strike," Hijazi told him. "No one will occupy the building. They fear another attack."

"Looks like twenty-mike-mike cannon—" Vatsek pointed to a hole in the wall, then a corresponding crater in the concrete slab foundation of the garage. The hundreds of holes indicated multiple strafing runs. "Armor piercing. Hebrews did a job on this place. Arab air-conditioning."

"Many people died here."

"Yeah, no doubt about it. IMI—" He used the initials of Israeli Military Industries—designs to kill."

"Many workers. And there were only a few Syrians."

"There it is. Let the Syrians move in and the property values go to shit."

Working in a line, the Marines unloaded the truck. They immediately divided the weapons and equipment by task, Vatsek assembling silenced Beretta pistols, Alvarez finding the Revolutionary Guard frequencies and putting the headphones on Javenbach. Stark took the cameras and electronics.

Hijazi led Stark and Niles up a flight of blackened steel stairs to a third floor. Workmen had left brooms and scoop shovels in a concrete hallway that still stank of fire. Hot wind blew through the empty windows of the offices. Armor-piercing 20mm cannon and rockets had punched hundreds of holes through the concrete ceiling and walls.

At the end of the hallway, an office viewed the south. Only fragments of glass remained in the windows. Tangled reinforcing rod and pieces of concrete hung from the ceiling where a rocket blast had torn through the roof. Avoiding the windows, Hijazi went to a fist-sized hole through the outside wall.

"There are the Iranians."

Less than a kilometer away, across an expanse of open fields and the rooftops of shanties, they saw a two-story building surrounded by a wrecking yard of cargo trailers and junked trucks. The old fence showed sections of new chainlink. Coils of barbed wire shimmered along the top of the fence. Other than the new wire, the building and wrecking yard showed no extraordinary changes for security.

"Dogs?" Niles asked.

"Dogs are unclean," Hijazi answered. "The Iranian fundamentalists are very strict. Guards but no dogs."

"Alarms?"

"That, I cannot tell you. But I have sold him nothing to do with alarms."

Niles glanced at his watch. "Three hours to dark. We'll set up the receivers here. Tonight we watch them and try to get through that perimeter—"

"Captain," Stark interrupted. "There. Behind the garage. I believe I see activity."

Checking the angle of the sun, Niles raised his binoculars. He saw men running to a trailer. No—he corrected himself: a shipping container on a flatbed transport trailer.

Numbers blurred on the LCD of the calculator, the tenths of seconds becoming seconds. Muhammed Ali Foruhar watched the four Salvadorians run to the flatbed trailer. Lobo opened the padlocks on the doors and jerked on the locking lever. It did not move—last night, Foruhar had put two tubes of superglue into the pivot. He laughed as Lobo wasted five seconds trying to muscle the lever. But Victor—the skinny kid with the weak arms—found a stone. Lobo bashed the lever and broke the glue, finally lifting the lever and pushing it to the side. The doors opened.

The teenagers threw out the bus parts, metal and boxes falling from the container until they came to the plastic bags. Victor passed the bags out to Marco and Daniel. Crouching under the trailer, they ripped open the plastic and took out the folded Kalashnikov rifles, jamming the magazines in the rifles. They faced in opposite directions. When the time came for the launch in San Salvador, they would provide security for the critical minutes of preparation.

The gasoline motors popped, white smoke clouding from the container, Lobo and Victor adjusting the chokes for maximum rpm's. Lobo climbed up to the roof of the container first, the extension cord coiled over his shoulder, the heavy power wrench hanging from a sling like a rifle. Exactly as they had rehearsed, he went to the far end of the container, laying out the cord, before jamming the socket over the first bolt. Victor stayed with the generators until Lobo shouted to him, then he went up to the top with his electric wrench.

Scrambling across the metal, they removed all the bolts along the one side of the top. Lobo dropped on the far end of the container and powered out the line of bolts there. He ran back to the doors. Shouting a warning to the others, he used the second wrench and socket to remove the bolts from the cross-strut securing the two sides of the container. He switched on the electric motor to the jack.

And waited. The high-cyclic whine of the generators continued but the walls of the container did not move. Foruhar watched his calculator—Lobo wasted ten seconds before climbing into the container and checking the motor and gears. Thirty seconds, sixty seconds passed as he frantically checked the overload fuse and connections of the motor. Foruhar knew the boy could not trace the power loss unless he disassembled the motor—Foruhar had cut a wire inside the housing.

Jamming the crank handle into the gear box, Lobo strained and grunted, slowly forcing the gears to turn, each turn of the crank spreading the halves of the container a fraction of a millimeter.

A crack appeared. Coughing from the smoke of the generators, the teenager labored at the crank until the side wall of the container fell. The opposite wall and roof tilted, angling over as Lobo wrenched the crank around. After another hundred turns, the wall and roof fell.

The teenagers climbed onto the trailer and removed the lumber and the blocks of styrofoam protecting the tubes, finally freeing the rocket launcher. Foruhar flipped the power switch of the transmitter and the servo motors rotated the launcher, tilting the tubes—perfect. Then he interrupted the test program and pressed the stop button on his calculator.

"Eighteen minutes!" He shouted in English. "And twenty-three seconds! Say your prayers. If you got soldiers shooting at you, you are dead shit. And if you look this bad when your colonel comes . . . so put it back together."

Stark peered through the viewfinder of the Nikon as he gently shifted the framing of the 360-1200mm zoom lens to follow the graying Iranian. Leaning away from the eyepiece, he waited an instant, allowing the camera to steady, then pressed the cable release. The shutter snapped and the motor drive advanced the film.

"Got him?" Niles asked.

"Several exposures, sir. Portraits. This afternoon light, the slant of the light brings out his age. He is not a young man."

"And the crew? The launcher?"

"Most of the roll. I'll shoot another roll right now."

"I believe the Iranian is an alcoholic," Hijazi added. "The several occasions we met for business, he has always smelled of alcohol. Also hashish."

"A doper." Looking through a ragged hole punched through the concrete, Niles stared out at the distant wrecking yard. "A high-tech Iranian alky doper who's training a crew of Salvadorians, Nicaraguans, whoever—to hit Americans. With one-hundred-twenty millimeter rockets. I tell you this, gentlemen, that will not happen."

28

THROUGHOUT the afternoon, Lobo and the others worked in the equipment yard. They could open the doors of the cargo container and ready the rockets for launching in less than twenty minutes, but the work of reassembling the container took hours. Like the pieces of a puzzle, each piece of the plastic foam protecting the rocket tubes had an exact place. String held the foam blocks in place as they refitted the wood braces. The motors of the generators required cleaning. They coiled and stacked the extension cords, replaced the power wrenches and plastic-bagged rifles, and cranked back the geared jacks. Lobo took apart the electric motor and reconnected the wire their Iranian instructor had cut.

The positioning of the steel walls and roof required the power winches of tow trucks. Before the Iranians had seized the truck garage and wrecking yard, the mechanics had used the cable winches of the tow trucks to lift overturned diesel trucks and trailers. The Salvadorians used two trucks to first lift the single wall, then they backed the trucks into position with the sidewall. Lobo scrambled through the equipment and trucks with a wrench, securing the wall with a few bolts. They repeated the careful maneuvering of the trucks with the roof and the other wall. But the Salvadorians had practiced with the container for a month and the walls had bent. To line up the long pattern of bolt holes where the single wall joined the roof, Victor backed a tow truck boom against the container and eased back a millimeter at a time, Lobo directing him with shouts. Lobo powered the bolts into the roof as the sun faded in the west. Loading the clutter of boxes and bus parts into the container, they finally locked the doors.

"Almost the last time," Lobo told his campañeros. "You heard him. The colonel is coming. Then we go."

"Did he say when?" Marco asked.

"It must be soon. We are ready."

"Ready for the shit pile," Daniel cursed. "I joined to fight. Not to do this shit work, over and over and over again for months."

Lobo laughed. He had an easy smile and joking manner that masked his years as a combatant. "Did you join to fight? Or to kill? You can fight with an old rifle. Maybe kill a soldier or militiaman. But this—" He slapped the steel wall of the container, "You know this will not be shot at some garrison in the mountains. The National Palace, the American embassy. They would not tell us, but we know, yes?"

The others returned to the garage. Lobo went to the water tank and stripped off his coveralls. Inside the garage, he heard the clatter of tools. The Iranians assembled another container—but they had loaded that one with rockets. He turned on the faucet above his head and the sun-warmed water flowed over him. As he scrubbed his body with the soap, washing away the stink of oil and dust and his own sweat, he thought of Mejicanos, the streets stinking of rot and shit, smoke always hanging in the air, drunks shouting, children crying as diarrhea and malnutrition wasted their bodies—and a few kilometers away, the rich in Escalón and San Benito enjoyed the bourgeois luxuries of their homes and cars and romances, wasting the wealth of Salvador to import the decadence of the North Americans and Europeans.

From his earliest memory, his parents had wanted that decadence for him. They worked in the homes of the rich, his father a chauffeur and mechanic to a rich politician, his mother a maid to an old banker. He wore the discarded clothes of the rich children and ate the garbage of the banker. But he grew strong and his parents had money for school and books. He learned to read and write. Then his parents sent him to a Mormon school, to learn English from the blond, blue-eyed North Americans who wore slacks and white shirts with ties, who talked of the Bible and led the classes in prayers for the souls of the unfortunates of El Salvador and world. Pedro Diego Gutiérrez, eating the garbage of the rich and wearing their rags, believed the lies of the North Americans. He learned their language and played their baseball. He wore the uniform of the foreigners—black pants and white shirt with the tie. Walking through the trash and stink of Mejicanos, he ignored the other boys. He scorned their soccer as a game of the uneducated—denying his own mixed Spanish and Nahua heritage to mimic the North Americans.

In the white shirt, carrying his books, Pedro Diego became a target of the older boys. They threw filth on his school clothes and taunted him. But his intelligence and strength defeated the neighborhood gangs. When they outnumbered him, he ran, his long legs and healthy lungs taking him away from the gangs. When they ambushed him, he fought and ran and threw rocks with the speed and accuracy of a speedball. The gangs left him alone.

Sometimes he worked with his father, reading repair manuals in Spanish or English while his father worked with the engines. He tried to avoid dirtying his hands with labor but his father forced him to learn mechanics. With his strength and his literacy and the exacting discipline learned from school, he developed a quick skill with American cars and trucks, then moved on to the new Japanese and European cars appearing in Salvador.

Then the police took his father. For years, to pay for the school and the books, his father had stolen from the rich family. He had pocketed a few colones a week, sometimes cheating the family of twenty or thirty colones by repairing an engine with a rebuilt part and charging the price of a new generator or carburetor. He listened to his father pleading to the judge that the money had gone to educate his son. The family who had employed his father for ten years did not attend the hearing.

With his father in prison, teenage Pedro Diego went to work. His mother found him work with a wealthy family. Appearing on time, in his black pants and white shirt with a tie, he presented himself for work—and they laughed. Why had he worn his best clothes to work in the yard? But he could read and write and repair their American car, he told them. Laughing at the proud thirteen-year-old boy who dressed like an evangelist, they sent him away. He went to garages and asked for work, telling the mechanics he could read and write and repair American, European, and Japanese cars. The mechanics offered to pay him centavos a day to wash the cars and sweep the garages.

Leaving the capital, he went to work in the fields. He picked coffee and cotton with the campesinos. The foremen drove the workers like animals, but they paid him a man's wage. Then he made the mistake of helping a foreman with the English instructions on a can of pesticide. The foreman asked, Why does a boy with intelligence and schooling pick coffee like a stupid campesino? Why not help the owner? There are communists here. Listen to workers and remember who talks communism, write the names—

He told the owner the truth—no communists worked there, only campesinos. The communists went to the university.

Go, boy, listen to them, there are communists in the fields talking unions and socialism.

He did listen. The campesinos talked of pains and hunger, of their sick children, of the wealth of their cousins in the United States. The women prayed and gossiped, the men chased the wives of other men and raved in alcoholic rages. Politics and ideology meant nothing to them. A Spanish priest visited the towns talking of Christians cooperating to improve their lives through reading and voting—but the priest said nothing of communism.

When he told his foreman all this, the hard-eyed ex-sergeant of the Treasury Police cursed him and pursued him, punching and kicking the boy. The campesinos warned him to leave. Losing a week of pay, he returned to Mejicanos. Word came of the disappearance of the Spanish priest. People in the slum told him of other disappearances. He saw bodies dumped on the roads.

Fleeing north, he worked in the United States, picking flowers in California, digging ditches for sprinklers in suburban lawns, understanding the nonsense on the radio of North American politicans talking of communism in Central America. They knew nothing of his country. He remembered the teaching of the Mormons and realized they had offered nothing to improve his country, only the drug of their evangelism.

Immigration officers took him. An informer identified him as a Salvadorian. The officers threatened him with prison if he did not sign a form authorizing his immediate return to Salvador—which meant death for him. Unlike the other illegals, he understood what the officers said to one another and he understood the language of the form. He refused to sign. They imprisoned him at a camp in El Centro, California, with hundreds of other Central Americans.

There, in the crowds of men squatting in the sun and talking, he received another education. The prisoners had no library, no workshops, no visits, only talk to pass the time. Many Salvadorians—teachers, union men, students, professional radicals—had fled the repression and the disappearances. He listened to a clique of radicals and he believed what the radicals told him—Salvador had no chance to enter the twentieth century under the domination of the United States. Had he not seen exactly what the radicals told him? The American multinationals wanted only cheap labor—campesinos to pick the export crops, workers to assemble products. The American government, as an extension of the companies, would always support the regimes oppressing the people of his country. Oppression kept the price of labor down. Until a progressive junta seized control of Salvador and drove out the North Americans, his people would always remain slaves. Only revolution offered hope.

When his immigration hearing finally came, he had no lawyer and no argument. The judge asked his age—sixteen—and immediately ordered him deported to be reunited with his family. Despite his fears, the authorities at Cuscatlán International processed him in a few hours and he took a bus back to San Salvador. He found his family ruined. His thirteen-year-old sister had disappeared. His father drank all day. His mother stoically continued cleaning the house of

the old banker in Escalón, returning home at night to watch
North American melodramas on a flickering television
junked by the banker.

Pedro Diego Gutiérrez took a bus north into Chalatenango. Where the bus stopped, he started walking. He
avoided an army patrol the first afternoon, slept, and the
next morning followed smoke to the cookfires of a unit of the
Popular Forces of Liberation. They sent him farther into the
mountains for training. Within a month, he had won his rifle,
a heavy G-3 pocked by the scrap-iron shrapnel that had
killed the soldier who had carried the rifle. The rifle had
excellent accuracy. Pedro trained himself to hit soldiers
from three-hundred meters. Working alone on the roads, he
killed officers and sergeants, leaving the draftees to hide in
the ditches as he slipped away. He took the fighting name of
El Lobo, the Wolf.

After years of war and leading small units against difficult
targets, a political officer recognized his courage and intelligence. The officer asked if Lobo wanted specialized training.
He accepted. A plane took him from a dirt airstrip, over
mountains, over the ocean to an island, then through the
night to another airstrip—where, he did not know. The one-
eyed, one-armed colonel welcomed him and introduced him
to the instructors who taught him of sniping rifles, plastic
explosives, American and Soviet detonators, and radios and
codes. The offer of the trip to Lebanon came at the end of his
course.

Lobo had come so far from the stink of Mejicanos. Only
nineteen—and the colonel honored him with this responsibility of the launcher. If the Mormons only knew! The colonel
had chosen Lobo because of his excellent English. Now, the
boy who had worn the black pants, white shirt with tie, who
had prayed to be one of the bourgeoisie, soon he returned to
Salvador with rockets to kill the fascists and their American
bosses.

The one strike would not win the war, would not drive out
the Americans. But he had studied the victory of the Vietnamese. The Vietnamese inflicted thousands and thousands
of casualties throughout the decades, never destroying the

American war machine, but always bleeding their forces. And in the end, the Americans finally abandoned Vietnam.

Kill an adviser, kill a Marine, destroy their embassy. Make the Americans tired of body bags and cripples returning from insignificant El Salvador. And when the Americans abandoned their puppet regime of Duarte and the generals, the regime would fall.

Voices and radio music came from the shanties lining the fields, wind carrying melodies and the scents of cooking. In the warm evening, with the dry wind sweeping down from the hills, families gathered outside their homes, kerosene lanterns lighting groups in yards and alleyways. Children ran from house to house with flashlights in their hands, the beams waving over walls, packed earth, and gardens.

In the fields, a rising moon created voids of shadow and areas of blue light, the footpaths looking white, the tall weeds an uneven expanse of light and darkness and half-tones. The wind carried dust and rattled the corrugated sheets of the shanties lining the fields. Papers appeared from the shadows and wheeled across the trash strewn fields, catching in the weeds, then lifting away and spinning into the shacks on the far side.

The Americans zigzagged from path to path, trying to stay in the shadows, only risking the fields when they must. Alvarez and Javenbach walked several steps ahead of Niles. Javenbach wore the fatigues of the Revolutionary Guard, Alvarez the camouflage uniform of the Syrian Army. Niles also wore Syrian camouflage. They carried flashlights but walked with the lights switched off.

For hours, from late afternoon until after the call of evening prayers, Niles had lain on the rooftop of the bombed warehouse. First, he memorized the footpaths and alleys of the area. Then, he studied the people—the women walking on the paths with bags of bread and vegetables, the teenagers stripping a junked car of fender panels, children playing in the alleys, a lone Revolutionary Guardsman who paced along the fence to the wrecking yard where the Salvadorians? Nicaraguans? worked on the shipping container. Niles saw no police or military patrols in the area.

Alvarez watched the highway and reported Syrian trucks passing, but no patrols. The Syrians and Iranians considered this area secure. After several hours of watching, Niles had decided to risk the footpaths to the wrecking yard.

Niles counted off the meters as he walked. Javenbach and Alvarez looked their roles. They carried their tools and their canvas packs of scanners and transmitters in blue plastic bags—the same bags the local women used to carry home their purchases from a neighborhood market. Niles had darkened his face and hands but he knew his camouflage and basic Arabic meant nothing if a patrol stopped him. But for a distance of only a kilometer, he judged the risk acceptable.

English startled him. On the other side of a board fence, a scratchy shortwave broadcast carried the British voice of an announcer describing Chicago politics. Another voice repeated words from the program, stumbling over the pronunciation of "Michigan," repeating the word, then trying another word, "lakeside"—a student learning English. Past the student, in another yard, two men argued the expense of a blown-out tire in Arabic, one man repeating numbers and the other man saying, "It made no difference, no difference."

Sound alerted Niles before he saw the sweep of light. Feet kicked through papers, the beam of a flashlight appeared. Two boys walked out of an alley. They saw the three soldiers and faltered a step. The Americans switched on their flashlights and put the beams in the faces of the two boys, effectively blinding them. One of the boys smiled and saluted. The Americans said nothing as they passed.

A wide band of tire-rutted earth separated a block of houses from the chain-link and barbed wire of the wrecking yard. The Americans continued along a footpath, then Niles pointed to the weeds and shadows near a concrete wall. They stepped off the trail and went flat. Javenbach slipped on the headphones of a scanner. Behind them, through a curtained window, they heard the crying of a baby.

Scanning the fences and the roofline of the garage, Niles searched for sentries. Naked bulbs set in the side of the building cast light on the asphalt between the building and the fence. Trailers had been parked against the fence. At the back, beyond the light, he saw the ember of a cigarette appear and disappear as the guard walked through the junked trucks. Niles guessed that the Iranians had changed guards—the man during the day had not smoked.

"Make the noise," Niles whispered.

Alvarez took a slingshot out of the market bag. Unfolding the wrist brace, he fitted the frame around his arm and stretched back the surgical tubing. The hex nut whistled through the night. Even from a hundred meters away, they heard the steel-on-steel impact. The cigarette scratched through the darkness as the guard went to check the sound. A second man appeared.

"Radios?" Niles asked Javenbach.

"Nothing."

"The fence."

Hooking a piece of scrap re-bar over the slingshot pocket, Alvarez arced the re-bar across the open ground, hitting the fence near the highway. The iron clicked off the chain-link. Watching the fences and the garage, they saw no movement. No alarm sounded.

For the next hour, they watched and listened. Sentries paced around the garage. Sometimes one of the Revolutionary Guards paused at the fence and looked out at the fields, the red point of a cigarette rising and falling in the darkness. But none of the Iranians stood sentry on the roof, where the high angle would look down on the fields.

Traffic became infrequent on the highway. The sounds of the radios and children and families faded, people blowing out the lanterns and switching off lights. The radios and cassettes went silent. In the quiet, the Americans heard the noise of power equipment from the Iranians in the truck garage.

Niles plotted a path across the open ground. Weeds had grown in the tire ruts, offering a few bands of shadow. Trucks had dumped loads of trash—the piles seemed to waver as the wind whipped tattered plastic bags from side to side. Even with the rising moon, he saw no problems if they went slow and quiet.

Laying down his Kalashnikov, unbuckling his Soviet vest of magazines, Niles took out the silenced Beretta he carried.

He checked the lock on the suppressor, then jacked back the slide to chamber a 9mm subsonic round. Hand-loaded by Vatsek, the cartridges in the auto pistol had only enough powder to drive the bullet out the muzzle at 300 meters-per-second, less than the speed of sound. A steel penetrator core in the bullets, designed by Vatsek to separate from the lead sheath and continue deep into the body of the target, compensated for the loss in power.

Javenbach and Alvarez put down their rifles and stripped off their unneeded Kalashnikov magazines. Like Niles, they also had silenced Berettas. They slipped on the canvas packs of electronics and tools. Gathering trash from around them, they tucked scraps of plastic bags into the webbing straps and belts.

Angling across the ruts, Niles went first, his body flowing in slow motion over the hard earth. He found a line of weeds and followed the shadows, stopping when the wind paused, continuing when the wind put the weeds in motion. Behind him, Alvarez and Javenbach watched the fences and monitored the frequencies of the Iranian walkie-talkies. If the Iranians somehow spotted him, he would have warning. He moved slower as he approached a splotch of open sand. Pressing aside dry grass, he watched the fence for minutes. Two guards passed. Niles waited, watching the fence and the hulks of the trailers, listening, then he snaked across the sand. He made cover in a minute. From there, the weeds and trash gave him concealment as he bellied to within a few meters of the fence. Then, with a small metal detector, he searched the ground for sensors. He found only nuts and bolts and bits of scrap wire as he advanced to a point at the fence where a trailer and a cargo container stood like a steel wall. The height of the wheels created a shadowed crawl space from the fence to the asphalt of the work yard. Niles signaled Javenbach with a click of his hand radio.

The crossings of Javenbach and Alvarez took another hour. Alvarez checked the fence for an alarm circuit. Nothing. Only then did they cut the fence, using heavy bolt cutters to snip a flap in the chain link. Niles went through with the metal detector, searching for sensors inside the fence. Javenbach and Alvarez followed quickly, pulling the flap closed behind them.

Again, they waited, sprawled in the shadow under the flatbed trailer and container, watching the area, timing the passings of the sentries. They heard voices from the front gate, but no sound inside the garage. Wind rattled the corrugated metal roof and walls of the garage, gusts sometimes making loose panels swing and crash.

Niles looked for access to the roof. The micro-transmitters they had brought required placement within normal listening distance of the subjects to be monitored. Satellite photos had shown skylight windows in the roof of the garage. Niles intended to place the microphones on the skylights, where the microphones could pick up the words of anyone below. The satellite photos had shown exhaust fans, water tanks, a stairwell, and plank walkways leading across the corrugated metal of the roof—but no ladder up the outside walls. From where he watched, he saw no ladders, no handholds, nothing to take him up to the roof. He glanced at his watch—nearing eleven. With dawn at five, he needed to place the equipment and get out.

The sentries walked circles around the garage. They stopped to talk with the guard at the gate, they paused to smoke cigarettes—the time of each circle varied.

"Can't trust their schedule," Niles whispered to Alvarez. He took the canvas pack of electronics and used wads of plastic and wind-blown paper to silence rattles, then slipped the straps over his shoulders. One last detail—with the point of his knife, he traced the lines in the soles of his ComBloc boots, flicking out rocks that had jammed into the tread patterns.

Waiting until the two sentries passed, Niles stepped out. The angle of the garage blocked the sight of the sentries at the gate. He calculated his path, looking for uneven asphalt or parts on the pavement—anything that could make a sound—then continued in a rush through the weak light of the bulbs, gaining distance on the sentries, then dodging into a shadow and repeating his search, then rush.

At the corner, he paused. The boots of the sentries faded.

He leaned out and saw the rear of the building. Scanning the area, he searched for the guard who had paced the back fence. But nothing moved in the trucks and trailers. Niles waited, slowly sweeping his eyes from side to side, trying to use the edges of his vision to find forms in the darkness.

In the quiet, Niles heard the accordians and quick thumping bass beat of a polka—no, a Mexican ranchero song, the bass line played with the peculiar six-string bass common to bands in northern Mexico. A woman sang a high nasal ballad that he remembered from Los Angelos and Tegucigalpa. He listened, hoping to hear the voices of the Latins, while he watched the rear of the wrecking yard. But he heard no voices and the guard did not appear.

Niles stood and walked through the light, his pace slow, casual. He came to an oversized door, high and wide enough for trucks. Inside, he saw clapboard walls to the right and left. The windows of what had once been offices overlooked the work area. Faint light glowed through torn paper shades. Past the offices, in the open work area of the garage, moonlight through the skylights showed another of the modified containers, the tubes of the rocket launcher exposed and angled up. He saw no lights, no motion inside the work area. From a stairwell to his right, at a position corresponding to the stairwell shown in the satellite photos, he heard the Mexican music.

If he went up the stairs to try to place the micro-transmitters on the skylights, he risked encountering the Latins face-to-face in a narrow passage. Even if he escaped, he lost the chance to place the transmitters and maybe brought a house-to-house search on the area . . .

Walking straight ahead, one slow, silent step at a time, Niles entered the half-darkness of the garage interior. His senses expanded, taking in the forms and sounds and smells of the garage. The walls and roof of a cargo container hung by chains from overhead winches, pre-positioned for the assembly of the container. Work benches lined the walls and—

A man snored. Niles froze in midstep. Wind rattled the corrugated sheets of the walls and roof. He heard the breathing of several men. Scanning the concrete floor, he saw the dark forms of men on pads, their boots standing in pairs, clothing and weapons within reach. He saw none of the men sleeping near the flatbed trailer and the modified container. Continuing around the trailer, he dropped to a crouch beside the wheel.

Slipping off the backpack, he found the plastic cases of the micro-transmitters by touch. In the darkness, he searched for a niche in the electrical conduits of the rocket launcher, then stuck the unit in place with the self-adhesive backing.

Tools and components covered a work table. Moonlight from the skylights allowed Niles to examine the several cases and boxes on the table, searching for an ideal placement for the next micro-transmitter. He saw metal tool boxes and two plastic carrying cases. Touching the plastic of one case, he felt the letters, SONY. The other case had chrome letters reading, NAGRA. He turned back to the trailer. Running his hands over the frame of the flatbed trailer, he found the hollow reverse side of the I-beam bumper. He placed the second transmitter there.

Going to the walk-in door of the garage, he felt inside the structural beams of the steel doorframe. His hands came away covered with dust and filth. Cleaning a spot, he stuck the third micro-transmitter in place.

Footsteps approached the door. Pivoting, Niles dropped to a crouch. The Beretta clanked against the steel wall but the rattling of the opening door covered the noise. The two Iranians passed Niles and crossed the garage to the sleeping men. A flashlight waved. He heard voices and the rattling of rifles—the changing of the guard shift. Several minutes later, different voices talked as two other men walked out the back of the garage. Niles glanced at his watch—twelve midnight, less than five hours until morning prayers. He had another micro-transmitter to place, then the booster unit, but he could not move until the two Iranians slept.

Thirty minutes passed before he chanced returning to his pack. There, he stopped and listened. He heard only snoring and regular breathing from the Iranians. The Mexican tape no longer played in the room on the second floor. Taking the last micro-transmitter out, he checked the pack for rattles and slipped on the straps, shifting his shoulders slightly to double-check for noise.

Quickly, he walked from the work-table and trailer at the center of the garage. He passed the sleeping Iranians and continued to the rear door. He stuck the micro-transmitter in the steel doorframe. One step outside, he crouched and listened for minutes, waiting for the pacing of the sentries. He heard only the wind and the banging of sheet metal. Easing back between two oil drums, he risked whispering into his hand radio.

"Where are they?"

"Went past fifteen minutes ago."

"Key me if you hear them."

Watching for movement, listening, he eased clear of the oil drums. He walked to the corner of the building, stepped into shadow, then dropped flat on the asphalt. He peered around the corner.

The series of bare bulbs bathed the asphalt in weak light. Three trailers away, almost fifty meters, Niles saw the shadow where Alvarez and Javenbach waited. He glanced in both directions, then stepped into the light. Four steps out, almost across the open asphalt, he felt the hand radio click. He continued another step and dropped under a trailer.

Boots ran. Desperate, Niles looked for concealment—and saw sheets of wrapping plastic caught on the trailer wheels. He tore the plastic loose and the wind took the thin, almost weightless sheets. In the light, the plastic drifted along the asphalt, floated out of sight, returned, then swirled out of sight again. Then he grabbed a handhold on the chain-link and dragged himself up between the chain-link and the trailer. The canvas of the pack caught on the wire. He kicked up and braced his boots on the trailer, pivoting, hiding his body between the trailer and the fence.

The boots stopped. Flashlight beams swept under the trailer. The men talked as they searched the area, the beams passing under Niles several times. He heard one man run, then the thrashing of plastic.

Niles breathed again as the boots and voices receded. But he did not leave his concealment. Hooking the strap of the pack over a bolthead, he used the pack as a sling. He hung there for another twenty minutes, waiting until the sentries passed again. Then he dropped and crawled under the trailers to Alvarez and Javenbach.

"Thought they had you," Alvarez whispered.

"So did I. Luck was with me."

"Lucky for them." Alvarez tapped his silent Beretta. "They could've died tonight. We had them in our sights."

"Tonight, tomorrow night, next week—they are all dead. I just have to think of how to do it."

29

WAITING in a Dodge taxi, Atallah watched the crowds of the Hammadiya souk, the vast sprawling marketplace at the center of Damascus. A thousand years old when conquest brought Islam to Syria, this souk had dominated the trade between the Mediterranean and the distant capitals of Baghdad, Mecca, and Teheran. Where the Roman quartermasters once bought supplies for their legions, merchants sold Czechoslavakian batteries for smuggled Japanese cassette players, farmers argued for a few more devalued Syrian pounds for their crops, and Iranian women in the black chadors of widows bought perfume from Taiwan.

His lieutenant appeared. Lieutenant Qaddam wore the traditional work clothes of a Syrian villager—keffiyah, long cotton shirt, and earth-stained pants. He did not look back or acknowledge the Colombian following him. Vendors recognized the foreign features and European suit of Alejandro Vásquez and they called to him, their words lost in the noise of the voices and generators and stereos. An old man fell into step beside Vásquez and showed the pages of a tourist pamphlet, his withered hands gesturing in the direction of Umayyad Mosque. Vásquez ignored him, keeping his eyes on Qaddam.

"Start the engine," Atallah told the taxi driver. The recent developments—the kidnapping and murder of Pazos, the possibility of surveillance by American or Israeli counterterrorist agents, the chance that the Colombian worked for the Americans—required him to meet this Colombian in the

278

streets, rather than in the security of his office at the Daraiya base. Nor could Atallah offer the convenience of helicopter transport from Damascus to Baalbek. The situation even denied the small comfort of his Mercedes. The threat to the operation now required civilian vehicles and disguises when he met newcomers. Atallah wore the threadbare suit of a humble merchant, a trusted sergeant wore the ragged clothing of a taxi driver.

Qaddam jerked open the door and paused. Vásquez stepped inside the taxi, Qaddam followed him, and in seconds the sergeant had put the old Dodge in motion, easing through the walking people, then accelerating into traffic. Qaddam looked back, watching the vendors and chador-draped women and the farmers with their hand carts of vegetables. He glanced to Atallah and shook his head—no surveillance.

"Perdóneme, Señor Vásquez," Qaddam apologized as he took out an electronic wand of the type used by airlines. He waved the loop over the shoes and clothing of the Colombian, finding coins and the Sheraton room key but nothing else.

Only then did Atallah introduce himself: "I am Colonel Atallah. May we speak in English? My aide speaks Spanish, if there is any difficulty with that language."

"If you want, we'll speak English. Or Spanish."

"Indeed, your English is quite excellent! It has not a trace of my unfortunate British accent. Did you attend an American university?"

"Berkeley." Alejandro Vásquez looked like a young banker, his pale features slight, almost effeminate, his shoulders narrow in his tropical-weight pin-striped suit. As a sub-comandante with the Armed Forces of the Colombian Revolution, he negotiated the purchases of weapons for the fighters in his organization. "Where are the rockets?"

"Ah, forthright and to the point. The missiles are, of course, not here in this city. We must drive to Lebanon. And circumstances are such that we cannot simply drive directly there. Please forgive me for the inconvenience of the next few minutes."

The sergeant swerved across four lanes of traffic, braked, then whipped into a narrow street, bumping and lurching over broken pavement. Old tenements, gray with a century of soot and decay, stood on both sides of the street. At the next corner, the sergeant swung wide around a donkey cart and accelerated, flashing past a field of broken stone and earth movers. Qaddam watched behind the taxi. Making two more turns, the sergeant skidded to a stop. Atallah motioned for Vásquez to follow.

Leaving the taxi, they walked through a street market, Qaddam a step behind them. Old women sold vegetables and plastic housewares from baskets. Chickens squawked from cages of woven cane. Long sticks held up sheets of plastic for shade against the sun. Atallah pushed aside flaps of plastic, weaving through the narrow corridor in the center of the street.

"A traditional market. Is it not the same in Colombia?"

"Only in the slums. We shop in supermarkets."

"Very American."

Atallah stepped into an alley. Qaddam rushed ahead and unlocked a rolling metal door. Inside the garage, he started the motor of another yellow Dodge taxi, indistinguishable from the taxi that had brought them from the souk. "Now to the Bekka. We will have a few hours. If you would be so kind, can you tell me more of your organization?"

Javenbach crouched in the shattered hallway, his eyes staring into the flash-scorched concrete as he monitored the transmissions from the garage a kilometer away. He wore headphones, his hands sometimes pressing the earphones hard against his ears as he strained to follow conversations. Beside him, a miniature reel-to-reel tape machine simultaneously recorded all four channels. Javenbach penciled down notes from time to time.

Switching on the monitor speaker, Niles heard Farsi, then the whine of an electric drill. He glanced down at the note pad—and saw that Javenbach wrote in Farsi.

"The tools and work noise are eating the tape," Alvarez told the captain. He broke the cellophane seal on a box and took out another reel of recording tape. He set it beside the machine, ready. "I've got a voice activated cut-off on line, but there's always noise to keep the recorder—"

"Captain!" Stark called.

Niles hurried to the office. Stark manned the camera, peering through the viewfinder. He leaned back and snapped a photo with the cable release. Niles scanned the garage compound. At the barbed wire gates, the Iranians searched a yellow Dodge taxi, looking under the frame and throughout the interior. Through the binoculars, Niles read the name of a Damascus company on the doors. The taxi went through the gates and two men stepped out. One man wore a cheap wrinkled suit, the other man—a foreigner? Latin American? Spanish?—wore a business suit. The camera snapped and whirred.

"The leader," Javenbach announced from the hallway, "is telling all of his men to leave. And in English, he tells the others."

The graying Iranian appeared. He escorted the strangers into the garage.

"Got them?" Niles asked.

"Full face and profile."

"English," Javenbach continued. "He is telling the colonel and the Colombian of the rockets."

" . . . and the rockets home in on this," Foruhar explained, lifting a gray metal case from the work bench. He lifted the lid to show the Colombian the components resting in the foam padding. "I don't want to get way too technical—"

"That looks fragile," Vásquez interrupted. "How could that survive transport and handling?"

"It can't. That's why I've got it in this box. It'll be built into—" Foruhar glanced at Atallah. The Syrian shook his head. "It'll be built into something else. Hidden, you know? This elminates about a million dollars worth of electronics in each rocket. When I worked for the Shah, cost did not mean shit. Hawk missiles, Shrikes, Harm missiles—whatever. He bought the best the Americans had and that was that. But for my rockets, I had to develop my own system. And this is it. It provides the aiming signal for the launcher computers.

And I tell you, it is absolutely accurate. Your man presses the button and within a minute, the launcher is locked in. Paradise hits at Mach Two."

"That is something we discussed on the long and very trying drive here." Atallah gestured to the rockets and the transmitter. "For his purposes, he desires a modification which will allow an agent to place the unit at the target and then retreat to safety."

"I can put a timer in there. An hour, a day—whatever. That's why I didn't use micro-circuits for the switching. Cut the wire, splice a timer in there—whatever. You want it, you got it."

"Could the target trigger the launch?" Vásquez asked.

"Like a super high-tech booby trap?"

"In a car, in an airplane, or a—"

"Say they switch on the car radio and wham! A world of shit comes down on their head? I thought of it. I could do it. But that means the rockets have got to be ready."

"If they were not ready, what—"

"Nothing happens. They won't launch inside the container. If your people had the rockets ready and the American ambassador came cruising along, listening to the New York stock prices and dreaming about how to sell out your country and he gets in range and wham! Great idea, but—"

"Within eighteen or twenty kilometers?"

"Right, right. But it wouldn't work. Car moving sixty miles an hour? The rockets don't maneuver like that. Maybe if he's parked, maybe if he's in a parade—there, that's it. If you slow the man down, you can hit him. Get him rubbing bellies with El Presidente and blow them away."

"In my country, the guards always open briefcases that officials take into government offices. Could this be concealed in a briefcase so that—"

"The door man searching the briefcase throws the switch? You got it. But you know, whoever's carrying the briefcase is not going to live through it. There won't be any time to walk away or hide. One minute, down they come. Forty rockets. Every other one of those warheads is armor-piercing with a one-second delay on the fuse. They'll go through the roof of a place and punch through to the basement before going off. And that means nothing but dead people."

"But what of the concrete and stone? Will that not block the signal?"

"No. I got that worked out."

"And will not the radio signals bounce off other buildings and confuse the rockets?"

"You got all the good questions. What you're talking about is signal propagation. But I worked it all out. The transmitter puts out signals on several frequencies. If the transmitter's downtown and the signals are bouncing, then the computer averages out the bounces and launches at the approximate source. Then the rockets have got a perfect straight-line drop on the transmitter. I took it out in the mountains and tried it ten times. Sometimes the rocket's correct one hundred per cent, sometimes it's only ninety-five. But forty missles? That means the target gets hit thirty-seven or thirty-eight times and other rockets come down close. Is that okay?"

"That is pinpoint accuracy? Are you telling me that all the rockets will hit that small thing?"

"I've done it. I can shoot one rocket and have it hit this box dead on. But I built in a dispersal factor so that the rockets don't stack up nose to tail on the way down. I decided on a strike diameter of fifty meters. That means forty rockets hitting within twenty-five meters of the signal. And that, man is that."

"Twenty-five meters? What if it is an assembly? A mass event?"

"Like if it's the inauguration of El Presidente? Then I can step up that dispersion factor. For something like that, you'd want to change the load, forget the armor-piercing and go with all impact fuses. With shrapnel jackets on the charges. No, maybe I could work out proximity fuses, get airbursts above the crowd. Shit, man. A slaughter."

Vásquez paced to the center of the garage and continued around the trailer, looking at the conduits, the computer components, the servo-motors of the launcher platform, then the rack of tubes containing the rockets. Above his head, the side panel hung from a hoist, ready for positioning and assembly.

"This is ready to fire?"

"Loaded."

"I want it fired. If it does what you say, we will take it."

"Not that one. That one goes out tomorrow."

"To where?"

"My friend, I cannot say."

"Then I am to return to my commander and tell him what you told me? Without actually seeing the performance of these rockets. That is not the way we—"

Atallah cut off the Colombian. "My dear friend, of course there will be a demonstration. Watch your television and your newspapers. In only a few weeks, you will see the demonstration in the news of the world. When you are convinced of this weapon, communicate with me again."

"Tomorrow?" Niles asked. "I heard that correctly? He said those rockets are going out tomorrow?"

Stark snapped a photo of the Iranians and Latins at the back of the garage. Then he shifted the tripod and aimed at the entry of the garage. "Yes, sir. Tomorrow."

Vásquez waited in the taxi as Atallah went back to the garage. Standing in the doorway, beyond the hearing of the Colombian in the taxi or the Iranians returning to their tools, Atallah asked Foruhar:

"Will that be ready"—he looked at the container in the center of the work area—"for the truck as scheduled?"

"It'll be ready. You don't want the colonel from Salvador to see it?"

"No. The man is no fool. What if he examines it closely? It is necessary that it leave as scheduled. Without fail."

"We close it up tonight. I've got to set all the fuses on the rockets and the demo charges and then I want to run a last check on the circuits and back-up batteries and then—"

"And what of the launcher for the demonstration?"

"I'll load two or three rockets and we'll take it out to the desert."

"And the guidance unit? You at no time can betray what will actually happen when the woman switches it on."

"She won't know shit. I'll cut out the trigger sequence. And use another transmitter to launch the rockets. There'll be a signal unit at the target. When she pushes the button, she'll see the rockets go up and come down."

"And the guidance units we will send with her to El Salvador?"

"A real camera and video recorder. Exactly what the news crews use. They walk into the embassy and take pictures, down come those rockets. But I had to screw around with the sound recorder. A cassette recorder didn't give me the room for the transmitter. So I got an old Nagra. Old but they still use it for interviews and movies. I built the thing into it. They turn on the camera or recorder—wham!"

"Then it is done. The commander and his woman are in flight now. I will radio from Daraiya when they come."

"How will they get back to Salvador?"

"Airlines. Why?"

"From Beirut? They'll lose it all! If they don't get robbed on the road, they'll get robbed at the Beirut checkpoints, or they'll lose it at the airport. Can you give them bodyguards to Jounieh? Then they take the ferry and can hand-carry it through Larnaca."

"No."

"You're risking my primo equipment! There'll be a delay of weeks if they lose those guidance—"

"Calm yourself. They will fly from Europe to Daraiya by private jet. I will bring them to you for the demonstration, then we will return to Daraiya. They will return by private jet to Europe. Does that satisfy your security concerns?"

"Didn't want to lose my equipment to a baggage man."

"Nor did I wish for Lebanese or Cypriot or European customs officers to note that they possessed that camera and recorder."

"Yeah, right, customs would—"

"I will return tomorrow or the next day with the commander. You tell the Salvadorians that their performance is to be perfect. And I will tell you, I want a perfect demonstration, for perfection will answer all their questions."

"Daraiya . . ." Niles watched the taxi exit the gates and turn south on the highway. Accelerating, the taxi quickly faded to a point of yellow in the heat shimmer. But Niles kept the binoculars fixed on the speck until it disappeared into the south. Niles glanced at his map of Lebanon and Syria, then rushed into the hallway, where Javenbach and Alvarez continued monitoring the voices from the garage.

"So we got it straight," Niles started. "That the gang they're training is Salvadorian. I heard that in English. And you, Alvarez?"

"As they were clearing out, someone said in Spanish that they'd at last be going back to Salvador."

"And that tells us where they're going. Javenbach, what did you hear?"

"Many things." He leafed through the pages of notes. "Many personal details of the Pasdaran. Names, villages, the Ayatollahs they respect. They have a very low word for the Salvadorians. They are glad all the Salvadorians will be killed."

"They will all be killed? How?"

"That was not said."

"Alvarez, the Salvos talk about the Iranians?"

"Call them, *traperos,* 'the ragmen.' They can't even talk with them. One of them, Lobo, does the translating. He speaks English to the main man, Muhammed. None of the Iranians speak Spanish, only Muhammed speaks English."

"About those guidance transmitters. With the equipment you brought, what can you do?"

"The kit has radio detonators, electric matches, caps, C-four, det-cord. I can place a charge that will destroy it when they turn it on. End of game. As Mr. Muhammed says, wham."

Niles shook his head. "My thinking is this. If you wire the C-four to the power switch, who knows who'll turn it on? One of the Iranians, maybe Mr. Muhammed. That will not destroy the organization. What if they don't switch it on until they're standing at the embassy? Or waiting in a crowd.

What if they try to take it on a plane and dogs or electronic sniffers pick up the C-four? They end up in a jail in Greece or France or Italy and stay about a week before they're out again. We want this organization destroyed. Can you put radio detonators on the units?"

"No problem with a radio-pop. But the C-four. How much can I load in there? If they're holding the recorder, they'll be blown away. But what if they put it in the trunk of a car? Chances are, no score."

Niles nodded. "No, won't do that. You heard what he said about putting a timer on the switch? Think you could wire a radio detonator to the switch? And turn it on?"

"No cap? No charge? The radio unit just receives the coded pulse and switches on?" Alvarez paused. In the quiet, the monitor carried the voices of the Iranians working in the garage. The reels of the recorder continued turning. "Yeah, I can do that. Maybe. But why?"

"I want you to go through every component you got. I want you to talk to Hijazi. He has that stereo shop in town. I want to know exactly what you can do tonight with the materials available to you. Because we'll be going back in there tonight."

"Thought we were scheduled to get out tonight."

"Radio out for a delay."

Niles went down the stairs to the trucks. At the heavy doors to the warehouse, Hijazi stood guard, watching the highway and fences.

"He-jazz. You know all about business here—"

"No, sir. My experience is very recent and therefore quite limited."

"You move cargo to Damascus?"

"In the future, perhaps. At the present, my business is limited to selling to Syrian officers. They transport the merchandise to their country."

"Only the Syrians smuggle?"

"No, sir. Many Lebanese are also involved in the trans-portation of goods to the markets of Syria. However, it is very difficult. I told you of the disappearance of the Saada father and son."

"Selling weapons to the Iranians."

"They were very knowledgeable in their work. I had hoped to become their associate and perhaps profit from their experience and contacts, but that is impossible. I must limit myself to business with Syrians until another opportunity arises."

"The Saadas did business across the border?"

"Yes, sir. Very frequently. Very discreetly. And very profitably. They had a loading point in the village of Ain el Fije, only a few kilometers from Damascus. I was very much saddened to lose the opportunity to become an associate."

Unfolding his map, Niles found the village. He calculated the distance from the village to Damascus, then traced the lines of roads from the village back to Baalbek.

"What is this road?" he asked Hijazi.

"The Zebdani road."

"It goes to Ain el Fije."

"Yes, sir. It is traditionally a route for untaxed goods—"

"Smuggling?"

"Yes, sir. As there is very little regulation of traffic, the Syrians also use that way to transport Iranians and their weapons into Lebanon."

"Is there a customs office?"

"Syrian customs. There is no office of the Lebanese government."

"Paved?"

"It is a gravel road to Zebdani, then pavement to the Beirut-Damascus highway."

"A good road then?"

"Very good. The Saadas moved many cars and trucks. A very profitable route for their concern."

"Could you take a truck to Ain el Fije and park it?"

From the Nile Hilton, the taxi took Quezada and Rivas through the evening traffic of Cairo, along the same boulevards and expressways they had traveled only an hour before on their arrival in Egypt. The driver had known their names. After that, he had said nothing, ignoring questions Rivas asked in English. Quezada slept. Exhausted after a day and a night of travel from Central America to Europe and across the Mediterranean, Rivas stared at the flashing scenes of light and darkness and old, old city until she slept also and then she started awake to the scream of a jet turbine.

The driver guided the taxi through a maze of steel hangers. Rivas woke Quezada by brushing his hair with her hands. She straightened the lapels of the wrinkled sports jacket he wore, then studied herself in her pocket mirror.

"You are very pretty," he told her in his peasant Spanish. "They will think I am very sharp with women."

"You are? I have nothing to say in my own life?"

"You are now in Arabia. Hold your fire if they treat you as only a pretty girl."

"The Syrian—" She caught herself. Did the taxi driver understand Spanish? "Our friends the Lebanese will be modern men."

"They are the enemies of the Americans and they are giving us weapons. If the weapons are modern, that is enough."

The driver stopped at a doorway. "In there."

Leaving the taxi, they walked into a hanger. A twin-engined corporate jet waited. The logo of a Korean construction company marked the tail. A chair scraped back, the noise echoing in the cavernous interior and a crewman in blue slacks and a blue jacket called. He motioned for Rivas and Quezada to follow. The starters whined as they went up the stairs to the cabin.

Minutes later, they flew over the darkness of the Mediterranean.

30

AGAIN, Niles entered the darkness of the truck garage, his steps slow and silent on the concrete. Nothing moved in the garage. Looking up at the windows of the second-floor office, he saw faint light shifting and flashing on the paper shades, the light repeating in rhythms. But he heard no sounds there, no footsteps, no voices, no music.

Like the night before, a dry wind from the mountains rattled the sheet metal of the garage. Niles continued past the plywood walls of office and storage rooms and his hearing distinguished—through the rattling and faint rushing of the wind—the slow, steady breathing of sleeping men. He stopped, standing for minutes as he listened for movement in the garage. Outside, as the wind shifted, staccato noises came from the wrecking yard, metal scraping and banging against other metal.

The white cargo container stood in the center of the work area, the sidewalls and roof in place, the doors closed. All throughout the afternoon, the micro-transmitters had carried the noise of the Iranians shouting as they struggled with cable winches. The #1 microphone—the microphone placed on the rocket launcher itself—had failed as the Iranians bolted the container closed with power wrenches. Niles carried another micro-transmitter to replace the one sealed in the cargo container.

At the sides of the garage, the work benches seemed the same—cluttered with tools and boxes. The Iranians slept where they had the night before. Niles studied their forms, watching for the movement of a hand, the turning of a head, any movement indicating shallow sleep.

Boots scuffed concrete. Niles shifted sideways, dropping to a crouch and easing between an oil drum and the tanks of a welding kit. For an instant, the lights outside silhouetted a Revolutionary Guard. The man appeared at the side of the rear door of the garage, then flowed into the boxes and equipment, disappearing without a sound. In that moment, Niles had seen that the man held no rifle—Javenbach.

The sentries passed, the sounds of their boots and the clicking of their weapons loud as they passed the door, then fading into the background noise of wind-rattled metal. Niles signaled Javenbach to wait. Niles resumed his watching and listening. Ten minutes later, he signaled Javenbach to follow him. They walked through the center of the garage, passing the sleeping Iranians. On the other side of the trailer and container, Niles signaled Javenbach to watch the Iranians.

Niles saw that the work table had been moved to the side of the garage. He went to the bumper of the trailer and found the #2 microphone. Twisting the adhesive-backed micro-transmitter away from the metal, he crossed to the table and pressed the micro-transmitter in place behind one of the angle-iron legs.

On the top of the table, the tools had shifted. Niles did not see the cases of the camera or the recorder. He searched through the clutter of the tools and boxes, reaching into shadowed shelves under the table and tracing the outlines of boxes with his fingertips. He went to the work benches mounted to the garage walls. Moonlight from the skylights allowed him to move quickly past the tools and vises and drill presses, glancing at the boxes, touching some forms. He went to the opposite side wall and searched the other work bench.

But he did not dare to search near the sleeping Iranians. He returned to Javenbach. Cupping his hands, he whispered, "Video recorder, sound recorder gone. May be there—" He pointed to the work benches near the sleeping men.

Javenbach nodded and started away. Niles stopped him

and hand-signed for him to take off his boots. Javenbach unlaced his heavy Soviet combat boots. Knotting the laces together and hanging the boots over his shoulder, he crossed the floor barefooted. Absolutely silently, Javenbach stepped over the Iranians. A man shifted. Javenbach went still, standing motionless as the man coughed. After minutes, the breathing of the Iranian slowed into a snore and Javenbach continued the search. He did not find either of the cases.

The Marines had maintained their surveillance of the Iranians throughout the day and evening. Muhammed—the English-speaking technical director—had not left the garage compound. The microphones had transmitted his voice up until eleven P.M., when Niles, Javenbach, and Alvarez started from the warehouse. If Muhammed had left for Beirut or Damascus, Stark would have radioed Niles immediately. Also, Niles reasoned that the Iranians had not sent the recorders to another location—Atallah and Muhammed had talked of the comandante of the Salvadorian group coming to take the video unit and the sound recorder.

If he could not find those recorders, Niles lost any chance to hit Atallah.

Niles hand-signed for Javenbach to go to the rear door. Then he took off his own boots and left the work area. Javenbach crouched in the equipment and oil drums, waiting. Niles ran his hand across the steps to the second floor and felt patterned steel. Signaling Javenbach to wait, Niles went up the stairs, slowly transferring his weight from one step to the next, easing his weight down, feeling the steel flex slightly under his foot. The noises of wind-rattled sheet metal covered the faint squeaks of the steps. He measured time in long, slow breaths, not allowing himself to rush any of the eighteen steps to the second floor.

Moonlight came through a dirty skylight. Windows lined the outside wall, the security lights casting a weak yellow glow through the windows. Niles paused at the top and scanned the second floor. To the left, a walkway led to an open area cluttered with stacked tires and shipping crates. Another flight of steel stairs led to the roof. In front of Niles, plywood sheets partitioned the second floor into rooms, the sheets not rising as high as the corrugated steel and skylights of the roof, leaving the rooms without ceilings. Planks served as a floor. Niles slid his feet across the planks, feeling the wood sag with his weight.

Cloth hung in a doorway. Niles heard snoring inside. In a second door, soft light flashed and wavered. He watched for a minute and realized the rhythmic light came from a television. Four more slow steps took him to that doorway. He listened and heard snoring.

He parted the curtain. The room stank of alcohol, hashish, and putrid body filth. Inside, Muhammed Ali, the Iranian technician who had engineered the rocket launchers, sprawled naked on a pad, blankets tangled around him. A videocassette deck, a television, and stacks of cassette tapes covered a table. A sex scene played on the television. A coil-cord stretched half-way across the room, the music of a soundtrack coming from headphones.

Across the room, Niles saw the two carrying cases. The television light shimmered on the chrome word NAGRA. The cases stood next to a ComBloc transceiver.

The planks creaked. A man coughed. Feet shuffled on the planks and a belt buckle rattled. Niles stepped through the curtain as a man left the other room, his feet thudding along the planks and then banging down the steel stairs. Niles stood with his back to the curtain, studying Muhammed and the interior of the stinking room.

In the blue light from the television, the white flesh of the Iranian looked dead. He had passed out with a remote-control handset in his hand. At the side of the pad, a knife and a cigarette lighter lay next to a plastic bag of hashish. Several black spots marked the pad, old burned marks. On the floor, a vodka bottle had overturned.

Niles thought of killing the Iranian now, jamming the blanket down his throat and pushing his face down into the filthy pad until he choked to death—as if he had died in a drunken, doped stupor. But killing the Iranian would not kill Atallah. The Syrian would only find another technician to modify the Soviet rockets. Then again, the Iranian might open his eyes and see the intruder staring down at him. . . .

If the Iranian woke, Niles killed him. If he slept, he lived another day.

A voice shouted out in Farsi. Boots ran across the asphalt. Another voice answered in Spanish. *¡Hijos de puta! ¿No puedo orinar?"*

The wrecking yard went quiet. Niles watched Muhammed, waiting for him to move. But the Iranian slept. The movie ended, the screen freezing the last frame of the film, the credits rolling past, the music from the headphones fading away. The screen finally went to static as the tape player switched off. Muhammed groaned and fell sideways on his face, his snore faltering.

Still cursing, the Salvadorian returned to the room. Niles listened as the man stripped off his pants and lay down on the floor. Waiting, Niles calculated his moves, counting the steps across the room and estimating the weight of the two cases. He used the time to stick the replacement micro-transmitter directly above the doorway, on top of the framing lumber bracing the plywood partition.

Minutes passed before he risked taking the four slow strides. He touched the edges of the cases, checking their locks, then felt their undersides, searching for dangling cords. Lifting the both cases simultaneously, he turned and left the room, pushing through the curtains and slowly, very slowly, one long slow step at a time, he crept to the stairs. The weight and bulk of the case containing the video camera and recorder forced him to sidestep down the stairs.

Then he moved fast. Javenbach emerged from the shadows and signaled the position of the guards. Niles whispered, "Check them."

Javenbach ran barefooted across the asphalt. He came back and took the sound recording case as Niles dashed from the garage. They dodged through the junked trucks to where Alvarez waited in an empty cargo container, handing the two cases through a sheet of black plastic serving as a light trap.

Working with a butane-powered soldering pen, Alvarez disassembled the switches of the recorders and wired new components into the circuitry.

As the shriek of the engines faded, the copilot swung open the cabin door and extended the steps, the clanking of metal and the noise of the slowing tubines reverberating in the reinforced concrete hanger. Atallah waited at his Mercedes. Unlike that morning, when circumstances forced him to wear the rags of an impoverished merchant, he now wore a perfectly tailored Yves Saint Laurent suit—not his best, but more than adequate to impress a comandante from Nicaragua.

The comandante stepped out. A sinewy man, he looked like a fighter—a scarred fighter. He wore a cheap, wrinkled suit. A black string held a patch over his left eye. His left sleeve hung empty. Atallah noted how the man scanned the hanger with his one eye, missing nothing. He nodded to Atallah, then turned and spoke to a young woman who appeared behind him.

How lovely! That girl killed Americans? She wore fashionable jeans and a tight sweater, as revealing of her body as if she stood naked. He remembered the flowery words of Pazos. The Cuban had raved of the beautiful girl and cursed the Nicaraguan who enjoyed her attentions. Atallah saw why the Cuban spoke with such frustration. In truth, how could anyone explain why that young beauty embraced a maimed soldier? What could he offer her? Other than death?

Fixing a smile on his face, Atallah rushed to the Nicaraguan. "Colonel Quezada, I am Colonel Nazim Atallah. Wecome to Syria. What a pleasure to finally meet you. A hero of your nation's revolution and fighter in the continuing war against American and Zionist imperialism. I am truly overwhelmed by this honor."

"*Mucho gusto,*" Quezada stammered. He looked to the woman.

"I am Marianela. The colonel does not speak English. I am to translate. Or would you like to provide your own translator?"

"Miss, I am charmed. Of course you may translate. I have come personally to take you to your quarters for the night and to arrange for your comfort."

"We are in Syria? Damascus?"

"That is not important. Tomorrow morning, we drive to the Bekaa."

* * *

As they rode from the hangar, she watched the Syrian colonel watch her as he spoke. The Syrian praised Quezada in his fluent English, then waited as Rivas translated. He told of his interest and admiration of the Nicaraguan revolution. But always the Syrian spoke to her, wooing her with his ideological rhetoric and reptilian smile.

Soldiers at checkpoints glanced at the Mercedes, then shone flashlights through the windshield to confirm the identity of the colonel. No soldier required that the colonel produce his identification. Yet Rivas saw the soldiers checking the passes of other officers. High fences and gates separated the hangar area from the barracks, then another fence and a gate secured an area of offices and communications towers. Soldiers patrolled the perimeter of the complex. A Soviet transport helicopter waited on a helipad. Soldiers and plainclothes security men stood at limousines, talking and smoking.

"That is the entourage of Rifaat," Atallah explained. "The brother of our President. If I did not have more important concerns, I would be in attendance. But my esteemed comrades in the struggle of course take priority over a merely formal meeting of party executives."

"Is he not the commander of the national security forces?" Rivas asked.

"Yes, yes, he is. Do you follow the very Byzantine political affairs of my nation?"

"Only in the newspapers."

"There are no other sources of information. Of course the information is invariably incorrect. But the journalists are not to be faulted. My government does not favor the publication of information concerning our state matters. All the decisions of our President and his aides are secret, all actions are secret. And there are secrets within secrets. Much like this operation. Perhaps it comes as a surprise to you that the plane took you not to Lebanon but to Syria, that a Syrian colonel and not some bearded mullah is the commander of the operation. But do you think my President would entrust vital operations to fanatics? If you were not proven, trusted allies you would indeed meet only with fanatics. But that is not the case."

She translated all this for Quezada, then turned back to the Syrian and asked, "But what is the secret within this secret?"

Atallah laughed. "The Cuban talked of you. He said you are very intelligent and that is certainly true. You and the esteemed colonel are the secret. Here are your quarters—" He parked the Mercedes at an apartment building near the offices"—we cannot risk allowing you to stay in a hotel. You will travel tomorrow to the Bekaa and return. Then you will return by jet to Egypt. If the Americans noted your departure from Nicaragua or the Mossad learned of your arrival in Egypt, they will know nothing of your true destination. Libya? Yemen? Iran? Syria? They can guess nothing of your intentions."

"And if they kill us," she added, "nothing connects us to Syria. If they take us alive, Syria denies everything."

"Of course. Come, I think you will find the rooms satisfactory."

Atallah showed his guests a suite with a conference room, bedroom, two bathrooms, and a bar stocked with wines and liquors from around the world. Changes of clothing hung in the closet. Later, after the Syrian left, Quezada turned on the stereo loud and questioned her in whispers on the details of what Atallah had said.

"I told you everything in the car."

"But what of Pazos? I heard him say—"

"He said the Cuban talked of me. That pig must have talked, the Syrian must have a file on both of us, so what?"

"I have no confidence in all this. Trusted friends, shit! Why would he compromise his country by bringing us here? To impress us with the airplanes and helicopters and his Mercedes Benz? That is not it."

"He said this insured security. I believe that. The jet and this base are absolutely secure. You saw it. No one but the Syrians will know we are here."

"This is a bad sign. If we had gone to Lebanon, I would not think this. But now . . . after the attack, if we are ever captured, if we ever talk, we compromise them. They will not allow that. This marks us."

"The Cubans. Could the Cubans know about Pazos?"

"Maybe. Maybe the Cubans want us dead. But the Syrians want us to hit the Americans. They don't care about some Cuban functionary. They want the attack to go forward. But after the attack . . . from this moment on, we must be very, very cautious. Tomorrow, I will talk of future attacks. I must convince him of our value to Syria past this one attack on the embassy. Or, for whatever reason—the Cubans wanting revenge, these Syrians wanting to silence us, who knows?—I think we will be liquidated."

In the next hours, as she tried to sleep, Rivas considered what he told her. And she remembered what Pazos had told her that night weeks ago in the limousine—Octavio Quezada could be replaced with a phone call. Octavio even confirmed that. The Cubans and the Nicaraguans placed no extraordinary value on the life of a hero. Did they intend to use him for this attack, then reward him with death? And what of her? When Pazos had offered advancement in the struggle if she took him as her lover, she refused him. Why should she leave a man of proven revolutionary valor, who had dedicated his life to training fighters for the freedom of her country? Why accept that Cuban pig? That coward? Pazos had served only the role of the functionary, taking commands from his Cuban superiors and relaying instructions to the various underlings, a functionary without commitment to El Salvador and no future in the international revolutionary struggle. That night in the limousine, listening to his talk of advancement, she had considered his promises—and told him to take his hands off her.

But now, she must reconsider her loyalty to Quezada. Her love and respect meant nothing if the Cubans or the Nicaraguans or Syrians intended to liquidate him. She must put the struggle above her own emotions.

Atallah actually directed this attack against the Americans. If the attack succeeded, she would gain the recognition of the leadership. She could finally advance in the organization and take command of a force. Atallah controlled the rockets and her future.

The Marines, her comrades in the unit, Pazos the functionary, now this Syrian—they always displayed their fanta-

298

sies like neon. Quezada had not—his discipline or pride kept him distant until that day she embraced him.

She had heard the talk of her taking him to exploit his rank. Lies. She had respected him first, then come to love him. But now she considered manipulating the Syrian. She had used her body to attract the Marines and score a victory for El Salvador, why not use her body to take the rank she deserved in the international struggle?

Like Quezada had told her, she must talk to the Syrian of future actions—to convince him of her value in the future.

31

ALVAREZ paced. He saw dawnlight beaming through the walls of the shattered warehouse—and he had not slept. Despite his fatigue, the three nights and two days without a straight four hours of sleep, his nerves and adrenaline kept him moving. He checked his Soviet web gear again, running his hands over the canvas of the vest of Kalashnikov magazines, jerking at the straps of his load-bearing suspenders and checking each buckle. He reached to the small of his back and slipped the Beretta out of the clip-holster. He kept the silencer and two spare magazines of 9mm subsonic rounds in his left thigh pocket. Without the silencer, he could almost conceal the auto pistol under his web belt.

For the tenth time, he paused at the stairs to the third floor. Farsi came from the monitor speaker in the hallway—but he did not hear the noise of a diesel engine. Going back to the Land Rover, he gulped from a can of Coca-Cola smuggled in from France for the rich of Syria. Hijazi slept behind the steering wheel. He wore torn and patched Lebanese army fatigues and cast-off American web gear. Arabic verses painted on the stock of his Kalashnikov identified him as a member of the Hezbollah.

Turning the side mirror, Alvarez studied his face. He put on his sunglasses. But his sharp Yaqui nose and high cheekbones did not look Syrian. Then again, this *vato* don't look no Anglo. Did the Syrians know what a Mexican looked like? He put on his ComBloc helmet and pushed the helmet forward until he had to tilt his head back to look at himself. A form moved behind him.

"Looking fine, Hey-zoot," Vatsek commented.

"Like a righteous soldier of Assad should."

"Problem is, you stink."

"Sorry I offend you. Want to run down to the laundromat for me? Take your white face and your phony Russian uniform into downtown Baalbek with a bag of dirty cammies? Wait four hundred forty-four years for the state department to get you out of Baalbek? Or what's left of you, after the faithful give you a few thousand lashes."

"Shit. You think those mother-fuck professors, you think they'd pay the price of a long-distance phone call for a Marine? We're here on our own. Live or die, on our own, alone. Think I will walk into Baalbek. Came here to kill ragheads. And there is nothing going on at all. Got no count in Nicaragua, now this looks like a zero count."

Vatsek continued on his rounds of the warehouse, peering out through the cracks in the plank doors, watching through the 20mm holes in the concrete. He carried his PKM like a rifle, the heavy machine-gun proportionate to his bulk.

The steel of the stairs clanged under boots. Javenbach ran down with a can in one hand and a bayonet in the other. He pointed at the doors with the bayonet. Alvarez reached into the Land Rover and shook Hijazi awake.

"Truck's in motion! Roll the doors!"

Hijazi started the engine and revved it, smoke clouding. Alvarez jumped over the side of the open Land Rover. He shoved aside a loaded RPG launcher and checked the pedestal-mounted PKM again, jerking back the cocking lever to eject the cartridge already in the chamber.

Scraping the inside of the can with the bayonet, Javenbach licked fava bean paste from the knife. He threw the can. "I listened to their words. They will go to Tripoli. The captain instructed us not to take the truck until after Deir el Ahmar, in the mountains. That is twenty kilometers."

"Only twenty clicks? A semi can do sixty or eighty miles an hour. Get in, Akbar. They got guards?"

The roar of a diesel truck passed, the garage shuddering with the low-cycle vibration.

"There are two cars of guards. Pasdaran from Baalbek that—"

"This will be a no be-bop cruise. Could get serious. Godzilla-man, loan us your weapon."

"Hey," Vatsek interrupted. "I want in on this."

"Stay where you are, sergeant," Niles said. "Open those doors and continue with your watch. You do not look like any kind of Arab I ever saw."

Vatsek passed his PKM to Javenbach. "That's my personal weapon, Corporal."

"I will care for it."

"Then kill someone with it. It's hungry."

"Wait until the mountains," Niles stressed. "Stay back, then hit the follow car and the lead car. They must be out of walkie-talkie range of any checkpoints or other militia units when you hit them. And there are to be no prisoners or survivors. If one of them escapes, we're all gone. And bring that truck and trailer back undamaged, you understand?"

Hijazi put the Land Rover in gear and drove out of the factory, bumping over the broken concrete of the bomb-cratered equipment yard. For the first time in days, Alvarez felt the heat of the sun. He looked back at the building, seeing the shattered walls and the fire-blackened concrete. Only the plank doors revealed the renovation of the building into a warehouse. Then he looked around at the junk littering the pavement—wrecked trucks, rusting equipment dumped by the workmen, a collapsed loading dock.

"East Los Angeles!" He told Javenbach, "All this time I thought I'd left the U.S. of A. But here I am. Back in the streets."

But Javenbach only stared at him. Hijazi deactivated the alarms on the perimeter fence, then drove the Land Rover out, rekeying the alarms before accelerating into the early morning traffic on the highway. After a few kilometers, the highway forked. Hijazi followed the highway to the left, away from a Syrian army checkpoint.

Workshops and clusters of shacks lined the roadside. Passing the town of Latt, Alvarez saw groups of militiamen boiling morning tea on fires. He slid down low in the back seat and watched the fields and towns. He remembered

Beirut—the narrow streets and ruined apartments, the shoulder-to-shoulder crowds in the markets, the loudspeakers blaring the calls to prayer and European disco rhythms. In contrast, the Bekaa looked like another country, another century. Here, all the women wore the chador. Stenciled Khomeinis stared from the walls.

Alvarez thought of Sonora, the state of Mexico where his grandparents still lived, the endless expanses of desert, the bleak towns on the highways. The Bekaa looked like a good section of Sonora—which meant the difference between zero and *nada*. Why would anyone fight for this place? Or Beirut?

"There." Javenbach pointed to the white truck and trailer a few kilometers ahead. The highway ran straight into the valley, then veered to the north. Greenery and light reflecting from windows marked Deir el Ahmar. Mountains walled the western horizon.

Maintaining his speed, Hijazi stayed far back. Alvarez wanted him to floor it, get it over with. Red line it. My brain is red lining, my nerves are burning. I'm no Niles, cold and quiet as ice, not a thought in his head as he goes walking through the dark like a cat. That man rode through Revolutionary Guard checkpoints. Talked French to the Pasdaran. Took their pictures! I'd jump out of my skin. Walking through Hayy al Sollom that night. Walk in, walk out, I said—insane.

Javenbach reached into a box on the floor and brought out Soviet grenades. He passed two of the grenades back to Alvarez. Alvarez stowed the two grenades and watched as Javenbach straightened the cotter pins of other grenades, pocketing the grenades in his shirt pockets. That kid is cool. What did he do in the revolution? Here I am, veteran of Colombia, Salvador, West Beirut, East LA, and he's cool.

Finally, where the highway veered, Hijazi floored the accelerator. Alvarez watched the needle of the accelerator moving to the right. He saw only open highway ahead. The white trailer appeared from time to time between hills. Buckling the strap on his helmet, he sat up. He held the grenades in his hands. Look cool, wear your shades. Before they look twice, they die.

The Land Rover shook with speed, the roadside blurring. As the highway cut through hills, Hijazi slowed and swerved and accelerated, powering through every turn at maximum speed, braking and swerving to avoid an oncoming car, then accelerating again. A van came into sight ahead. The steep uphill grade slowed the diesel truck and the guard cars. Gaining on the cars. Hijazi maintained an even speed until he closed the gap, coming up on the bumper of the battered Japanese van.

Turning in their seats, Iranians looked back at the Land Rover. One man spoke into a walkie-talkie. Other men shifted, the muzzles of Kalashnikovs appearing—they did not point the rifles, but they held the rifles ready.

"Be cool, He-Jazz," Alvarez almost shouted. "They're going slow. They know it. Pass them when you can. Make like you're the normal, state-of-the-art Beiruti insani. Pass them. Keep going. If I say stop, hit the brakes, like you got a car coming, you know."

"And then?" Javenbach asked.

"Do it. But don't even look at them unless I say it. If they stay sharp, we'll go past them, try for the lead car. Pass them now!"

Easing into the other lane and accelerating, they passed the van. Alvarez looked over and saw the muzzles of Kalashnikov rifles in the open windows of the van. The bearded, scowling gunmen did not point the rifles, but they watched the Land Rover, ready to aim their weapons and fire. And Hijazi braked suddenly, the gunmen jerking up the rifles, then lowering the rifles as Hijazi slowed and swerved back into the lane.

A motorcycle flashed past, followed by a Syrian troop truck. Hijazi waited, following the curves through the hills. Drop-offs appeared as the road switchbacked across mountains. When they came to another open stretch, Hijazi tried to pass again.

And again the Revolutionary Guards held their rifles ready, glaring at the three men in the Land Rover. Alvarez stared back. One of the Revolutionary Guards raised his rifle to his shoulder and laughed, the others in the van laughing as Alvarez flinched.

Horn blaring, a Fiat came head-on. The tires screeched as Hijazi braked and swerved again, the swerving throwing Alvarez hard against the PKM pedestal, a bolt tearing his arm. The laughing Iranians flashed past.

Far ahead, the road doubled back. The truck slowed and down-shifted, laboring against the grade. Beyond the railing, Alvarez saw only blue sky. Jerking the RPG off the seat, he tore off the safety cap. Hijazi glanced back.

"Rocket?"

"Forget the strategy. Time to get serious."

Hijazi stepped on the accelerator, holding the Land Rover straight and steady. The Iranians looked back, still laughing. Their faces went slack as Alvarez stood and fired from a distance of twenty meters, the rocket screaming into the rear door of the van.

Flame and glass exploded from the van, the roof and side panels suddenly distorted. Back-blasted glass showered Alvarez. Hijazi braked to avoid the van and Alvarez hit the dashboard. Javenbach grabbed him and shoved him back. Trailing flames from the shrapnel-torn gas tank, the van drifted to the left, hitting the end of the guard rail and overturning, tumbling sideways down the slope. Hijazi whipped past and accelerated through the wide turn, flooring the pedal, gaining speed until the next curve, down-shifting, side-slipping through the curve, coming within a hand's-width of the guard rail.

Alvarez reloaded the rocket launcher in the back seat, the whipping Land Rover battering him between the side panel and the steel of the machine-gun pedestal. Forcing the wax-coated shaft of the rocket into the launcher and locking the shaft under the hammer, he looked up to see the white steel doors of the cargo container looming over him as Hijazi tried to pass the truck.

The truck driver watched them in the rear-view mirror. Alvarez saw the driver speak into a walkie-talkie. If he's talking into the radio himself, Alvarez reasoned, that means he's alone in the cab. He's got no man riding shotgun.

Looping the sling of his folding-stock Kalashnikov over

his shoulder, Alvarez slid the short rifle around to his back, leaving his hands free. "Don't pass the truck, stay tight on his ass, but don't pass."

"What?"

The truck driver down-shifted for the next switchbacking turn, Hijazi braking almost to a stop. Alvarez jumped over the side of the Land Rover and hit the asphalt running, stumbling, not falling, sprinting across the asphalt and broken concrete to the side of the truck and leaping onto the running board. The driver started at the sound of his boots hitting the truck and stared at the Syrian soldier in sunglasses looking through the window at him.

In the second the driver stared, Alvarez tried the door handle. Locked. Then the driver reached for a pistol. Gripping the handle in his left hand, Alvarez swung away as the pistol fired through the window. The next bullet punched through the metal of the door. The clutch lurched, the truck wove as the driver fired with one hand and tried to steer with the other, the steering wheel demanding too much strength. As the driver gripped the wheel with both hands, Alvarez jerked the Beretta from the holster behind his belt, fired wild, the pistol jumping in his hand as he pointed and fired as fast as he could bring the pistol on line and pull the trigger, scrambling through the window and almost touching the driver with the muzzle as he fired again and again, slugs punching through a hand, an arm, gouging across his face, knocking his head to the side, killing the driver before Alvarez stopped firing, the driver falling to the side.

Alvarez clawed at the steering wheel, dragging himself through the window by the bicep of his left arm as he fired a last shot directly into the dead driver's face, then he grabbed the steering wheel in both hands and kept the truck and trailer on the road. He wrenched open the door and pushed the dead man out, almost dropping the body in the Land Rover as Hijazi passed. Javenbach now stood behind the pedestal-mounted PKM.

The Land Rover skidded through a curve. Alvarez strained at the blood-slick steering wheel, managing to muscle the truck and trailer around the curve, the truck cab shaking with the lurching of the clutch. He ground the gears as he down-shifted and accelerated, bringing up the speed as the road straightened.

Five hundred meters ahead, an old Mercedes sedan had pulled off the road. Bearded gunmen stood at the side of the road, firing at the Land Rover. The windshield of the Land Rover spidered with a hit, then the popping of automatic fire came. Hijazi braked, tires smoking, Javenbach trying to hold onto the pedestal but falling between the seats.

Alvarez continued forward. The gunmen waved for the truck to pass. Only as the truck came within a few meters did they look up and see the helmeted Syrian driving the truck and then Alvarez swerved, the bodies of the gunmen thumping the truck, then metal screeched, the truck pushing the Mercedes along the guard rail.

The Mercedes pitched over the edge. Alvarez jerked the truck back onto the pavement. In the rear-view mirror, he saw the Land Rover, Javenbach behind the PKM, the muzzle flashing. He looked in the right-hand mirror and saw dust puffing around a man laying prone with a rifle. The gunman flipped and did not move. Javenbach raked the other bodies with bursts from the machine gun. Alvarez saw the Land Rover pull over—to throw the bodies off the road.

Following the highway for a few kilometers, he found a side road leading into the valleys. He managed to turn the truck and trailer around. Shaking with nerves and adrenaline, he sat behind the steering wheel and laughed.

You are one *vato loco, sus socios son locos,* there it is, *socios locos.* Traveling with Captain Niles, this is too extreme!

Then a thought stopped his laughs.

What will the captain do with these rockets? He didn't say destroy them. He said, take them. Why?

Hijazi and Javenbach arrived minutes later. Alvarez called out, "Back to the warehouse?"

"No. To Ain el Fije."

"Where's that?"

"Syria."

Through binoculars, Niles watched the Salvadorians kick a soccer ball. They reminded him of the teenage soldiers he had trained in Honduras. Thin and wiry, without the mature strength of men, but very intensely motivated in combat, killing and dying for the cause of their nation. Yet they played like boys, taunting whoever lost a point, mimicking one another, strutting when they kicked a trick shot.

The monitor speaker carried the voices of the Iranians and the noises of power wrenches inside the garage. A tape machine recorded their conversations—later, Javenbach would review the tapes. But Niles had an approximate schedule of the activities of the Syrian, Iranians, and Salvadorians. The micro-transmitter placed near the long-distance radio had monitored the cryptic exchanges between the Iranian and the Syrians at Daraiya. A Syrian had reported the arrival of "the comandante" at dawn. The Syrian told Muhammed Ali to expect a meeting later in the day.

That meant the demonstration, when those four boys would go through a final rehearsal for a murderous and criminal attack on the American embassy in San Salvador. Or the American ambassador's residence? Or the National Palace? To murder in one strike all the American diplomats stationed in Salvador and the highest political leadership of their nation.

A crime? Or war? A terrorist attack on American diplomats in revenge for the United States's sponsoring the defense of El Salvador? Or an act of war? A desperate and brilliant attempt to decaptitate the forces opposing the revolution? He had monitored the talk of those boys. They had fought face-to-face against the army of El Salvador. They talked of the fascists and the regime and the imperialists.

Jargon. Yet they had earned their bravado.

Niles intended to destroy their gang. If that action required killing those boys, so be it. They served with a gang that murdered Americans. But Niles did not fight for payback, corpses for corpses. He fought to win. First he destroyed Atallah. Then, if he could capture and interrogate those teenagers, maybe reindoctrinate them and return them to El Salvador as agents working for Salvadorian intelligence, they lived. A telephone call might break another gang or save the lives of Americans targeted in a future attack. But Niles guessed—he would bet money—even if he took them prisoner and offered them their lives for cooperation, they would refuse.

Stark interrupted his thoughts. "Hijazi and Alvarez reporting back."

"They all right?"

"No casualties."

"And they took it?"

"It's parked at Majdalon. Javenbach stayed with the truck."

Rushing down the stairs, Niles saw the bullet-shattered windshield of the Land Rover. Alvarez stood near the plank doors, hosing blood from his Syrian fatigues. Hijazi spread out papers on the hood of the Land Rover. Rolling a form into a portable typewriter, he printed numbers on lines.

"The driver of the truck carried these documents. They carry the seal of the Lebanese military command. But I do not recognize the signatures of the officers."

"Any problems with your documents?"

"My documents will have the signatures of Syrian military commanders." He pointed to the form in the typewriter. "The soldiers will know the names."

"The truck in good shape?"

"Some small damage. Nothing important."

"Then take it through."

"Sir," Alvarez asked. "What is going on? Why are we going into Syria?"

"You're not. It'll be Hijazi and Javenbach."

"Into Syria? Two guys? You expect to see them again?"

"Sounds one-way to me," Vatsek commented.

"They can make it. Hijazi has got it all arranged."

"Then send me with them. They need back-up."

"A Syrian asks you a question, you're all gone. Go, Hijazi. Park it, open it up, cover it. Then get out."

"Sending those rockets into Syria? Captain, what are you doing?"

Niles shook his head. "You don't want to know."

Atallah coordinated the demonstration from his office, calling the Nicaraguan, then ordering an aide to radio the Bekaa to alert the Iranians. Changing from his uniform to the threadbare suit of the merchant, he left his office and walked through the afternoon heat to the apartments.

The Nicaraguan answered the door. He wore the simple clothes of a field worker, coarse pants, a shirt, and a keffiyah.

"¿Está bueno?"

"Very good. No one will give us a second glance."

"And is this appropriate?" Rivas asked.

Even in the chador of a peasant girl, she somehow looked enticing. The draped cloth of the long dress and long-sleeved blouse did not hide the slim form of her body. And she held the head-covering at her throat, emphasizing the oval of her face and her perfect features.

"How lovely."

As Muhammed Ali received the radio message from Daraiya, Niles listened a kilometer away.

Shouting and waving his arms, Muhammed Ali ran through the garage, his voice echoing from the steel walls as he directed the Iranians. One man raised the main door, others went to the cars and trucks outside. The Salvadorians gathered at the tractor and trailer. Behind the steering wheel, Lobo tried the controls. Muhammed Ali saw Lobo in the cab of the Mercedes tractor rig and shouted:

"What are you doing in that truck? Out!"

"But is not this show to prove to my comandante that we can—"

"Shut up. Get out. My man is driving the truck. You can't even read the dash."

"True, it is German and Arabic. But a man does not need to be a scholar to understand trucks. A truck is a truck. I can drive it."

"Get out of there! We've got an hour to get in position."

Muhammed Ali continued outside. He argued with an Iranian driving a wrecking truck. Lobo talked with his comrades in Spanish. "Even after all these weeks of working together, he has no respect. The commander told me before we left the base to be very careful of these foreigners, to watch and think of what they did. Today when I see him, I will tell him of these things. Are you in agreement?"

"They think we are shit," the stocky Daniel spat out. "I cannot know what they say, but I watch them. They care nothing for our fight. They want only to kill Americans."

"And for that they need us," Victor countered. "Who cares what they think? You tell the colonel they are not friends, but the rockets are good."

"Why did they not allow us to watch the work?" Marco asked. "That is a question I have. Are there rockets in the box they sent to Salvador?"

"There are rockets." Lobo nodded. "I saw that."

"Then why did he not allow us to work on the assembly?"

"They think we are too stupid," Daniel answered.

A shout from Muhammed Ali stopped their talk. "Out! To the car. We got an hour to get this ready."

Lobo told the others in a low voice, "The colonel will hear of all this. Now we will be good soldiers. They trained us and we will show what we learned. . . ."

Niles noted the comment of the one teenager: Muhammed Ali did not allow the Salvadorian crew to observe final assembly of the rocket container—why?

In the cab of the truck, Hijazi watched the Syrian soldier question Javenbach. The other Syrians had not left the shade of the concrete and sandbag border post. Wind from the mountains swept through the narrow valley, clattering the sheet-metal roof of the post and scouring clouds of dust off the road. Wrecked trucks and armored personnel carriers rusted on both sides of the road, remnants of skirmishes and accidents. Israeli jets had hit columns of Syrians here during the 1982 invasion, the Syrians and the Iranians had fought with Lebanese militias, and smugglers like Hijazi had tried to run the border during the night to avoid paying the guards—all the conflicts had left scrap metal littering the fields.

The soldier pointed at the spider-shatter of the Land Rover windshield. Javenbach gestured back to the Bekaa, as if geography alone could explain the bullet—and geography seemed to answer the soldier. He fingered the plastic tape over the bullet hole in the glass, then motioned for Javenbach to continue. Hijazi eased the tractor and trailer forward. At the guard post, the other soldiers finally left their chairs. They laughed and joked among themselves as they spread out along the roadside.

"Documents!"

Hijazi handed over the forged travel permit of Rashid Saada. The soldier glanced at the photo. Another soldier brought a notebook with pages of names—some typed, others handwritten. Hijazi said nothing. The Saada father and son had conducted honorable trade between Lebanon and Syria, earning an honest profit and making several Syrian bureaucrats rich men. They had paid the expected bribes without fail. Hijazi did not fear the list of names.

The soldiers paced the trailer, slapping the steel sides. Finally the sergeant commanding the post stepped to the truck, "The documents for the truck and the cargo. What are you carrying?"

"It is all here." Hijazi folded a U.S. ten dollar bill into the papers—the going rate for a sergeant passing a truckload of merchandise.

As the sergeant leafed through the forms, the bill fluttered to the ground. One of the soldiers grabbed the money. The sergeant looked from the money the soldier held to Hijazi. Then he passed the forms back to Hijazi.

"Go."

As the heavy truck and trailer left the checkpoint, the Syrian sergeant returned to his office. He dialed the number of military intelligence in Zebdani.

"There is a truck—" He described the Mercedes tractor and the trailer, then read off the license number. "The driver is Rashid Saada. His identity card lists his work as merchant. And the documents list the truck and its merchandise as his property. But this truck, I have seen it many times. It is a truck used by the fanatics of Iran to take their weapons and munitions into the Bekaa."

"And now it is returning for another load? Why do you call with this information?"

"Because the truck is returning loaded. And the documents declare the destination to be Damascus. Why are the fanatics talking their weapons to Damascus?"

Minutes later, agents of Syrian Military Intelligence parked on the road south of Zebdani. They watched for the truck and trailer.

32

SPEEDING north on the Baalbek highway, Rivas translated the questions asked by Quezada. The difficulty with languages required that she share the back seat of the Dodge taxi with Atallah. Quezada sat in the front with the driver, the man named Madaya—the Spanish-speaking Arab who had gone to Managua. Rivas listened carefully as the Syrian colonel spoke, then she summarized the answers in Spanish for Quezada.

For the hour of the drive from the military base, she had questioned and observed Atallah. She knew that he lied. Behind his mask of smiles and courtesy, his mind calculated the intent of every question, then manufactured elaborate and seemingly factual responses to reassure and flatter Rivas and Quezada.

" . . . though the Cuban revolution matured through its role as diplomatic leader of the Third World, it has also remained the vanguard nation of the Western Hemisphere—much as Syria remains the vanguard nation of the Arab League. Therefore it was without surprise—but with joy nevertheless—that I received the inquiries of our esteemed associate Emilio Pazos—may he always be remembered as a hero and a martyr."

"It was Pazos who began all this?" Rivas asked. "He told us the Iranians offered the rockets after the killing of the Marines in Salvador."

"He was so modest! He came to me after the great victory of the Shiites over the American Marines in October. He had approached someone in my government—it remains uncertain who, though I believe he may have encountered them at

314

an embassy affair. That unknown person directed him to me."

"Why you? Do you work with the Iranians?"

"I am not so fortunate. It is only my responsibility to identify the many foreigners traveling through my country. Though I knew almost nothing of the Iranians in Lebanon, I directed him to the groups of devout young men organizing the Islamic resistance. After that, Pazos did not require my assistance to pursue his alliance. Why should he, as a Cuban and revolutionary, require my help to fight the Americans? It was in his blood."

Rivas summarized his long answers in quick translations. Quezada nodded and watched the fields and mountains of Lebanon. She wanted to add that Atallah lied but could not. The driver Madaya spoke only broken Spanish, but how much did he understand? Her evaluation of the statements by Atallah must wait until they had a moment away from the Syrians. Quezada asked if Atallah would not take the place of Pazos in the organization as the coordinator and commander?

"How could I take the place of the heroic Emilio? How could I, a low-ranking officer reduced to the clerkdom of a petty bureaucrat, take the place of a genius like Emilio? Who brought together the most far-flung and foreign of comrades in a common struggle for freedom. I am serving only to accomodate his many friends in this time of terrible grief. Must I allow the mercenaries of the United States a victory over the people of the world? If I can accommodate the many friends of my dear Pazos, if I can introduce one fighter to another so that they may continue the struggle as allies, I deny victory to the Americans. Their crime will not defeat the work of the one hero they struck down because many, many heroes will close ranks to continue the struggle."

"Who are these other friends? Latins?"

"We will talk of the others another time. Their loyalties and indeed their identities remain in doubt."

"We will work directly with the Iranians?"

"Do you think that only Iranians and yourselves struggle against the imperialism of the United States? Do you discount the contributions of the Lebanese and the Palestin-

ians? Today you meet Iranians. Lebanese and Palestinians—
I was told by my dear Pazos—also played a role in this strike
against the Americans, though I am not aware of what role.
Perhaps if you ask the Iranians, they will explain."

"And we will deal directly with our comrades the Iranians
in the future?"

"With some provisions for security, I am sure, but nevertheless, direct. I cannot continue to play this role as go-
between. I cannot involve myself in affairs beyond my rank
and ability. Though my heart yearns for the field of valor, I,
unfortunately, must leave the struggle to free the Americas
to fighters like you and your brave colonel—"

The taxi turned onto a side road of gravel and broken
asphalt. "Finally, we are leaving the highway. Now we drive
only a few kilometers. I am sure your victory in Salvador
will be a great inspiration to all the other revolutionary
movements. You will, in fact, be celebrities in the international struggle, leaders without equal, perhaps commanders
of the struggle to free all the Americas!"

Rivas translated that statement for Quezada and the
scarred veteran laughed. In Spanish, he commented, "Celebrities? Commanders of the war for the Americas? And not
the war for the moon and the stars? Ask him who will finance
this war to free the Americas . . ."

Hijazi guided the truck and semi-trailer through the white-
washed village of Ain el Fije. The afternoon heat had cleared
the streets, the few merchants retreating deep into their
shops, chador-draped old women scuttling through the
shadows, a group of ragged boys throwing stones at a dog.
Though Ain el Fije viewed the sprawl and pollution of
Damascus—only thirty minutes away by car—the village
remained isolated. Second-class buses came only in the
mornings and evenings, the infrequent transportation forcing men who worked in Damascus to commute on motorcycles.

The Saada father and son had exploited this contradiction
of isolation and proximity. The family compound of a rich
farmer became their warehouse and vehicle storage yard.
The house had long ago burned, but the animal sheds, the

walls, and the heavy plank gates remained. They parked rows of smuggled and untaxed motorcycles in the security of the walls, often using local men to deliver the motorcycles to buyers in Damascus. Cars stolen in Beirut received a new coat of paint and Syrian license plates. And when they purchased weapons from the Syrian army, the Ain el Fije compound allowed the Saadas to move the weapons from the government warehouses and then wait for a favorable time to move the truckloads of weapons through the Bekaa. After the disappearances of the father and son, one of their associates had looted the compound of cars and motorcycles. Hijazi had inspected the compound without informing the family—if they decided to sell the property, he wanted to negotiate with the strength of knowledge while pretending disinterest.

Stopping on the wrong side of the road, he opened the gates, then drove the rig to the back of the compound, swinging wide across the oil-soaked ground to maneuver behind the walls and foundations of the long-ago burned house. Javenbach secured the gates with a heavy padlock while Hijazi broke the padlocks off the container.

"It is all here. As the captain said."

The two men threw out the boxes of bus parts. Finding the power wrenches and electrical cords, they started one of the generators. Hijazi climbed to the top of the container.

Beyond the orchards, beyond the low hills, across the wide green plain, beyond the black band of the highway to Beirut, he saw Damascus. He remembered the tapes of Muhammed Ali and the Colombian talking of using the rockets to murder an ambassador traveling in a car. Captain Niles had refused to explain the attack on the Syrian colonel. But Hijazi knew one thing—the Syrian colonel died today.

Hijazi put the socket over the first bolt and triggered the motor.

A few hundred meters from the compound, two cars stopped. Syrian agents stepped into the shade of trees. With a direct line of sight on the compound, they sent the cars to wait in the village. They tested their walkie-talkies and then sat down to wait and watch.

317

"This, for the purpose of the demonstration, will be the transmitter." Atallah held a metal case of exposed electronics in his hands. "Of course the transmitter for the Americans will be very much different in appearance. The technician prepared two, a video camera and a sound recorder. But that is for later, when this demonstration has convinced you of the value of our gift to your revolution. And this—" He held up a second metal box "—will launch the rockets. Who will place the transmitter? And who will stay here for the demonstration?"

The Iranians had parked the truck and semi-trailer in a field. A line of trees screened the field from the highway. A hundred meters away, the Salvadorians leaned in the shade of the truck and semi-trailer, waiting for instructions. Rivas translated the questions for Quezada. Not answering immediately, he squinted at the sun, then glanced at his watch.

"Does he have binoculars?"

Atallah recognized the Spanish word and passed binoculars to Quezada. "Spanish and English are so similar. With my little knowledge of French, I can sometimes understand your Spanish. Not at all like Arabic."

"Would Arabic be difficult for me to learn?" Rivas asked.

"Difficult, but rewarding, for Arabic is the language of the Koran."

"And the language of our allies. If we are to work together in the future, it would be good to speak your language."

"Would you learn Persian also?"

"Why not? I will do whatever is required."

"You are a very determined young woman."

Quezada pointed to the foothills. "There. Where that road cuts that ridge. Tell him to send a man there with the transmitter. We do not have time to go there ourselves."

After she explained to Atallah, he relayed the instructions to an Iranian. Atallah went to the Iranians waiting at the wrecking trucks. As the Syrian and the Iranians talked and pointed at the hills, Quezada told Rivas:

"I did not want to risk you. Who knows what screw-ups are possible?"

The Iranians drove away in their battered Mercedes. Atallah returned to Rivas and Quezada. "They will place the transmitter. The road is good and it will only be a few minutes. May I suggest that we proceed with the demonstration? Your men are anxiously awaiting your order."

Quezada threw a rock at the Salvadorians. "Show me what you can do! Why are your waiting?"

As their commander paced around the truck, the Salvadorian crew opened the cargo container. The teenagers moved through their duties with speed and precision, unlocking the doors, unloading the stacks of boxes and parts concealing the generators and tools. Weeks of practice made talk unnecessary. Marco and Daniel took their positions with the Kalashnikovs. Victor started the first generator and Lobo climbed to the roof of the container with his power wrench.

Rivas watched from the trees, Atallah answering her questions.

"As you can see," Atallah explained, "it is entirely self-contained. Tools, power, rifles. Then there is an entirely independent power supply for the launcher."

"There cannot be an accidental firing?" Rivas asked.

"Impossible."

"Why is it impossible?"

"First, the box must be opened. Then there must be the signal from the transmitter. And finally, the signal to fire."

"There can be no accident with the signal to fire?"

"That will be your responsibility. You will have the aiming transmitter. Then there will be the firing transmitter. If you have the firing transmitter in your possession, there can be no accidents."

"Would it be possible to withdraw to a distance before sending the rockets?"

"It would be very wise!" Atallah laughed.

Rivas imagined waiting in the top floor bar of the Sheraton, at the long windows viewing all of the city. There, if she pressed the button, she could watch the rockets fall on the American embassy. Perhaps she could videotape the attack—summon news crews for a media event, wait for them to start their cameras, then press the button. Could she also appear in the broadcasts? Stand in front of the cameras and denounce the United States as she killed Americans?

Steel clanged, dust clouded as one side of the container fell away, exposing blocks of styrofoam braced with wood. The teenagers cut twine and the styrofoam fell away, exposing the tubes of the rocket launcher. Driven by a motorized jack, the other wall and the roof tilted to the side.

"Now, that falls away . . ." The steel panels crashed to the ground. " . . . the switches close. The computers are now ready to aim the rockets. When the transmitter sends the signal, the computers will immediately aim the rockets."

Motors whirred. Sweat streaming down their bodies, the Salvadorians staggered back from the truck and trailer. They stood with Quezada, talking, watching the launcher. Styrofoam fell away as the launcher turned, the tubes angling upward. Then the motion stopped. The rocket tubes stood exposed and ready.

Atallah searched the foothills with the binoculars. "They are driving away. They seem to have placed the transmitter. Here—"

Scanning the road, Rivas saw dust clouding behind a speck. The car moved down the hills, sunlight reflecting from the windshield. She called to Quezada, "It is ready!"

"Then fire it."

"Is it safe?" she asked Atallah.

"If there is an error in the guidance computers, it is far better that we discover it now." He passed her the second transmitter. "And was it not the Iranians who devised this weapon? If there are casualties, why not they?"

Rivas unsnapped the cover. Inside, she saw two switches. Tape over one switch read, ON-OFF, the label over the second, FIRE. She watched the launcher as she flipped both switches.

In one roar, three rockets flashed away, the backblasts throwing a storm of dust and grass. She raised the binoculars and watched the distant hill. Even as the supersonic shriek of the rockets in flight came, she saw the crest of the hill explode. She held the optics steady, expecting to see two other explosions. Then she realized that the three rockets had hit simultaneously, blasting a section of the ridge many times wider than the road, sending a churning cloud of dust high above the hill. She imagined the shock and devastation of forty rockets striking the American embassy.

"Are you decided?" Atallah asked. "Will you take this weapon?"

Rivas nodded. Across the field, the Salvadorians cheered. Quezada shook hands with all the teenagers. Atallah called out, "Is the colonel impressed? Does he want the rockets?"

Lobo shouted back, "When do we kill the Americans?"

"Then back to the garage. Your rockets left for Salvador today. You leave tonight."

33

VOICES woke Niles, the Salvadorians talking of leaving the desert and the gang of ragmen. He stood, wiping the dust and sweat from his face, slapping dust from his Syrian fatigues. Stark worked the Nikon, clicking photos, the motor drive zipping film through the camera. Niles went to a hole in the concrete wall and squinted into the late-afternoon glare.

A van had returned. A yellow Dodge taxi eased through the gates and parked. Niles checked the angle of the sun, then stepped back from the wall to prevent the sun from flaring off his binoculars. Five people left the taxi—he immediately recognized Atallah and Muhammed Ali. Then he saw the woman in the chador and the man with the hanging left sleeve—Colonel Quezada and Marianela, the Salvadorian woman.

"So, they're here . . . take a gang shot. I want them all in the same picture."

The Nikon clicked. Stark adjusted the zoom lens, then clicked other photos. "Got it, sir. With duplicates."

"Syrian and an Iranian, a Nicaraguan, a Salvadorian. Think that qualifies as an international terrorist plot? Why don't we print up a few thousand postcards and send them to Congress and the Europeans?"

"Are you serious, sir?"

English came from the monitor as Atallah entered the garage, telling the others, "The rockets are scheduled to be loaded on a freighter . . ."

* * *

". . . perhaps they are already embarked on their transport to El Salvador."

"How and where will the rockets enter Salvador?" Rivas asked. She and Quezada toured the garage, their footsteps echoing in the steel building. Quezada went to a cluttered work table and examined a circuit board.

Atallah did not answer. "Tell the colonel those are all American and Japanese components."

"What port and when?" Rivas repeated.

"Allow me to transmit that information later. First, let us send the crew into the country. I have already reserved seats on a flight from Beirut. It is arranged that they will fly from country to country. It will then be your responsibility to see to the final transportation. Will they return to Nicaragua before they travel to El Salvador?"

Rivas translated the question for Quezada. He shook his head. He dropped the electronics and walked away, leaving her with Atallah and the Iranian.

"A very withdrawn fellow," Atallah commented. "He spoke very little during our drive from Daraiya. I would think he would be elated following the demonstration. But then, men of genius are often moody."

"I am elated. I can tell you that Octavio does not want to work with any foreign groups. But I do. I want your weapons. I want your communications, your experts, your spies. I want whatever is required to defeat the Americans."

The Iranian laughed. Atallah silenced him with a look.

"I can't speak of this with Octavio present," Rivas continued. "But if we can talk at another time, I want to plan for the future."

"With or without the colonel?" Atallah asked.

"If I must, I will start my own organization. Octavio and I don't agree on tactics. He is very idealistic. I am not."

"Our departed friend Emilio Pazos told me once that you were a killer, that you killed even those who some would call innocents, if the killing served your purpose. Is that—"

"This is a war. There are no innocents. I do what I must."

Atallah stepped close to her, so close that the Iranian could not hear. His hand went to her back, pressing her closer to him as he spoke quietly, almost whispered, "We will talk of this . . ."

She did not recoil from his touch. The scent of his French cologne and American cigarettes, the strength of his hand, the scar at the side of his eye—his face and his strength held her for a moment and she accepted that he would use her and she would use her body again to advance the revolution, to gain her rightful place in the struggle to free her country.

" . . . but later. After the strike in El Salvador. After you have killed more Americans. Then I can approach my superiors with a proposal for your organization."

And then he stepped back, suddenly formal and courteous again. "Is it possible you can bring back the colonel for a few minutes of consultation? We very much need to discuss how the crew will return to the Americas. Only a last few details of logistics."

Leaving Atallah and the Iranian, she felt her heart racing. She had won again. Perhaps Quezada had guessed right, perhaps the Syrians intended to liquidate the others—but not her. She would command her own organization, her own force of terror against the Americans. Only a few weeks remained until she took command. First she attacked the embassy . . .

Muhammed Ali laughed. "She thinks she's got a future!"

"Say nothing!" Atallah warned him. "Or do you volunteer to carry the transmitter into the American embassy? Now, the transmitters are ready? The camera and recorder?"

"Ready for days."

"And the container went as scheduled?"

"You see it here?"

"And the charges were set as you were instructed?"

"Hundred kilos of C-four. Jammed in a ring around the container. They launch those rockets and they die. Won't be nothing but scrap metal left. And then those rockets come down and she dies—"

Niles jerked away from the wall. Running into the hallway, he saw Alvarez noting the number from reel-to-reel digital display. "Did you hear what the Iranian said?"

"I heard it," Alvarez nodded. "A hundred kilos, two

hundred twenty something pounds of C-four. If they are still there when—"

"They won't be."

"I don't know your secret plan in Syria—" The voices of Muhammed Ali and Atallah moved away from the micro-transmitter at the work table. Alvarez turned up the monitor volume, checked the meter reading on the signal, then took off his headphones. "I don't know your secret plan, sir. I don't know why you sent them into Syria. But do you have a margin of hours worked into that secret plan, Captain? You absolutely positive there's no way Hijazi and Javenbach will be there?"

"They won't be there because—"

"I'll take a motorcycle—"

Niles shook his head. "I sent them in. I'll tell them to get out of there."

"Sir, you can't go. You don't look right. First checkpoint, they got you."

"First time they ask you a question, you're gone."

"I look the part. And you don't."

"I sent them, I'll warn them. On a motorcycle, I can go around the Syrian checkpoint. I got it worked out already, Alvarez. I think I can do it. I'm no martyr. If I didn't think I could get away with it, I wouldn't risk it—"

"Sir," Stark interrupted. "It is an unjustified risk. Javenbach is a corporal, Hijazi a UCA. If they are casualties—"

Niles laughed. "You hear that, Hey-Zoot? He went to college. Javenbach's only a corporal. Hijazi's only a unilaterally controlled asset. Lieutenant Stark, don't talk like an agency man. I sent those men in, I get them out."

"Sir, if the Syrians take you, it will be a serious intelligence loss to—"

"Intelligence! Me? What do I know? Later, gentlemen. Hey-zoot, push the button on those guidance units, then code out for extraction at the railroad. Same place as last time. You heard me? When that taxi leaves, you push the button."

Niles took his rifle and helmet, his Beretta, then rushed down the stairs to the parked trucks. Going to the collection of uniforms and weapons, he found a keffiyah. He smoothed brown camo paste over his face, rubbing the waxy color into his tanned skin, using the paste to darken his eyebrows and hair.

In the motorcycle sidebags, he found Hijazi's goggles and gloves. Then he wrapped the keffiyah around his face. As a final prop, he put a case of cigarettes on the luggage rack and lashed the box down with cords.

Racing south on the side roads of the Bekaa, dust clouding around the motorcycle, Niles looked like any other Syrian on leave. He did not take the Zebdani road, the traditional smuggling route to Damascus. Instead, he continued south past Britel, passing militia checkpoints at Haour Taala and Khodor. The bearded teenagers saw his Syrian uniform and did not leave the shade of the trees where they maintained their watch for enemies of the faith.

A kilometer before Nabi Chit, Niles veered off the road and moto-crossed on the rutted dirt lanes dividing the fields. He avoided the towns of Nabi Chit and Saraain. Farmers watched him pass without interest, not pausing in their labor in the rocky fields.

Maps showed a broken line winding through the mountains between Rayak and the town of Serghaya on the Zebdani road. A dust-pale appeared in satellite photos. Niles cut cross-country until he found the road. The tire tracks of cars and trucks indicated others used the route. He followed the tracks, crossing the Syrian border.

Behind the wrecked trucks and the rusting trailers, beyond the hearing of the Arab who understood Spanish, Quezada questioned his fighters about their time with the Iranians. He listened carefully to what they told him, measuring their memories against their anger, judging the meaning of every detail against the facts of different languages and different cultures. After several minutes of stories, Daniel raving, then Victor talking and Marco arguing, he held up his hand for silence.

"They did not treat you as comrades, I understand that—"

"They would not touch what we touched!" Daniel held out his hands. "If they touched us, if they touched what we touched, they washed their hands. Like we are diseased. We did not mock their praying or their priests. We were good students, we did as they said—"

"I understand. But I have questions. I watched the show with the rockets. And you all did very well. You were very fast, dividing up the work, then two standing guard—"

"That is one good thing the head ragman did," Victor added. "The first day, he took us into the mountains and fired a rocket. He showed us so that we knew what we would do. So we learned, we practiced, no matter how the rags insulted us."

"But what were you trained to do after you fired the rockets?"

"After?" Daniel asked. He laughed. "We need no training in that. After we shoot, all the police and soldiers in the world will be searching for us."

"What do you do with the launcher? And the steel box and the truck?"

"We burn it," Lobo answered. "Pour gasoline on it and burn it to make the investigation difficult—"

Footsteps approached. Rivas came through the wrecks, holding the headcloth closed over her face, only her eyes showing as she searched. She saw them and called, "He needs to plan the transportation. He wants to talk with you."

"An Arab woman who speaks Spanish?" Victor asked.

"She is one of us." Quezada went to Rivas. "Why does he want to talk now? We will have time in the car to talk of that."

"He said—"

"What he said is a lie. The truth is that he does not want me talking with my men. Tell him I will come soon. Go, they should not see you."

Quezada called back to the young man. "Lobo! Come, we will talk." He paced the wide asphalt lane beside the garage and the empty fields, thinking of what the others had told him before he spoke. "I have many suspicions. I have decided that you will not do exactly as the Iranians tell you."

"What suspicions? They hate the Americans. Why would they betray us?"

"Not betray. I suspect that they want none of us to live through this."

"They will kill us?"

"Or you will be killed by the regime. I do not have much time to tell you this. It may happen that I will not talk with you again—"

"Why?"

"I have my suspicions. Hear me. When you return to Salvador, when you have the rockets, forget the instructions they give you. Use your own head. Do not make the attack until you think it is right. Then do it."

"Colonel, we can radio you. Or send a message."

"If you radio, the Americans can intercept. If you send a messenger, he can be taken. But if they have eliminated me, you will be alone. Be ready to work alone. Keep contact, but put a distance between you and whoever you must contact."

"Why would they kill us?" Lobo pointed to the cargo containers lining the fence. "They do not want to hit the Americans once only. This is a factory. They want to hit the Americans again and again and again. They need us to fight their war."

Quezada continued walking, considering his words, finally telling the teenager, "There are many fighters in the world. In Salvador, in Guatemala, in Colombia, in Chile—everywhere. And everywhere, young men and women, they risk their lives to attack police and soldiers. With only a rock or a knife or a bottle of gasoline. They do not think that by killing a policeman or a soldier they will free their country. They only want a pistol, maybe a rifle, so they can fight. Brave ones die every day. They see their friends die. And then come the Arabs with these rockets. The Arabs will have many fighters, they will have more fighters than rockets. And no one will remember if we lived or died, only if the rockets killed Americans—what is . . ."

"You are right," Lobo nodded. "Do I tell the others this?"

Not answering, Quezada rushed to the next trailer in the line. His eye had seen a difference in the dirt and litter. Scanning the asphalt lane, he studied the windblown trash and the weeds under the trailers and along the fence. The

Iranians had not cleaned the area. Trash had collected under the trailers and tangled with the fence.

In one area, dust and papers and stones looked different. Motions had buffed the asphalt, leaving the asphalt black in spots but dusty in other places. But—in violation of all logic—the trash and small stones remained, scattered about randomly. Quezada squatted down and looked under the trailer.

The tension on the chain-link fence varied, flowing tight and flat from one steel pole to the next—then the chain-link jagged behind wind-blown newspapers. Quezada eased under the trailer and ran his fingers over the weathered, dry paper.

Sticks and twists of trash plastic secured the newspapers. Quezada carefully examined the paper. By touch, he found the sharp points of cut steel. The points formed a rectangle. He looked past the fence.

Broken weeds stood upright. Movement had snapped off weeds at the dry earth and crushed the fragile networks of twigs and dry leaves. But the weeds had sprung up again— impossible. A narrow path of crushed and restored weeds led from the field to the fence.

At the fence, in the trash, he saw no monofilament lines or disturbed soil. He checked the fence for trip-lines, then slowly, carefully, he eased the dry papers away.

Shears had cut a rectangular flap in the chain-link. He examined the gleaming, sharp ends of the wire. A bit of green thread hung on the metal. Each cut had required only one clean snap—meaning that the intruders used specialized tools, levered shears or bolt cutters.

A man or men had crossed the field, cut through the fence, and entered the garage area. Turning, Quezada studied the area—the asphalt, the trash, then the underside of the trailer.

He saw a dull black box jammed between two steel struts of the trailer frame. Tape secured the box. Wires led from the box and tape secured the wires—antennas.

During his training in Cuba, his East German and Soviet instructors had demonstrated the devices of electronic sur- veillance. Modern technology allowed engineers to reduce microphones and transmitters to the size of buttons. But radio physics and batteries limited micro-transmitters to very short ranges. Micro-transmitters required signal amplifiers to increase the transmission range. He now stared at an amplifier.

Quezada crawled from under the trailer. Motioning for Lobo to remain silent, he stepped between the trailers and scanned the area—the highway, the shacks, the bombed ruin of a building over a kilometer away. Lobo looked under the trailer, then stood behind Quezada.

The three-story building towered above the low shacks. The empty windows of the building looked into the compound. The height of the building also allowed a straight line of transmission from the signal amplifier to any receiver placed there. Quezada motioned for Lobo to follow and they walked away from the breach in the fence.

"This area," Quezada whispered, "has been penetrated by agents. I think there are microphones placed. Inside, maybe outside here."

"Americans?"

"I think the Israelis. But what is the difference? All the plans of the Arabs are compromised. And you must get out of here while they are still running the surveillance. Because then come the commandos."

"Will you tell the Arabs and Iranians?"

"Why? I will say nothing and let them take their chances with the commandos." He took his wallet out of his jacket. "There is a thousand dollars there. Take it all."

"But you need money—"

"The Arabs bought our tickets. The money was for an emergency. This is an emergency. Take the thousand dollars. Take the tickets the Arabs give you and go. But once you are in the Caribbean, you must disappear—"

"Colonel!" a man shouted. They turned and saw Madaya walking to them.

"Take the money. Hide it. Go to Honduras or Nicaragua by boat. Then go to El Salvador. You must risk their tickets to get out of here, but once you are close to El Salvador, change all the plans. Use your head and stay alive—"

"Colonel! We must go!"

With his one arm, Quezada embraced the young man, the warm brotherly embrace of one fighter for another—brothers who might not live to see one another again.

"But you?" Lobo asked. "What of you? What will happen to you?"

Quezada laughed. "One eye? One hand? Can't even use a rifle? What does it matter what happens to me?"

And he walked away, not looking back.

"Go with God, Colonel! I will always remember you and what you taught me. I will always try to be as brave as you!"

Madaya looked from Quezada to the shouting teenager. "What does he say?"

"Slogans. Where is the woman?"

"At the car. We go now."

Rivas sat in the back of the taxi with Atallah. The open case of a video camera lay across her legs and she ran her hands across the plastic and metal of the camera, touching the camera like she had once caressed his scarred body. That lovely girl, that woman who had slept beside him for so many months, she looked from the Syrian to the camera to the Syrian, smiling, talking in English, laughing—but she did not look up from the camera as Quezada sat in the front seat of the taxi. Unaware of Quezada, laughing at some joke, she grasped the arm of Atallah and leaned to him, touching her forehead to his shoulder like a woman laughing with her man. Atallah remained correct, smiling at the joke, but greeting Quezada with a nod. She sensed his difference and looked to his face, then started when she saw Quezada watching. She explained the joke to Quezada in Spanish and he nodded as if he heard, but he turned away, staring straight ahead as the taxi left the gates.

He had lost Rivas—if he had ever had her. Maybe he had only allowed her to exploit him. Every man had vanity and desire. A beautiful student had become his woman. The instructors at the camp could not question his personal life and he had not allowed the woman who slept with him to claim any privileges over the staff or students. Yet, as he came to depend on her intelligence and cunning, he delayed sending her back to the war in Salvador. When she did return to the war, by her own demand, she followed her instructions and completed her work without difficulty—proving herself cool and calculating, the equal of any unit leader. With him again in Nicaragua, she took the vague scheme of the Cubans to kill Americans in Salvador and planned the strike against the off-duty Marines. The idea had come from Pazos, but Rivas had gone to Salvador and plotted every detail. She became a leader—but dependent on Quezada for fighters and Pazos for money.

Now she had transferred her loyalty to the Syrian. The Syrian had weapons and money. With money, Rivas could make an organization. With weapons, she could recruit fighters.

It had ended. Maybe she had exploited him, maybe not. But it had ended. Maybe she would try to make a false front and continue as his lover, but he wanted none of it. He did not hate her. He would not do as traditional honor demanded of him and kill her. Let the Syrian take her.

It had ended.

Watching from a kilometer away, Alvarez pressed the button of the pulse transmitter, the pulse switching a relay in the modified digital units, the micro-circuits switching on the transmitters in the tape recorder and the video camera.

Lobo looked across the fields to the ruin. From those windows, spies had monitored the preparations for the rocket attack on the Americans. They had defeated the colonel and Lobo and his friends before they ever left Lebanon. When the information of the shipment of rockets went to the Americans, the Americans would seize the rockets.

What if the Americans never received the information? What if Lobo acted now and killed the spies? Maybe the spies had already reported the shipment of the rockets. If so, killing the spies meant Lobo and Victor and Marco and Daniel gained time to escape. But if the spies had not reported to their headquarters today, then the rockets reached Salvador. Even with the treachery of the Arabs and Iranians, Lobo still might lead the attack against the Americans.

Kill the spies—he made the decision as he ran back to the others. They still waited at the back fence. But he took no chances. Motioning for them to be silent, he wrote out what the colonel had discovered. They read that note while he wrote the next.

We take rifles, we go there, we kill them.

Vatsek put all the equipment in boxes and threw the boxes into Syrian army transport. Every piece of military and personal gear would go to the helicopter. Only the video duping machines—remanufactured by NSA technicians to record days of sound on videocassettes—would remain to continue monitoring the micro-transmitters placed in the garage of the Iranians. In time, Hijazi would transfer the other frequency-monitoring machines from Baalbek three kilometers away. Hijazi intended to convert the third floor of the warehouse to a music and videocassette factory. The lower floor would become a warehouse and truck garage. But when the workmen returned, nothing could remain of the Marines' stay in the building.

On the third floor, Alvarez and Stark continued listening to the transmissions from the garage while changing the recording over to the remanufactured video duping machines. All the portable equipment would go out in the truck.

Disco music came from the monitor speakers, echoing in the quiet of the concrete warehouse. Vatsek finished loading the boxes of equipment. He took a few minutes to walk the rounds, glancing out at the gate and the fences, the heaps of junk, the fields in the back—he saw nothing moving. No one had shown any interest in the warehouse—not the neighborhood kids, not the Syrian or militia patrols. Invisibility proved the best security here.

Slinging a Kalashnikov over his back, Vatsek policed the interior of the building, picking up trash and searching for anything—paper, equipment, or personal article—that might betray Hijazi. This meant life or death for Hijazi. In a few days, the Americans would be in Honduras—but Hijazi had to work in Baalbek. Vatsek found only Arabic-printed bottles and cans. He bagged the trash and went to the back of the warehouse to burn the bag.

A shadow streaked across a wall and Vatsek reacted, spinning, the muzzle blast of a rifle smashing his ear, his right arm instinctively flailing out with the bag of bottles and cans, hitting a form, someone gasping, the rifle firing again, a slug ricocheting off concrete. Vatsek sprang back, the strength of his legs converting his panic-spin into a rush and he front-kicked the moving form, impact lifting the man off the ground, slamming him backward against the wall, and Vatsek continued forward, one arm down blocking the Kalashnikov and grabbing the weapon, his right hand clawing into the man's face, gouging out an eye, gripping the face of the screaming man and jerking back, then pistoning forward, smashing the skull of his attacker into the concrete of the wall, once, twice, blood spraying—

The corridor flashed red with the fire of another rifle and shock sent agony through his back. Vatsek staggered, his back arched with agony, the dying man and the Kalashnikov still in his hands.

A rifle flashed again.

34

A JET shrieked over the highway. Madaya flinched and the taxi swerved. Atallah jerked at the door. Rivas saw Quezada looking behind the taxi as the second jet flashed overhead, the overwhelming shriek of the engines coming simultaneously and continuing, the metal of the car shaking with the noise. Rivas turned in the seat and saw the tailpipes and wings of a fighter bomber so low that the jet seemed to skim the asphalt of the highway.

Shock rings radiated from the horizon and the booming of the explosions came. Flame rolled into the sky, the horizontal light of the sunset dull red on a churning ball of smoke. She heard a voice screaming incoherently and saw the face of Atallah twisted with panic, his mouth wide, his eyes rolling, his head whipping in all directions as he looked for escape. Gravel rattled the fenders as the taxi drifted off the road and Quezada lunged for the steering wheel with his one arm, managing to hold the taxi on line as he moved across the seat and put his foot on the brake. Madaya finally stopped the taxi on the side of the highway.

Atallah threw open the door, a truck roaring past, then he ran across the highway and crouched in a ditch, his eyes searching the sky for jets. A dull roar came from the distance, a cacophony of explosions and firing, tracers streaking upward from Baalbek. In the front seat, Quezada gripped Madaya by the jacket, keeping him in the taxi.

No other jets came. Quezada told her, "Get the Arab back in the car. Those planes hit our men."

"How could the Americans know?"

"Call that coward back! Get him!"

But Atallah had already returned to the taxi. "The Jews didn't strafe the road this time. Many times they have machine-gunned everything they saw, killing everyone. However, I fear for my associate Muhammed and your fighters. We must return—" He directed Madaya to turn the car.

"How could they know?" she asked Atallah. But he did not answer as they raced back to Baalbek.

Ahead, against the deep blue of the dusk sky, a column of black smoke towered above flames. Flares floated in the smoke. Tracers streaked into the darkening sky, the sound of antiaircraft guns a roar without end.

Vatsek staggered, his back twisting with agony. He spun, falling, trying to use the skull-crushed, dying man as a shield, the other gunman's rifle flashing point-blank, the muzzle-blast slamming him in the face. The Kalashnikov tracked Vatsek as he fell backward, his back hitting the concrete of the corridor, the rifle slung over his back jamming into his wound. He screamed with pain and adrenaline. Concrete hit his face as a bullet whined away and then the roar came, the noise shrieking through his consciousness, the concrete floor leaping under his back—he thought the gunman had hit him, the noise of the roar of a bullet killing him, but he rolled to the side, grabbing the Kalashnikov from the dying man.

Stark looked up from the Nikon and saw the jet hurtling at his face. For a long instant, he stared into the air scoops and cannon barrels, then the jet flashed above the warehouse, the belly only meters above the roof, the shriek of the turbines hitting Stark in a wave of two-hundred-decibel noise.

Across the kilometer of fields and shacks, fire boiled from the open doors of the garage, the walls of corrugated steel sheets disintegrating into hundreds of individual rectangles thrown outward by expanding napalm fire. Stark saw the second jet come in higher. Two cylinders dropped from the wings. Parachutes blossomed, fireflare tinting the cloth red.

The cylinders seemed to pause in flight, then fell exactly into the flaming skeleton of the garage.

A hemisphere of flame and debris rushed outward and the shock slammed Stark back. He staggered a step, the concrete of the warehouse shaking under his boots, then steadied himself against a wall. The jet scream faded to the west.

In the horizontal light of the sunset, Stark saw a field of flames and debris where the garage had stood. Nothing remained of the steel structure. Flames and black smoke churned into the sky, steel sheets spinning in the air like ashes, flashing with the light of the setting sun. Three tiny parachutes drifted in the clouds of smoke, each parachute carrying a point of magnesium white light—flares to draw infrared-seeking sensors of Soviet antiaircraft missiles.

Alvarez rushed into the office and looked out at the devastation. "Oh, man. . . ."

"The Israelis."

"We could have been in there."

Rifles echoed in the warehouse, then the entire world seemed to fire weapons at once, the hammering of machine guns becoming a roar.

Bullets tore through the head of the dying man, throwing the corpse against Vatsek. The shrieking roar of turbines and explosions shook the concrete passage and Vatsek turned the Kalashnikov, firing one-handed, sweeping the narrow space with a long burst, the flashing muzzle lighting a bullet-jerked form in stroboscopic instants. His left hand found the foregrip and Vatsek fired another burst through the man—a man? he looked thin and young, a teenager.

The Salvo gang.

Another form moved and Vatsek pointed and fired, the legs of a running man jerking with bullets. Then Vatsek rolled, pain searing across his back as the rifle slung on his back gouged into his wound, but he jumped up and rushed the teenager.

Blood bubbled from lung wounds, but the teenager still moved, his hands trying to grip his rifle and Vatsek brought down his boot in a perfect breaking-strike on the teenager's face, bones crushing, a sobbing scream spraying blood as

Vatsek continued past, charging the third man who twisted and whined with the pain of his bullet-shattered legs.

An arm reached out to drag the wounded man back into a doorway, the hand closing on his shirt. The fourth man glanced out, saw Vatsek. Vatsek recognized him as the leader of the Salvadorians, the one who went by the name of The Wolf. He kicked, but misjudged the movement of the Salvadorian teenager, his boot glancing off the face of El Lobo and staggering him back.

The leg-wounded teenager raised his Kalashnikov and Vatsek pivoted and shot him point-blank, the burst punching through his chest, a hole appearing in his throat, a last bullet hitting him in the eye and exploding out the back of his skull.

Vatsek pursued El Lobo. Semi-conscious, the Salvadorian staggered backward from the doorway and fell against the wall, blood flowing from his mouth and broken nose. But he still held a Kalashnikov. Vatsek snapped his rifle to his shoulder and aimed at the center of the teenager's face, shouting out, "Surrender!"

"No . . ." And El Lobo stepped toward Vatsek, bringing up his rifle.

Pulling the trigger, Vatsek heard the bolt slam on the empty chamber. He lunged forward and smashed the other rifle aside, the rifle firing, a bullet gouging away flesh, then he whipped the stock across, hitting the teenager's shoulder but breaking off the stock of the rifle. Swinging the empty rifle by the barrel, Vatsek clubbed him with the steel of the receiver, staggering him back another step, his head hitting the concrete wall, his left arm gone limp as he tried to raise his rifle with his right hand. Vatsek smashed rifle against rifle, knocking the teenager's arm down, swung again, the rifle breaking ribs, doubling the teenager. Vatsek let him fall, then put his boot on the back of his head, pressing his face into the concrete as he gasped for breath.

A row of barred windows, jagged with shattered glass, ran along the outside wall. Vatsek unslung his folding-stock Kalashnikov and saw a bullet crease in the stamped steel of the receiver. The bullet had slammed the rifle into his back, leaving bloody bruises on his spine, then fragments of the bullet had slashed his back. Blood streamed down his back and pants, but the wounds felt shallow. Pain throbbed from another wound, blood flowing from the gouge in his side, the skin flecked by powder from the muzzle-blast.

Outside, machine-guns fired thousands of rounds, the sound a continuing roar. Vatsek glanced out the windows and saw tracers arcing across the dusk sky. Then he heard metal scrape concrete in the corridor. Vatsek jacked back the cocking handle of his rifle to confirm the operation of the bolt, then stepped toward the door. The teenager on the floor reached out for a rifle. Vatsek stomped on his hand, breaking bones.

"Godzilla!" Alvarez called out.

"Stay low!"

"What happened?"

"Salvo punks came to visit. I got four. Could be more."

Zigzagging through the corridor, Stark rushed past. A boot slammed a door open. Alvarez dashed into the room. He crouched in the doorway and covered Stark.

"We have got to get out of here—that one's still alive."

"What the fuck is going on out there? The ragheads throwing a mad-minute?"

"Israelis did the number on the rocket factory."

Stark returned. "Nothing out there. I thought there were automatic alarms on that fence—"

The rotor noise of Soviet helicopters approached. Alvarez looked up, as if he scanned the sky through the concrete of the warehouse and offices.

"First the Salvadorians come check us out. Now it's the Syrians. Time to get out of here."

Rotors threw ashes and scraps of scorched metal. In the glare of spotlights, Syrian soldiers rushed from the ramps of two Soviet MI-8 troopships, officers directing the soldiers to positions around the smoking wreckage. Atallah held up his identification as he walked to an officer. Quezada watched the soldiers take Atallah to the senior officr.

Only concrete and wreckage remained of the steel garage. The Israeli bombs had sheared the structure off at the foundation, shattering the concrete slab, leaving the highway and fields strewn with twisted beams and tangles of blackened corrugated sheets. Trailers and upended cargo containers lay everywhere, upended in the wreckage, thrown into the fields by the blast. Small fires continued, flames leaping up from burning debris—tires, wood, insulation. A pall of smoke drifted from the wreckage, reducing the illumination of helicopter spotlights and truck headlights to a gray glow. Individual soldiers waved flashlights over objects in the wreckage.

Quezada recognized the overwhelming stink of benzene and styrene—the Israelis had first napalmed the structure, then dropped high-explosive, the flaming chemicals and the blast of the explosives devastating the garage and the compound.

No one had survived this bombing. Quezada had lost his four men. The soldiers searching the devastation would find none of the Salvadorians alive, maybe not even a corpse. Quezada collapsed on the taxi seat, closing his eye against the defeat, knotting his fingers into his close-cut hair. Grief tore at him. Those four men—only boys, none of them yet twenty years old—and already lost, anonymous ashes in that devastation.

"Who will open up the box of rockets?" Rivas demanded, her voice rising to a shout. "How quick can we get another crew and send them for the training? The rockets are on the way, we have transmitters, any target in Salvador is ours— we must get another crew now! Answer me! When can we send Atallah more men to be trained?"

Years of hope and courage, risking their lives in the streets and the mountains to struggle for the liberation of the masses of their nation from the exploitation of the regime—and their lives ended here, in this Arab town, in a junkyard at the side of a highway. All the dreams of revolution—only ashes.

And the woman who now served the Arabs demanded more young men.

Finally looking up at Rivas, he saw her rushing away. She had not waited for him to answer her demands for more men—more brave young men to squander in the schemes of the Cubans and Arabs. In the smoke, she became a gray figure going from soldier to soldier, one soldier grabbing her arm and jerking her back. The noise of the waiting helicopters covered her voice as she struggled.

Atallah appeared. They stood together, surrounded by the soldiers, shouting to one another in the noise. Quezada watched her, knowing she talked with the Syrian of assembling another group of fighters. Another plot. If Quezada did not supply the men to support her try for glory, she would use the money of the Arabs to recruit fighters.

And in an instant of clarity—the vain macho sadness of losing his woman gone, forgetting the grief of losing his men—he realized he must count Rivas as an enemy. She might try to maintain a false front, but she now worked with the Arabs.

Oh, Octavio, he thought to himself, you came too far. You wanted to play baseball but you fought a revolution. They took your arm and your eye and left you with only your love of the people. Why did not the Guardsmen kill him and spare him these long years of fighting? To be a dead hero, beyond all the schemes and lies and betrayal, to be a name on a school, to be far beyond pain and loss—it did not seem so bad.

Atallah and the lovely Rivas walked to the taxi. Watching them approach, Quezada felt calm take him. Without fear or anger, he thought, It means nothing what happens to me. If you kill me, I win peace. If I live, if I out-maneuver you, if I kill you, I will continue fighting until someone else finally gives me peace.

"We can do nothing here," Rivas told him. She reached into the taxi and grabbed the sound recorder. Atallah took the case containing the camera and video recorder. "We are going back. By helicopter."

The Marines dragged the Salvadorians to the troop truck, propping the dead men against the boxes of electronics and equipment from the warehouse. Despite a broken arm and a crushed hand, the last man—the teenager called Lobo—continued struggling, trying to escape. An injection of sedatives calmed him. They laid him near the tailgate of the truck, a bandage over his bleeding face.

Blood from the corpses had splotched the Syrian uniforms of Stark and Alvarez, the Soviet uniform of Vatsek.

"Hey, do we look like we got bombed?" Alvarez asked. "I mean, are they going to ask us any questions? The bombs came down and then a truckload of fucked up *vatos* shows up . . ."

As Alvarez spoke, he wrapped a bloody bandage around Stark's head, concealing his black features, leaving only one eye hole for visibility. Stark got in the back of the truck with the dead and wounded.

"Sergeant Vatsek, you do have that map memorized, correct?" Stark asked.

"Don't get nervous, Lieutenant." Vatsek pushed open the doors of the warehouse. "I'll get you around the checkpoints. Unless we run into some raghead militia shit who speaks Russian, we are out of here."

"How can they say no?" Alvarez asked. "We all definitely look like we need a hospital. But you don't look quite fucked-up enough . . ." Scooping up a handful of clotting blood from the concrete, Alvarez slapped it on the side of Vatsek's head. "There, a head wound. This truck is an ambulance, they won't even slow us down—"

"But lock and load," Vatsek added. "If they stop us, that is it. We joined the Corps to fight."

Alvarez laughed. "Hey, be cool, Godzilla. This is time for escape and evasion. No crash cars. They shot you twice already, isn't that enough?

Sirens wailed. A flashing red light streaked past on the highway. Alvarez locked the warehouse, then the gates. As he got into the cab of the truck, Vatsek passed him the PKM machine gun.

"Like I said, lock and load."

Hijazi and Javenbach worked as a team, Javenbach holding the flashlight, Hijazi locking the socket of the power wrench over each bolt and torquing the bolts out, then moving on to the next. They had worked without pause for hours to open the cargo container, the blazing afternoon fading to dusk, then to evening as they struggled to match their instructions to the unfamiliar equipment and tools.

The noise of the gasoline generator hammered against the night of the village. No cars moved on the dirt lanes, the sounds of radios remained quiet and private—only the sound of a passing motorcycle equaled the noise of the generator and power wrench.

To the south-east, lights defined the sprawl of Damascus.

"That is the last one," Javenbach told Hijazi.

"At last." Wiping sweat from his face, Hijazi stood up straight, the muscles of his back aching but the wind from the mountains cooling his sweat-soaked fatigues. He looked at the lights of Damascus and the lines of headlights traveling the Damascus-to-Beirut highway.

Had Captain Niles correctly anticipated the route of the Syrian? What if the Syrian remained in the Bekaa tonight? What if he had already returned? God willing, these rockets punished that murderer.

Then he climbed down to the open doors. Javenbach walked along the roof of the container, waving the flashlight over the seam between the roof and the wall, checking for any remaining bolts.

The gasoline-powered generator filled the interior of the container with smoke. Hijazi coughed in the smoke as he searched for the electric jack. He found the jack shafts, then the motor and gears, then he traced the conduit to the generator. A switch interrupted the line.

"Akbar!"

Hijazi waited for Javenbach to jump down and run for cover, then he flipped the switch. The motor and gears whirred, the shafts slowly, slowly moving outward against the frame of the container wall, the steel creaking with the stress.

As Hijazi stepped back, an arm locked around his throat, a pistol went to his head.

Rivas shouted over the turbine shriek of the Soviet helicopter. "This cannot stop us. If the rockets go to Salvador, I can give instructions to some men. There will be no need for training. We can attack immediately."

"Will Colonel Quezada support your decision?" Atallah asked.

"What do I care what he says? I can get the fighters to do this. This will be my attack against the—"

The noise of the turbines changed, the lights of the Daraiya air force base appearing as the troopship angled down to the landing pad. Crewmen went to the side door as the wheels touched down on the pavement.

"We will speak of this in my office." Atallah looked across the helicopter to Quezada. "Will it be necessary to include your colonel in this discussion?"

"Why?"

And Atallah smiled, the glare of the landing lights harsh on the scars and age of his face, making his face a gray rictus mask of skin stretched over a skull. His hand touched her thigh, moving over the thin cloth, caressing the curve of her thigh to where her thighs met.

Shuddering with revulsion, she imagined the flight of the rockets.

Hands slammed Hijazi against a wall. The steel muzzle of a pistol went to his head. He heard a grunt as boots slammed into a body, a fist slapped flesh, someone cursed in Arabic, then fists pounded his ribs and gut. The pistol remained against his head and Hijazi only raised his hands to protect his face, allowing the fists to beat on the muscles of his torso.

Several men surrounded him. To his side, in the fan of light from a flashlight on the ground, he saw forms fighting. A man cried out and fell holding his crotch. Then men shouted and a pistol flashed, the muzzle flash pointed into the sky. The fight continued. A man with a rifle rushed into the melee and drove the stock at one form. The stock thudded into flesh but the man with the rifle staggered back, gasping.

Javenbach fell, stunned. The attackers overwhelmed him, beating him, kicking him. One arm rose and fell with a pistol, the steel of the pistol clattering against Javenbach's head.

"Who are you?" a voice shouted at Hijazi. "What is in that trailer?"

"Are you thieves? Why do you attack us?"

"We are the police—"

Syrians. Hijazi had brought hundreds of dollars—he still had a chance to survive this confrontation. But he must bribe them and send them away before they saw the rockets.

"Answer the question. What is in—"

Steel smashed to the ground as the one side of the cargo container fell away. Dust and trash swirled in the darkness. The hammering of the gasoline generator continued, the electric jack powering the other side of the container away from the rockets.

"What is in the trailer?"

"Cargo for a very important person. A man of stature in the government. If you will allow me to present my papers, you will see that you have committed an error. We can resolve this problem with the payment of the customary fees to the correct officials, can we not?"

"Perhaps. Who is your superior?"

Shouts came from the Syrians near the trailer. Flashlights moved and spots of light reflected from the brilliant white of the styrofoam protecting the rockets. A few of the Syrians remained with Hijazi and Javenbach, the others went to examine the truck and trailer.

"What is that machine doing? Stop it now."

"It is only opening the shipping container. Please call your men back, they may be injured if the—"

"Stop it—" The Syrian lurched forward, falling, the pistol slipping from his hand.

Even as the man beside him gasped and fell, Hijazi realized the falling men had already died. He stepped back against the wall, grabbing the pistol of the last man, guiding the pistol past him as he jerked his knee into the Syrian's crotch, the pistol firing, the man whining with sudden pain, then Hijazi slammed his knee into the man's face, crushing his nose, teeth breaking, the man's hands going loose for an instant and allowing Hijazi to take the pistol as both men fell. Hijazi pushed the pistol against the head of the Syrian and fired, a flap of skull and scalp flopping away as the bullet exited.

Other pistols fired, the bullets pocking the concrete behind Hijazi. Hijazi pointed the dead man's pistol at the Syrians standing over Javenbach and fired at their silhouettes, then at the flashes of the pistols firing back at him. Men dropped, bullets sprayed blood from the dead man covering Hijazi, then a bullet punched into his leg, a ricochet slashing across his arm. His pistol went empty and he scrambled across the bodies, finding another pistol.

But the Syrians holding Javenbach had dropped. A pistol flashed again. Hijazi aimed but he saw Javenbach holding the pistol. The Marine crawled away from his captors as Syrians shouted all around them, calling for the dead men.

The second section of the container crashed to the pavement, the steel flexing with a sound like thunder. Hijazi watched for Syrians as Javenbach took cover against the wall. The wall blocked the fire of the Syrians near the trailer. He heard the sound of ropes snapping. Styrofoam blocks fell away. He snapped a glance over the wall the the rocket tubes rotating.

"Akbar!" Hijazi whispered in English. "Stay down, the launcher will fire the rockets!"

"He-Jazz! Corporal!" a voice called. "Hold your fire! Don't—"

A form dashed from the opposite side of the burned-out house. Pistols and rifles fired, bullets sparking on concrete and buzzing away, then the form sprawled on the concrete slab, scrambled to one knee and sprayed a burst of Kalashnikov full-auto at the Syrians. The fire stopped.

"Get out of here!" Niles shouted out. "There's a hundred kilos of C-four in the—"

The Syrians fired again, bullets from pistols and rifles ripping overhead, chipping at the concrete, men shouting as they rushed.

Orange light lit the scene, dust exploding from the pavement, blocks of styrofoam flying through the air as the solid fuel motors of the rockets flashed, the rockets screaming away on streaks of flame.

In the instant of orange glare, Hijazi saw Niles jam his

palms against his ears and drop flat. Hijazi copied him and the concrete leapt up, unconsciousness taking him into the darkness.

As the rotor blades continued turning, Atallah gripped the heavy case containing the video equipment. He followed Rivas across the heli-pad, marveling at her beautiful, womanly form as the rotor wind pressed the cloth of her chador tight against her body. At the entrance to the office tower, he motioned for the security men to pass the young woman. Then he told the officer, "That one. The foreigner with one arm. Take him to an office and hold him there until I issue instructions."

The officer glanced at the heli-pad. Quezada slowly walked across the asphalt, looking around at the office tower, the helicopters, the limousines waiting for the commanders inside the offices.

"He is to be considered an enemy," Atallah continued. "Under no circumstances is he to—"

A flash-shock slammed Atallah. He staggered as a roar enveloped him and then came silence, his body seeming to float through light, his eyes open and staring as the hundreds of windows of the office tower sprayed millions of glittering jewels outward, then the walls moving outward, slabs of concrete spinning. He stopped but felt nothing. Staring into the black of the sky, he saw the spinning fragments of concrete coming down and his reflexes tried to move his arms and legs but only his throat responded, his lungs exploding with a scream—

Niles dragged Hijazi free of the broken concrete, then returned for Javenbach. The foundations and wall of the ruined house had blocked the force of the blast. Nothing had protected the Syrians. Placed in the base of the cargo container, the plastic explosive had simultaneously destroyed the container and rocket launcher while throwing fragments of torn steel outward at a speed of five thousand meters per second. The blast had leveled all the sheds, chopped trees off at the ground, and knocked down sections of the earth and brick wall. Bits of twisted metal and flaming plastic continued to fall as Hijazi staggered to his feet. He and Niles helped Javenbach walk.

Blood ran from cuts on the Marine's head and face. Niles checked the wounds by touch and felt welts and lumps the shape of pistol frames—the Syrians had tried to beat the young man unconscious.

A steel beam had ripped through the Land Rover, entering one side, tearing through the engine, and continuing out the other side. Other fragments had flattened the tires. Niles found a leg in the back seat as he stepped inside and took the PKM machine gun from the pedestal.

"Out to the street. There are cars there—"

The padlock held the gates closed. But a section of the wall on the side had collapsed. They stumbled over the broken bricks to the street. Nothing moved in the street or the fields. All the houses had gone dark, all the people remained in hiding—they did not want to lose their lives in a conflict between the factions of militias or the security forces. Only dogs barked as the three men staggered two hundred meters to the parked cars.

Niles pulled a dead Syrian from behind the wheel. "He-Jazz, you okay? You think you can drive?"

"Yes, sir. I am not injured."

"Then get moving—"

Racing from the village, the car passed over a rise and Niles looked to the southeast. Eighteen kilometers away, just outside of the lights and urban sprawl of Damascus, flame and smoke marked Daraiya.

35

ATSEK followed rutted dirt lanes, the high beams of the truck lighting farms and orchards and stone walls.

Inside the houses of scattered villages, lanterns cast a yellow light over dinner gatherings, men seated at the tables, women serving. Children ran in the cool of the evening. At one farm, a man worked under a truck, a gasoline generator providing power for an arc welder. A portable stereo blared out the news in Arabic.

"General mobilization," Alvarez translated. "Israelis attacked Baalbek . . . and Damascus."

"Damascus?"

"A rumor. Unconfirmed report."

"The Old Man did it!" Vatsek laughed. The instrument lights made the triangle of his face seem to float in the dark, his white Russian features reptilian and evil. "He hit Syria. Payback on those raghead shits."

"Maybe."

"Then who did? The Israelis? They don't want a war with Syria."

"And we do?"

"Which way is Syria? Ready to go?"

After another kilometer, the dirt track intersected with a two-lane paved road. A battered Japanese pickup truck passed. Children and sheep crowded the back of the pickup, the fenders rattling as the axles of the overloaded truck banged the frame. Vatsek turned south, accelerating to a hill. He switched off the engine and headlights as the truck came

349

to the crest, gravity braking the truck to a slow roll. They scanned the landscape to the south.

Alvarez glanced at a map Niles had drawn. He pointed to lights two kilometers away. "That's Taibe."

"No, Britel."

"Look." Alvarez put a penlight on the map. "Captain knows this place."

"It's in Arabic! How am I supposed to read that shit? Where's Britel?"

"Three clicks past the Taibe crossroads."

"Then we got a checkpoint in front of us." Vatsek started the engine and accelerated downhill, driving the curving road without headlights. They passed isolated farms, each house surrounded by stone walls. Fields of grain shimmered under a half moon. Dirt roads cut through the fields, following the contours of the land and dividing property. Vatsek swerved the troop truck off the paved road and followed parallel ruts. Grain brushed both sides of the truck.

In low gear, Vatsek eased over the rocks and holes. Dust swirled. The truck lurched and swayed, the springs squeaking, the fenders sometimes clanging with rocks, but the slow pace made the truck quiet. On hills, Vatsek paused, scanning the landscape, listening before continuing.

They heard the turbinewhine of helicopters approaching from the south. Vatsek waited as the noise of the Soviet troopships passed. As Vatsek put the truck in gear, orange streaks scratched the sky over Baalbek, then they heard the distant hammering of antiaircraft guns. Tracers arced over Baalbek as gun crews searched for the helicopters with heavy-caliber slugs. White searchlights appeared in the sky, red and green flight beacons blinked on and off—the helicopter pilots trying the signal the gunners to cease fire.

"Do it to them." Vatsek laughed.

"That is not funny. Those Syrians are seriously nervous and I got to call in a helicopter."

"Call for a gunship. Start the war."

Vatsek zigzagged across the fields, following grass-choked roads, even footpaths, as he angled toward the main highway. Finally, he cut through an orchard. Branches dragged and snapped on the sides of the truck. Coming to a paved road, without switching on the headlights, he turned west and idled through the darkness. Orchards lined both sides of the road.

They saw the red points of cigarettes a second before flashlights lit the windshield. Men called out in Arabic. Vatsek jerked the headlight knob, the glare catching several militiamen in the road. Other men stood at trucks parked under the trees. Hands banged on the fenders, the voices demanding that the truck stop.

Pain came in shocks, every movement of the truck throwing him into a moment beyond pain, his consciousness coming and going. Lobo heard groans rasping from his throat. Every breath brought a knife stab to his chest. Slowing his breathing, fixing his mind on the idea of escape, he tried his body. Bandages covered his face, blinding him. Agony came with any movement of his left arm. He could not move his smashed right hand. But his legs worked. He turned his head and the bandages shifted—the Americans had not taped the bandage.

If he could only get out of the truck, he could see and he could run.

Lobo concentrated on consciousness, listening to the rattling of rocks under the tires and the metal-on-metal sounds of the truck. Sometimes he heard the voices of the Americans. But he heard no voices or movement in the back of the truck—the Americans had killed all his comrades. He had seen Daniel take a bullet to the face. And when the Americans had dragged him to the truck, his comrades had remained still, their bodies without life.

Of all the comrades, only he remained alive. Only he remained for the Americans to question. His faith and courage meant nothing to the American interrogators—prison meant an eternity of questions and torture and chemicals before they put a bullet in his head. He would try to run, he would try to escape, but if he could not, duty required that he take his knowledge of the rockets into the silence of death.

Slowly, slowly, he gathered his resolve. He felt the truck

leave the rocks and ruts for the pavement of a road. Maybe he could throw himself out of the truck without the Americans seeing him fall.

Then Arabs shouted and the truck stopped.

Bearded faces leaned in the windows, men talking and questioning in Arabic. Vatsek answered in Russian, pointing to Alvarez and to the back of the truck. Alvarez had slumped against the seat, his eyes closed. He gasped out a few words of Arabic and held up a bloodstained hand.

A leader pushed militiamen aside. Hard-faced, older than the others, he wore new Syrian fatigues painted with verses in Arabic. Studying Vatsek, he held out his hand for documents. Vatsek pointed to the insignia on his shoulder, the radar-disc and lightning flash of a Soviet antiaircraft technician. Then he tried to speak the Arabic word for hospital,

"Mus-tash-fa. Mus-tash-fa. Ray-yak."

"Rayak? Baalbek?"

"Ray-yak."

Boots walked on the planks of the cargo deck. The leader shouted to the man in the back of the truck. The man answered and the leader motioned for Vatsek to continue. Vatsek pointed ahead and asked again,

"Ray-yak?"

The leader used the universal language of directions, pointing straight ahead, then to the left. Vatsek nodded and saluted, putting the truck in gear and leaving the militiamen.

"Americans!" A voice cried out in English. "Americans!"

"What the fuck?" Vatsek looked in the side mirror and saw the men crowding around a form on the asphalt. He pressed the accelerator to the floor.

A moment later, the militiamen shouted. Vatsek switched off the lights and kept the accelerator down, the engine racing to maximum rpm's. Rifles fired, the first bursts aimed high, to warn. Vatsek shifted and gained speed, hurtling through the darkness, the truck rattling and banging on the weathered asphalt. Bullets slammed into the truck, the sounds of the rifles coming an instant later.

Desperate, Vatsek watched the sides of the road—no escape. Trees and fields blurred past, then clusters of houses. He managed to keep the truck on the narrow road. Behind him, he saw the headlights of cars and pickups driven by the militiamen. A rifle popped from the back of the troop truck, the lieutenant firing single shots, then careful two- and three-shot bursts. Alvarez looked back through the glass of the cab window. He grabbed the PKM and looked at the roof of the cab, the door, out the door at the side of the truck.

"Got to get in back there. Can do serious damage with this. But not from the—"

Headlights came directly at the front of the truck, Vatsek straining against the steering wheel, steel shrieking as he side-swiped the car, stones beating the fenders, the truck smashing a parked pickup. Muscling the truck back to the center of the road, Vatsek saw the steaking headlights of the highway ahead. But a sandbag and oil drum bunker guarded the intersection. Lanterns lit Arabic banners with portraits of the Ayatollah Khomeini and Ayatollah Sadr.

A Hezbollah militiaman with a rifle stepped out in the road, his hand raised. Vatsek down-shifted and braked—to slow for the turn, not to stop. The militiaman misjudged the speed of the truck and waited too long before rushing for the protection of the bunker. Vatsek cut the corner, the ragged steel of the fender catching the running man, severing an arm and hooking his torso, the surprised face of the militiaman staring through the windshield for an instant, his eyes wide, his mouth gaping with a scream, then his body fell under the wheels as Vatsek careened across the highway, the truck shuddering and skidding. An oncoming driver panicked and locked his brakes, the tires smoking, the headlights drifting sideways. Alvarez screamed and clutched at the dashboard as Vatsek used all his strength to hold the truck in the turn, a roadside stand disintegrating, lumber and sheets of corrugated steel shattering the windshield, a Fiat and a motorcycle suddenly a single mass of tangled metal, then Vatsek wrenched the truck straight on the highway, shifting and accelerating.

Laughing and bopping his head, Vatsek slapped out a beat

on the steering wheel. "Did you see that shit's face—wah wah, wah, this is the Martyr Delight, we deliver!"

"Turn coming up! Get us to that LZ without that gang behind us or we'll be the martyrs—"

"There they are." Looking in the mirror, he saw the distant points of headlights leaving the side road and speeding throught the slower traffic. Vatsek came to the Majdaloun road. Down-shifting, braking, down-shifting again, he managed to force the truck through the turn, the mangled fenders clattering as the tires bounced on the stones.

A few shops and garages clustered at the intersection. A few hundred meters from the highway, Vatsek saw fields bounded by stone walls. He let the truck slow as he found the Beretta and put it in a thigh pocket, then grabbed the backpack of PKM drums off the floor of the cab. Shifting into neutral, he opened his door.

"Don't leave without me—"

"What the fuck are you thinking?"

"You work the radio, I don't. Take the truck. Code out and wait."

Taking the PKM, he stepped out of the moving truck. He staggered a few steps, Alvarez shouting behind him. He heard the brakes squeal, then the gears clashed and the truck lumbered away. A hundred meters farther on, Stark jumped from the truck. He sprinted to Vatsek:

"Sergeant, this is less than—"

"I didn't ask you to get out of that truck."

Ignoring him, Stark repeated, "This is a less than ideal ambush. I thought you might need back-up."

"Yeah?" Vatsek jumped over a ditch and vaulted a wall. Kicking the piled stones, he made a firing position. He did not extend the bipod—the bipod would only slow him down. "You, a college man. I thought you were smart."

Accelerating and braking, Hijazi beat the Mercedes against the rocks of the Serghaya road, ignoring the damage to the stolen sedan as he swerved across the ruts. Niles braced his boots against the firewall and watched the road ahead. They passed the point where he had cut onto the smuggling road, Niles recognizing his own motorcycle tracks on a hillside. But he did not stop Hijazi. This Mercedes could not cut across the fields.

Niles smelled the village—the smoke of cooking fires, the stink of animal pens—before he saw the lights of houses on the hillsides. Beyond the small farms, he saw the town of Nahri. Pavement allowed Hijazi to speed. He weaved past motorcycles and slow trucks, flashing his lights.

"There will be a checkpoint," Hijazi warned him. "On the road to Rayak. Perhaps in the village."

"We got to chance it."

"Perhaps not."

In Nahri, Hijazi turned off the road and followed the narrow streets of the village, cutting through the alleys. They heard a loudspeaker blasting the voice of a mullah. As Hijazi whipped through a right turn, they saw rows of concrete blocks in the avenue. Bearded young men gathered at the sidewalk tables of a café. With rifles in their hands, they left their drinks as the Mercedes approached. Hijazi reached under the dashboard and flipped a switch—

A siren overwhelmed the loudspeakers. Niles held out a wallet with Syrian identity cards bearing the seal of the G-2 office. The militiamen shouted for the car to stop but Hijazi continued, weaving through the concrete obstacles.

"They will not shoot—" Hijazi swerved onto the main road north and accelerated, the siren still wailing. "God willing . . ."

Looking back through the dusted rear window, Niles saw the militiamen returning to the café.

Vatsek watched the headlights. Twenty meters farther along the wall, at a gate, Stark sprawled in the dirt. Vatsek clicked off the safety of the PKM as he watched the headlights approach—a pickup, a car, followed by a second pickup truck. He squinted into the glare of the first pair of headlights and waited.

At fifty meters, he raised the PKM and aimed, but waited, tracking the pickup truck in the sights until he heard the voices of the men in the back and he fired, almost point-blank, raking the truck with the heavy steel-cored slugs as the truck continued past, the front tire flapping, the door panel buckling with hits, a tracer punching through the cheap Japanese steel and continuing through the legs of the driver and passengers, the militiamen in the back taking through-and-through wounds, then Vatsek shifted his aim to the next car. He fired at the headlights and held the machine gun on line as a headlight popped, steam clouded, the windshield shattered. The bullets passed through the grill and hood, through the windshield, continuing through the men inside the car. He counted two tracers into the car, no less than ten rounds.

The pickup truck at the end of the line braked, skidding sideways on the road. Vatsek put the sights on the driver and killed him, then raked the length of the truck.

Bullets rang off the stone walls as a militiaman fired wildly, not aiming his rifle, only pointing and holding back the trigger. Then other rifles fired as gunmen tried to find the ambushers, bullets tearing in all directions. One rifle answered with single shots—Stark.

Sighting low on the last pickup, Vatsek put a long stream of rounds through the undercarriage and tire. Rounds punched through the gas tank and a tracer ignited the gasoline, the yellow light of the flames illuminating dead men and militiamen crawling for the ditches.

Vatsek shot the wounded, then jerked the machine gun clear of the wall and ran. Bullets tore past him. Stark exchanged fire with two militiamen crouched behind the first pickup, the gunmen spraying the wall and gate with bursts of unaimed fire. One man rushed Stark and Vatsek fired point-blank into the running man. The next burst went into the wreck of the pickup, the heavy slugs passing through the thin sheet metal and knocking the militiaman back. Vatsek aimed for the fuel tank of the truck, dead men jerking, wounded crying out, the slugs holing the tank—long jets of flame flared from the sheet metal of the fenders as the vapor burned.

A grenade popped, dust clouding around the gate. Vatsek grabbed Stark's web gear and dragged him a few steps before the lieutenant scrambled to his feet. A form jumped up from behind the wall. Stark pointed his Kalashnikov with one hand and fired on full-auto without breaking stride as the dead man fell. Vatsek alternated with Stark, running and stopping and covering each other, until they gained the wall of the next field.

Crouching behind the wall, Vatsek changed magazines on the PKM, snapping the steel cartridge drum in place by touch, snapping the head of the new belt to the tail of the belt in the machine gun. Stark watched the flaming trucks and the fields, sniping at movement, until Vatsek signaled him.

Then they ran. After several hundred meters, they saw the railroad tracks. A service road covered with weeds and grass paralleled the rails. In the moonlight, Vatsek spotted two lines of crushed weeds weaving along the road. Where gullies cut the road, the truck had scraped the suspension, leaving the earth furrowed.

Rotor noise came from Baalbek. Vatsek and Stark ran southwest, following the tire marks. Looking back, they saw a Soviet MI-8 troopship circling the flaming wrecks. A spotlight swept the scene, the xenon white beam a sudden-noon glare on the road and the fields. Mini-guns sprayed streams of tracers at ditches. The helicopter flew several circuits, firing two more streams of fire at shadows before descending. A second helicopter stayed above the fields, beaming down white light. The Marines moved fast, scanning the road ahead, turning to check on the helicopters, running.

One helicopter followed the road to the west, its spotlight glaring down on the road. The other helicopter flew slow passes over the fields, the xenon beam projecting ahead, searching for movement along the walls and ditches. A single line of tracers scratched the darkness, a doorgunner firing random bursts into trees and brush.

And along the roadside walls, flashlights waved as soldiers tracked Vatsek and Stark.

The Marines made a kilometer before the white beam approached. Dropping, crawling into a stand of weeds and wild grain, Vatsek molded his bulk to the earth. He kept the

PKM free—if they spotted him, he would kill the doorgunner before the pilots killed him with the mini-guns.

Xenon white light illuminated every leaf and stem. Vatsek waited for the bullets but darkness returned, the turbine-shriek passing over him. He allowed his eyes to adjust before looking up. The troopship passed against the stars, the weeds and grass whipping with the rotor wind.

Waiting until the noise faded, they rushed ahead, covering another kilometer before they heard the helicopter returning. This time, they went to ground early, finding a dry stream bed for concealment. Again, the white light passed. Past the gully, the ground angled up. Vatsek remembered the gully and the slope from January, when melting snow and mud had slowed the truck taking the Recon squad to the highway—only a few hundred meters remained until they reached the LZ.

Stark pointed back. Near the side road, Vatsek saw the flashlights waving in the fields.

"So what? We are out of here." Vatsek broke into a run, his eyes watched the fields for other soldiers. Gray in the moonlight, the gravel band of the railway cut across the darkness of the fields. Vatsek looked for the truck—but he did not see it. He continued running.

The slope eased. Vatsek saw the lights of speeding traffic—the highway to Jounieh. A line of headlights had stopped at the side of the highway. The tiny points of flashlights wavered through the fields.

Syrians came from the highway, platoons of soldiers combing the fields and the railway.

But Vatsek did not see the truck.

From the east, the turbine/rotor whine of the helicopter returned. Vatsek crouched in the darkness, anger and panic simultaneously coursing through him as he realized Alvarez had abandoned him.

"Where's the truck?" Stark whispered.

"Forget the truck. We're on our own. The ocean is fifty clicks that way—" Vatsek pointed to the west. "You ready to go?"

They watched as the helicopter passed five hundred meters behind them. A machine gun fired. The MI-8 hovered over the stream bed, the doorgunner firing long bursts into the gully and the weeds. A light flashed, the pop of a grenade coming an instant later. Then the helicopter continued the search of the fields to the east.

Headlights left the highway. Two jeeps mounted with spotlights low-geared along the road paralleling the railroad. Vatsek saw Syrian soldiers walking in the headlights, following the tracks of the troop transport.

"That's the wrong way, you dumb fucks. You're coming straight to me. Hey, Lieutenant Strak-man. What did they say about this at college?"

"The studied and experienced opinion of my instructors would be to escape and evade."

"Yeah. But that's back at school. We got fifty clicks of Syrians, raghead Shiites, and the Phalange gangs between us and the beach. Let's come to an agreement here. They don't take us, right?"

"No."

"Then that's it. Escape and evade. Or zero. Here they come."

Silhouetted against the headlights, soldiers thrashed through the weeds. Vatsek and Stark crawled into the fields, going low in the furrows. The standing wheat concealed them. Parting the stems with the muzzle of the PKM, Vatsek watched the Syrians search the weeds and ditches. He calculated the path of the soldiers and saw they would pass without stepping on him—he and Stark might get a chance to survive this yet.

Then he saw the soldier standing in the back of the lead jeep. Braced against the pedestal-mounted machine gun, the soldier turned from side to side, his torso and head turning like radar. A soft red light blinked from his hands—

An infra-red viewer. The soldier shouted and pointed at Vatsek and Vatsek killed him, two hits throwing the spotter backward. The next burst killed the driver and the officer in the front seats. Holding the trigger back and finding targets, Vatsek hit three soldiers, then the Syrians had dropped to the ground. Rifles flashed on full-auto, soldiers firing in the direction of his PKM, slugs slashing through the fields, tearing over his back as he crawled away, shifting his position.

A Syrian in the second jeep fired a burst from a 12.7mm Degtyarev heavy machine gun. Designed to hit aircraft at up to two thousand meters of altitude, the armor-piercing slugs shook the ground, spraying dirt and rocks. Vatsek rolled back, scrambled in a low crawl, wanted to get up and run away from that monster earth-pounding weapon. Then the Degtyarev went quiet, Stark knocking down the gunner with a three-shot burst, a second burst killing the driver. Soldiers fired at the muzzle flash, trying to find Stark as he followed Vatsek in retreat.

Helicopters converged on the firefight, one from the east, the other from the west.

Vatsek sprawled on his back, staring up at the black dome of the sky. Bullets ripped through the field. Here, far from Beirut and Damascus, only the few thousand electric lights of Baalbek paling the night, the night and the stars continued forever, the distance unknown and impossible to know, the stars above him the definition of infinity. Vatsek thought of his father and grandfather beating the gulag for Fontana, his brothers beating Vietnam for Fontana—but he didn't beat Baalbek for Fontana. So it goes—

Xenon interrupted his moment of philosophy, the helicopter from the east roaring overhead, the light past before the pilots spotted him, the field seething with the rotorstorm. Vatsek found the xenon with the sights of the PKM and fired behind the spotlight, raking the troopship.

A tracer ricocheted from the armored belly. The troopship wheeled against the stars and Vatsek sprinted three steps, riflefire ripping past him until he dived, the receiver of the PKM slamming him in the face, blood filling his mouth as he crawled, trying to make distance before the Soviet troopship returned with the mini-guns. He covered only a few meters before the xenon returned—and found Stark.

The doorgunner fired a quick burst and then a loudspeaker voice boomed out in Arabic. Vatsek sighted on the black-on-gray rectangle of the side door and fired, holding the trigger back, tracking the slow moving helicopter, two tracers scoring on the door.

Turbines shrieking, the troopship pivoted. The roar of mini-guns, the turbines, the rotors, the firing of the PKM, the hammering of his heart—the noise overwhelmed his senses. He did not feel the machine gun jackhammering against his shoulder, he could not hear his own long scream of rage and panic and fear as he watched the single string of tracers touching the troopship, the troopship turning, four cones of tracers spraying from the mini-gun pods on the side of the fuselage, the fields seething with impacts—

And coming from the west, the second helicopter overflew the first, spraying the troopship with an instant of mini-gun fire, hundreds of slugs punching through the aluminum top of the fuselage, the five rotor blades flying off the hub, the turbines exploding in thousands of fragments, the troopship suddenly falling scrap metal. The second helicopter continued past as the flames splashed across the fields.

Vatsek stared, not believing what he had seen. All the riflefire stopped, the Syrians silent as the wreck burned. Vatsek laughed. Ammunition in the mini-gun pods exploded in chains of staccato bursts. Vatsek laughed loud, not trying to hide his noise, betraying his position, laughing at the spectacle of Soviet-Syrian incompetence.

The second troopship returned, the xenon beam racing across the fields. Vatsek checked the magazine of belted cartridges. Only ten or fifteen cartridges remained. He did not bother to try to load another length of belt—he would not live that long. Shifting his position, he watched the troopship over the sights of the PKM.

But the pilot veered away from Vatsek. Again the mini-guns fired, the cones of orange tracers killing the platoons of Syrians, destroying the jeeps, the mini-guns going silent for an instant as the troopship continued to the highway and destroyed the parked trucks, rifles flashing in futile self-defense, the platoons of Syrians dying in one banking pass as the pilot cranked a hard bank to return to Vatsek and Stark.

The xenon spotlight found the Marines, then went black, the Soviet troopship descended. Vatsek saw men standing in the side door. A light went on for a moment, showing Captains Niles and Alvarez, then went dark, Vatsek already sprinting through the waves of rotor-whipped grain.

A hand reached out for him, he took it, and he stepped into the turbine-loud interior and Stark jumped inside and then he felt the helicopter lift away, the flames of the wrecks receding into the distance.

Niles shouted into his ear, "Sorry to interrupt your good times down there, but I got a message from the colonel that we got some action coming up. You want to volunteer?"

Vatsek spat blood on the deck. "Ready to go."